# Search for the Signet

## An Orion Labauve Novel

by

# L. L. Blacke

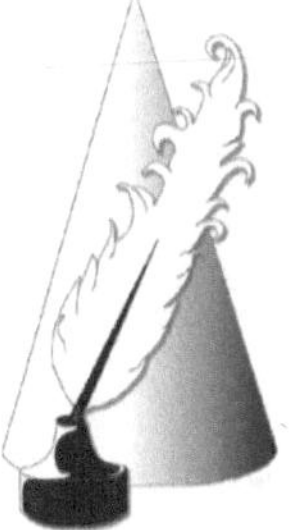

Foolscap & Quill

ISBN 978-1-938143-63-2

Foolscap & Quill
P.O. Box 1018
Morrison, CO 80465
http://www.foolscap-quill.com

# Table of Contents

# Chapter 1

# A Finding Job

The revelations of the past few weeks churned in my mind, leading me to question the very foundation of my closest relationship. Cyrus, my supposed best friend, had kept the most important secret from me and everyone, shattering my trust in him.

I raced the old Chrysler New Yorker up the plantation dirt road, skidding on the loose, muddy pavement, the vehicle weaving precariously back and forth as it quickly moved over the private driveway. Panic surged as I approached the mansion too fast. I stomped on the brake, closed my eyes, and held my breath, realizing I may have waited too late to stop. The brakes could not slow the heavy automobile fast enough, and it careened through the plantation's front picket fence, smashing it to the ground, pickets snapping and breaking, crushed beneath the vehicle's tires.

I opened my eyes and inhaled, relief washing over me that I had narrowly missed the massive oak tree's trunk by inches.

I threw open the car door and ran to the plantation house. With trembling hands, I fumbled for the door key in my pocket. My mind was consumed with apprehension and thoughts of losing everyone I cared for, unsure how to stop it.

Bursting into the vestibule, I urgently yelled, "Cyrus!" willing him to appear.

The ghost materialized, and I shouted, "Where is it?"

I was angry with him about what I had discovered at my father's grave.

"Where's what?" he replied, irritated at being forced to appear.

"You know what I'm talking about."

I was tired of Cyrus's constant deflection.

He feigned ignorance, a façade I refused to entertain any longer.

"It's in the bedroom where you left it this morning. Orion, why is that so important?"

Ignoring his question, I sprinted up the stairs two at a time to my room and desperately searched every surface until I spied the precious item and seized it. My hands trembled as I stared at it, struggling to believe it had been in plain sight all this time.

Holding the charm, I realized the depth of my grandmother's manipulation. She had planned everything—this was the key to powers I hadn't even known I possessed. The power she sought to wield through me was daunting. My grandmother had been manipulating the Labauve family for decades to produce an heir—ME—with the unique capabilities she required to use the power of this charm over spirits.

My life has been intertwined with spirits at the L'Enfant Haven estate since I was three, their presence a constant companion, shaping my reality. I never questioned their presence—they were as real to me as sunlight through the shutters. They raised me to become the man I am today—Orion Aniston Labauve, Finder of Things and People— at least, that's what my business card says. My life has changed drastically over the last several weeks since my twenty-fifth birthday and I became aware of the true extent of the extraordinary talents given to me by my '*God*' father.

☗— ☗— ☗—

Several weeks before I discovered the L'Enfant Haven secret, I was returning from a Finding Job—that's what I call them '*Finding Jobs*'—locating lost jewelry at a mansion in Georgia. This one was an unexciting job compared to some. Andy, my attorney, would usually pick me up at the airport in Shreveport, Louisiana, the closest to the estate. But he couldn't today—something about family issues—so I took a cab, which cost me a pretty penny for the hour-long drive from the airport. At least I can write it off my taxes. The yellow cab dropped me off in front of the mansion.

While sitting in the back seat of the cab on my way home, I reflected on the events of the job. In this Finding Job, the household matriarch had concealed valuable jewelry under the floorboards of her bedroom for forty years without revealing its location. After her passing, the family became frantic about finding the luxurious, expensive jewels. Confident that the items were in the house, they reached out to Andrew "Andy" Butler Jr., my attorney and agent, after learning about my services from a family friend.

I receive a negotiated percentage of the value of the items I find. Andy handles the negotiations for me. He gets fifty percent of the finder's fee, so he'll negotiate long and hard to maintain that substantial percentage. He also takes care of all the business matters, accounting, taxes, bookings, travel reservations, etc. He does a lot for me, so I'm happy to give him fifty percent. This payday should be exceptional— my best-paying job to date.

I had sensed a few apparitions hanging around when I entered the Georgia mansion. A peculiar sensation washes over me when spirits are present. It's difficult to describe: a combination of a tingle in my chest and sinus pressure. There were no significant manifestations at this residence—active specters that move things and make noises— just a couple of sad family members who stood and viewed the others in the household. Having ghosts in the area ensured that finding items was easier and faster. If apparitions are near, I can speak with them and gather information to help find what I am searching for. That's only one of my unique abilities: talking to the dead. I've been able to do this since I was three and encountered my first ghosts.

An unusual sensation in my stomach occurs when I search for the missing item or person and I'm headed in the right direction. When I'm close to what I'm searching for the nausea builds, like a compass with a cruel sense of humor. The moment I touch it the stomach issues are gone and I'm back to normal.

My investigation inside the Georgia mansion was uneventful until I found the spirits—a short man with gray hair and a plain-looking, brown-haired woman.

I approached them and asked, "Hello, I'm wondering if you can help me?"

They both looked at me, surprised that someone recognized them and wanted to speak with them. They both smiled, and the woman said, "Sure, what do you need?"

"I'm searching for some jewels that Miriam Adams hid in the house. Do either of you know anything about that?"

The man shook his head, but the woman recalled something.

"Many years ago, she took a large jewelry box into her bedroom and never brought it out."

I thanked her and entered the bedroom. The odor of disinfectants and medication lingered. The old woman had been sick for a long time and preferred to stay at home rather than in a hospital.

The nausea hit me immediately as I moved toward Miriam's bedroom and it was worse by the bed. I searched the bed and under the mattresses, but found nothing. Crawling under the bed, I held my hand an inch above the floor, moving it around. I almost puked when I found the spot. I couldn't see much in the dark and moved the bed away. When exposed to the light, a dark line around a set of floorboards on the hardwood oak floor could be seen. Kneeling and trying to keep my stomach in check, I pounded on the boards and one end popped up. I got my fingers under it and removed that section. In a cubby hole under the boards was a jewelry box covered in dust and cobwebs. I pulled it out, and the nausea disappeared. I knew I had found what I was searching for.

I blew and brushed the dust and cobwebs away from the red velvet lid of the ornate box. Flipping the latch up, I opened the box and beheld opulent, extravagant jewels and jewelry of every kind—necklaces, brooches, earrings, and loose gems of all types—that resided inside. Points of light flashed off the jewel facets as I moved the box around to look at the contents. I closed the lid, went downstairs, and handed it to the waiting family members.

The family was shocked at how quickly I found the precious, expensive items and showered me with thanks and gratitude. I always feel weird when this happens and prefer to leave soon after the job is complete, claiming that using my psychic abilities tires me. It doesn't, but the clients always accept that excuse and someone drives me back to my hotel.

When no local ghosts are present to talk to, it can take me much more time to find things, sometimes even days, especially if the item is being moved by someone or something. I wander through a house or property until I become queasy. Occasionally, I even have to walk around a neighborhood to determine where to go for what I'm searching.

# Chapter 2

# Home Again

During the hour-long drive back home, I noticed the taxi driver reacting uneasily to me in the back seat by glancing in the rearview mirror more than was expected. This usually happens when I'm around people. It also occurred on the plane returning to Louisiana. The heavyset guy sitting in the aisle seat next to me kept glancing over and fidgeting, trying to get as far away from me as possible, but being heavy meant he couldn't move much. I ignored him and read my book, but his constant adjustments irritated me. After the airplane took off and we could release our seat belts, he stopped a flight attendant and asked if he could move to another seat, claiming that the seat was uncomfortable. She found him a seat in the back row, and he quickly moved.

I don't have any close living friends. Most people find me foreboding and feel unsettled when around me. They get ominous sensations when I'm close because of my exceptional abilities. I guess it gives them the creeps. I don't know. I only recently discovered why this happens.

As the driver approached the house, Norman said—I saw his name on his cab license hanging from the rearview mirror—"Wow, nice place you have here. Is this all yours?"

I smiled, happy to be home with people I love, even if they were dead.

"Yeah. It's been in the family for two hundred years. Can I get a receipt?"

"Sure thing."

He scribbled out a receipt and gave it to me. I handed him the cash with a decent tip and exited the cab, glad to be in the fresh air. The vehicle's air conditioning wasn't functioning, and the driver produced some heavy body odor despite the open windows. He should have had one of those pine tree air fresheners hanging from the rearview mirror, but he didn't. At least it was springtime, and the temperature was decent.

He said, "Thanks. Have a nice day."

He turned the dinged and dirty yellow taxi around, heading back up the plantation's private road.

As I walked up the flagstone path, the temperature dropped in the shade of the enormous oak trees that stood as sentinels on either side of the trail, keeping the front of the mansion cooler.

I said hello to Paul, the yardman, who was on his knees, leaning over to remove unwanted weeds from the decorative flower beds. He looked up.

"Good day, sir," he said in a strong Southern accent and gave me a broad smile.

An earthy aroma arose from the overturned dirt around the various colored zinnias, marigolds, rudbeckias, and salvias in the garden as he pulled weeds. He always does a beautiful job and should, being the oldest spirit on the property. He has been doing the same work for over 170 years. Paul had lived—and died—on this land. He was hanged from the left oak for a crime I still don't believe he committed. Now, he tends these gardens like they're sacred.

Cyrus, my best friend, and the next oldest ghost on the plantation, who had traveled with me for this Finding Job, made a smart-ass comment to Paul.

"I think you missed one over there."

Paul scowled at him with loathing. He didn't like Cyrus. I never understood their animosity, but I would later discover the reason.

Cyrus Labauve was the only ghost who could leave the estate; the other ghosts had to stay on the property. When I was eleven, I found the unique spirit linked to an amulet in a spacious chest in the attic. He could manifest within fifty feet of the jewelry piece and not be detected by anyone but me. Sometimes he would help me find stuff for my job, and sometimes he was a pain in the ass, but he was fun to have around and someone to talk to when no one else would speak with me.

I asked Cyrus, "Why do you say things like that to Paul? He does a wonderful job."

"It goes way back. You wouldn't understand, being raised in these modern times."

He put his hands in his early nineteenth-century pants pockets and moved on.

I pulled out the ancient front door key from my front jeans pocket, unlocked the massive door, and stroked the nose of the brass lion head knocker, which always seemed to be smiling at me. The lion's snout is now polished, shiny and bright after all the years of doing this little ritual since I grew tall enough to reach it.

As I entered the ancestral home, I was greeted by the familiar warmth of the ghostly inhabitants. Their unwavering support had sustained me through tumultuous times, fostering a sense of belonging amidst the chaos of my upbringing. I placed my small suitcase on the always spotless and waxed hardwood floor.

Philly, one of the ghost maids, rushed up and said, "Nice to have you back home, Mr. Orion. I'll take the bag to your room, sir."

She curtsied, picked up the case, and went up the steps. She was a hundred years old but didn't appear a day over twenty-one; ghosts never age.

"Thank you, Philly."

Over the years, I had learned to recognize the tiny differences between the twin spirits, Milly and Philly, the maids.

Delicious aromas of cooking food wafted up the hall from the kitchen. Bertha always provided a meal when I walked in the door. She had been the best cook in the parish eighty years ago before she passed on. She told me stories about often winning the local cooking contests in those years.

10

# Chapter 3

# From Flophouses to an

# Ancestral Sanctuary

When I was three, my mother and I moved to the L'Enfant Haven estate in the late spring of 1960. I thought the ghosts occupying the plantation house were just other people staying with us. That was what I was familiar with—a house full of people. It didn't register in my young brain that the people in the new place were dead. I found out later that some of the occupants were relatives of mine, going back as far as 170 years; some were ex-slaves, and some were ex-servants.

My mother inherited the ancestral mansion from Great Aunt Gretchen Labauve, a spinster and the family's matriarch. As stipulated in the will, my mother had to live in the house to receive the monthly annuity from the L'Enfant Haven trust associated with the property. The $500.00 per month allotment—generous in the 1950s, when the will was created—is now poverty level in 1982. That's why I must work; finding things and people is my peculiar specialty.

Haunted by memories of a turbulent past, I found sanctuary at the plantation house amidst the echoes of bygone eras. The ghosts on the property became my family. They loved and cared for me as I did for them. They were always available for emotional support and helped me whenever possible when my mother failed in this maternal responsibility, which was most of the time. However, there were rare occasions when Mother demonstrated her love for me.

I didn't hate her for the lack of concern and neglect; I accepted it as usual. As a young child with limited exposure to live people, I didn't realize other familial relationships existed. When I was older, I learned from reading books, watching television, and observing other kids at school and their reactions to their parents that my family life was different. In some ways, it was diminished due to the neglect from my mother, but in other ways, it was enhanced by the ghosts always being there when I needed a shoulder to cry on or someone to listen to me. But the spirits taught me to be a kind and amiable individual to other people, no matter what they might say about me, and my being peculiar in people's eyes meant they talked a lot about me.

No other ghosts I've met can do the things my ghost family at the L'Enfant Haven mansion can do, like cooking, cleaning, repairing items, gardening, or driving—the same things they did when alive—but only on the plantation property when a Labauve heir was present or within a few miles of the property. Things will get done if the heir isn't near, but at a much slower pace. I'm unsure why this is, but it's somehow connected to the curse. Oh, there's a curse on the L'Enfant Haven plantation; that's why the ghosts are on the property.

Each ghost instructed me in the exceptional skills they exhibited daily at the plantation. Having people, whether dead or alive, who wanted to be with me and help me grow into a man was a blessing. I didn't realize this until I was almost an adult. I'm sure I wouldn't have survived in the toxic environment my mother exposed me to in the drug flophouses before we moved to the L'Enfant Haven plantation.

I did a lot of hiding in the drug flophouses, constantly wary of what the other people would do. Sometimes they would be happy, dance, and play with me; sometimes they would yell, scream, and try to hit me. I was smart, had a great memory, and learned early to run and hide to survive when anyone was in one of those moods—I could move fast for my age. I soon recognized when a bad mood was coming on someone—the shaking, hand-wringing, the voice getting louder and higher-pitched—and would stay out of the way. I would find a secure location and not exit for hours, frightened of what might happen—listening to the screaming and yelling of the person having a meltdown.

While hiding, I often wet my pants and sat in that spot, smelling the acrid odor of my urine, afraid to move out of the hidey-hole. When I left my secret place, my mother would spot my wet pants and yell at me for it, change my clothes, swat me on the butt, and make me sit in a corner facing the wall. I would sit with tears running down my cheeks and sniffling. She would never listen to me about why it happened, usually missing most of the terrifying occurrences while loaded on her drugs.

To amuse myself while stuck in the corner, I would pick paint chips off the wall, trying to make the spot look like something. Finally Mama would take her pills and fall asleep, and I knew then I could get up and find something else to do. I can still tell when something is wrong with someone and they are ready to go over the deep end. I still try to avoid these situations and don't like being among many people, suspicious of what to expect from them.

Sometimes, when staying in the flophouses with my mother, I would have bad dreams and wake up crying. I would cuddle close to Mama's body, hoping her unconscious presence would make the nightmare go away. It never did, and she never awoke when this happened.

The dreams always consisted of a black woman with deformities on her face standing over me. She wore a bright-colored scarf around her head, a colorful skirt and blouse, and lots of jewelry around her neck. Her appearance terrified me for some reason. She never attacked me; she would stare at me as if evaluating me for some nefarious purpose and say things like, "He's not ready yet." I would start crying and wake up. These nightmares stopped when we moved into the old plantation house.

Now, I know her name. And I know why she watched me from the shadows of my dreams.

14

# Chapter 4

# The Inheritance

Andrew Butler Sr. tracked my mother down before we moved into the L'Enfant Haven mansion. How he found her in our dangerous Shreveport neighborhood remained a mystery until I was allowed access to his diaries years later. He knocked on the flophouse door, gray suit pressed, briefcase in hand—completely out of place. One of the girls living in the house answered the door. There were so many people in and out of that house that I don't remember most of their names.

Mr. Butler said, "May I speak with Marie Labauve?"

"Who?"

"Marie Labauve."

"Oh, Marie. Yeah, right. Marie, some suit wants to talk to you! Is she in trouble or something?"

"No. She isn't in trouble," Mr. Butler reassured her as the girl left the door half open.

Mother stumbled out of our room to the front door, opened it wider, and said with slurred speech, "Oh, it's you. I haven't seen you for years."

Mother's blond hair was darker than usual, not having been washed for over a week, and stuck out at weird angles because she had just gotten out of bed, which consisted of an old, stained mattress on the floor. Her once-beautiful face was now drawn and pale, her blue eyes dulled by drugs and neglect. She wore filthy clothes, a testament to our living situation.

I hid, peeking around the corner, wary of who was asking for my mother. The old man with pale hair, a short white beard, and glasses stood on the porch and lingered as if he wasn't going anywhere until he spoke with her. I had never seen anyone that old before. I didn't leave the house much.

Mother leaned against the door.

"What do you want?"

"Your Great Aunt Gretchen passed on and left you the plantation house and fifty acres."

He stared at her with a disappointed expression.

"It's about time that fucking old bitch died!" she exclaimed, as she ran her shaking hand through her messy, long hair and searched behind Mr. Butler as if expecting someone or something else to be present.

Mr. Butler ignored her unusual reaction and comment, almost as though he had anticipated it, and asked, "Can I come in to discuss the will with you?"

"Sure," she said.

She pushed open the screen door—half the mesh dangling loose— and let him inside. He surveyed the dilapidated structure, peeling wallpaper and paint, ripped, filthy, and stained—you don't want to find out what with—carpeting and a few ancient couches with torn cushions. He twitched his nose at the odor of unwashed bodies, decaying foods, urine, and vomit that permeated the place.

He found an intact cushion on one of the sofas and sat down. My mother reclined on another couch across from him. Joey, one of the guys who resided in the house and was friendly to me, slept on a third couch while they talked.

I peeked around the corner from what should have been the dining room—but now contained multiple stained mattresses strewn on the floor, with one person asleep on one—and listened, not understanding what was being discussed. People never showed up asking for my mother. I was curious and stayed hidden, unsure of what to expect from this unusual encounter.

Mr. Butler opened his brown leather briefcase and pulled out a stack of papers. He shuffled through them and said, "Your Great Aunt Gretchen left you the plantation house, fifty surrounding acres, and a monthly allotment of $500.00."

My mother shouted, "$500.00 a month, that's fantastic, and if I sell the place, a lot more money would come in!"

"You can't sell the property."

"That's bull shit. If it's mine, I should be able to sell it."

She crossed her arms with a defiant scowl.

"The trust owns the estate, so you can't sell it. You inherit the right to live on the property until you die, at which point your next of kin will inherit the rights."

"I don't want to live in that place. That's why I left; I didn't want to stay in that house with that bitch and all the weird shit that goes on there."

"If you don't live in the house, you'll not receive the $500.00 allotment. The trust also funds utilities, property maintenance, furnishings, automobiles, and other farm and yard equipment. The fifty acres are currently leased to a local farmer who plants cotton. I'm sorry, Miss Labauve, but those are the stipulations in the will. If you don't accept it, the next in line would be your second cousin, Herman Labauve."

"Herman! He would get it—that idiot. Like hell I'll let that happen. So, if I die, my next of kin would be my son?"

"You have a son?" he said, his voice indicating shock at discovering this information.

"Yes. Ory! Come in here."

I stepped into the doorway, apprehensive about the old man. My grimy black shorts and a green T-shirt with holes hung on me. Oversized, they were things Mother had found for me, being thrown out as rags from the thrift store.

Mr. Butler said in a gentle tone, "Hello, son. What's your name?"

Looking at the floor, I said, "Ory."

Mother piped in and said, "His full name is Orion Aniston Labauve."

"He doesn't have his father's last name?"

"No, we didn't stay together long and were never married."

"He's a cute little fella with those black curls, not a Labauve trait. You all were always blond or light brown-haired. Those blue eyes are yours, though."

Mother said, "Come over here, baby."

I ran over, climbed onto the couch, pulled my bare feet up, and cuddled close to her, not taking my eyes off the odd man. She put her arm around me.

She asked, "Do you want to move to a big new house? You would have lots of room to play inside and outside."

I didn't know what to say and just nodded.

She eyed Mr. Butler.

"I remember how fun that place used to be until...."

She trailed off and went no further. Butler didn't press her to continue; I think he understood.

Mother paused for a few moments, staring at me, and said, "Okay, I guess I have to return to that hellhole."

She pulled me closer. I'm unsure if she did this instinctively to protect me from whatever frightened her in the house or if having me near helped her cope with moving back to someplace that terrified her.

"You need to sign these documents to agree to the stipulations in the will and trust for L'Enfant Haven plantation."

He handed over the articles, and my mother signed them.

"When do we have to move in?"

Uneasy, she frowned at the action being forced on her.

"I'll post the articles with the parish clerk, and once that is processed, you get the keys. Do you have a phone number I can call and let you know when you can move?"

"No, we don't have a telephone. Give me your telephone number, and I'll call you."

"The paperwork will probably take a couple of weeks to complete."

He handed over his business card. She took it and put it in her jeans pocket.

"Okay, I'll call you then," she said, sounding reluctant.

After Mr. Butler left, Mother's demeanor shifted, and she retreated into herself. I could sense her anxiety about returning to the place she had fled years ago. When she got like this, she would take the pills she said I couldn't touch, and would be in bed for a long time.

Some other people in the house asked her what was happening with that old guy.

She said, "I'm moving in a few weeks," and went to our room and locked the door.

# Chapter 5

# L'Enfant Haven & Ghostly Encounters

Two weeks later, Mother took my hand and we walked down the street to the grocery store to use the pay phone and call Mr. Butler. The telephone booth's broken windows left plastic shards on the floor that crunched under our feet, and torn pages from the phone book were scattered everywhere. We were fortunate the telephone still worked.

"Hi, Mr. Butler, this is Marie Labauve. Have the house documents been processed at the parish yet?" she asked, fidgeting.

"Yes, they have. I just got the confirmation today. You can come by any time and pick up the keys."

"I don't have any way of getting there. Can you take Ory and me to the house?"

I peered up at her as she talked to Mr. Butler, seeing a worried expression in her eyes.

"I don't have a truck to move your stuff."

"We don't have much, just a couple of boxes," she said sadly.

"Okay, I'll come by tomorrow morning and get you two."

"Thank you. See you then," she said and hung up the phone.

She glanced at me and smiled.

"We'll move to the new house tomorrow. Isn't that exciting?"

She wasn't excited and had a fake smile.

I nodded but got a weird sensation in my tummy. This house was different somehow. We returned to the flophouse and packed our meager items into two cardboard boxes.

Mother dressed me in unstained clothes: tan pants and a black T-shirt—the best I had, which wasn't saying much. She wore her nicest things: clean blue jeans and a bright floral pullover blouse. Mr. Butler drove up in a black Buick, wearing new jeans, a blue button-up shirt, and a leather jacket. He took one of the containers while Mother took the other, and they placed them in the back seat. Mother put me in the back seat next to the boxes. This giant car made me feel tiny.

We took off with a pall of silence draped over the front seat on the way to the new house. Mother stared out the window while Mr. Butler frowned most of the time. I got up on my knees to peer out the window as we drove for what seemed like hours, but in reality, only an hour passed. I saw the countryside for the first time, with farmland, growing crops, and farm animals.

I got excited when I recognized cows I had seen in a picture book, yelling, "Look, Mama, cows, lots of cows!"

My mother answered, "Yes, baby. Cows."

We arrived in a town and passed through its center. Later, I learned it was Madreville. We traveled down a parish street onto a dirt road and reached the house. It was the largest house I had ever seen—of course, I hadn't seen many homes at three years old—a grand yet dilapidated mansion loomed before us. Once more I felt a strange sensation in my stomach.

We parked on the tall grass next to the dirt driveway in front of a picket fence, gray and chipped, with some pickets fallen off. Mother and Mr. Butler exited the car, walked around, and stood before the gate, gazing at the house.

Mother commented, "The bitch let the place get run down."

"This only happened since she perished six months ago. It was in good shape until then," he said, glancing at the house.

"Six months? I thought you said she had just died," she said, facing him with a questioning furrow on her brow.

"It took me that long to track you down."

Mother shrugged and continued to inspect the house, glancing up at the third floor.

"But how can the house have gone this bad in six months? It looks like it hasn't been touched for years."

"I don't know. It looked fine the last time I was here, when she was alive, seven months ago."

Still in the back seat, I tried yanking the door handle several times to open the car door, but I wasn't strong enough. Mother turned, looking for me and realized I wasn't out of the Buick. She opened the door for me. I rolled over onto my stomach and slid down to the ground. I walked over to the gate and peered between the pickets at the old house.

The ancient mansion featured four enormous columns in the front. The structure had been painted white but now appeared an unkempt gray, peeling in several places. I thought I saw someone standing at a window on the third floor.

Two massive, ancient oak trees stood in the yard, their enormous, curving branches almost reaching the lawn. Spanish moss draped from many of the branches. Each tree dominated either side of the overgrown stone path, where grass obscured the flagstones underneath, leading up to the front porch. Two gray wicker rocking chairs rested on the patio behind the columns. The four columns supported a balcony on the second level above. The flower beds in front of the porch were filled with dead flowers and weeds.

Mother and Mr. Butler pulled the boxes from the back seat and closed the car door. I jumped, startled, having been focused on the structure and feeling the sickness in my stomach. Mr. Butler held a box in one hand, opened the gate with his other, and stood to the side—always the gentleman—allowing my mother to enter first. I followed closely behind her, unsure what to expect. We all walked up to the door.

Mr. Butler placed the container of our items on a chair and retrieved a three-inch ring of keys from his coat pocket. He tried several keys and found the one for the front door, an old brass key. The teak wood door was impressive, standing eight feet high and four feet wide, with a brass knocker shaped like a lion's head holding a ring in its mouth at the center.

I thought the lion looked at me and smiled. I held my mother's leg while staring at it, feeling uneasy and apprehensive about a lion smiling at me. Mother put a hand on my head. She could occasionally be caring when not loaded on drugs.

He turned the key, and I heard the lock unlatch. It echoed from inside the house. He pushed the door open easily, which was surprising given its age. We all entered. The place emanated an old, musty odor. Mother placed the box she carried on a chair next to the door.

A woman wearing a funny old maid hat peered around the corner at the end of the stairs. I giggled and she disappeared. She was the first ghost I had ever seen, though I didn't realize it at the time.

My mother turned and asked, "What are you laughing at?"

"The lady with the funny hat."

She glanced around suspiciously; no one was there, yet she said nothing and asked no further questions. Mr. Butler looked at me with an almost knowing expression but remained silent.

He said, "I dropped off groceries earlier and put them in the kitchen for you and Ory. If you want more, call Jordan's Grocery and order whatever you want. The number is next to the phone on the side table."

He pointed to a long, narrow, fancy table in the hall with carved legs and a telephone.

"They'll deliver it, but only to the front porch. The delivery person will not enter the house. Jordan will send me the bill. Do you need me to show you where things are around the house?"

Mother frowned.

"Did the bitch change anything in the last six years?"

"No, not really."

"Then I remember where everything is."

The attorney gave her the ring of keys, placed the container on the floor, and left, closing the door behind him. With the door shut, it felt like being in another world. The outside seemed distant. Every sound we made created a slight echo through the quiet structure.

Despite the mansion's grandeur, neglect had taken its toll. Dust covered every surface, and the air was heavy with the scent of abandonment. Yet amidst the decay, there were glimpses of something else—perhaps hopeful.

Looking around, I noticed that the stairs leading to the second and third levels were situated across from the entrance. The ceiling rose high, featuring elegant notches where the wall met the ceiling. An immense glass chandelier hung in the center of the front hall, with cobwebs and dust clinging to it, obscuring the crystal pieces of the once-exquisite lighting fixture.

A thick layer of grime covered everything. Our footprints were visible in the dirt on the floor. I shuffled my worn sneakers through the dust and spotted the shapes left by my shoes. I sneezed from the dust my shuffling disturbed.

Mother said, "I guess we should check the place out."

I could tell she didn't want to do this because of her nervousness and anxious expression. She placed the ring of keys on top of the box and took my hand. As we explored the house, memories must have flooded back for Mother. I could see her struggle with her emotions, as evidenced by the slight tremor in her hand, or was that due to her lack of drugs? The house was filled with echoes of the past for her, both joyous and haunting.

We walked through the house. White sheets covered and protected many pieces of furniture. Mother pulled me along, not allowing us to stay in any room for too long. To the left was a living room or parlor.

Mother told me, "This is the parlor, as the bitch Aunt Gretchen used to call it. I would call it the living room to piss her off," and gave a snide smile.

A massive fireplace was situated on the wall opposite the double sliding doors. The room contained several antique couches, chairs, and side tables covered with sheets, while a baby grand piano, also covered with a sheet, occupied a distant corner beside the windows.

We then entered the connecting library and office. This room featured another impressive fireplace, dark wood paneling, and bookshelves filled with books. On one side of the desk stood a tall cabinet with glass doors, filled with bottles and medical supply packages—a chemical odor lingered in the air.

A giant maple desk sat opposite the double sliding doors leading from the parlor. A balding man in an old gray business suit with a vest and sporting a gray mustache sat at the desk, wearing a sad expression as he stared at me when we entered. Mother quickly glanced in that direction and pulled me through another door into the hall.

Glimpsing back through the door, I asked, "Mama, who is that man?"

He was still staring at me from behind the desk. She didn't answer. We rushed into the kitchen across the hall. The old kitchen contained appliances from the 1940s, painted white cabinets, and yellow tiled counter tops. A heavyset, smiling Black woman wearing a black dress with a white apron and a white scarf tied around her head stood beside the stove—an odor of nondescript cooked food hung in the air.

My mother went to the refrigerator, inspected the contents, and said, "It seems like enough food for the next few days."

She ignored the woman next to the stove.

While Mother evaluated the refrigerator's contents, I asked the Black woman, "What's your name? My name is Ory."

She answered with a strong Southern accent, "My name is Bertha. I knew your name, Orion, when you came through the door."

She gave me a broad, friendly smile. I liked her.

With a surprised expression, Mother anxiously yelled at me, "Ory, get over here!"

I ran to her, and she grabbed my hand, pulling me through the swinging door into the dining room. As we passed through the door, I looked back at Bertha. She was still smiling at me.

We entered the dining room, adorned with ornate floral wallpaper and another fireplace featuring an oak-and-marble mantle on the outer wall. The room had once been quite grand and opulent. A large oak table was positioned in the center of the room, accompanied by chairs for eight people, along with additional chairs lining the wall. An oak buffet cabinet and a glass chandelier, both covered with cobwebs, hung in the dining room. The table and buffet displayed fine China soup tureens, bowls, and pitchers, all featuring intricate blue Chinese scenes painted on them. Dust and cobwebs veiled everything.

Wearing white full-length dresses with black aprons and silly white hats, the twin dark-haired maids stood in the corner, looking at us. I smiled at them, feeling a friendly, caring warmth in return. They smiled back at me. Mother rushed out of the room and around the corner, and we ascended the stairs.

I climbed the steps slowly because I had to hold onto the posts to help pull myself up. Mother picked me up, hurried up the stairs, and put me down. We went to the left, opened a door, and entered a fancy bedroom with a four-poster bed, white-painted walls, and heavy blue velvet curtains on the bed and over the windows. A white fireplace was on the far wall. Hearthside were two chairs with a round table between them, covered by sheets. A mahogany armoire, a dresser, and a daybed draped with a sheet next to a window were also in the room.

Mother said, "This was the old bitch's room, my Great Aunt Gretchen, your Great-Great Aunt. At least she isn't here. She must have died in the hospital."

I didn't know what she meant by that last statement until I got older and discovered that most ghosts stay near where they died.

We walked across the hall and entered another bedroom. This one contained a standard double bed with a bright floral bedspread. A white fireplace was located on the wall opposite the door. A smaller white armoire and dresser also filled the room. Old posters and movie star photos hung on the wall next to the bed, and a record player sat on a small table with 45 rpm records stacked below. A compact desk and chair were placed in a corner.

This room emitted a fresh scent, unlike all the other rooms that reeked of dust. It wasn't dirty or dusty like the others; it had been cleaned by someone or something. Mother didn't pay any attention to this fact.

Mother said, "She didn't change anything after I left."

She opened the armoire, and clothing hung from hangers. She rifled through the dresser drawers, pushed the clothing aside, and pulled out an old marijuana joint, putting it in her pocket.

"All my clothes are still here."

Mother said again, "She hasn't touched anything since the day I left. Look, my sweater is still on the chair where I left it six years ago."

Tears streamed down her cheeks. She sat on the bed, covering her eyes with her hands. I went to her and hugged her leg, unsure why she was upset or what to do. I didn't realize that she had once lived here; this had been her room.

I'm still not sure why she was crying at the time. Was she frightened, or did she realize that Aunt Gretchen loved her so much that she couldn't move anything in the room in hopes that Marie would return one day? I read this in Aunt Gretchen's diaries years later. I didn't find out why Mother got so frightened in the house until the day she died.

She wiped the tears from her eyes and sniffled. She took my hand, and we went through the other rooms on this level. They were just additional standard bedrooms with fireplaces and attractive furniture.

The whole house contained exquisite furniture; there were no ripped, torn, or stained cushions, broken chairs, or tables. Everything was in excellent condition, only dusty.

We went up to the third floor, which had four smaller rooms. The first two rooms on the left were small bedrooms, and the two on the right were the nursery, as Mother called it.

We entered the first room, and she said, "This is the nursery, your room."

I had never had a room of my own, but I liked it and smiled. This room had two twin beds, one with a light blue quilt and the other with a pink quilt. Against the far wall, there was a small light-blue armoire, a dresser for clothes, and white bookshelves filled with many toys, books, and stuffed animals.

Confused, I couldn't believe that all of this belonged to me.

I asked Mother, "Whose stuff is this?"

"It's yours now, baby."

I went over to the shelves, pulled a red toy truck off the lower rack, and stared at it, still not believing that all of this was mine. The room was also spotless, with no dust. Still holding the truck, I followed her into the connecting room.

She told me, "This is the playroom and schoolroom."

More toys were scattered around the adjacent room for both boys and girls to play with. This room was immaculate. Two small wooden school desks were positioned on one side of the room, facing a blackboard on the wall. There was another bookshelf filled with numerous books. In a corner sat an adult-sized desk with a stack of paper and a cup of sharpened pencils.

Mother bent down and picked up a doll with brown hair, a red dress, and a white apron, and a smile came over her face. I now realize she remembered playing with it when she was young and lived here.

"Oh, Beauty, you're still here."

She straightened the doll's dress and noticed a small tear on the apron that had been hand-sewn and repaired. She placed Beauty back where she had found her.

A woman wearing a black dress that hung mid-calf, with a white lace collar, her brown hair pulled back into a tight bun at the back of her head, stood and smiled at me in the doorway. Mother noticed me looking at someone and turned, but the woman had vanished.

Mother said, "Let's unpack our boxes."

I placed the toy truck on the floor. She lifted me up and carried me downstairs. She grabbed both containers with the ring of keys on top and hurried up the stairs to her room. I followed her, climbing the steps.

Someone—I now know it was Nanny—came from behind and assisted me up the steps, lifting me with each step to help me climb them.

Mother yelled, "No! Put him down!"

She ran down the stairs to me. I dropped and landed on my knees on one of the steps. Mother grabbed me and ran up the stairs. We went into her room, and she slammed the door. I didn't understand what had happened or why Mother was so upset. She lay on the bed, hugging me with her cheek on top of my head, crying and shaking.

We lay on the bed for what felt like an eternity. At last, Mother calmed down, sat up, and went to the boxes. She pulled out some items, put her clothes in the dresser, and hung others in the armoire. She set aside my things and placed them in a separate box.

I told her, "I need to go to the potty."

I had been holding it for a while, and it was getting urgent. I didn't want to be yelled at for wetting my pants.

She went to the door, opened it, poked her head out, opened the door fully, and motioned for me to come to her. We dashed down the hall to the bathroom. Elegant black-and-white tile patterns stretched along the floor and halfway up the walls. She set me on the toilet, and I went, relieved that I didn't go in my pants. She relieved herself, and we hurried back to her room.

When I returned to the room, I told her, "I'm hungry."

Two Baby Ruth candy bars were in the containers, and she pulled them out.

"Here ya go."

That was our dinner on our first night in the mansion. The delicious candy bar alleviated my hunger pangs for the time being. We didn't leave the room for the rest of the day and night except to go to the bathroom. She played records and we danced. Mother tried to appear as if she was having fun, but I could tell she wasn't.

She never explained why she was so frightened. Was she afraid of the others in the house? They seemed friendly enough to me, much nicer than those in the flophouses where we stayed. Mother had that faraway stare again as she looked out the window, took some of her pills, and fell asleep on the bed.

A Black man wearing loose white pants and a pullover shirt stood beside one of the oak trees in the front yard looking up at me. I waved to him, and he waved back, smiling. I wanted to go out and talk to him, but I thought Mother might be mad if I left the room, so I didn't. After a while, I got tired, cuddled beside her in bed, and fell asleep.

That night I dreamed about the people I encountered in the house. They stood in the room with others I hadn't met yet, but would over the next few days. They all smiled, which made me feel cared for and somehow secure. When I woke I was excited and wanted to play with the toys in the playroom. I knew they were waiting for me to come and play with them, and they were all mine.

⛏— ⛏— ⛏—

The Voodoo Imperatrice had been meditating for the last hour, inhaling the hypnotic herbal smoke from the small brazier on the table in the darkened room at the back of her house in New Orleans. A drummer sat on the floor in the corner, beating a continuous cadence. She moved back and forth to the rhythm.

She held the wooden bowl containing the divining pieces and shook it; the bones rattled inside, and she tossed them across the table's surface. As she studied the bones and observed the configurations swirling before her eyes, she sensed their meaning with her now open and receptive mind.

"The boy has arrived," the Imperatrice murmured. "The spirits owe penance—they will shield him. The mother is broken. She cannot. We must wait until he is twenty-five to achieve his full power; then, we can move forward with our plan to find the Labauve family signet and induce the boy to use his special abilities for our purposes."

The ghost of Rose, a former voodoo priestess standing in the corner, nodded her head, aware that by providing the Voodoo Imperatrice information about the power residing in the signet, she was getting closer to releasing her son's spirit.

All the cursed L'Enfant Haven plantation ghosts, except for the one in the attic, stood in Marie Labauve's bedroom while the boy and his mother slept.

Paul hopefully asked, "Do you think he is the one? The one to break the curse?"

Doc Albert said, "I don't know, but there is something special about this kid. I can feel it."

Bertha agreed, "Yes, I feel something too. He could see and speak with all of us. No Labauve has ever been able to do that."

Helen Jones said, "It doesn't matter if he is the one; he's a child, and we must protect and help him however we can."

Walter Sherman said, "I agree. We have to look after him."

Hugo Evans said, "I like the kid. I got a good feeling the minute he stepped on the property."

Milly and Philly both said, "He looks so sweet. It's too bad what has happened to his mother. She was such a beautiful child."

Helen Jones said, "I think he knows we're here. We should leave him to sleep."

All the ghosts left the room and went about their duties to prepare the house for the new heir and her extraordinary son.

# Chapter 6

# Spectral Meals

The aroma of Bertha's award-winning fried chicken wafted down the hall, promising yet another unforgettable meal. Whatever she cooked would be something exceptional.

Doc Albert, also a ghost, stood in the library doorway as I passed on my way to the kitchen.

"What's up, Doc?"

He smiled, now understanding the reference to the cartoon I liked on television.

"Glad to see you home, Orion."

Cyrus did the Porky Pig stuttering, "Th ... Th ... That's All, Folks," as he went by.

Albert didn't respond. The other ghosts don't like Cyrus much.

Entering the kitchen, I wrapped my arms around Bertha's ample waist, eager to discover tonight's menu.

"What's for dinner?"

With a smile and a pat on my left arm, she said, "Your favorite, fried chicken,"—I was right—"mashed potatoes, gravy, fresh green beans with bacon, biscuits, and apple pie."

"Mmm, that sounds wonderful. I'm going upstairs to wash up and get out of these sweaty clothes; I'll return in a jiff for the meal."

I went upstairs to the bathroom, used the toilet, and washed my face and hands.

Nanny Helen, another ghost, taught me to always clean my hands before eating. Her absence was keenly felt.

As I washed up, I couldn't help but notice my reflection in the mirror. Nanny Helen would have chided me in French for my unruly curls covering my ears—a testament to her meticulous grooming standards.

She would have said in French, "Time for a haircut. A gentleman always needs to have his hair trimmed."

We always spoke French to one another to help me learn and practice the language. I learned it quickly when she began teaching me at three. Nanny always said I was brilliant and could remember everything.

Yet despite the need for a trim, I couldn't deny the allure of my olive skin and piercing blue eyes, reminiscent of my mother's before her struggles with drugs took their toll.

Amazingly, my nose remained narrow and straight, considering all the fights I had in junior and high school. Some skirmishes occurred because Cyrus insisted I talk to him when people were around.

I went to my bedroom and shed the sweaty clothes I had worn on the airplane and in the hot taxi. I stood in front of the mirror on the back of the door and admired my well-conditioned six-foot body. A handsome man, I attracted women easily until they caught me talking to someone invisible, discovered I lived in a haunted plantation house, or sensed something ominous about me. Sometimes, I wouldn't bring Cyrus's amulet if I thought I had a chance with a girl. His constant smart-ass comments and criticisms of the women I liked were hard to ignore.

I threw on clean jeans and a white tee before heading downstairs. As always, just one place setting waited at the head of the long dining table—a tradition that Nanny insisted on. Dinner, no matter what, belonged in the dining room. While I ate, I recalled the first time Bertha cooked for me.

⚷— ⚷— ⚷—

After sleeping beside my mother on our first night in the house, I woke up excited to go upstairs and enjoy all the playthings. I was enthusiastic about all these toys—never having had more than two or three, usually broken, and now an entire room full—the most thrilling and joyous experience of my short life. I jumped out of bed, ran to the door, opened it to leave, ready to head for the playroom, but the lady from the third floor stopped me. She stood in the hall, waiting for me.

She stared at me, "You must have breakfast before playing."

How did she know what I was thinking?

"Okay," I said.

My stomach growled when she mentioned breakfast. I seldom had a morning meal because Mother always slept late. The woman took my hand and led me to the bathroom, where I relieved myself. She instructed me to wash my hands before a meal and held me up to the sink so I could accomplish this task. We then continued to the stairs.

She asked, "Can you make it down the steps?"

"Yes."

I sat down and scooted on my bottom until my feet touched the step below. Then, I stood up and repeated the same process for each step. It took me a while to descend the stairs, but I eventually made it. As we continued down the steps, she told me her name.

"Orion"—she always called me by my full first name—"my name is Helen Jones, but you can call me Nanny or Nanny Helen. I am your governess and here to care for and teach you."

"What are you going to teach me?" I asked, not knowing what a governess was.

"How to take care of yourself, grow up to become a fine gentleman, your manners, and how to read and write both English and French, how to read music and play the piano."

"I get to read and write? I like books. I like the pictures."

"Well, I will teach you to understand the books and learn what they say. There are numerous books in this house, with fun stories."

"Oh, good. I like stories."

She smiled, glad to have an excited and bright pupil after so long.

When we reached the bottom of the steps, all the cobwebs and dust on the elegant glass chandelier in the front hall had been cleared away. The crystal pieces sparkled and flashed with the light streaming through the now clear windows on either side of the door, creating mesmerizing rainbows on the walls. Having never witnessed anything like this before, I watched in awe as the prisms of color danced around the room.

I glanced at the floor; the hardwood looked freshly waxed, with no dusty footprints. Everything was clean and fresh, all grime eliminated.

Sheets no longer covered the parlor furniture, and the antique Victorian pieces stood polished and clean.

The governess took my hand and led me down the hall to the kitchen. On the table sat a bowl of oatmeal, raisins, maple syrup, and milk, ready for consumption. I inhaled the aroma of maple and my stomach rumbled. The sweet scent combined with the hunger pangs in my tummy made me yearn to grab the food and start eating.

I stood waiting to be told what to do, unsure if the food was for me or someone else, not wanting to be yelled at if it belonged to another person. As I mentioned, I was smart and had learned to be cautious while living in the flophouses around unstable people.

Bertha stood over me with her hands on her ample hips and said with her strong Southern accent.

"Sit at the table, child, and eat your breakfast."

Happy to hear this statement, I climbed onto the chair, but the table surface was too high. I got on my knees for better access to the delicious food. Nanny Helen approached me with a massive pillow to prop me up, bringing me high enough to eat from the bowl. This tasty meal was the best I had ever had at that time. I finished the cereal, and Nanny Helen helped me back upstairs to play with the toys in the playroom.

Mother awoke in a panic and yelled for me, realizing I wasn't in her room. Thinking I would want to enjoy the toys, she rushed up the stairs and stood in the playroom doorway, panting.

She shouted, "Ory, come back to my room!"

"But I want to play!" I yelled my defiance.

"No, you're coming with me."

She picked me up, went down to the second floor, took me to her room, and slammed the door. I cried and fought to escape her grip the entire way. I wanted to go back to the nursery and play with the toys.

She told me, "Stop crying. You have to stay here with me."

"Why? I want to play!"

I sobbed, shouted, and stamped my foot.

Mother never gave me an answer, just a swat on the bottom, and said, "Now, be quiet!"

I sat on the floor with my knees drawn up to my chest, tears still streaming down my cheeks, sniffling and feeling unhappy. Mother took her pills again and collapsed onto the bed.

The door opened a crack, and Nanny Helen stuck her head in and waved for me to come out. I smiled and left the room, ready to return upstairs to the playroom. I played all morning, jumping from toy to toy, distracted by each new treasure I discovered in the room. This episode taught me not to fight Mother, let her take her medication, and sneak out later.

36

# Chapter 7

# Living at the Estate
# & Driving Lessons

While enjoying my fried chicken dinner, the ghosts gathered to listen to my Finding Job narration. They loved hearing about the people in the outside world and how I helped them. Most of them couldn't leave the property.

I outlined the events of the job for everyone. The ease of this Finding Job disappointed some of my spirit family. They preferred the complex jobs that took me to different places, sometimes lasting several days. After eating, I went into the living room and turned on the TV. Most of the ghosts enjoyed watching television, as it allowed them to learn more about the outside world. I watched a movie, went to bed, and read a French novel for a while before falling asleep.

I still actively use the French language that Nanny Helen taught me. While in high school, I took the advanced French classes offered. Being exceptional in French made the course easy for me. My French teacher, Miss Beaumont, gave me personalized reading assignments and introduced me to current French novels. I had already read a few of the classics.

Andrew Butler Sr. had been the Labauve family counselor for over fifty years. He was the only person outside the family to enter the L'Enfant Haven house without hesitation. His son Andy Jr. would only enter the haunted house when necessary. Butler Sr. was involved in several unusual episodes at this property. As I got older, I learned about some of them, though I'm sure not all. The L'Enfant Haven mansion and the Labauve family share quite an interesting, colorful, and tragic history.

Mr. Butler Sr. brought the first black-and-white television to the house for Mother and me on the first Christmas we stayed in the mansion. Mother didn't realize it was Christmas until he arrived with the gift. He set it up in the parlor—now that there was a television in the room, I think the parlor officially became a living room. Having never seen a TV—there were none in any of the flophouses we lived in—I sat in front of it, mesmerized for hours on that first day. Mother ignored it and returned to her bedroom.

Because she was on drugs most of the time, the spirits learned not to manifest around her, so she no longer freaked out when I wasn't with her.

Nanny Helen didn't care for television. She believed it distracted me from personal creative playtime, schoolwork, and piano practice. She limited the amount of TV I could watch each day.

⚷— ⚷— ⚷—

When I got up the following day, I shaved, brushed my teeth, dressed in jeans and a button-up plaid short-sleeved shirt, had a hearty breakfast made by Bertha, and went to the garage to check on the restoration of the 1939 Rolls-Royce Phantom.

Walter Sherman, the chauffeur and automobile mechanic from the 1940s, was a ghost who died when he crashed an older Rolls-Royce into one of the oak trees in the front yard. He worked on the vehicles. When I was away from the property, the work progressed slowly. Walter had another fender sanded. I would help him if no other Finding Jobs came around.

⚷— ⚷— ⚷—

When I was six, I stole the ring of keys from my mother's room and tested several until I found the right one to open the carriage house garage. Covered with canvas tarps, the vintage automobiles waited to be admired, cared for, and driven. I pulled the drapes off the cars, and my eyes widened in amazement. The old vehicles included a black 1939 Rolls-Royce Phantom, a red 1949 Jaguar XK120, and a black 1950 Chrysler New Yorker. I was in heaven. I got behind the wheel of each car and pretended to drive, making vrooming sounds.

Walter walked up and said, "Nice, aren't they?"

"Yeah, I like them."

I was happy to have access to the vehicles.

"Well, when you're a little older, I'll teach you how to drive them."

"How soon?" I asked eagerly, my heart racing with anticipation.

"In a few years, when you can reach all the pedals."

"All right."

After that, the drapes stayed off the vehicles, and Walter kept them clean, waxed, and operational.

Walter brought over an old bicycle and said, "Until then, you can use this. I'll fix it up."

The bike had been my mother's when she was a little girl.

"But I don't know how to ride one."

"I'll teach you."

The next day, Walter brought out the cleaned bicycle with inflated tires. I thanked him and hugged him. He brushed my curls out of my eyes and said, "You're welcome."

He explained what to do and held the back of the bike while I learned to balance, going back and forth on the dirt road. I got the hang of it and would zip up and down the plantation roads as fast as possible, producing dust clouds behind me if it hadn't been raining, and jumping over drainage ditches.

For a few years, the bike was my primary mode of transportation around the estate on the dirt roads. It kept me busy and entertained. Mr. Butler purchased a new bicycle for my eighth birthday. The shiny new bike sported a basket on the front, and sometimes I would ride into town on errands to pick up small items from the grocery, hardware, or auto parts stores.

The old cars in the garage were not just part of the trust for the property; they were a part of me. I might drive the vehicles, but I could not sell them. Why would I want to sell them? I loved operating these vintage automobiles.

Walter taught me how to drive when I was ten; it was my birthday present from him. I couldn't drive on the state or parish roads but was allowed to drive around the estate's private dirt roads. Other kids could only dream of what I got to do every day. I told my classmates that I drove cars around the plantation, but they thought I was lying—none of them dared to come see for themselves.

Walter also taught me how to maintain automobiles and fix their parts. Again, I learned quickly. We would spend hours in the garage. Sometimes, Nanny Helen would be upset because my schoolwork wasn't finished and I was always covered in dirt and grease. I loved every second of it. While I emerged covered in grease, Walter's crisp black chauffeur uniform stayed spotless—ghost perks, I guess.

After graduating from high school, I worked as a car mechanic at Marti's Auto Shop in Madreville for a year to earn extra cash until regular job opportunities began to come in.

It took me a while to convince Marti Graceland that I knew how to work on older cars. I went to the shop daily and demonstrated how I would repair some of the older vehicles. I was determined to prove my worth, and he eventually agreed to hire me. I didn't bring the amulet with me so that Cyrus couldn't distract me, which allowed me to do a lot of productive work.

It upset Marti when I told him I was quitting because Finding Jobs took so much time. We are still friends, and he lets me use some of his specialized tools for vehicle maintenance, like his paint shack, to restore the Roll's body pieces as Walter and I work on them.

# Chapter 8

# Investigation Results

It was a beautiful, clear day, so I drove the red 1949 Jaguar into town. The Jaguar doesn't have a ragtop, so I can only drive it when there is no chance of rain. I went into Madreville to visit my lawyer's office.

People always stared when I drove through Madreville—maybe it was the car or the guy from the haunted plantation. I parked in front of Andy's office—on the second floor above the town's doctor, tucked into an aging brick storefront. I entered the door with the Andrew Butler Jr. sign, ATTORNEY AT LAW, and ascended the steps.

Doris Owens, Andy's secretary, sat at her desk, a Black woman in her fifties with flecks of gray hair and glasses that hung around her neck most of the time. She had worked for the Butlers for thirty years. A six-inch clear crystal mounted on a wooden base sat on her desk; the decoration had always been there. I asked her about it once, and she said it was a lucky charm. It fascinated me when I was little; she let me hold it while my mother talked to Andrew Butler Sr. I felt a slight tingle from the crystal but never told her anything. Even as an adult, if I have to wait to get in and speak with Andy, I'll stroke the crystal, enjoying its sensation.

She glanced up and said, "Go on in. He's waiting for you."

When I entered Andy's office today, he smiled widely. He seemed excited, yet something else was happening. I couldn't identify it, but something felt off. I could sense it in my stomach.

Andy, a handsome man in his sixties with graying brown hair and warm brown eyes, always wore a smile and maintained steady nerves. He had lived in Madreville his entire life and followed in his father's footsteps to become a lawyer. He had known me since I was three and had helped turn my strange gift into a career.

He married a local girl, Vivian, his high school sweetheart, and the couple had three children who now live outside Louisiana. Andy, a kind-hearted man, had several pro bono clients—probably too many—but since we established the Finding Job business, things have improved financially for both of us.

After I found the Rowen kid, who had been missing for two weeks, when I was eighteen, word spread, and my unique talent became sought after. He realized I was different, having worked with his father and knowing me since I moved to the estate at three. The money that Finding Jobs offered was too tempting, so he set up the business, with me as the Finder and him as my agent and business manager.

He said, "Got the appraisal. Biggest payday yet—the check's going out tomorrow."

"Fantastic. Any word on my father?"

"Yes, I discovered he succumbed to an overdose, like your mother. I found this out from your grandmother, his mother. She wants to meet you."

Was that a slight tremor in his voice? Something must be wrong.

"Okay. Where does she live?"

I noticed the new crystal on his desk and unconsciously rubbed it, again getting a tingling sensation.

"Is this new?"

"In New Orleans. Here is her address and phone number. Yes, Doris said my office needed some decoration."

I nodded, took the small piece of paper and stuffed it into my pocket.

"Thanks for doing this for me. Before she passed, I promised my mother I would find him."

I had been sitting on this for over five years, unsure if I wanted to meet my father. But thoughts of my mother and what she said on her deathbed had been coming to mind in the last few weeks since my twenty-fifth birthday. I asked Andy if he could explore this issue for me, because for some reason I don't understand, I can't locate things for close relatives like my mother or maybe my father.

My mother always lost her car keys, and I would try to find them for her, but I never could. I would have located them in seconds if anyone else had been looking. I knew tracking my father down would be a challenge.

"I'd think twice before meeting her. She calls herself a voodoo witch. Probably makes a fortune off tourists in the Quarter."

There it was again, a slight tremor in his voice. Something wasn't right with Andy, but I decided not to say anything. It might be a private matter.

"I'm not stupid. I'm not handing her any cash. I want to talk to her about my father and some things my mother told me about before she died."

"Okay, I understand. Just be careful."

"No, you don't understand. But, maybe one day, I'll tell you everything."

I left his office, unaware that the phone call would never happen.

44

# Chapter 9

# Past Whispers at the White Rabbit Club

As Orion Labauve left his office, Andy Butler Jr. couldn't help but feel a surge of insight.

'I know more than you think,' Andy mused. 'More than you ever will. Some things I wish I didn't.'

On his deathbed, Andrew Sr. told Andy strange stories about the L'Enfant Haven plantation—stories he had never dared to speak aloud before. He insisted that Andy come to his room each day to divulge as much information as possible before passing away, leaving Andy to inherit the family business.

Discovering his father's diaries hidden in a safe behind a wall panel in the office added another layer of revelation. His father had never mentioned or granted him access to the personal diaries, perhaps assuming Andy would eventually find them. The safe opened with the birthdate of Sebastian Gaines—his father's closest friend. That alone spoke volumes.

The journals revealed shocking information about his father, especially his secret homosexuality. While initially disturbed by this, Andy started to piece together specific actions and mysterious trips his father had taken over the years.

Despite being a loving father and husband, societal norms of the time compelled his father to conceal his sexual orientation. Sebastian Gaines, his father's lover since college, shed light on the frequent trips to New Orleans for "business" purposes.

Gretchen Labauve discovered him and Sebastian in New Orleans when she saw them together at a private club during her visit to the establishment. She was looking for someone to exorcise the ghosts from the plantation.

Gretchen Labauve had heard whispers about the White Rabbit Club, a mysterious establishment rumored to fulfill any desire. Determined to solve the haunting plaguing her estate, she spared no expense to join, receiving the elusive password and gaining entry through the red back alley doorway. Wearing a sleek black sequined dress, Gretchen surveyed the club's dimly lit interior, watching couples sway to jazz melodies.

Dim lighting and small candles burning on each table provided customers with enough light to see others at their table while creating shadows for those who preferred not to be observed. Gretchen recognized her attorney—blond-haired, handsome Andrew Butler—and another dark-haired, rugged-looking man kissing in a booth.

Sauntering over, Gretchen interjected wryly, "What a romantic rendezvous."

Andrew stopped kissing Sebastian, shocked that Gretchen Labauve was beside his table.

He stammered, "I, I... Wh ... What are you doing here?"

"I have nothing to hide," Gretchen said, smirking. "But it looks like you do. I always had my suspicions. I'm searching for a voodoo witch to help me exorcise ghosts from my house. I asked you for assistance on this matter and you refused. I still need assistance, and you will give it to me, or else I will announce your homosexuality in the newspaper and make some claim of perversion."

Looking at Andrew, Sebastian asked, "What does she want you to do?"

"She wants someone who can determine why the L'Enfant Haven mansion is cursed and how to remove the curse, thus exorcising the ghosts."

The jazz music stopped and the musicians left the stage for a break. Gretchen slid into the booth with the two men to keep their conversation confidential.

She added, "I don't want to exorcise the spirits; I just want to allow them to move on. The spirits are all stuck there for some reason, and I need to find out why to help them."

Sebastian inquired, "Can't they tell you?"

"No, they can't talk to me, or at least I can't hear them. I can see them sometimes, but not always. They handle things, clean the place, and occasionally cook, which is strange."

Andrew said, "I don't know why you think I would know anything about voodoo."

"Oh, maybe because a voodoo witch raised you."

Shocked by this statement, Sebastian stared at his lover.

Andrew asked, "How did you find any of this out? I've never told anyone."

"The Labauve family used to be quite social around the turn of the century, and my Aunt Caroline was best of friends with your mother, Ann Christof. My aunt kept detailed diaries. I found them in the attic and read them. Your mother got pregnant with you via some illicit affair, and the family shipped her off to have you in secret. You were given to Josette Montaigne, who acted as your nanny and caregiver and was also a voodoo practitioner known as Mama Obeah Oracle."

Andrew explained, though reluctant to give Gretchen this information, "My mother handed me over to Josette Montaigne. She raised me. She was also a voodoo priestess—Mama Obeah Oracle. My mother continued to pay Josette to take care of me. I attended the most expensive schools in New Orleans and the most prestigious college in Louisiana.

"Josette raised me like her own son. To me, she was my mother. My real mother seldom came to visit. I left that world when Josette passed on and haven't contacted anyone since. Josette never allowed me to be involved in any of the ceremonies."

Gretchen said, "To continue your story: After you completed your bar exam and became a lawyer, your mother, Ann, asked her best friend, my Aunt Caroline, to take you on as an attorney for the Labauve family. This way, she could keep in touch with you by visiting occasionally. So she must have cared a little."

"I still don't understand why you think I would be able to find someone for you."

"Oh, you should remember associates of Josette's. I'm sure you can locate a practitioner if you try. Please try.”

Gretchen got up and walked away. As she left, she smiled, knowing he would take care of this task for her.

As Gretchen left, Sebastian inquired, “Is all of that true?”

“Yes. I’m sorry you found out about it this way. I was planning on telling you one day.”

“Do you know anyone who might be able to help her?”

“There is somewhere I can go and ask. Some may even remember me.”

The next day, Andrew stepped into the Occult Goods Shop, the scent of herbs and incense instantly transporting him back to his childhood, bringing back memories of Josette and how much he loved and missed his surrogate mother.

A loud female voice with a Caribbean accent came from behind the counter, saying, “Well, look who the black cat drug in! If it isn’t little Andy.”

The tall, dark woman, wearing a multi-colored skirt and a white blouse, was placing items on a shelf when she turned around with a wide smile. Marcella rushed around the service counter and gave Andrew a big hug.

Andrew said, “It’s good to see you, Aunt Marcie.”

She asked him, “What brings you back to N’Orleans? Don’t you live up by Shreveport?”

“Yes, in Madreville.”

“Ain’t you still working for La ... ?”

She tried to remember where he worked.

“The Labauve family, yes. And I’m married and have a son now.”

“Married? Hmm! I didn’t think that you swung in that direction,” she said with surprise.

“Well, one has to put up fronts these days.”

“That is the truth for the outside world, but if you had stayed here, you wouldn’t have had to. What can I do for you? I know you ain’t here for a visit.”

She was curious about his unexpected appearance.

“You always could read people. I need someone to help a client break a curse and exorcise ghosts.”

"Oh, not a small request, a real job. Will there be payment?"

She thought, 'This should be interesting.'

"Yes, quite generous."

"I'll ask around. Where are you staying?"

"At the Royal Hotel."

"I'll send a message when I find someone interested in the work."

Marcella thought, 'Whew, that place is expensive. He must make good money working for the Labauves.'

"Thank you. It was good seeing you again."

"See you later, Andy."

As Andrew left and returned to the Royal, he mused on how the reunion stirred memories of his past and the mysterious world he left behind.

While waiting for Aunt Marcie's call, Andrew paced the floor in his room. Sebastian observed Andrew walking back and forth, staring at the walls with concern.

Sebastian said, "Andrew, please relax and sit by me on the couch."

Andrew dropped onto the couch beside him. Sebastian wrapped an arm around his shoulder, sensing the tension still coiled in every muscle and the tiny twitches that demonstrated his nervousness.

Rubbing Andrew's upper arm to help him relax, Sebastian pleaded, "Please try to relax. It can't be that bad."

Andrew snapped back, "Yes, it can be. You don't understand how critical it can be. If I don't get a practitioner for Gretchen, she will publish something about me in the papers. That will ruin my life, my family's, and yours. If Aunt Marcie finds someone to break the curse, it might work, but there might be other problems if they aren't skilled at using the practice."

He sat with his head on Sebastian's shoulder and continued to worry.

Two days later, he received a note with an address and a time: 8 a.m. He dressed in jeans and a white T-shirt to avoid drawing attention in that neighborhood. While he prepared to leave, Sebastian knocked on the door to his hotel room. He opened the door and let his lover in.

Sebastian said, "I'm going with you."

"No, you are not. I don't want you exposed or involved with these types of things. It's best that you stay out of it."

"But you might be in danger," he said, worry showing in his eyes.

"I won't be in danger; the people in this area of town all know who I am and what Josette was to me. They know I have protective spells around me. They can't do anything to me, or the spells will return tenfold to them."

"Do you believe in all of this voodoo stuff?"

"Yes, I do. I've seen too many situations to dismiss them as fantasy. That's why I don't want you involved in any of this. They can do things to you. I don't want something to happen to you. That's why I want you to stay here. I'll be back. Everything will be okay."

As Andrew closed the door, tears of dread and concern brimmed in Sebastian's eyes, mirroring the fear and anxiety in his heart.

Andrew took a taxi as close as the driver could take him to the indicated location and walked the rest of the way. He approached the tiny house. Voodoo protective spells and charms made of feathers and bones, painted red and black, hung from the front porch rafters. They swayed despite the absence of wind.

A wave of apprehension washed over him, urging him to stop and walk away. Nonetheless, he forced himself to move toward the house, convinced that these oppressive sensations were a protective enchantment placed on the premises. He maneuvered between the talismans, being careful not to touch any, rapped on the door three times, and waited. Aunt Marcie answered the door.

"Come on in, Andy. The Voodoo Imperatrice is waiting for you."

Andrew stepped forward to enter but stopped when Marcie said, "The Voodoo Imperatrice ..."

He recalled Josette speaking of her with unease and how her power in the practice surpassed anyone else's in Louisiana.

Andrew intently stared at Aunt Marcie and said, "You don't mess around with finding someone to do a job."

He continued into the tiny house.

Marcella said, "I put out the word, and she's the one who answered, so there has to be a reason for it. There is always a reason. This way."

Andrew followed her into a back room. She drew back the beaded curtain from the doorway, and Andrew entered. His mind, filled with apprehension and anxiety, made his heart rate and breathing accelerate faster than usual, leaving him slightly dizzy.

Black candles flickered in the gloom, shadows danced across walls concealed behind heavy drapes. The air reeked of cloves, marijuana, sage, and something older, leaving a faint smoky haze in the small space.

A female voice with a strong New Orleans accent and a slight lisp emerged from the deep shadows.

"Sit, Andrew Butler, or should it be Andrew Christof?"

Renee chuckled, "Na, Butler is right; your daddy was a butler."

Andrew didn't know this but said nothing. He sat down.

"Tell me more about this exorcism."

"My client owns a plantation in Madreville that has been haunted for 170 years. Several ghosts occupy the house. She would like the curse on the house removed to allow the spirits to move on."

"Does she want this to help the ghosts or her?"

"I don't know for sure. She said it was to help the spirits."

The Voodoo Imperatrice didn't reply; she moved into the light of a candle on the table and sat on the other side. Her face was partially in shadow, and Andrew could tell it was somewhat distorted. Her hair was wrapped in a colorful scarf, the rest of her clothing was dark and difficult to distinguish in the shadows. She wore several necklaces around her neck that clattered and jingled with her movements.

Renee, the voodoo priestess, picked up a wooden cup and shook it; something rattled inside, and she scattered tiny items across the table's surface. She examined the configurations of the divining bones.

"You're telling the truth," she declared. "I'm getting that this needs to be done, but not by me. Someone else will come later. We must prepare for his coming. I will come to this plantation and speak with the owner. Make the arrangements, but don't tell her what we talked about. Just tell her I want to see the place first. You can call Marcella when things are ready. Now go."

Andrew stood up and left without asking any questions, as Josette had taught him never to question the Voodoo Imperatrice. He entered the tiny front room, where Aunt Marcie was waiting.

He said, "I need your phone number. She wants me to contact you when I have arranged for her to come to the estate."

Marcella wrote down her number and gave it to Andrew. He stuffed it into his pocket, left the house, and walked down the street in a daze. What was all that about?

'Someone else will come.'

The words clung to him like cobwebs. He shivered—and didn't know why.

# Chapter 10

# The Cursed Assault

Renee Broussard exited the back room and observed through the window as Andrew walked down the sidewalk. A thirteen-year-old boy left the bedroom and stood next to his mother.

Antoine asked, "Why did you want me here when that man came for a reading?"

"He will take us someplace important. You will meet a person who will be special to you."

Antoine Broussard knew better than to question his mother; her exceptional capabilities frightened him. Antoine glanced toward the corner. His father's ghost stood there—always watching. He hated it. He hated that his mother insisted it was necessary. And he hated her for it.

Renee returned to the divination room and commented, "It's started."

The black voodoo priestess spirit in the corner walked into the candlelight and nodded her head.

Renee returned to the living room. Her son, Antoine, and Marcella had already left. Marcella would drive him back to Josephine's. She went to the bedroom to lie down for a while, contemplating the next steps in her plan. Knowing she had to be patient, she believed everything would unfold as she envisioned the future. However, the past crept back into her thoughts.

⚿— ⚿— ⚿—

Renee Broussard was a child prodigy in voodoo practices. Her mother, Angelique, began teaching her at the age of twelve, and she learned effortlessly to perform the ceremonies, create gris gris

53

(charms), and be possessed by spirits. She always understood what to do without needing instruction.

Paid well, Renee's mother conducted rites and crafted talismans for several affluent businessmen. Renee recalled the terrible events that occurred when she was fourteen.

On a dismal rainy night, one of Angelique's clients, Webster Turner, came to their house, angry that the ceremony Angelique had initiated for him was unsuccessful. He lost substantial money on a bad investment and blamed her

Drunk, smelling of alcohol, Webster kicked the door in, yelling, "You better fix this, you witch bitch!"

He smacked Angelique multiple times. Receiving flashes of satisfaction from these actions, he progressed to beating her with his fists and kicking her repeatedly. Angelique writhed on the floor as Webster's rage took control of him, and he beat her mercilessly. She later died from her devastating injuries at the hospital.

Renee leapt onto the assailant's back, screaming. He flung her off and struck her hard across the face. As she fell to the floor, she crawled to the coffee table and picked up a ceramic figurine. She swung the statue with all her strength and hit him on the head. Slightly dazed, his anger was reignited by this action. He turned to her with a crazed, manic expression and punched Renee in the face, knocking out her two front teeth. She fell unconscious. He continued beating her mother.

When Webster tired of pummeling her mother, he turned to Renee. She woke with him standing over her and a fist moving through the air, hitting her face. He struck her again and again—until her vision blurred and darkness swallowed her. He ripped off her dress and underwear and viciously raped her, grunting with each thrust and a deranged, possessed glint in his eyes. When she awoke, it was to pain, blood, and the hollow echo of her own voice screaming into silence.

After he left, Renee crawled to the phone and called the police. The blaring sirens and flashing lights of the police cars arrived, and officers searched through everything in the house.

The policewoman asked, "Who did all of this?"

Shaking, Renee replied, "A strange white man broke down the door, forced his way in, beat both me and my mother. He raped me and left."

She gave them very few details. She swore vengeance against this man, which only she would have.

The police investigation progressed with little to no information about the perpetrator. They ultimately closed the case. This type of incident occurred often when voodoo was involved, as the police department lacked the time or manpower to dedicate to those who believed in supernatural occurrences.

After a week in the hospital because of the horrible beating, Renee learned she was pregnant.

Her face would never fully heal. Her nose, having been severely broken from the beating, now displayed a large knot that rose above the natural bridge. Two of her front teeth had also been knocked out, and her left eyelid drooped continuously due to muscle damage from the beating.

Her aunt Bernadette took her in, but they had no money for surgery.

Renee stopped wishing for repairs. Instead, she embraced the mirror's reflection—each scar a vow. They served as a constant reminder of that horrifying day and what she must do to exact her revenge and ensure it could never happen again.

She continued to study voodoo under various practitioners, learning as much as possible from each. Her ability to influence the voodoo realm grew to levels unmatched by any other practitioner. She learned to perform a glamour spell on her face when she didn't want people to see her deformities.

She cursed Webster Turner and his body deteriorated with the most excruciating cancer imaginable. He suffered for months. As part of her revenge, she further cursed him never to have peace, never to be able to move on, forcing him to follow the child he sired, doomed to watch him forever.

After the devastating death of her aunt and uncle, her hatred and vengeance toward the group that committed the crime festered into a self-centered obsession with power and control. Any love she might have had for Antoine was buried—locked away with the rest of her memories from that night. He always reminded her of the horrific night when her mother died and she was raped. She utilized her son's natural talents to perceive spirits whenever needed, never caring about how he felt.

Her quest for voodoo's influence over ghosts and people led her to search for the ultimate Spirit Speaker—someone who could observe apparitions, communicate with ghosts, contain spirits within themselves without being possessed, and, most importantly, control these spirits. If she found this individual and gained domination over them, she would influence every aspect of the voodoo practice.

Her meditations led her to a previous Voodoo Queen, Rose. Renee called Rose from the other side and manifested her spirit to learn more about Rose's unique abilities to create potent charms.

One of Renee's special powers was her ability to divine the future and perform remote-viewing activities from long distances. She learned that the Spirit Speaker she desired would be born to a fair-haired, white woman who could see ghosts. Her son, Antoine, would be the father. When news of the ghost exorcism job for the Labauve plantation, haunted by multiple spirits, reached her, she recognized this as the next step toward acquiring the talents of the Spirit Speaker.

# Chapter 11

# The Voodoo Consultation

Almost in tears, Andrew opened the hotel room door and collapsed into Sebastian's waiting embrace.

"What happened?" Sebastian inquired, hugging Andrew and holding him up.

"I met the Voodoo Imperatrice," he said, shaking.

"The Voodoo what?"

"The Voodoo Imperatrice. The most powerful voodoo practitioner there is. It was terrifying. She wants to come out to the estate and see for herself before she commits to doing anything. I must go back and talk to Gretchen about this."

Andrew slid the closet door open, pulled out his brown leather suitcase, and tossed it onto the bed. He took a light-blue short-sleeved shirt from the hanger and buttoned it over his sweat-soaked T-shirt. He removed his other clothes from the hangers and the drawers and stuffed them into the suitcase.

"You're leaving right now?"

"You don't understand. You don't make that woman wait. I must leave now. I'm sorry. I'll call you when I know more about what's happening."

Andrew kissed Sebastian, closed the suitcase, and left the room. He checked out of the hotel and requested that his car be brought around. As he waited for his vehicle, a shiver ran through his body. He needed to hurry back to the estate. When his vehicle arrived, he threw his bag in the back seat and sped away.

The tall doorman, dressed in a long dark blue coat with gold piping and a top hat, verified that the important blond man had driven away. He walked over to the pay phone and called a number. The Voodoo Imperatrice answered.

The doorman said, "He left."

"Thank you."

She hung up the telephone and thought, 'Mama Obeah Oracle taught him good.'

Andrew traveled faster than the speed limit back to Madreville. He went straight to the plantation mansion. Nearly five hours after leaving the Royal Hotel, he parked the car in front of the L'Enfant Haven house and rushed to the entrance. While driving back, his mind was consumed by the frightening, strange woman's words. He couldn't shake the feeling that the Imperatrice hadn't just agreed to help—she'd set something in motion. Something neither he nor Gretchen could control. What had he done? What had Gretchen Labauve forced him to do?

Using the lion-head knocker, he frantically pounded on the door, striking the brass ring against the metal plate several times. As he waited for someone to answer, he took several deep breaths to calm himself, so Gretchen wouldn't suspect that something was bothering him.

Marie Labauve, Gretchen's great-niece, and a pretty twelve-year-old blonde girl who would be beautiful when grown, opened the door. Her parents had died in a car accident. Gordon Labauve Jr., her father, had been Gretchen's favorite nephew; he would have inherited the plantation, but now it would go to Marie's older brother, Robert. Gretchen doted on her niece and loved her dearly.

Marie, who had a sweet disposition, stood at the entrance, smiling. "Hi, Mr. Butler, come on in."

Andrew entered, saying, "I need to talk to your aunt."

"She's on the back porch having a lemonade."

Andrew walked down the hall to the back door and the veranda.

Gretchen sat leisurely on the screened veranda in a white wicker chair, holding a refreshing drink. A full pitcher rested on the small table beside her chair. She glanced up at Andrew.

She said, "I didn't expect you to be back so soon. Would you like a lemonade?"

"No. No. I managed to make the contact you requested."

"See, I knew you would come through," she said snidely.

"She wants to come here to view the place and talk to you first before she commits to anything."

"She wants to figure out how much she can flim-flam me for."

"She doesn't haggle. If she takes the job, you pay what she asks—no questions."

"Okay, when can she come?"

"I will call, and she will give me a date and time. That will not be negotiable either."

"My goodness, she certainly has you nervous," she said, noticing him fidgeting.

"She's the Voodoo Imperatrice. She has incredible power."

"What should I expect if she agrees to perform the rite?"

"She'll decide the best day, time, and place to perform the ceremony in the house, and several of her followers will accompany her to assist. You'll have to be involved in some way as the house owner, especially since you are the oldest living descendant of the Labauve family. I don't know what will happen during the ceremony; as I said, my mother never allowed me to participate in them."

"Okay, make the call. Set it up."

Andrew walked into the hall and called Marcella—Aunt Marcie.

"I have spoken with Gretchen Labauve, and she is willing to let her come here to see the place before commitment."

Marcella said, "Hold on."

Then she put the phone down.

Sweating, Andrew stood waiting for her to return. After what felt like an eternity, she picked up the receiver.

"She will be there sometime the day after tomorrow. Give me the address."

He told her the location and hung up the phone. He then informed Gretchen of the date when the priestess would arrive. She nodded her head.

Andrew left with his gut twisted; each step away from the house served as a reminder of how deeply he'd fallen into something dangerous.

When he got home, his wife could tell something was wrong, but he wouldn't talk about it, saying, "It is nothing for you to worry about, dear."

Marie was in the kitchen during Aunt Gretchen and Mr. Butler's discussion. She froze when she heard Mr. Butler mention a voodoo priestess. With her eyes wide, she tiptoed through the dining room and then bolted up the stairs to avoid being caught.

The spirits on the property all knew and were concerned about what this visit by a voodoo priestess meant. Trouble always followed when voodoo occurred here.

# Chapter 12

# The Mansion & Ghost Viewing

Renee Broussard arrived at 5 p.m. with her son Antoine. Throughout the day, Andrew Butler paced, his nerves fraying with each hour the Voodoo Imperatrice failed to arrive. When Marcella knocked on the door, Andrew answered.

He said, "Come in," and bowed his head in deference and respect as Josette taught him.

Renee Broussard rubbed the lion-head knocker on the nose as she entered. Andrew noticed that the deformities of the Voodoo Imperatrice he had seen at her house were no longer visible. She was beautiful. Renee wore the same colorful scarf wrapped around her head as when he visited her home. She was also dressed in a flowing red full-length skirt and a light-blue, low-cut blouse, with many necklaces rattling and jingling as she moved.

Andrew advised Gretchen earlier to answer the door and bow her head to the Voodoo Imperatrice.

"I'm not bowing to a voodoo witch," Gretchen scoffed.

Andrew sighed.

"Then don't expect miracles. She won't lift a finger if you insult her."

"Money talks," Gretchen muttered. "We'll see."

Andrew shook his head, knowing he wouldn't change Gretchen Labauve's mind.

Andrew led Renee, Antoine, and Marcella to the veranda and introduced them to Gretchen Labauve. Gretchen sat looking up at the Voodoo Imperatrice and pointed to a chair.

As the priestess sat, Gretchen asked, "Would you like some refreshments?"

The priestess said, "Why, thank you. I believe I would."

The hostess filled the glass with lemonade.

Renee told Andrew, Marcella, and Antoine, "Please wait in the parlor while Miss Gretchen and I come to an understanding."

They all left, went to the parlor, and waited on the couch. Marie came down the steps.

Andrew said, "Ah, Miss Marie. Why don't you take Antoine out front and show him around the plantation grounds?"

Antoine's eyes opened wide when the attractive, fair-haired girl descended the stairs. He stood and followed her outside.

Andrew asked, "Aunt Marcie, do you think the Voodoo Imperatrice will perform the ceremony? I told Gretchen she should answer the door and bow her head, but she refused."

"I don't know; she's the only person I can't read."

They both sat in silence.

Gretchen asked Renee, "What is your real name? I feel silly calling you Voodoo Imperatrice."

The priestess laughed, "Renee Broussard."

She sipped the refreshing drink as they talked.

Renee continued, "This is perfect lemonade. Give my compliments to your cook."

"Thank you, I will. What do you need to take this job, Renee?"

"Why do you want to get rid of the ghosts?"

"I feel sorry for them, stuck here all this time, not able to move on. My Grandma told me about the curse. It started back in the 1810s because of the death of a child. The plantation name was changed to L'Enfant Haven because of that terrible incident; it used to be called Oak Manor. From my research, one of my ancestors did something that resulted in a jinx placed on the house. All the spirits are here because they either did something that caused the death of a child or failed to do something that could have saved a child."

"Maybe they deserve to be stuck here and punished forever."

"I don't want to believe that. They have all been tortured enough and need to move on."

Renee stood up.

"Show me around the house. I want to see all the rooms."

Gretchen said, "There are also ghosts outside the house in the workshop shed and the carriage house. Do you want to see those too?"

"Yes."

Gretchen walked to the back door. The screen door spring screeched when the door opened.

Gretchen pointed to the left and said, "This is the kitchen. Bertha Baudin is here most of the time."

Renee inspected the kitchen; Bertha resided beside the stove and the priestess acknowledged her. Bertha nodded back.

Across the hall, they entered the dimly lit library. Gretchen nodded toward the desk.

"Dr. Albert Labauve is usually here. He rarely leaves this room."

The ghost scowled at the intruders, arms crossed, unimpressed and disapproving of the idea of a witch in the house. The priestess acknowledged him, but he didn't react. They walked through to the parlor where Andrew and Marcella waited. They both stood when Renee and Gretchen entered. The priestess wandered around; no ghosts were present there.

They went to the dining room, where Milly and Philly stood in the corner with worry in their eyes.

Renee said, "Hmm, twins."

"Yes. Milly and Philly. They were the maids."

Marie and Antoine returned through the front door. The voodoo priestess inspected Marie up and down.

Gretchen said, "This is my great niece, Marie Labauve. She lives here with me."

Renee said, "Exceptional."

She glanced at her son, a knowing smile on her face. They turned and ascended the stairs. Marie and Antoine continued to the parlor, sat on a small sofa, and whispered.

The two women went to the second floor.

Gretchen said, "My bedroom, Marie's room, and two other bedrooms are on this level. I have never seen a ghost on this level."

The priestess inspected each room.

"You may not have seen them, but they have been here. Does Marie see spirits?"

"She has never mentioned seeing any."

"She will soon."

They went to the third floor.

Gretchen said, "The governess, Helen Jones's spirit, has been observed many times in the playroom."

Renee looked in and saw Helen standing next to the window. Renee acknowledged her, and Nanny nodded back.

They ascended a set of narrow steps to the attic. The loft contained two small servants' bedrooms along with several storage chests and boxes. A few other apparitions were present on this level. Still, only one substantial ghost, Cyrus Labauve, feigned disinterest in the women, not wanting another voodoo witch to notice him as had occurred in his past life.

Renee stopped before the old chest. Cyrus sprawled across it, eyes narrowing.

"You're interesting," she said without flinching.

"You're not wrong," he replied, but his usual smirk faltered.

She couldn't understand the words, but she sensed his resistance.

The other minor apparitions in the attic were not associated with the curse.

Renee said, "Show me the outside ghosts."

They descended the stairs, exited through the back door, and headed to the backyard. Gretchen brought the priestess to the workshop and shed. She looked inside and saw Hugo Evans standing in a corner. She acknowledged him, and he nodded back.

Renee scrutinized the property for other apparitions or supernatural entities as they approached the carriage house garage door. None were observed. Gretchen unlocked the garage door, and they entered. Renee moved around the draped vehicles and found Walter Sherman leaning against the Jaguar. The priestess confirmed his presence, and he nodded back.

As they left, Gretchen said, "That is all of them."

Renee asked, "What about the one in the front yard?"

"What one in the front yard? I have never seen one there."

"I saw him when we drove up. He's standing next to the oak tree on the left."

"Hmm, I have never observed him. Perhaps he is the one who

always takes care of the lawn and flower beds. I always thought it was Hugo, the handyman."

They returned to the house via the back door and went to the parlor.

Renee informed Gretchen, "I'll be back at the full moon. The moon ceremony will happen on the moon's rise. You will make a sacrifice to the lunar goddess. A payment of $5,000 in cash must be made. It may not work, but it is the strongest way to break the curse. Are you agreeing to the sum?"

"I do."

"Then I'll see you in two weeks. Marcella, Antoine, we are leaving."

She went out the front door with the others following.

Andrew, Gretchen, and Marie watched from the porch as the Voodoo Imperatrice drove away.

Behind the windows and among the shadows, the ghosts watched her leave. They sensed ominous happenings approaching. When the voodoo priestess returned, something would change. But not their freedom.

66

# Chapter 13

# The Moon Ceremony Aftermath

Two weeks after the initial inspection of the L'Enfant Haven mansion, the Voodoo Imperatrice returned to the estate with a significant entourage of followers. They moved all the furniture in the parlor, set up a large brass brazier in the middle of the room, and started a fire inside it. The drummers began the ritual cadence, and the followers danced and chanted. A foul-tasting drink in a wooden bowl was passed around, and everyone drank from it. The concoction made Andrew dizzy and eager to move to the beat of the drums. Gretchen also swayed to the rhythm.

The ritual continued; the priestess called for a sacrifice, and a scream echoed from the hall. Gretchen jumped up, hearing her niece's cries. When she noticed the red streaks on her niece's pajama bottoms, she realized what caused the stains and took Marie upstairs.

The Voodoo Imperatrice said, "The sacrifice has been made. Virgin menstrual blood is the strongest."

Andrew didn't understand what she meant by that statement.

The followers cleaned and packed everything back into the vehicles. When Gretchen came down, she paid the priestess, and Renee departed.

Andrew asked Gretchen, "What was wrong with Marie?"

Gretchen told him, "Marie started her period, and it scared her."

Andrew left soon after, finally understanding what the priestess had meant when she said, 'The sacrifice has been made. Virgin menstrual blood is the strongest.' He felt sorry for the poor child and what she would endure.

In the years that followed, Marie's fear hardened into resentment. She avoided the ghosts, loathed the house—and eventually loathed her aunt. Her innocence, her safety, her sense of self—taken, all under the guise of a ritual she hadn't consented to.

That was the real sacrifice.

What for? Andrew could never be sure.

Gretchen called and asked Andrew to purchase a Jaguar for her nephew Robert's graduation present. It cost a considerable amount. The expensive vehicle was delivered two days before Robert was to return home. However, Robert never returned to the plantation; he died in a drunken car accident with his friends, celebrating the end of school, by going off a bridge into the river below. This tragic death sent poor Marie into an even deeper depression, marking the start of her drug use.

Grief transformed Gretchen. Seemingly overnight, she decided to sell all but fifty acres of the estate and place the remainder into a trust. Andrew tried to dissuade her, but she insisted. The house would remain with the family—but no heir could ever sell it.

"There must always be a Labauve here," she said. "The estate needs one of our blood."

Andrew never understood what she feared—or what she knew.

A monthly allotment of $500.00 would be given to the heir. This would ensure that a Labauve or a close relative of the Labauves would permanently reside on the estate. She created that clause because she feared that a non-family member would gain control of the assets at some point in the future. Andrew never understood this unwarranted fear and where it originated.

After Gretchen died, Marie inherited the right to live in the L'Enfant Haven mansion. Andrew Butler could track Marie down through his contacts with Aunt Marcie. He found Marie living in a hippie flophouse. Thanks to the protection spell his voodoo priestess mother placed on him, he could move through the unsavory neighborhood where Marie lived.

Andy read about these incredible events in his father's diaries. Now he understood why Marie Labauve had been a drug addict and felt sorry for Orion, who suffered from his mother's neglect due to this voodoo ceremony. He was unable to help Orion because the deranged voodoo witch would harm his family if he did anything. The guilt of providing Orion's grandmother the information she wanted created a massive knot in his stomach, making him feel sick just thinking about it.

70

# Chapter 14

# The Rowen Finding Job

Leaving Andy's office, I jumped over the car door, slid into the driver's seat of the Jaguar, and peeled out of Madreville. My desire to speed down the town's main road was tempered by the ever-watchful local sheriff, who held a grudge since I outshone him in finding the missing Rowen kid.

As I leisurely cruised down Main Street, I passed Marti's service station and auto repair shop. Marti, a tall Black man in his forties, waved as he pumped gas, evoking memories of friendly times and appreciation from my former auto repair job. I waved back. Sometimes, I find myself almost regretting quitting that job.

At eighteen, I worked at Marti's Auto Repair for about six months when Evan Rowen went missing. The boy was last seen riding his new bicycle around town the day he disappeared and never made it home for dinner. Worried, his parents, Howard and Sharon Rowen, called everyone they could think of, asking if anyone had seen their son.

Howard Rowen contacted the sheriff's office at 10 p.m.

He frantically reported, "My Evan is missing; he's been gone all day, and no one we've contacted has seen him for hours."

Sheriff Titus Warren rushed to the Rowen house and documented all the information. He dispatched officers to search the areas surrounding Madreville but found no clues about where the child might be. The next day, the sheriff organized a complete investigation, inspecting every building and home in Madreville.

He came to Marti's, and I stood nearby listening to them talk. As the sheriff turned to leave, he paused, removed his sunglasses, glared at me accusingly, and said, "You're that Labauve kid from the plantation, right? Have you seen Evan Rowen anywhere?"

"No."

"Maybe I should check out the plantation. People always say weird things happen at that place. Something may have happened to Evan there."

"Any time you're curious, Sheriff. The ghosts don't mind visitors."

He thought I was joking. I wasn't.

He laughed, put his sunglasses back on, and said, "We'll see how it goes. Maybe I will come out."

Days went by with the boy still missing. The sheriff decided to announce the search for Evan Rowen to the media. Newspaper and television reporters arrived to interview people around town. Organized searches of properties across the fields and woods found no signs of the child.

It had been almost two weeks since the boy disappeared, and people said he must be dead. I didn't think so. I didn't know how, but I sensed he was alive somewhere. The sheriff put out a call for another full-scale investigation.

Marti agreed to participate and asked me, "Why don't you come and help? People say you can find things."

"Yeah, I'll help."

I went along to the organizing meeting.

The sheriff outlined where they would explore and what to do if anyone found anything. I disagreed with his planned search locations, feeling a sensation in my stomach, and stood at the back of the crowd shaking my head. He noticed me doing this and furrowed his brow.

After the announcements, he approached me and said, "You disagree with where to search?"

"Yes."

"Where do you think we should look?

"In the forest."

"Why is that? Do you know something you aren't saying?" he asked, suspecting I might be involved with the boy's disappearance.

"I just have a feeling."

"My son told me about you. You find stuff for the kids at school."

"Yeah."

"I don't believe it. You probably steal the stuff, hide it, and then say you would find it for them."

"That's been said before, but it's not true."

"The plantation is starting to sound more interesting to me."

"You can come over any time you want."

The sheriff walked away and yelled at some officers, his hand circling above his head to signal the start of things. They organized the search teams, and everyone moved out. I joined Marti's group. We trudged through the fields beside the forest. Every time I faced the woods, I felt a wave of nausea in my stomach, indicating that the thing I was searching for was in that direction. I knew the boy was somewhere out there.

I headed for the trees and Marti yelled, "Where are you going? We are supposed to stay in this area."

"I'm going over here. I think he's over here."

"How do you know?"

"I find things. ou know that."

I kept walking toward the woods and the ache in my insides worsened. Marti paused for a moment and decided to follow.

He jogged beside me and asked, "What are you feeling?"

"I feel sick when I move in the correct direction to find what I'm looking for. And I'm sick right now and it's getting worse."

We ventured into the woods, stopping a few times to turn around until the sensation returned. We traveled quite a distance into the forested area and approached the road on the other side; the nausea intensified.

I said, "He's close by."

He's near. The nausea spiked—I nearly puked. I knew we were right on top of him.

I inspected the location. An old cypress tree had fallen and sprawled across the forest floor, obscuring a large section. I moved the branches aside and revealed broken boards on the ground beneath the tree.

I yelled for Marti, "Over here!"

We removed additional tree debris and wood slats, uncovering an old well that decayed gray boards had concealed.

We stared down the dark abyss, and I shouted, "Evan! Are you down there?"

Marti pulled a flashlight from his pocket and shone it down the hole. The light reflected off the water at the bottom of the well, while the odor of decaying plant matter rose from the depths. Something moved. He adjusted the flashlight, revealing a bicycle. A hand appeared on top of the bike seat.

I yelled, "Evan, Evan!"

The hand twitched, and a weak "Help me!" emerged from the depths.

"We found him!" Marti exclaimed. "You were on the track team, run back and get the sheriff."

I took off running back the way we came, weaving and bobbing between the trees and underbrush, getting stinging slaps in the face several times from tree branches. I entered the field, panting, and searched for the volunteer group. They were heading back toward the cars. I ran to the group, trying to say, "We found him," but I was so short of breath I couldn't speak.

I stumbled into the clearing, gasping, hands on my knees, barely able to speak.

The sheriff chuckled, arms crossed.

"What happened, kid? Get lost out there?"

I straightened up, chest heaving, and growled, "No. We found Evan. He's alive. He's in the woods—down a well."

The laughter died instantly.

Disbelieving, he retorted, "We've already been through the forest and didn't find anything."

"Marti's with him. The boy is down an old well covered by a cypress that fell on top of it. Does someone have some rope so we can pull him out?"

A guy in the back of the group replied, "Yeah, I have some right here. Let's go."

The two of us moved out, and after a moment, the others followed, leaving the sheriff trailing behind—mostly because he was too heavy to keep up with the rest of us—not believing anything I said. We trudged through the humid woods and arrived at the fateful location.

Marti stood up, hearing us coming. You couldn't see him until he rose.

He shouted, "It's about time you guys got here! He stopped talking."

The EMTs with the team took charge.

One EMT said, "Here, tie the rope off on that oak over there."

He tied the other end around his chest, and the group lowered him into the well.

Others in the group moved the fallen cypress out of the way. The EMT removed the bike from Evan's body and checked him over. He was still alive, lying at the bottom of the well with about six inches of water. The EMT discovered that both of Evan's legs were broken and he had a concussion. His bike had fallen on top of him and cracked a couple of ribs, making it difficult for him to take deep gulps of air to yell for help.

The EMTs sent someone to call the fire department, and the fire engine and ambulance came up the road close to the well's position; they brought a stretcher and more ropes. Strapped to the bed, they lifted Evan from the well. When they investigated that section of the forest, the search team parked in the exact location where the fire engine was parked. They never inspected the toppled tree. The sheriff's reputation suffered after that incident, and he has despised me ever since.

The word spread quickly: I found Evan Rowen and saved his life. A cypress tree fell on Evan as he rode his new bike through the woods, striking him on the head and causing him to plummet to the bottom of the well. While in the well, the boy drank the putrid water to stay hydrated. Due to a concussion, he moved in and out of consciousness, failing to hear the rescue team calling his name.

Evan's parents came to Marti's to thank me.

Howard said, "Thank you so much for saving our son; if you need help with anything, call me. I don't care if you live in a haunted house; I'll come and help."

Howard owned a construction company in Madreville.

"Thanks. I might call you for repairs on the house. I can make sure the spirits won't bother you."

I grinned, making it appear I was joking, but I wasn't. They both smiled and left.

The reporters gathered around the auto shop, wanting to talk to me.

I told them, "No, you talk to my lawyer, Andrew Butler Jr."

We conducted an interview that Andy supervised with the New Orleans Times-Picayune newspaper. Following that, calls flooded in, requesting that I locate various items and individuals. That was when my attorney organized the business, which has thrived since then.

# Chapter 15

# The Jaguar Crash &

# Dreams of My Parents

As I cruised by, I spotted a police car tucked along a side road—and those signature mirrored sunglasses told me exactly who was behind the wheel: Sheriff Warren, still nursing his grudge.

The sheriff trailed me, hoping for a chance to catch me for speeding. Turning onto the private estate road, I floored the gas pedal, reveling in the freedom from his jurisdiction. Cyrus flipped him off from the passenger seat, laughing like a maniac. The sheriff couldn't see it, but it made us both feel better.

Zipping down the dirt road and throwing a vast dust cloud behind the sports car, I decided to make the circuit of the property. I loved driving fast with the top down and the wind blowing through my hair. Cyrus, sitting next to me, laughed the whole time. Speeding in automobiles was one of the most exciting things for him to do.

I popped the clutch, dropped it into a lower gear, pulled the handbrake, and skidded around the first corner. I straightened the vehicle and shifted through a couple of gears, increasing speed with each change.

Then the sports car hit something in the road. Going this fast, I didn't even see what it was. I found out later that the farmer's tractor created a depression during a rainstorm, getting stuck in the mud and making a hole in the road. The Jag's front right tire smashed into the edge of the hole, and because the automobile sits so low to the ground, the car careened out of control and flipped end over end.

There were no seat belts in a '49 Jaguar. When the car flipped, the door flung open, and I was launched like a rag doll. My hands were out before me as I came down, and my right hand hit the dirt first, snapping my arm. My head came down onto a rock in the road, which caused a severe concussion. I blacked out, and my body tumbled uncontrollably several times across the road, landing in the drainage ditch.

The farmer plowing the field near the accident saved me. When I barreled down the street, he gawked as the Jag tumbled down the road, then hurried back home and called for an ambulance. If he hadn't been on-site, who knows how long I might have lain in the trench before someone found me.

They located me in the ditch with my face just outside the runoff water.

I opened my eyes; Cyrus hovered over me.

"There you are. Hold on, EMTs are here to help."

He disappeared as the paramedics splashed through the water to pull me out.

I blacked out again and didn't wake up for two days. They took me to Christus Hills Medical Center, a hospital in Shreveport. Initially, they weren't sure I would make it when they examined me.

Two figures stepped through the mist, emerging from a tunnel of golden light. Somehow, the glow itself radiated peace and love—don't ask me how, but I felt it in my bones. The woman was my mother and she looked beautiful. Her long, golden hair shone brightly. I somehow knew that the light-skinned, handsome Black man beside her was my father.

My father said, "Be careful of the Voodoo Imperatrice; she will try to trick you and use you for her purposes."

Mother said, "You've always been gifted, baby. I didn't see it when I was alive, but I know it now. You have a unique ability to work with spirits and to have them help you."

My father said, "Don't let the Voodoo Imperatrice corrupt your talents for evil. She will tell you she is right and you are wrong. Don't be fooled by what she says; fight against it. You have power she doesn't know about. You can use the ghosts to stop her."

Mother said, "The Voodoo Imperatrice used me and your father to produce what she wanted: someone like you who can talk to the spirits and have them do things for you. We must go now, baby. Remember what we told you."

I jolted awake, head pounding, tears already streaming.

"Mama, don't go," I cried, the dream still clinging to me like smoke.

Leaning over the edge of the bed, Cyrus stared at me. His charm was in my pocket when I crashed the car, so he followed me to the emergency room. I tried to move my right arm, but I couldn't without pain shooting through it. Using my left hand, I wiped away the tears.

I asked, "What happened?"

I rubbed my head and touched the bandage on the right side of my forehead. The slight pressure of my touch sent a bolt of agony through my head. I winced and moaned.

Andy leaned over the bed through Cyrus—not realizing he existed—and said, "You crashed the Jag on the dirt road. You've been out for two days. What did you say before that?"

Cyrus said, "You did a number on the poor Jaguar," using a modern accent and colloquialisms he had picked up from being around me so much over the past fourteen years.

I replied to Cyrus, "It'll keep Walter busy fixing it."

To Andy, I said, "I was having a dream."

But he heard both statements together.

Quizzically, he asked, "Who's Walter?"

"My mechanic."

Which was true, but he didn't know he was dead.

I said, "All this talking is hurting my head."

"I'll tell the nurse you are awake and in pain."

I nodded. As Andy left the room, he passed through several apparitions.

I asked, "Who are all of these people?"

Seven spirits wearing hospital gowns—what they died in—were staring at me.

Cyrus explained, "People who passed on here at the hospital and had things that kept them on this plane."

"Make them go away. I don't want them standing around."

As those words exited my mouth, Andy and the nurse walked through the ghosts. Cyrus shooed them out of the room.

The nurse asked, "Make who go away?'

I answered, "All the other people in the room."

I was still out of it and not thinking straight. Usually, I could create some other story.

Andy whispered to her, "I think he's seeing things."

She replied, "It's possible with a severe head injury."

She handed me two white pills and a plastic cup of water. I downed both, hoping they'd knock me out fast.

"These will make him sleepy."

He said, "I'm leaving now. I'll be back tomorrow morning."

"Okay, see you then. Can someone turn the lights down? They're hurting my eyes."

"Here, I will close the curtains. The concussion causes sensitivity to light."

After they left, Cyrus said, "I thought you were going to join this crowd for a while. If you're going to go, try to do it at the house. At least you would have a better chance of being there with the rest of us."

The drugs were starting to kick in, and I said, "But I haven't hurt any children, so I don't think I'd stick around. I got to see my mother and father. They were telling me to beware of the Voodoo Imperatrice."

Cyrus winced.

"Damn, that was cold—talking like that about dead kids."

He tilted his head.

"Voodoo Imperatrice? What are you talking about?"

His image wavered, fading at the edges.

The drugs pulled me under again.

# Chapter 16

# Hospital Rehabilitation

When I woke the next morning, the pain had dulled. My head wasn't pounding as before, but my broken arm throbbed, and my whole body ached from being tossed across the road like a rag doll.

Cyrus came over; he was still semi-transparent because of the pain medication.

"Morning, Sleeping Beauty. Any more visits from the Voodoo Imperatrice?"

"No. No other dreams that I remember."

Andy walked in.

"Talking to yourself in here."

"A habit I've gotten into from living alone."

"How are you doing today?"

"Still got a headache—not as bad as before. Everything else feels like I got tackled by a freight train."

"That's understandable. You were covered in bruises when they removed your clothes. I had the Jag towed to the garage at the estate. I figured it was better there until you figure out where to send it for repairs."

"Thank you. I may work on it myself."

Walter would begin the repairs, but progress would be slow without me—and we would definitely need to order parts.

"I noticed that you have been restoring the Rolls."

"Yeah, when I have time."

The nursing assistant brought in a tray with breakfast, which included scrambled eggs, sliced tomatoes, toast without butter, and orange juice. As I sat up, the room tilted slightly, and a wave of dizziness swept over me.

After being spoiled by Bertha's excellent cooking, I chewed a few bites of food but couldn't stomach the institution's bland fare. I pushed it away.

Andy asked, "Are you going to eat that?"

"No, you can have it if you want. It's pretty tasteless."

"Sure, I'll take it. I didn't have anything this morning."

Andy shrugged and dug in, clearing the plate like it was his last meal.

"I don't think it's that bad."

"I'll invite you over for dinner sometime, and you can have food with real flavor."

"Who's cooking? The ghosts?" he said, thinking he was being funny.

"Sometimes, but I can cook. I'll cook for you."

The doctor came in with a smile and commented, "Excellent, you finished your breakfast."

"No, he did. I ate a few bites but didn't want any more."

The physician asked, "Dizziness and nausea?"

"Yes."

"It's to be expected. We will keep you here for a couple more days to ensure no other complications occur."

"Were there complications?"

"Some brain swelling occurred that we were worried about. But it has gone down, and you seem to be getting better. You have a small crack in your lower right frontal bone, and you broke both the ulna and the radius bones on your right arm. Luckily, they were clean breaks."

The doctor checked the chart and left the room. I knew precisely what he referred to from the anatomy that Doc Albert taught me.

Cyrus piped in, "See, I told you, you almost checked out."

Andy said, "The Masonville, Georgia, job payment came in this morning. I deposited it in the checking account and wrote myself a check for half the amount, my cut."

"Thanks, but most of that will probably go to paying this hospital bill."

"And whose fault is that?"

"Yeah, yeah. I know."

He was right; I shouldn't have gone barreling down the road so fast.

"Do you want me to bring you anything?"

"Something to read."

"I'll see what they have in the store downstairs."

He left, walking through a ghost.

I looked at the apparition, "What do you want?"

A middle-aged man with a weary expression and thinning brown hair peeked around the doorway, his gaze heavy with sorrow.

The spirit answered, "I've never seen anyone like you."

"What do you mean, like me?"

"Someone who can see us and talk to us. You're special."

"Yeah, that's what my mother says, too."

I remembered my mother saying this in the dream. Or was it a visitation?

I asked, "What's your name?"

"Peter Johnson. I died of a heart attack here three months ago."

"Why don't you move on?"

"I wanted to ensure my wife was cared for, but I can't leave. Can you help me? I think you can."

"I don't know how I can assist you. I'm sorry."

He turned and walked away, disheartened.

Cyrus said, "That's too bad. He seems like a nice guy."

A little later, the nurse arrived and said, "Let's check the stitches on your head."

I sat up slowly as she gently pulled the tape away from my skin, exposing the wound. She inspected it.

"It's coming along well," she said. "I'll put some antiseptic cream on it. We must keep it moist so it doesn't dry, crack, and bleed."

She retrieved a tube of cream from her pocket and dabbed some onto the sutured injury. I winced at the irritation her gentle touch caused.

She said, "I'm sorry, but it will hurt for a while."

"Is there a mirror? Can I see it?"

"Oh, sure."

She rolled the tray over and lifted the center section to reveal a mirror. I stared at the jagged two-inch gash held together with dark stitches, surrounded by a bruise the size of my palm. It looked like someone had tried sewing shut a purple balloon.

"That's going to leave a scar."

"Probably," she said with a smile, covering it with a clean bandage and tape.

I turned on the TV and enjoyed a show until Andy returned with a thick paperback novel and a few magazines.

Holding the chunky book, I said, "This should keep me busy for a while."

He smiled.

Andy left for work, and I opened the book to read the novel. Cyrus hovered over my shoulder, squinting at the words. Every time I tried to flip the page, he muttered, "Hold up. I'm not done yet."

I waited.

"Okay," he'd say.

We had a rhythm.

As we read, it began to rain outside. I watched the rain for a while and thought, 'I hope Andy is okay driving through this.' This continued for an hour until I grew tired.

"Here, you continue; I'm going to take a nap."

I gave him the book, and he placed it on the rolling tray next to the bed before continuing to read. I rolled over and went to sleep, my head and body still aching. The nursing assistant woke me up for lunch.

Hungry and ready to eat, I dug into the food, but once more, it was terrible. This time I ate a bit more, but only slightly. The next few days unfolded like this: Andy visited briefly in the mornings, eating breakfast, reading, having lunch, taking a long nap, enjoying dinner, watching TV, and sleeping again.

After a few days, the doctor said, "I think everything looks good, and you can go home today."

"Wonderful, doc; I'll check if someone can bring my car here."

"No, you shouldn't drive for a couple of weeks. You'll still have dizzy spells and headaches for a while. You must leave the cast on your arm for at least six weeks. You can go to your physician to have it removed. They're bringing some pain pills and antiseptic cream from the pharmacy to take with you."

"Thanks, Doc. I'll call Andy for a ride—since I'm apparently grounded."

I called Andy.

"Can you bring me home from the hospital? The doctor says I can't drive for a couple of weeks."

He said, "I'll be over later this afternoon. I have another client who is coming by soon."

"Okay, see you then."

I dressed in the dirty, torn clothing I had come to the emergency room in. I didn't even bother to ask him to pick up some clean things. That wouldn't have happened without my being with him. He was not as brave as his father, Andrew Butler Sr., who would walk straight into the house without hesitation. When Andy arrived at the hospital, it was 5 p.m. and raining. He drove me home, and we didn't say much during the trip. Upon arrival he carried my small bag of personal items to the door as we navigated the path in the rain.

He asked, "Can you take care of yourself, okay?"

"Yeah, I'll be fine."

I opened the door and could smell something fantastic cooking in the kitchen. My mouth watered. Andy's eyes widened. He also noticed the aroma. He handed me my bag and watched as I entered.

I turned, grinned, and said, "Dinner's waiting," then stepped inside and shut the door behind me, leaving the scent of home—and ghosts—to greet me.

86

# Chapter 17

# Visiting Mother's Grave

Still aching, I shuffled into the kitchen and found Bertha at the stove, just where she always was. She gave me a sidelong glance.

"Dinner's almost ready. Pot roast, potatoes, carrots, biscuits, salad, and apple cobbler."

"Sounds like heaven. Hospital food was awful—inedible, really."

I rubbed my face.

"I'll wash up here. If I go upstairs, I might not come back down."

I washed my face and hands, dried them with the dish towel, and entered the dining room through the swinging door. A place setting awaited at the head of the table. I sat down, and the meal arrived soon after. The aroma alone stirred something alive within me. After days of bland mush, this was a feast. I praised her as I ate, and she simply smiled. While I was enjoying the delicious dinner, Doc came over and checked me out.

"Hmm, a broken arm and a severe concussion. You're lucky that was all that happened."

"I'm also bruised from head to foot."

He asked, "Did they give you something for the pain?"

"Yeah, here."

I pulled the bottle out of my pocket and gave it to him. He examined the label.

"Be careful with how much of these you take. It's the same stuff your mother was addicted to."

That hit hard.

"Thanks for the warning. I'll take a couple tonight—just to sleep. Is the air conditioner on in my bedroom?"

Milly said, "Yes, sir. I turned it on just before you came home."

"Thank you. I'm going to bed after dinner; I'm still tired."

Doc said, "That's the concussion. It makes you tired."

After dinner, I climbed the stairs slowly, each step eliciting a dull protest from my battered body. When I opened the door to my bedroom, a rush of cool air washed over me. The air conditioner functioned flawlessly. I closed the door to maintain a consistent temperature in my room.

Pulling everything out of my pockets, I discovered the paper with my grandmother's name, Renee Broussard, along with her address and phone number.

'If I feel better tomorrow, I might call her,' I thought to myself.

I placed everything in the crystal bowl on the dresser: my wallet, a handful of change, the bottle of pain pills, and Cyrus's amulet.

The amulet featured an oversized sapphire with a crest engraved on its surface, centered within a silver fleur-de-lys. Quite appealing, it was attached to an intricate silver cage with a loop at one end of a blue velvet ribbon, which had a button on one side and a buttonhole on the other. The ribbon allowed it to be connected to a belt or threaded through a large buttonhole. Ornate and ancient, it radiated history.

I removed my dirty, torn clothing and threw it in the corner. It could go into the trash. I stood before the full-length mirror on the back of the bedroom door and studied my bruised reflection. I'd lost weight—hospital meals and pain will do that. Yellowing bruises and dark purple blotches told the story of a body still recovering. A bandage covered the sutured gash on my forehead. I'd take it off in the morning. Those were the ones that hurt the most.

I took two pain pills with a glass of cool water, which Milly and Philly always provided in a pitcher on the side table each night. I removed my dirty underwear and lay on the bed naked, with just a sheet covering me. Soon, I fell asleep.

I dreamt that my mother stroked my curls back from my face and spoke to me.

"You're gifted, baby. You can fight the Voodoo Imperatrice; I know you can. You have the power with you. I am here with you always. I will help where I can."

I woke up crying, "Mama, Mama, don't go," with tears rolling down my cheeks.

Why was I having these dreams of my mother and crying? I never cried this much, even watching her die in the hospital five years ago.

She's buried in the Labauve family plot on the estate. Maybe I should take some flowers to her grave today. I knew she wasn't a ghost. She is not in the house and she wasn't in the medical center. She died in the same hospital I was in. I would have felt her there if she were. Were these actual visitations by her spirit in my fantasy or were the dreams my subconscious feeling guilty for not doing more to get her off the drugs?

I got up from the bed, my body still aching all over, and padded naked to the bathroom. I never worried about spirits being around when I roamed the house without clothing; it never bothered them, so why should it bother me? I went to the toilet and turned on the shower to access hot water from the cellar to the second floor.

Looking in the mirror, I slowly peeled the bandage from my forehead. The swelling had subsided. The bruising remained deep, and the sutures puckered slightly at the edges.

I stuck my hand under the shower head; the warm water felt refreshing as I stepped in, holding my right arm above my head to keep the moisture off the cast. I washed it as best I could using only my left hand and dried with a towel. I brushed my teeth, shaved, ran my fingers through my damp curls to improve their appearance, and applied antiseptic cream to the suture line on my head.

When I returned to the bedroom, my dirty clothes were missing, and breakfast was served on a tray. I picked up the food tray and placed it on the small table beside the daybed. I enjoyed a delicious morning meal consisting of eggs, bacon, sausage, biscuits, gravy, and fresh orange juice. With Bertha's cooking, I should quickly regain all my lost weight. I dressed and went downstairs.

Always aware of my thoughts, the spirits had provided a glass vase with cut flowers from the front garden and placed it next to the phone on the hall sideboard. I picked up the flower vase, went out the back door, and headed for the Labauve family plot.

The ancient graveyard, enclosed by iron posts, fleur-de-lys finials, and cross beams, held many of my family's remains. The gate, untouched since my mother's burial, let out a long, rusty screech as

I opened it. The oldest graves were near the entrance to the family graveyard, with Cyrus being one of the most senior.

I moved past generations of names—family names etched in stone. The newer graves were toward the back. The latest ones included Great-Great Aunt Gretchen Labauve, her brother Gordon Labauve and his wife, their son Gordon Labauve Jr. and his wife, my mother's parents, Adeline, Joseph, and Robert, my mother's siblings, Helen Jones, Nanny, and Marie Labauve, my mother. I suppose when I die, I'll be next to my mother. The space where I would be placed was evident.

MARIE LABAUVE, 1938 to 1977

I set the flowers down at the base of the stone and stood there, memories creeping in like fog. Her last words echoed in my mind. Grief cracked open in me, raw and sudden. I hadn't realized how deeply I missed her until now. A sob broke free, then another. I stood there, weeping, grief five years delayed, finally breaking free—a testament to the depth of my loss and the enduring bond with my mother.

I remembered how good it felt when she would hug me and call me 'baby.' I don't think she would have called me that if she hadn't cared for me.

I recalled when I was little, if she wasn't too loaded, she would pull me to our room with a big smile and give me a new toy she had found for me. I knew that when the smile came, something good was coming. I miss that beautiful smile. Even though she rarely left her room at the mansion, knowing she was just upstairs remained comforting.

Despite everything, I had loved her. Even when she forgot me, even when the drugs stole her away, she had gotten me to the plantation. That was something. My love for her, despite her struggles, was unwavering.

Considering their limitations, the ghosts raised me as best they could and did an excellent job. They showed me more love and care than my mother could. They became my family.

She never believed me when I told her about the spirits. The drugs clouded her thoughts until every shadow felt like a threat. I wish I had the chance to tell her the truth—that she wasn't mad, just overwhelmed by what she couldn't understand.

What she told me on the day she passed away helped me understand why she was so frightened. I could have explained the spirits and why they were in the house, but she would never listen to me or anyone else. The drugs muddled her brain so much that she believed everything she saw was the truth, but it wasn't. She died before I could tell her the truth. I'm sure she knows everything now; maybe that is why she is returning to my dreams.

When I returned from her grave, I mustered the courage to open Mother's room for the first time in five years. The room was frozen in time, a silent witness to the day I closed the door. A fallen bottle of pills rested on the night stand, clothes piled on the chair, and the dust-free room stood as a testament to the ghosts' care despite my mother's reactions. How did they manage to clean around the pills? The ghosts still cared for my mother, and it was a painful reminder of her absence.

Retrieving a cardboard box from the cellar, I packed her clothes and other items. I found some drug paraphernalia and threw it into the wastebasket. Her 45 rpm records and the pictures on the wall went into the storage container. I took the box to the attic and archived it with the other containers belonging to past relatives and occupants of the plantation.

The last time I was in the loft was when I took over Aunt Gretchen's bedroom and stored her belongings there. I remembered that her diaries, which were in one of those cardboard boxes, mentioned a voodoo priestess. I dug through the boxes and pulled out all the journals.

At ten years old, I found most of her journals in the safe in the library. Doc Albert remembered the combination. When I first searched the house, I read several of her journals for information about ghosts. However, I never reviewed all of them; at ten and eleven, they were dull reading. Perhaps now, being older, I would find things more interesting, especially anything to do with the Voodoo Imperatrice my parents told me to beware of in my dreams. I took the diaries to my bedroom.

My broken arm throbbed with each step as I carried the diaries to my bedroom. A dull headache had settled in, reminding me that I needed to slow down and take care of myself for a while.

# Chapter 18

# Marie's Early Life &

# Introduction to Antoine

Five years ago, on the day I received the call about my mother's overdose, I had just walked into the house covered in motor oil from overhauling the Rolls-Royce engine all day with the ghost mechanic Walter Sherman when I noticed the light flashing on the phone answering machine. I rewound the tape and listened to the fateful message.

"Mr. Labauve, this is Officer Mike Osborn with the Shreveport police department. Your mother has been taken to the Christus Hills Medical Center in Shreveport due to an overdose. You can call the hospital for information on her condition. Thank you."

I shouted, "Oh, fuck!" and my stomach plummeted.

Taking two steps at a time, I sprinted upstairs to clean up and change my clothes. As I hurried out the door, the house ghosts and Cyrus were crowded in the vestibule near the entrance, appearing concerned. They cared about my mother, having watched over her as a young girl living in the house. Even though she hated seeing them now, they remained distressed about her being in the hospital.

The spirits all realized I was upset as I flew out the door, jumped into the Jag, and headed for Shreveport, exceeding the speed limit. I'm amazed I wasn't stopped by the police along the way, and it wasn't raining.

I parked the car, ran into the hospital, and went to the front desk.

"Marie Labauve was admitted here today. I'm her son. What room is she in?" I demanded, wanting the information immediately.

The receptionist searched for her name on a list and said, "She is on the fifth floor, ICU room 525."

"Thanks," I said and rushed to the elevator.

I waited impatiently for the elevator, bouncing on the balls of my feet and running my hand through my curls.

A group of people had to exit the elevator first. I pushed past the last person, pressed the fifth-floor button, and anxiously awaited as the chamber ascended at a snail's pace, stopping at the third floor for another individual.

Finally, the elevator arrived at the fifth floor, and I ran down the hall to her room. A doctor and nurse were present. My mother looked pale, with dark circles etched under her eyes.

The last time I saw her was two days earlier, pulling away in the old Ford she had bought from Andrew Butler Sr. not long after we moved into the plantation house. She claimed she was visiting friends in Shreveport, but I knew better. She was chasing stronger drugs; pills weren't enough anymore. She had moved on to heroin. I never confronted her, though I should have. As she left, I remembered thinking the Ford needed an oil change and I would take care of that when she returned.

The doctor looked up and asked, "Are you her son?"

"Yes, I'm Orion Labauve."

"She's been asking for you."

"What's wrong with her?"

"She took an overdose of heroin. We were able to restart her heart, but all the years of drug addiction have severely damaged it. It's fragile, and we are unsure how long she will last. She wants to talk to you; she keeps saying it's important. All you can do is be with her until the end."

"Thank you, doctor."

I approached the bed, took Mama's hand and sat in the chair.

"Mama, it's me, Ory. I'm here."

Her eyes fluttered open. She looked exhausted, as if every word was a weight.

"Ory, baby, there are so many things I must tell you before I go. I know I don't have much time. I want you to understand what happened to me in the house and why I did what I did."

"That's okay, Mama. You don't have to tell me."

"No, baby. You don't understand. I want to tell you so the same thing doesn't happen to you."

When Marie Labauve was seven, tragedy struck her family. Her parents died in a car accident. Two of her older siblings had perished in a fire before she was born. Left mostly alone, she found solace in her great-aunt Gretchen. However, tragedy seemed to cling to the Labauve name, and as they buried Gretchen's nephew and his wife, the weight of the loss felt unbearable to the matriarch.

Marie and Gretchen cried as hired help lowered Gordon Jr. and Eloise's caskets into the ground at the burial plot on the L'Enfant Haven estate. Robert stood on the other side of Aunt Gretchen, trying to be a man at twelve and not cry. The funeral attendees didn't realize it, but five ghosts on the property also attended the solemn event.

The troubled girl hugged her aunt and sobbed, her face buried in Gretchen's dress. Gretchen rubbed her great-niece's back and dabbed her eyes with her handkerchief. They left with the other family members, friends, and spirits, returning to the house as the hired mortuary hands shoveled dirt into the graves. Several wreaths of flowers surrounded the gravestones.

Marie sat dutifully in the parlor on a chair beside her aunt and brother, looking down; the profound sadness in her heart caused tears to stream down her cheeks.

People would approach Marie, her brother, and her aunt, saying, "We are so sorry for your loss."

Food and drinks were available on the oak dining room table. Mourners stood around, ate, drank, and talked.

Marie could hear people saying things like, "Poor children. Both their parents are gone; what will become of them?"

"I heard they will be living with Aunt Gretchen; Gordon was her favorite nephew."

After a while, Gretchen glimpsed Marie, sitting with her eyes closed.

She asked Marie, "Are you tired, dear?"

Marie nodded.

Gretchen said, "Excuse me, I need to take Marie up for a lie-down."

She gently helped her niece stand. They walked up the steps to the third-floor nursery. As they ascended the stairs, Gretchen glanced back at the family and friends who came to the funeral. She was surprised by how many attended, considering most avoided the plantation house like the plague because of the haunting. The number of attendees at the funeral demonstrated how much both family and friends loved her nephew, just as she did. A tear ran down her cheek at the thought.

The girl sat on the edge of the twin bed with the pink quilt, and Gretchen removed her shoes.

"Lie down and try to sleep, dear."

Marie placed her head on the pillow, closed her eyes, and fell asleep. The matriarch returned downstairs. The attendees of the somber event gradually trickled out. After everyone left, Gretchen went straight to bed, thinking she would clean up in the morning.

Marie woke up, hugging a stuffed rabbit and wrapped in a light blanket. She assumed Aunt Gretchen had given her the bunny to cuddle with in bed and had covered her. She squeezed the bunny tightly and buried her face in its soft, plush fur. Somehow the toy made her feel comforted and protected.

She changed out of the black dress she had worn for the funeral and put on the plaid play dress that she thought her aunt had pulled from the armoire and laid across the chair for her to wear today.

She went downstairs, and two bowls of oatmeal with raisins, maple syrup, and milk sat on the kitchen table. She ate breakfast, again assuming Aunt Gretchen had prepared it for her and Robert. After the morning meal, she went out onto the veranda, sat in a wicker chair, and stared across the backyard at the family plot where her parents were. She thought about how she would never see her parents' warm, loving smiles or receive their hugs when she came home from school, and she cried. Robert didn't come out of his room all day, grieving in his own way.

In the morning, Gretchen dressed, came downstairs feeling heavy, and forced herself to move. She went into the dining room to clear all the food and dishes from the table. Everything was clean; Gretchen knew the ghosts performed this charity. She looked at the spotless surface and murmured, "Thank you" to the spirits.

Gretchen walked out onto the veranda and saw Marie crying for her parents. She thought, 'Why am I feeling this bad? Look at what this poor child has to suffer.'

The girl looked up at Aunt Gretchen with tears running down her cheeks. "I'm sorry," unsure of what someone is supposed to do after their parents die.

Gretchen said, "Don't worry yourself. You cry as much as you want and need. I've been sobbing, too. If you need anything, you tell me."

Marie nodded and sat missing her parents. Her chest felt tight and her face sore from so much crying.

Sitting beside her, Gretchen said, "Come, sit on my lap."

Marie got up, climbed onto her aunt's legs, and cried. Gretchen hugged and rocked her, understanding what the child must be going through and feeling the same loss. She pulled a handkerchief from the pocket of her dress, dabbed her eyes, and handed it to her niece.

Marie blew her nose and said, "Thank you."

The two comforted each other on the screened porch, grieving and hugging.

Robert returned to boarding school the following week. His father had paid for him to attend until he turned eighteen. He only came back to the plantation for holidays and for one month during the summer.

After a couple of weeks, things settled into a routine. Marie always got up early and found something for breakfast on the kitchen table. On a typical day, she played outside, rode her bicycle up and down the dirt road in front of the house, or enjoyed the toys in the playroom.

Gretchen would call her for lunch, which consisted of a sandwich and fruit. In the afternoon, the girl read on the shaded screened back porch with a fan blowing over her. A glass of lemonade was always available when she came down with the book she had chosen to entertain herself.

Aunt Gretchen enrolled her in the local public school, as she did not want to send her to boarding school and needed to keep the child close for some reason. The bus picked her up each day at the end of the dirt road. Gretchen would accompany her, wait until the vehicle arrived, and wave goodbye. When Marie came home, milk and homemade cookies were always waiting on the kitchen table. The house was always tidy, the yard well-manicured, the flower beds maintained, and all weeds removed.

Marie did well in school and enjoyed learning new things and reading. When she first attended the school, some kids would make mean comments and call her "ghost girl" because she lived in the haunted house.

Angry, she said, "You are being mean. I have never seen a spirit at the house. It is just me and Aunt Gretchen. Stop calling me ghost girl."

The children calmed down after that, wondering if perhaps their parents were mistaken, but how could they be? None of her schoolmates would ever visit the house. Aunt Gretchen would organize birthday parties for Marie at the local ice cream parlor, where everyone attended the celebrations for the free ice cream.

Things were peaceful and happy for the next few years at the L'Enfant Haven estate.

On Marie's tenth birthday, Aunt Gretchen told her, "You are growing up and need to move out of the nursery. I will have the bedroom across the hall set up for you."

Gretchen called a construction company in Shreveport because no one from Madreville would come out to work on the plantation house. Workers arrived at the house, painted the room, and transported new furniture to the second floor and Marie's room.

When she came home from school, Aunt Gretchen met her at the front door with a smile and said, "Come and see your room."

She took Marie by the hand to her room.

Marie was so happy that she jumped up and down, shouting, "I love it, I love it!"

Together, they moved all the girls' clothing into the new space. Marie felt more grown-up than she ever had.

As Marie grew older, she noticed unusual occurrences around the house. She never found Aunt Gretchen cleaning, yet the house was always tidy. Occasionally, she would see Gretchen cooking, but only for certain meals. She never questioned how all the work was accomplished.

One day, Marie asked her aunt about this curiosity, and Gretchen told her, "People come in while you are out and do work."

The girl didn't believe this explanation.

After these questions became more frequent, Gretchen sent the girl to summer camps for two months to prevent her from witnessing astounding occurrences in the house. When Marie was home, she eavesdropped on Aunt Gretchen's telephone conversations, hoping to find a clue to the mystery.

On an unusual day, Mr. Butler visited their house, not dressed in a suit as usual, and wanted to speak with Aunt Gretchen. He appeared worried and upset. Marie listened from the kitchen while the adults discussed a Voodoo Imperatrice.

Two days later, three Black individuals arrived at the estate. Marie watched them park an old tan Ford in front of the house. A peculiar woman wearing a colorful scarf wrapped around her head, along with a brightly colored skirt and blouse, exited the Ford. Another woman, dressed entirely in white, and a boy in jeans and a T-shirt also left the vehicle. They all walked up the path together. The woman with the head wrap paused momentarily to look at one of the oak trees before continuing on her way.

Marie silently opened the door to her bedroom, stood at the second-floor landing, and watched and listened as Mr. Butler greeted the woman with his head bowed. She wondered why he did that. He escorted the unusual guests to the back porch where Aunt Gretchen lounged. She waited until Mr. Butler, the woman in white, and the boy entered the parlor before coming downstairs to find out what was happening.

Mr. Butler asked her to show the boy around the yard, so she took him outside.

"What is your name?"

"Antoine."

He detected the aroma of the soap the girl used in her bath that morning. The slight lavender scent lingered around her, one of his favorite scents, making him even more attracted to her.

"Mine is Marie."

As the two walked through the yard, she asked, "Why is that lady here talking to my Aunt Gretchen?"

He answered in a southern New Orleans accent, "My mother is talking to your aunt about doing a job for her."

"A job? What sort of job?"

"I don't know, but it will be something with a voodoo."

"You're lying. My aunt doesn't have anything to do with voodoo."

"Maybe you don't know, but that's what my mother is doing."

The two young teens strolled around the yard. Antoine's eyes were always on Marie. He had never been as attracted to someone as he was to her—her beautiful face, hair, the way she walked, and the way she spoke. So mesmerized by Marie, Antoine never noticed Paul, the ghostly yard man beside the oak tree.

They returned to the house, and as they entered, Gretchen and the Voodoo Imperatrice were leaving the dining room. The priestess inspected Marie from head to toe. The girl felt a shiver run down her spine. Aunt Gretchen and the priestess ascended the stairs.

Marie and Antoine went into the parlor and sat on the settee. They whispered.

"Why did your mother look at me that way? It gave me the shivers."

"I don't know. She's always planning something. She never tells me anything. I hate her."

He glanced over his left shoulder, and the spirit of his dead father stared at him. He hated ghosts.

"You are lucky you have a mother. My mother and father died in a car accident."

"My mother only wants me around when she needs something from me. She doesn't love me. My father is dead, too, but he is still here."

Marie looked quizzically at Antoine, not understanding his last comment. 'How could his father still be here?'

"That's too bad that you feel that way. I love my parents."

Marie's legs touched Antoine's as they sat there and he liked the sensation.

Finally, Aunt Gretchen and the strange lady returned to the house, having gone out to the backyard.

Antoine's mother said, "I'll be back at the full moon. The Lunar sacrament will happen at the Moon's rise. You will make a sacrifice to the Moon. A payment of $5,000.00 in cash must be made. It may not work, but breaking this curse is the strongest ritual. Are you agreeing to the fee?"

Aunt Gretchen said, "I do."

She watched them drive away. Mr. Butler also left after that.

Marie asked her aunt, "What did that lady mean? She will do a Lunar ceremony?"

"It is nothing for you to worry about, dear. She will be blessing the house."

"But the woman said something about a curse?"

"It is just something the Labauve family has done every few years to keep curses from happening. Many people don't like rich people and try to do bad things to us. You don't have to worry about all this nonsense. This has nothing to do with you."

Marie felt a queasy sensation in her stomach and suspected her aunt was lying. If possible, she would try to sneak down and watch when the ceremony took place.

# Chapter 19

## Marie's Tragic End

My mother took a drink of water and continued telling me about her tragic life.

Two weeks later, the moon rose over the plantation, casting silver light across the estate as the ritual night arrived. Gretchen dressed in white as instructed—a simple blouse and skirt—and then went to Marie's room and gently knocked.

"Stay in your room tonight, dear. No exceptions," she said.

Marie nodded, but once the door closed, she muttered under her breath, "Like that's going to happen."

Several cars arrived and parked along the road in front of the house. From her window, Marie observed the people in white, loose-fitting clothes exit the vehicles, pulling out a large kettle and several boxes of items. Andrew Butler also came dressed in white pants and a shirt. This would be the first and last voodoo ceremony in which he would participate.

The voodoo priestess' followers entered the house and assembled in the parlor. Renee Broussard, the priestess, instructed them to move all the furniture into the dining room and library. Once the space was empty, the devotees transported the bronze brazier on metal legs with wood pads on the floor and placed it in the center of the parlor. Candles flickered in every corner, casting dancing shadows along the walls.

They opened the tall windows to let the wind flow into the room and the lunar light to pour in from the east. The disciples formed a circle around the fire. Drummers began playing a low, pulsing rhythm that stirred something primal in the air.

Gretchen stood in one corner. They closed the paneled entryway, and the ceremony began.

Marie observed all the preparations from the second-floor landing.

Antoine left the parlor and took a seat in a chair beside the front door. The drumming continued, and chanting began. Antoine saw Marie tiptoe down the stairs, appearing to float like an angel in her pink satin pajamas.

She approached Antoine and asked, "Why are you out here and not in there with the others?"

"My mother said I should stay here. I don't know why."

Marie said, "Let's sneak a peek," and turned toward the double doors.

Antoine grabbed her arm.

"No, you shouldn't."

"I want to see what is going on," she said, pulling away from him.

Pushing the panels apart by an inch, just enough to peer inside, she stood there watching the ceremony, not understanding what it all meant. A circle of devotees chanted and danced around the kettle, with a fire burning in its center. One follower poured a liquid from a bottle into a wooden bowl. The assemblage passed the mixture to each person, and they all drank, including Aunt Gretchen and Mr. Butler.

The mingled scents of various herbs she couldn't identify wafted from the large brazier, floating through the crack between the panels. Marie liked the aroma and inhaled deeply, feeling a bit dizzy.

The drums maintained an addictive rhythm. Aunt Gretchen stood in a corner, swaying back and forth to the beat. Marie, too, unconsciously moved in time with the drumbeats as she observed the mysterious activities. The lunar orb began to rise on the eastern horizon. The priestess picked up mystifying items at various moments, danced with them, and sang in a peculiar language, shouting and screaming. The moon ascended higher. The cadence quickened, the chanting intensified, and it grew louder.

Gretchen knelt on the floor in front of the fire. She swayed to the drumbeats. She accepted the fetishes offered by the priestess, kissed each one, and pressed them to her forehead. Two followers jumped from the circle of dancers, yelled, and gyrated frantically, their eyes rolling to the tops of their heads. The pale orb continued to rise above the horizon. The dancing, singing, and screaming continued.

The Voodoo Imperatrice shouted, "The sacrifice must be made."

She again called, "The sacrifice must be made," holding her arms over her head.

The moon rose above the horizon.

Marie felt something warm running down her leg. Glancing down, she noticed a red trail marking her pajama pants between her legs. She screamed at the sight.

Aunt Gretchen jerked from her trance. Hearing Marie's scream, she rose from her knees and ran to the sliding doors. When she opened the panels, she saw Marie, who was screaming and looking at the redness on her pajamas, terrified and confused about what was happening.

Gretchen grabbed her by the shoulders.

"It's okay. There is nothing wrong."

Marie looked up at her and sobbed. Gretchen wrapped her arm around Marie's shoulder and led her upstairs to the bathroom, frustrated with herself for delaying the explanation of the uncomfortable topic of women's cycles.

The Voodoo Imperatrice said, "The sacrifice has been made. Virgin menstrual blood is the strongest blood there is."

The supporters started extinguishing the fire and candles. They loaded everything into the cars and rearranged all the furniture in the parlor. The Voodoo Imperatrice sat on the sofa and waited for Gretchen to return.

Gretchen removed Marie's pajamas and cleaned her with a warm washcloth. Then she went to Marie's room to get clean night clothes and underwear. When she returned with the clothes, Marie appeared in shock, sitting on the toilet and staring at the wall.

Gretchen explained to Marie about women's menstrual cycles and how to use and dispose of sanitary napkins.

Marie stared at her aunt and shouted, "You caused all this! You are a witch!"

She ran into her bedroom.

Gretchen felt terrible for not having explained this to her sooner. She thought she still had a couple of years left. She went downstairs, and the Voodoo Imperatrice sat on the couch, waiting for her payment.

Gretchen approached her.

"I'm sorry the ceremony was interrupted," she said. "Do you want your fee?"

The priestess nodded her head.

Gretchen said, "I'll go get it."

She entered the library, slid the secret panel aside in the bookshelf, and opened the wall safe. She pulled out the $5,000 as promised. The hidden storage compartment also contained her diaries from over the years.

She handed the money to the voodoo priestess, "Do you think the curse is broken?"

"We will see what happens. Maybe yes, maybe no."

Gretchen understood that the ceremony likely didn't work because the girl interrupted the ritual with her outburst. The Voodoo Imperatrice stepped outside and took a seat in the front of one of the parked vehicles, smiling as she realized that the sacrifice had been accepted. The mysterious entourage drove away.

Andrew Butler approached Gretchen and asked, "Is Marie okay? What happened?"

"Marie started her period, which scared her because she didn't know what it was. It's my fault for not explaining it to her sooner."

Andrew didn't say anything. He understood now what the Voodoo Imperatrice meant when she said, "The sacrifice has been made. Virgin menstrual blood is the strongest blood there is." The girl was the sacrifice. He walked out the door to his car and drove home, still feeling strange from whatever they had made him drink. He felt sorry for the poor child and what she would endure for years.

When Marie woke up in the morning, she went to the bathroom and changed her sanitary napkin, just as Aunt Gretchen had demonstrated. She got dressed and went downstairs for breakfast. While sitting in the kitchen, she noticed a heavyset Black woman standing at the stove cooking. The woman turned, smiled at her, and placed a bowl of oatmeal with raisins, maple syrup, and milk on the table for her.

She asked the Black woman, "When did you start working here?"

The woman didn't answer and stood next to the stove.

Aunt Gretchen walked into the kitchen and said, "Good morning, dear. Do you feel better today?"

Marie asked, "When did you hire a cook?"

"I haven't hired a cook. What do you mean?"

"That woman over there just made my breakfast."

"Oh, you can see her now? Renee said you would begin seeing them soon."

"Seeing who?"

"The ghosts, dear. She's a ghost."

"What ghosts? There are spirits in this house and you never told me. You never told me anything!" she yelled as she ran from the kitchen into the hall.

Dr. Albert Labauve stood in the library doorway. When she saw him, she screamed, ran to her bedroom, and slammed the door. She jumped into her bed and pulled the covers over her head. Following her, Gretchen opened the door and entered Marie's room. She placed her hand on Marie's shoulder, covered by the blanket, and Marie screamed, believing that one of the ghosts had touched her.

Gretchen said, "It's me, Aunt Gretchen. I didn't tell you about the spirits because I didn't want you to be scared."

Marie cried, "It is all your fault. Everything was fine until you had those weird people come over and do that voodoo stuff. You're a witch. You called the ghosts. You made me bleed. It is all your fault."

And she cried.

"No, dear, the spirits are here because of a curse on the house. They have been here for over a hundred years. Some of us Labauves can see them; some can't. Most of us don't start seeing them until about thirteen or fourteen. You started younger. It is nothing I did."

"I don't believe you! Get out of my room. I don't want to talk to you."

Gretchen departed the room, and Marie lay in bed for the rest of the day and night, paralyzed by fear. She only came out to use the bathroom and change her napkin. Gretchen brought a food tray to her room and knocked on the door.

"Dear, here is dinner. Please eat something."

After Gretchen left, Marie pulled the tray into her room, famished, and ate the meal.

After finishing the meal, she realized, "Oh, my god, the ghost may have cooked this."

She felt nauseous and vomited the food into the wastebasket, placing the dishes and trash receptacle outside the door. Milly came by later, picked them up, and took them to be cleaned, which would have freaked Marie out if she had known.

On Monday, Marie went to school. She dressed, ran down the stairs, out the door, and down the road as quickly as she could to catch the bus. She didn't want any ghosts or Aunt Gretchen to observe her. Their loathsome stares made her feel dirty. She didn't take her lunch with her; the spirit might have made it. She used the little money she had to buy her meal at the cafeteria.

When she came home, she went straight to her room and locked the door. This continued for about a week. After her cycle stopped, Marie felt a little better but was still terrified of the apparitions. She would come down for dinner, flinching at the slightest noise. Always on the lookout for apparitions, she would return to her room if she saw any. On weekends, she stayed outside to avoid seeing the ghosts in the house. She didn't realize spirits were elsewhere on the property.

Marie became so depressed that she lost focus in school and failed to complete her homework. She often got into fights. The school contacted her Aunt Gretchen several times about these issues.

When Marie turned thirteen, her brother Robert died in a car accident, just like her parents. While celebrating his graduation with friends, they all got drunk, and the driver hit a wet spot on a bridge, causing the vehicle to crash through the railing and into the river, killing all five boys.

She didn't leave her room for two days, devastated by her brother's death. They buried Robert next to his parents in the family plot. After Robert's demise, she felt an overwhelming loneliness, believing this was proof that Gretchen was a witch. As the years passed, Marie's life spiraled into depression and darkness. The ghosts she once feared became a haunting presence, driving her to drugs and rebellion.

She hung out with the tough kids to compensate for her fear. Introduced to drugs and marijuana by this unsavory group, she soon realized she didn't see the apparitions if she came home loaded. She began stealing money from her aunt's purse to pay for the illegal substances.

Her aunt tried everything to help Marie understand what was happening at the house with the ghosts, but Marie wouldn't listen. As Marie got older, she often didn't return home until late after school and argued aggressively with her aunt when she was there.

At sixteen, she met an older boy, Darren Smith, who was nineteen. Desperate to escape, she ran off with him, believing she had found someone who cared about her. She never returned until Gretchen departed.

Marie lived in flophouses with Darren for a few months until he left with another girl. Marie felt deeply betrayed. She vowed never to care for another man. She drifted from one group of drug users to another and took temporary jobs here and there to make ends meet.

Unexpectedly Antoine Broussard reentered her life in one of the new flophouses. They were immediately drawn to each other, recalling the circumstances under which they initially met and now sharing similar backgrounds. They stayed together for several months; she became pregnant and gave birth to a beautiful baby boy. Antoine mysteriously disappeared before the child was born, leaving Marie feeling utterly hopeless.

It happened again; she thought she had someone who cared about her, but he ran off. She didn't understand why he had disappeared. He had just gotten a job, and they were both trying to cut down on drugs, knowing it was unsuitable for the child. She reduced her drug use to only marijuana while carrying the baby. She wanted Antoine to see and hold his son but couldn't find him anywhere when she asked around. After she gave birth to Orion, she returned to more potent medications to cope with the ongoing depression she felt.

After a year and a half of separation from Antoine, she met one of Antoine's friends, Nathan, whom she hadn't seen in a long time.

She asked him, "Have you seen Antoine? Do you know why he left before his baby was born?"

Nathan said, "Antoine told me his mother made him leave you and never return."

Marie reflected on everything that had happened to her over the past several years and realized that the priestess wanted them to come together. Antoine didn't need to attend the ceremony; his only purpose for being there was to meet her and for them to bond. Antoine shared how his mother exploited his ability to see ghosts, disregarding how it affected him. As he explained, his mother had plans; she needed them to produce a child.

However, she didn't understand why until they moved back into the mansion and she discovered that Orion could see and communicate with ghosts even at three. Both Marie and Antoine could observe spirits; that was why they both took drugs, to avoid seeing the spirits, and now their son possessed even more skills to interact with apparitions.

"Baby, I never wanted to live in the house. I never wanted to see ghosts. The Voodoo Imperatrice convinced Aunt Gretchen to do the ceremony so I would see the spirits, meet Antoine, and have you. You're special, baby. Find your father. He should meet you. He can tell you what his mother is planning for you. She has some plans for you. Don't let her use you."

"Mama, I know all about the spirits. They have been there for a long time. I saw them the first day we walked in the door. I'm not afraid. They have taken care of me all the years you couldn't. They are my family."

"The Voodoo Imperatrice wants you to love the ghosts and do anything to save them. Promise me you will find your father and talk to him. I was weak. You must be strong and fight her however you can."

"I will, Mama, I will."

She closed her eyes and never opened them again. I sat there with tears rolling down my cheeks, but not for long. None of this had to happen. She had no reason to fear the spirits to the extent that she did; they were there to help her, but she would never accept it. I did all the paperwork at the hospital and drove home in a daze.

The next day, I called the local mortuary in Madreville and arranged for them to come out and dig the hole in the family plot, had a simple gravestone created, and informed them which casket to use and when to pick up the body at the hospital. A week later, the funeral took place. The minister from the church conducted the services. The only attendees at the service were me, Andy Butler Jr., Herman Labauve, and the ghosts. No one else from the Labauve family came. With my mother's passing, the weight of her legacy as the new Labauve heir fell upon me, a burden I carried alone as we laid her to rest.

The attorney and Herman didn't know it, but the ghosts also attended. With so few of us at the funeral, no wake was planned for afterward. Everyone just went home. I went to my room on the second floor and went to bed.

In the aftermath, I couldn't help but reflect on yet another tragedy that unfolded within the walls of our house. My mother's life, consumed by fear and regret, ended as it began: haunted by the ghosts of the mansion's past.

My life wasn't much different after my mother's death. I left her belongings in her room untouched, just as Aunt Gretchen had done when she first ran away from home at sixteen. Nothing changed since we moved into the house, and Mother reoccupied her former room, a self-imposed prison. After I came home from the hospital where she died, I closed the door to her room and never opened it until she visited me in my dreams.

# Chapter 20

# Fear of Thunderstorms

# & Nanny's Care

After I packed my mother's belongings and stowed them in the attic, I lingered there longer than intended, my fingers grazing the cardboard that contained my mother's life. The silence felt heavier than before. To lift my spirits, I went downstairs and spent some time playing the piano.

Milly asked, "Mr. Orion, would you like something to drink?"

"Just some ice water."

She came back with a glass.

The phone rang, and I got up to answer it. It was Andy.

Andy said, "Hi, Orion. How are you doing today?"

"I still ache all over, and I keep having dreams about my mother. So, I went to her grave and left some flowers this morning."

"I know what you mean. Sometimes memories just hit me out of the blue. I miss my dad too," Andy sympathized.

"She keeps urging me to fight against the Voodoo Imperatrice. She mentioned it even on her deathbed."

"You said the Voodoo Imperatrice?"

"Yes, that's what she said."

"She's your grandmother. She is supposedly powerful. My father wrote about her in his diaries."

"Well, I don't know if my mother's spirit visited me in my dreams or if my subconscious felt guilty about not doing more for her. She told me that the Voodoo Imperatrice was my grandmother, but I didn't realize she was that powerful. If her spirit comes again, I'll pay more attention to what she says. Each time she shows up in my dreams, it gets me depressed. I also packed all her stuff from her room today—something I should have done five years ago. I feel terrible about it."

"I understand. Don't be too hard on yourself. Grief has its own timeline," Andy reassured.

"While in the attic storing her things, I remembered Aunt Gretchen mentioning the voodoo priestess in her diaries. The first time I read them, I was eleven. I pulled the journals out of storage; I'll look deeper into Aunt Gretchen's diaries, and maybe I can learn more about my grandmother."

"Are you going to call your grandmother?"

"Yes, I will, but not right away. I want to find out more about her first. I'll research her in New Orleans and see what I can discover."

"How are you going to do that?"

"With ghosts," I responded cryptically before ending the call.

While performing Finding Jobs for clients, I learned that some communities have ghost towns. Some spirits hang around the houses they occupied when alive, and ghosts often linger in older homes and neighborhoods. I can send Cyrus to a location and have him ask for the information I need.

Sometimes the house spirits talk to other specters in the area, and those apparitions communicate with additional spirits. The word gets circulated, and I receive information whenever I pass through the community every few days. The phantoms are always willing to assist me. Mother meant this when she said I am unique and can compel ghosts to do things for me.

I decided I wouldn't do anything until I felt better. My right arm ached, and I had a headache from the day's work. The doctor said I shouldn't drive for a couple of weeks; I would have to wait to snoop around. I'd read Aunt Gretchen's diaries and help Walter repair the Jaguar.

A massive thunderstorm swept through while I was reading Aunt Gretchen's journals that afternoon. As thunder rumbled outside, the house seemed to whisper of old memories. I couldn't help but reflect on the first storm I experienced here.

⚷— ⚷— ⚷—

A few weeks after we settled into the house, Mother had me sleep in the nursery. She found some boys' pajamas, dressed me for bed, kissed me on the head, and said, "Good night."

She left to return to her room on the floor below to take her pills and pass out. I went to sleep but awoke later that night, hearing thunder and seeing lightning. A fierce storm raged outside. The wind blew so hard it made the oak trees creak loudly, branches threatening to snap. Torrents of rain pounded against the window. The lightning flashed and illuminated the nursery, casting strange shadows on the walls and ceiling. The thunder crashed and rumbled, sounding as if something would smash through the building at any second.

It frightened me so badly that I cried out, "Mama, Mama!"

My cries for my mother went unheard, drowned out by both the storm and her medication-induced slumber. I wanted to cuddle beside her and hide under the covers next to her body. Too scared to run downstairs to Mama's room, I quivered with the blanket over my head and cried for her, "Mama, Mama!"

Nanny Helen came, pulled the blanket back over my head, and pushed my curls back.

"It's okay. Here's Bunny to protect you from the thunder and lightning."

She gave me a large, brown, plush stuffed rabbit.

She said, "When lightning flashes, push your face into his tummy. He will protect you from the light. He is a good protector. He used to protect your mother when she was little."

I grabbed Bunny, hugged it, and buried my face in its stomach when the lightning flashed and the thunder boomed. She was right. Bunny did help. I looked into Bunny's glass eyes, and I swear they were smiling at me.

Nanny sat on the edge of the bed and rubbed my back.

She said, "I am always here to protect you; we all are."

I glanced up from the stuffed rabbit, and the others who lived in the house stood in my room, smiling at me. At that moment, I still didn't realize they were dead and ghosts, but knowing they were all there to be with me made me feel less frightened.

I fell asleep hugging Bunny all night. After that night, the stuffed rabbit became my constant protective companion and stayed with me each night. If I ever felt extra frightened or unsettled, I would call for Nanny, who would hold me until I stopped feeling nervous and anxious.

I never called my mother after that night. Even at that young age, I understood she would never be there to alleviate my fears and comfort me, but Nanny always showed up until the day she left. I slept with Bunny until I turned ten and then moved to a room on the second floor. I didn't need Bunny's protection as I got older, but I occasionally visited the nursery to hug Bunny.

It distressed me when Nanny departed; I always missed her availability. She played with me in the playroom and sometimes outside. When I was very young, I often played with the ghost slave children who lived by the old slave quarters, always playing tag. Occasionally, I wanted to play something else, but they could only play tag. The governess would throw the ball with me until Walter gave me the bicycle, which I rode all over the property.

The mornings were for playtime, while the afternoons were for school. My nanny taught me to read English and French when I was three. I learned quickly and brilliantly. By the time I entered public school at six, I was already two grades ahead of my peers. I think that may have been one of the reasons they didn't like me.

She also instructed me to read music and play the piano. Learning the piano took considerably more time because my fingers were too short. As I got older, my fingers grew, and I improved. I still practice every few days.

Early in September, at six years of age, the attorney came to the estate and informed my mother that I needed to be registered for school and receive my vaccinations. Mother was halfway presentable when he arrived and drove us to Dr. Wilson's office in Madreville, where I received the required vaccinations. When he poked me with the needle, I closed my eyes and tried not to cry. A few tears still escaped. Then Mr. Butler took us to the elementary school. My mother filled out all the paperwork, and I attended first grade the following week.

On the first day of school, Nanny walked me down to the end of the dirt road where it met the paved parish road—she couldn't go any farther—and there the bus would pick me up. She held my hand the whole way. Bertha made lunch and placed it in a brown paper bag. My lunch would be ready each day, sitting at the kitchen table. When the vehicle pulled up, I was still holding Nanny's hand, so it seemed funny to all the children on the bus, who saw my hand hanging in the air.

I got on the conveyance, and all the kids laughed at me and raised their hands like I had. I didn't understand at first, but I eventually realized they were making fun of me for holding Nanny's hand. Some kids continued to mock me after we arrived at the school, and I got into a fight on the first day.

Having not been raised around other children, I didn't grasp how cruel they could be, and my anger surfaced quickly. The principal sent a letter home with me about the incident for my mother to read. Mother never saw it, but Nanny did. She explained that children sometimes say inappropriate things and that I should disregard what they say. This was sometimes hard for me to accept.

When I was ten and moved to the second floor, I accidentally discovered why Nanny was a ghost. Nanny had suggested I move to the lower level. Early Saturday morning, while moving some of my belongings to the new room, I wanted Nanny's opinion on what I should bring and went looking for her. I found her facing a corner in what used to be her room on the third floor across from the nursery.

Occasionally, I noticed that each apparition, except Cyrus, faced a corner and did not respond to anything. At four years of age, I went to pull on Bertha's dress, wondering where my breakfast was. Bertha stood in the corner of the kitchen next to the stove. Nanny stopped me from touching her.

She explained, "Each of us has a private time, and you should not touch or bother them when this happens."

I accepted this explanation at the time. However, at ten, I wanted Nanny to answer my question, so I walked up behind her, touched her shoulder, and experienced what she was reliving.

On that day, I learned that on the anniversary of their deaths, each spirit vanished into a silent ritual—reliving their final moments, locked in the pain that bound them here.

# Chapter 21

# The Governess' Story

In June 1932, Gretchen Labauve hired Drew Merriweather as the new English butler at L'Enfant Haven plantation. Fifty, tall, and dashingly handsome, Drew Merriweather was refined, yet far less proper than he appeared. Oh, and that English accent could melt a lady's stockings off.

At thirty, Helen Jones, the governess at L'Enfant Haven, had never been so attracted to a man. She made excuses to visit the kitchen or the veranda, where he often relaxed. Always drawn to Mr. Merriweather, as he preferred to be called, Helen neglected some of her duties. She was less passionate about supervising and teaching the Labauve children—Joseph, six, and Adeline, seven.

Helen and Mr. Merriweather would converse, and he would make flirtatious comments to her. Men rarely paid much attention to her. Helen, a plain-looking woman with brown hair that she always wore pulled back in a bun, fell in love with Drew, and when the amorous comments escalated to kissing and grabbing, she allowed it to continue. They often made love in her room, far above where the Labauve family stayed. When around the Labauve family, both maintained a professional demeanor.

Drew would say, "Good morning, Miss Jones," and Helen would say, "Good morning, Mr. Merriweather."

The family never suspected the relationship between them.

One day, while the children were doing their schoolwork, Helen searched for Mr. Merriweather. She couldn't find him in the kitchen or on the porch, where he usually was. She went up the attic stairs to his room. She explored Mr. Merriweather's room, but he wasn't there.

Hearing grunting and moaning noises from the room next door, she peeked in. She pushed the cracked door further open to discover

Mr. Merriweather having sex with Alice, the maid, against the wall, with his pants down at his ankles and Alice's skirt crumpled between their chests with her legs around his waist.

Seeing this, Helen gasped, "Oh, my God."

The couple stopped, shocked, having been caught in this act of lust. Helen ran down the stairs to her room, tears streaming down her face. The children saw Nanny rush past the playroom doorway and slam her door. A short while later, Mr. Merriweather came to her door and knocked.

He whispered through the door, "Helen, open the door. I want to speak to you."

She said, "No, I don't want to talk to you. Go away."

"Helen, please let me speak to you."

"No, go away."

He left and went downstairs.

She didn't know Drew Merriweather was charming all the women in the house. His obsession with sexual encounters caused his dismissal from previous employment at an estate in New York City. He loved women of all types and couldn't get enough of them. His exceptional good looks enabled him to seduce anyone he desired.

Drew learned about the Labauve family needing a butler from Ann Christof, with whom he had an affair while serving as the assistant butler for the Christof family in New Orleans. Ann became pregnant and went off to have the child. He kept in touch and occasionally asked about his son.

He discovered that Andrew Butler was his son and the Labauve family lawyer, but he never revealed it. The boy thrived and grew into a fine gentleman. Andrew's rise above his father's station made Drew proud of him.

After a while, Helen regained control, wiped the tears away, and returned to the playroom, smiling to mask her feelings of betrayal and emotional devastation. Something was wrong with their governess, but the children didn't know what it could be.

Helen peered at them.

"Let's see how you are progressing with your work."

She glanced over their shoulders, commenting, "You are doing so well," distracting the children from recognizing her unhappiness.

She didn't go to dinner, claiming to have a sick stomach.

Helen avoided Mr. Merriweather whenever she could. One day, she walked past him to take the children outside to play. She tried to ignore him when he grabbed her arm.

"I want to speak to you about what you saw."

"Well, I don't want to talk to you."

"Helen, please. I feel terrible about what happened. I care about you and don't want that incident to come between us."

He said the right words. She stopped and peered at him, wanting to believe what he said.

She said to the children, "Go ahead and enjoy yourselves. I must talk with Mr. Merriweather."

The young ones played with the ball in the yard. They threw the red ball back and forth.

He said, "We can't speak here; let's return to your room."

They each went upstairs at different times to not attract attention. Helen sat on her bed. He came in, shut the door, and positioned himself beside her.

An expert liar, Drew told Helen the words she wanted to hear.

"I'm so sorry you found Alice and me. I had a weak moment. Alice had been pushing herself on me for weeks. When she pulled her skirt up, I couldn't stop myself. I hate myself for what I did. I only want to be with you. Please forgive me. It will never happen again. I want to marry you, Helen, but I didn't dare to ask."

Helen sat and listened to him. Her stomach jumped when he said he wanted to marry her.

She said, "It is hard for me to believe you after what I saw."

"I know. I'm a horrible person. I understand if you say no to my proposal."

"I'm not saying no. I want to marry you, too. I want your assurance that this will never occur again."

Knowing he won her over, he grinned and said, "Yes, I swear this will never happen again."

He kissed her, and she melted into his arms. While kissing, he undressed her, unbuttoning her dress and removing her underpants.

She said, "Not now. I must go out to watch the children."

"They are okay. We can make it fast," he continued.

Outside, the wind howled, unaware of the tragedy it was about to unleash.

They made love until an explosion occurred outside. The sounds of people yelling and the odor of smoke wafted up the stairs. They both jumped out of bed, got dressed, and ran downstairs.

As Joseph and Adeline threw the red ball, the wind picked up and caused the boy to miss the catch. It rolled over to the gardening shed and hit the wall. Joseph eyed the forbidden open door, wanting to enter. He walked over and picked up the toy before standing in front of the door. Adeline ran around and positioned herself next to her brother.

Remembering what Nanny said, 'You must never go in the shed.

But why couldn't they enter the building? They exchanged glances and silently agreed. They walked into the outbuilding and looked around. A strong odor lingered in the air. A gust of wind slammed the outbuilding's door shut; the latch fell into the hook, locking it from the outside.

The children jumped when the door slammed. They realized what had happened: the wind had blown the door shut, and they laughed. They continued to investigate the shed's contents. The small, filthy window didn't allow much light into the enclosure, and the strong scent grew more intense.

As a typical boy, Joseph said, "Here, I can use the matches."

He pulled three matchsticks out of his pocket.

Adeline said, "You aren't supposed to have those. Nanny Helen will be angry if she knows you have these."

"Then don't tell her."

Joseph struck a match on the tabletop. Holding the burning matchstick high above his head to better view the items hidden from them, the ember burned down the wooden stick. They didn't notice the puddle of liquid on the floor. As they searched around, the lit end of the match brushed against Joseph's fingers.

He shouted, "Ouch!" as he dropped the lit match.

The pool of liquid ignited into flames, and the children shrieked. They ran for the door, but it wouldn't budge. They didn't know about the pull line hanging through a hole in the door. If they pulled the cable, the latch would release from the hook holding it in place and unlock the door. The brother and sister, in complete terror, screamed, cried, and beat on the door.

"Help, help! Let us out!"

No one heard the children's pitiful cries for help. Their parents and Aunt Gretchen were visiting friends, driven by the chauffeur. The maids were in the basement doing laundry, operating a loud clothes washer, talking, and laughing. The cook was at the market. John, the handyman, was out front making repairs to the fence, hammering slats back onto it. He had left the door open.

The flames grew larger. The children continued to scream and beat on the door. The leaking gas can in the outbuilding exploded, destroying the shed and killing the boy and girl. Other chemical containers in the garden shed also burst from the heat of the initial fire.

Shocked by the explosions, everyone ran towards the source of the sound. John grabbed the hose connected to the water faucet in the yard and turned it on, trying to extinguish the flames. Helen and Mr. Merriweather were the last to leave the house. Seeing the burning structure with flames shooting high, Helen immediately shouted for the children and ran throughout the back and front yard, searching for them.

When she returned to the backyard, the servants crowded near the remains of the shed. The fire was out, but a few spots still smoldered and smoked. The air was filled with the acrid scent of gasoline, burnt wood, and charred meat. The charred wreckage of the shed lay scattered like bones, and atop it, two small bodies—blackened and still—broke Helen's world.

As the vision of the children's blackened bodies filled Helen's eyes, she fell to her knees, screaming. Great racking sobs erupted from her throat. She thought her heart would burst from the pain she felt in her chest. Mr. Merriweather took her by the shoulders and walked her into the house.

As they entered the house, he told John, "Call the police and tell them what happened."

He took Helen to her room and laid her on the bed. She could barely stand; the weight of her grief pressed heavily on her shoulders. The vision of the children's burned bodies haunted her thoughts. The tragic event felt entirely her fault. This wouldn't have happened if she hadn't been with Mr. Merriweather. The children were her responsibility. They were now gone because of her weakness and her surrender to carnal desires.

As the police and ambulance approached along the dirt road with sirens blaring, Mr. and Mrs. Gordon Labauve Jr. drove up behind them, unaware of what had transpired. They noticed smoke rising from the backyard. The old Rolls pulled into the driveway and parked in front of the carriage house. They jumped out of the Rolls and ran toward the source of the commotion.

The smoldering remains of the children's bodies were visible as they approached the source of the smoke. The women screamed and sobbed. Gordon held both his wife and Aunt Gretchen as they all cried. He took the women into the house so they didn't have to observe the horrific sight.

The sheriff questioned everyone.

John told them, "I left the shed door open. I was only going to be gone for a short time."

He sat on the back porch and sobbed, blaming himself for the deaths of the children.

Drew Merriweather informed the police, "I was in my room in the attic when it happened, and Helen was also upstairs in her room."

Gordon asked, "Where is Nanny?"

Drew said, "She was so upset I took her to her room."

They all understood.

Reported as a tragic accident, the police closed the investigation.

Later, Gordon went to Nanny's room and knocked. She didn't answer, but he could hear her sniffling.

He said through the door, "Nanny, none of this was your fault. It was an accident, a horrible accident. You can stay here at the house as long as you want."

Helen lay there, hearing his words but still blaming herself. Guilt anchored her to the bed. Grief soaked every breath. The maids would leave trays of food for her in the hall, but they were rarely touched.

A week after the calamity, the funeral took place in the family graveyard at the estate. Helen managed to attend the solemn event but stood apart from the family, believing she didn't deserve to be included. After the funeral, she returned to her room.

Sometimes at night, when everyone was in bed, she would walk to the playroom and longingly gaze at the children's belongings, wishing her young charges would magically reappear, hoping the horrors she had witnessed were just a bad dream. But the boy and girl were never there, and the overwhelming sensations of guilt and grief would once again engulf her. It was all her fault because of her selfish desires.

Drew tried to talk to her, but she wouldn't speak to him or anyone else. The Labauves worried about the governess and called a doctor, who recommended that she visit a psychiatrist. They were looking into this when the final tragedy occurred.

Nanny believed she should have been the one who died, not the children. She felt she must die for what she did. She took the sheets off her bed, tied them together, and made a slip knot at one end. Moving a chair under the light fixture on the ceiling, she attached the sheet to the light pole. Putting the slip-knotted end around her neck, she kicked the chair away from beneath her feet.

The following day, they discovered her hanging from the light fixture. They called the police again for yet another tragic event. They buried Helen in the family plot, next to the children she loved.

Nanny Helen materialized in the playroom. Paul, Bertha, Milly, Philly, and Hugo stood in the room with sympathetic looks.

Bertha said, "Welcome home."

Helen entered the hall and watched as the police carried her body away. The Labauve family held each other, crying as her body was covered with a white sheet and taken down the stairs.

Bertha explained in her Southern accent, "Your spirit has to remain here at the plantation because of a curse on the house. Anyone who caused the death of a child and died in the house, their spirit has to stay until either the curse is broken or the spirit could somehow save a child from dying."

Helen said, "I deserve to be left in purgatory for what I have done."

She returned to the playroom to look out the window while her body was taken to the funeral home for preparation for burial.

All this appeared in a flash, and I jerked my hand back. Nanny Helen didn't react to my touching her and continued to stand in the corner. I went to my new bedroom and lay on the bed, crying about what Nanny had suffered.

Being so young, I never thought about how the ghosts had once been alive, had their own lives, and why they remained in the house and on the property. After this, I began to consider all the ghosts from a different perspective. I now understood that each spirit had a tragic story that haunted them. We, the living, weren't being haunted by the ghosts—the ghosts were the ones haunted by their past.

I would discover all the spirits' stories except for Cyrus'. This was the first time I heard about the curse on the house related to the deaths of children. I searched through old items in the house, looking for clues to the ghosts' lives, family tales, and anything about the curse.

Through my searches of Aunt Gretchen's journals, I discovered that Mr. Merriweather left the plantation a few weeks after Nanny Helen expired. Gordon Jr. and his wife moved to New Orleans a month later, not wanting to remain on the property where their children had succumbed, leaving Aunt Gretchen living in the house with the cook, maids, handyman, and chauffeur for the next few years.

Gordon Jr. and his wife had two other children—Robert, one year later, and Marie, my mother, five years after that. I uncovered all this information in Aunt Gretchen's journals.

The following day, I tried to talk to Nanny Helen about what I witnessed when I touched her. She became furious.

"It is impolite to intrude on another person's thoughts and life. What you observed was only meant for me, not for anyone else. That is why each of us has a day to reflect on our previous lives. You must never do that again."

I nodded okay.

She didn't realize I had touched her shoulder and viewed her life until I spoke up. Despite Nanny Helen's initial anger at my intrusion into her memories, I couldn't shake my curiosity about the other spirits. I had unlocked one tragic tale, and there were others waiting in the shadows.

127

—

# Chapter 22

# Distressing Childhood Incidents

Sleep came slowly that night. Aunt Gretchen's journals had stirred too many memories, and my daytime dozing had scrambled my internal clock. The concussion made me tired, so I napped a lot. As I lay in bed, haunted by my mother's unsettling dream, memories of other distressing incidents from my past flooded my mind. My life seemed to be a tapestry woven with alarming occurrences.

March 4th marked my eleventh birthday, a day lost amidst the chaos of my mother's neglectful indifference towards me. Yet the spirits inhabiting our home remembered. They orchestrated a small celebration with homemade cake, ice cream, and even a heartfelt gift from the doctor: a stethoscope. It was a day of fleeting, bittersweet joy amidst my tumultuous childhood.

I thanked Doc Albert for the gift and gave him a big hug. He patted me on the back.

Albert taught me first aid and science. He allowed me to use this medical device to listen to my heartbeat, and I caught one of the chickens to hear the creature's rapid heart repetitions. Fascinated, I now had my stethoscope and pretended to be a doctor. I brought the device to Show-and-Tell Day at school, letting everyone listen to their heartbeats. I was popular for a day.

My teacher asked, "Where did you get the stethoscope?"

I told her, "It was a birthday present from a friend."

Mr. Butler, one of the few kind souls in my life, gifted me a box of comic books—a treasure trove of adventure that illuminated my dull world. His great-grandson was discarding them. Mr. Butler took the container and explained to his great-grandson, "I know a boy who doesn't have any comics and would love to have these."

When I opened the box of books, the scent of the ink on the pages erupted from inside. The kids at school talked about comics, but I never bought any because I had no money. After seeing how much I enjoyed them, Mr. Butler continued to bring them for me.

He also donated hand-me-down clothes from his great-grandson. When I was younger, many small boys' clothes were still available from when my mother's brothers lived in the house. However, as I grew taller, the items fit me less and less. The pants were often too short, leading the kids at school to make fun of me for wearing high-waters. These taunts angered me, resulting in many fights.

Milly and Philly mended any tears, let down the leg cuffs so that the lengths were a bit longer, and kept them clean, but there were limits to what they could do. Occasionally, Mr. Butler took me to the local thrift store and bought me some used clothing. I always had something to wear, though it was usually in poor condition.

Life at home was a delicate dance of survival. My mother, trapped by addiction and neglect, squandered our meager resources, leaving little for necessities like food. It was my responsibility to manage our small budget, navigate the intricacies of grocery orders, and endure my mother's wrath when finances ran short.

Mother used much of the $500.00 monthly annuity from the trust for her drugs and sometimes for food. I called in the food orders from a list Bertha provided me each week. I would have gone hungry for many days if it had been up to Mother. Jordan's Grocery would send the bill to Mr. Butler, who would deduct the costs from the $500.00 allotment. My mother would drive to his office, and he would pass on whatever the difference was. Quite often, she would be upset and return home to yell at me for spending so much money.

As I grew older and consumed more, our grocery expenses increased. Concerned that I wasn't getting enough to eat, the ghosts held a family meeting while I was at school and devised a plan to ensure that some food would always be available for my mother and me.

Paul proposed starting a vegetable garden to offset costs. Hugo suggested repairing the old chicken coop and getting some chickens. Albert informed them he had money in a secret drawer in his desk, which could be used to purchase a small flock of chickens. Bertha mentioned she could preserve any extra vegetables and fruits from the apple and peach trees on the property. The plan was excellent, and I never went hungry.

Albert gave me the secret cash, and I rode my bike to the closest farmer and bought six chickens. He tied the legs of three of the squawking brown birds together and placed them in the bike's basket. I rolled around to the plantation house's backyard, untied their restraints, and let the poultry loose in the enclosure. The next day, I pedaled back and got the remaining birds. The one rooster in the flock would produce a steady supply of chickens available to eat.

We now had poultry for eggs and for eating. We allowed some eggs to hatch, and little chicks ran everywhere in the yard. Within a month and a half, there were plenty of chickens to slaughter and eat. Released each day, the chickens foraged on the grounds, and I picked up a bag of feed at the hardware store to supplement their meals. In the mornings, before going to school, I collected the eggs.

But as I grew older, I desired my own money and took it from my mother's purse, little by little, trying not to make it obvious that cash was missing.

132

# Chapter 23

# Like a Guardian Angel

Another unsettling memory was the arrival of George Anders—a sinister figure shrouded in darkness and fueled by alcohol, drugs, and malice—who unleashed a wave of violence that shattered the fragile semblance of normalcy I clung to.

Mother went to Shreveport more frequently and sometimes stayed for a few days. One day—Friday, I believe—she came home with a man named George. He was tall and swarthy, with dark hair and a thick mustache that drooped down to the corners of his mouth. He resembled the villains in the comics I read. His teeth were in poor condition, with several missing.

Both drunk and loaded, my mother and he staggered into the house late at night. I could hear their commotion when they arrived and ascended the stairs. Mother didn't shut her door all the way. I got out of bed to determine what all the noise was about. Nanny Helen stopped me from peeking in her room.

She said, "That is your mother's private room and business; you should not eavesdrop or peek in."

Still curious about what was happening in her room, I walked away. Nanny closed my mother's door completely. I don't think either of them noticed the door closing on its own.

The next day, I exited my room and saw the slimy guy leaving my mother's room in his dingy underwear. His body odor wafted toward me from across the hall, almost making me sick.

He said, "Hi, kid. You must be Marie's boy. What's your name?"

"Orion."

I didn't like this guy and had an ugly sensation in my stomach.

He entered the bathroom while I went to the kitchen for breakfast. Bertha prepared enough grits for the three of us. As I finished eating, he came into the kitchen, now dressed.

He looked at me.

"I forgot to tell you my name; it's George Anders. Is there anything for breakfast?"

I pointed to the stove. He walked over and glanced at the pan.

"Is that all?"

I nodded.

"Guess that will have to do."

He went over and opened all the cabinets until he found the stacked bowls, pulled out two, and plopped cereal into each one. Searching the drawers for flatware, he took out two spoons. He returned to Mother's room with the bowls of grits. As he left the kitchen, Bertha, Nanny, and Doc stood beside me with scowls.

I recognized their expressions and said, "Yeah, I agree. I don't like this guy either."

I went to the garage and assisted Walter with the oil change for the New Yorker. After we finished, I went into the house to clean up for lunch. I caught George rifling through the drawers in Doc's office in the library.

Standing at the door, I asked, "What are you doing?"

He said, "I'm looking for a pen or pencil."

Walking over to the desk, I pulled a pencil out of the pencil box on top of the desk and gave it to him.

He said, "Thanks."

With a snide expression, he went back upstairs.

As he left the room, I thought he said, "Smart ass kid."

Doc Albert said, "He has been going through everything in the house."

"That figures."

I went to the bathroom, cleaned up, and returned to the kitchen. Bertha had prepared a chicken salad sandwich and sliced apples for my lunch.

George came down and asked, "What's to eat?"

I shrugged. Heading to the refrigerator, he pulled out a fried chicken wing and chewed on it sloppily, with pieces falling from his mouth.

I told him, "I think you should leave. We don't like you."

I said this, referring to the ghosts and me.

"You have been going through our stuff looking for something to steal."

"Your mother invited me to stay. And I don't care if you like me or not."

He took the plate of chicken from the refrigerator and slammed the door. He stomped up the steps and noisily closed my mother's door, not showing his ugly face until the next day.

The following day, while in the living room, I heard a loud thud reverberating from above, and I rushed to the second level.

George yelled at my mother, "Where's the cash at, you bitch? I know it's here in the house somewhere."

My mother cried, "I don't have any money. You took it all. I won't get any more until the first of the month."

A smacking sound and a thump came from Mother's room. Running into the room, I saw Mama quivering on the floor with her hand in front of her face, while George stood over her with his hand drawn back, ready to strike her again.

"Don't give me that! You lying cunt," and slugged her.

Her head was violently pushed to the side. I leaped onto his back, screaming. He flung me off like a rag doll. My head slammed against the wall. Stars exploded. Darkness flickered at the edge of my vision.

He hit Mother again, this time with a fist, and she fell unconscious. I ran at him; he struck me, and I dropped to my knees with pain shooting up my legs.

He lunged for me, saying, "Why, you little son-ava-bitch."

I rushed out of the room, yelling, "I'm calling the police!"

I took a step down the stairs, but he was quicker than he appeared and grabbed me by the shirt. He yanked me off the step and shoved me to the floor on the landing.

He shouted, "No, you're not!"

I stood, shaking, leaning against the banister. George's hand cracked across my face, and the world tilted. I was airborne, flipping backward over the railing—until a cool and firm hand caught me midair. Like a guardian angel, Nanny grabbed my arm and pulled me back. Dazed and unsure of what was happening, I only knew Nanny had her arms around me, holding me tight.

As I was going over the rail, George saw a woman appear, grab me by the arm, and pull me back.

Nanny held me and yelled at him, "Get out! Get out!" with such force that a wind came up and blew him against the wall.

With insane fear in his eyes, he bolted down the stairs, not understanding what he had witnessed. As he came to the bottom of the steps, all the other ghosts crowded in the vestibule and shouted, "Get out! Get out!"

All the ghosts appeared to him. His face distorted in terror, he screamed and stumbled in circles, surrounded by the spirits yelling at him. The door opened, and he jumped for the exit, racing across the front yard, and fell onto the picket fence, knocking part of it down.

Seeing the old Ford, he ran to it and sped away like a madman, skidding back and forth on the mud from the morning rain. Mother had left the keys in the ignition when they arrived drunk.

Nanny Helen saved me from going over the railing and dying. Getting up, she stood beside me. I was still on my knees when Mother ran up to me. She didn't see Nanny standing there, loaded with her pills. She knelt on the floor and hugged me.

Crying, she said repeatedly, "I'm sorry, baby. I'm sorry, baby."

Still sobbing, I peered over my mother's shoulder, and a bright light tunnel appeared, with the silhouettes of two children holding their hands out to the governess.

She looked down at me, her smile radiant through the tears.

"I have to go now. The children are calling me. Can't you hear them?"

And I could. Their voices echoed like wind chimes in the distance: "Nanny Helen! Nanny Helen!"

Approaching, she took their hands and floated toward the light.

She stopped, looked back at me, smiled, and said, "Thank you," and moved on until the tunnel disappeared.

Nanny Helen moved on to wherever a spirit goes when it transitions to the other side. She saved my life and broke the curse for herself.

Burying my face against my mother's shoulder, I sobbed even

harder. Mother knew nothing of this and thought I was crying because George assaulted me. After a while, she got up and put me to bed. Mother went downstairs, phoned Mr. Butler, and told him about the incident.

Mr. Butler called the sheriff and somehow persuaded Dr. Wilson, who was in the unit on the first floor, to come out to the plantation. They all seemed to arrive at the same time. Mother let them in. Sitting on the living room couch, she explained everything to the policeman.

"I met George at a bar in Shreveport. We got along well, I thought, and he came home with me. He demanded I give him money, but when I told him I didn't have any, he hit me several times. Orion came in and tried to stop him, and then he assaulted Ory and left, stealing the Ford."

While Mother spoke with the police, the doctor came to my room and examined me. I continued to sob about Nanny Helen. Bruises covered the areas where the creep hit me, but other than that, everything was okay.

The physician said, "That must have been very scary. You are going to be all right. You were courageous trying to help your mother."

With tears streaming down my cheeks, I nodded. He got up and went downstairs to check on my mother. Lying back on the bed, I buried my face in the pillow, crying, knowing Nanny would be the first to hold and console me if she were there, but she wasn't and would never be there again. The other spirits appeared in my room. Albert sat on the edge of the bed. He understood I was lamenting the loss of the governess.

He said, "I know you're upset because Helen is gone. You loved her, and she loved you. But you must understand she is at peace now, and her sins have been forgiven. She is in a better place and happy. You'll be with her again when it is your time to go. She is not gone, just away. You will always have her in your heart."

Bertha approached and gave me Bunny. Grabbing the stuffed rabbit, I pressed my face into his stomach as I had done the first time Nanny Helen gave him to me. I stayed in bed for the rest of the day and night, hugging the stuffed rabbit, sleeping, crying, and desperately missing Nanny.

The doctor from town checked on my mother. She was only bruised as well. After the police left, she and Mr. Butler looked into my room. They thought I was asleep, but I wasn't.

Mother closed the door.

Mr. Butler asked her, "Are you all right? Do you need anything?"

"No, I'm going to bed."

He said, "I'll come by tomorrow to see how you and Ory are doing."

"Okay."

Mr. Butler left, and Mother took her drugs in her room.

The following day, I woke up late and headed to the kitchen for breakfast. Two bowls of grits with melted butter were on the table. Mother came down and had breakfast with me. I stared at her; she had never come down to eat since we moved into the house.

She realized I was staring at her and said, "What, I can't have breakfast with my son?" and presented me with a beautiful smile, something I hadn't seen from her for years.

I smiled back, happy she had come out of her room to eat with me. While we ate, Mr. Butler arrived.

Opening the front door, he called, "Good morning!"

Mother called back, "We're in the kitchen."

He entered the kitchen.

"Good news. The sheriff phoned me and said the Shreveport police had already found George and your car. I authorized it to be towed back here. They discovered him drunk at a bar, talking about ghosts in this house. I told the sheriff he was crazy. I think they are going to be putting him away."

We all smiled.

After Mr. Butler left, Mother returned to her room and did not come out for a few days. With George's departure, a sense of normalcy returned to our home, albeit tinged with the lingering specter of Nanny Helen's absence. Yet her legacy lived on in the lessons she imparted, guiding me through the trials and tribulations of adolescence with unwavering support.

Studying hard, I always completed my schoolwork, knowing Nanny would want me to succeed in my studies. I received A's in most classes. Because I could run fast, I joined the high school track team and performed well. I still got into many fights because I wouldn't tolerate bullies, like George, and, of course, people thought I was strange. But I persevered, refusing to let their judgment deter me from my path.

Doc Albert took on the role of teacher after Nanny moved on, instructing me in medicine and science. He also asked the other ghosts to help guide me in their areas of expertise. Their presence, though ethereal, was a source of comfort and guidance, reassuring me that I was never truly alone.

I learned how to cook from Bertha, about gardening and plant propagation from Paul, general home repair from Hugo, and cleaning tips and sewing from Milly and Philly. I had already learned auto maintenance from Walter, but he had now delved more into the science of the internal combustion engine. Each day I didn't attend school, I learned something new from one of the ghosts. It was all fascinating, and I was eager to absorb as much knowledge as I could, often visiting the school library to find books on the subjects for more in-depth information.

140

# Chapter 24

# Aunt Gretchen's Journals

Still aching from the loss of Nanny Helen, I buried myself in Great-Great Aunt Gretchen's diaries the next morning, hoping to lose my grief in someone else's words. Everyone wrote in journals during that time. Some still do, but not as many. Written in French, the diaries took a while to translate. Ten volumes span the years from 1900 to 1960.

Reading Aunt Gretchen's journals gave me much information about this woman. She certainly had an exciting life.

8— 8— 8—

Aunt Gretchen's journals provided a window into a bygone era, illuminating the lives of those who came before me. Through her words, I glimpsed a world steeped in tradition and turmoil, where curses and spirits intertwined with the very fabric of everyday life.

Born in 1880 to Gregor and Jennifer Labauve, Gretchen Anne Labauve was the middle child of three, with one older brother, Howard, and a younger brother, Gordon. She kept diaries after returning home to the L'Enfant Haven plantation from Miss Veronica's School for Young Ladies. She attended the boarding school for six years and returned to the estate only for holidays and one month during the summers.

She decided to write her journals in French to practice the language she loved and specialized in at Miss Veronica's. It also prevented her family from reading her diaries, as most didn't know French well enough to understand them.

Her parents wanted her to marry soon after she returned to the estate, likely to get her out of the house. She was not interested in marriage and insisted on pursuing her own interests, refusing to be told what to do by a man or be burdened with a pack of children. It wasn't that she didn't like children; she just didn't want the responsibility and commitment that came with raising them.

She quickly became the most sought-after debutante in the parish, attending soirees with whichever eligible bachelor she fancied. She adored the dancing, gleeful frivolity, elegant dresses, and social interactions with the elites from that area of Louisiana.

Gretchen was asked for her hand in marriage several times by some of Louisiana's most eligible young men, but she always turned them down. Her parents never understood these refusals.

She would say, "I haven't found the right man."

Gretchen's grandmother, Flora, would tell her son and daughter-in-law to leave their granddaughter alone. She had plenty of time to marry; they should allow her to have fun. Time passed, and Gretchen never found the right man.

She occasionally perceived the ghosts around the house. She wasn't afraid, just curious. She tried talking to her mother about the apparitions, but her mother would say, "I have never seen any spirits."

But Gretchen knew her mother noticed evidence of their presence when things moved in rooms with no one there, or when places appeared clean even though the maids hadn't entered.

Gretchen asked her grandmother about the apparitions.

"Grandma, are there spirits in this house?"

Her grandmother smiled.

"Yes, dear. They have been here since the 1810s. Your grandfather's mother told me about them. Of course, there were only two then, the one in the front yard and the one in the attic."

"I have seen them. Do you see them?" Gretchen asked, curious.

"Yes, I do, dear. I have seen them since I married your grandfather and occupied the house. Sometimes they help me when I struggle to get out of bed."

"Why are they here, Grandma?"

"A curse was placed on this house in 1813," her grandmother whispered. "A child died—some say through negligence, others claim it was worse. Since then, anyone whose actions, or inaction, led to a child's death and who dies on these grounds... doesn't leave. They linger as spirits, trapped by the curse, until it's broken—or until they save a child themselves," her grandmother explained.

"That is horrible. Who are all the ghosts?"

"Well, let's see. There is Cyrus; he is the oldest. But he is only present in the attic. There are the two maids, Milly and Philly, from the 1880s. They used to work here when you were a baby. It was said they were with child and had them removed and died. Nobody knew who the fathers of their babies were. There may be another ghost in the front yard, but he is seldom seen. That's all I know of."

As Gretchen resided in the house, more ghosts took up residence on the roster. The best cook in the parish, Bertha Baudin, worked at the plantation from 1890 to 1902—she consistently won the cooking contests at the local fairs. In the winter of 1901, all three of Bertha's children died of pneumonia because she was not there to care for them. She was always at the estate working for the Labauve family and was not granted time off by Gregor Labauve to look after her children. Coming home from work one day, she found her children had died.

Bertha passed away from a heart attack in the kitchen the following year. After that, she appeared in the kitchen next to the stove. Sometimes she would cook something and scare the hired chef, who would then quit. It became increasingly difficult to keep cooks.

In 1923, Hugo Evans, the handyman working on the roof of the plantation house, left the ladder against the side of the house and went home for the night. The next day, Gordon Labauve's youngest son, Charles—"Charlie," as everyone called him—climbed the ladder to the roof, pretending to be on top of the world. Slipping on a loose tile, he fell from the top of his world and died. The family grieved but never blamed Hugo for the accident. Hugo began drinking more often and sometimes failed to come to work.

One day, he showed up to work drunk. A leak had developed on the roof due to rain from the night before. He leaned the ladder against the house to fix the leaking tile, but slipped on a rung near the top, fell, and died from a broken neck. His ghost appeared in the workshop and shed.

Gretchen hired Helen Jones as the nanny for Gordon Jr.'s two children. She hired Helen because she could teach her niece and nephew English and French. She enjoyed speaking French with the nanny to stay familiar with the language. After the death of the children and the nanny's suicide, Gretchen sensed that Helen was still present in the house. She regularly visited the playroom and spoke to Helen in French. Occasionally, she would see Helen looking out the window.

Gretchen's cousin, Albert Labauve, moved in with her in 1940. After experiencing a nervous breakdown, he needed a quiet place to recuperate. Happy to have her cousin Albert to talk to, she welcomed him into her home.

After a few months, Albert said, "I'm feeling good. I want to start my medical practice again here at the plantation."

He liked the place and wanted to stay.

Gretchen replied, "This is an excellent idea."

They converted the library into his office and examination room. Few people would visit the plantation for consultations with him, which led to his growing depression.

Gretchen never understood why Albert had a nervous breakdown until she received a letter from another relative explaining Albert's addiction to opium and an erroneous diagnosis, which led to the death of a child. He spent several months recovering in a drug rehabilitation center, but they referred to it as a "nervous breakdown."

Albert's depression worsened, and he began using opiates again to cope until he overdosed. Afterward, Gretchen would see his ghost sitting at the desk in the library.

A few years after cousin Albert passed away, the chauffeur, Walter Sherman, got drunk and died in a car accident, crashing the old Rolls-Royce into the oak tree in front of the house. You can still see the scars on the tree trunk where the vehicle struck it. He appeared in the carriage house garage. Gretchen never understood why Mr. Sherman's apparition lingered on the plantation, but she assumed he must have caused the death of a child at some point in his life. She bought a used 1939 Rolls-Royce Phantom, not wanting to incur the expense of repairing the old Rolls.

After so much tragedy, Gretchen decided she needed to take action. The house seemed to attract horrendous events and disturbed people.

With an abundance of information in the diaries, I occasionally skipped ahead to find a section about the Voodoo Imperatrice. It took Gretchen several years to learn about curses and how voodoo witches could sometimes break them. Remembering her Aunt Caroline speaking about this, she searched for her aunt's journals and read them.

When I read this statement, I stopped reading Gretchen's journals and went to find Caroline's diaries. Cyrus followed me.

I asked him, "Do you know where Aunt Caroline's diaries are?"

"Yeah, they are in the green steamer trunk."

Moving a few other trunks, I found the storage chest. Shifting the trunks around caused my broken arm to ache. I opened the chest, which was full of women's clothing from the 1910s and 20s, with an odor of gardenias. It must have been her favorite scent, permeating all her things. Digging through the items, I found the books at the bottom of the container—fewer volumes than Aunt Gretchen's journals. I pulled them all out and took them back to my room.

Dinner time arrived, and I decided it was an excellent moment to take a break from my research. After freshening up, I went to the dining room for the evening meal. A pasta casserole accompanied by a salad and peach pie smelled wonderful on the table.

I eyed the bubbling casserole with curiosity.

"This is new," I said.

Bertha beamed.

"I've been watching those cooking shows you like. Figured I'd try something modern."

I took a bite and smiled.

"Keep watching. This is fantastic."

She chuckled, clearly pleased, and I helped myself to seconds.

My arm throbbed from hauling journals and shifting trunks in the attic, a painful reminder of how much I'd already uncovered—and how much still lay hidden in this haunted house. It felt like déjà vu. Years ago, I started this search as just a boy curious about ghosts. That was when I first stumbled onto Gretchen's writings—and eventually,

Cyrus himself.  I never realized at the time how close the spirits were, or how deeply their stories would shape my own.

# Chapter 25

# Meeting Cyrus

I was eleven, digging through old trunks in the attic, searching for clues about my Labauve ancestors, when I encountered the ghost who would become my best friend.

Cyrus's chest was tucked away in a far corner of the loft, as it was the oldest. He wasn't visible at first. I cracked open a dusty old trunk in the corner, but the lid slammed shut on its own.

Grinning, my curiosity only deepened.

"Why don't you show yourself?" I called out. "Afraid of a kid?"

Cyrus popped into view. He was handsome, in his late thirties, with blond hair styled forward featuring messy, curly bangs. His bright blue eyes resembled those of my mother and me. He wore beige pants with two rows of buttons up the front, a white long-sleeved linen shirt unbuttoned at the neck and chest, left untucked from the pants, a dark blue unbuttoned embroidered vest over the shirt, and black knee-high leather boots.

He stared at me and said, "Boo!"

Laughing, I asked, "Are you trying to scare me?"

"Well, that is usually all it takes."

"I know all the ghosts in this house; why haven't I seen you until now?"

"I can't go far from here."

"Why is that? The others can go all over the house and property."

"I'm attached to an amulet and can't go more than fifty feet from it."

"Is it in this trunk?"

"Yes."

Opening the chest and rummaging through the contents inside, I experienced a severe stomach ache. I discovered some tie pins and a fleur-de-lys attached to a blue velvet ribbon featuring a large blue sapphire in the center and a symbol engraved on it.

I held it, and the stomach sickness stopped, and I said, "This is it."

He said, "How do you know?"

"I get a feeling in my stomach when searching for something, and when I find it, the upset stops."

"You are special. You can see ghosts, talk to ghosts, and find things. What else can you do?"

"I don't know. That is all I know I can do. What is your name, anyway?"

"I'm Cyrus Alexander Labauve."

"Oh, you're one of the earlier owners of the L'Enfant Haven plantation. I read about you in Aunt Gretchen's diaries."

"At your service, sir," he said and bowed to me.

I laughed.

He asked, "What is so humorous?"

"Nobody talks like that and bows now. You've been up here too long. Why don't you come down and meet the others?"

"I can't go down."

"Yes, you can—if I take the amulet with me."

"You would do that? Take it with you?"

"Sure, why not?"

Putting the charm in my pocket, I went down the stairs with Cyrus following me. I introduced him to the other ghosts, and they all said hello, but they didn't seem very happy to meet him. At the time, I didn't understand why.

I told him, "My mother also lives in the house and stays in her room most of the time. She's afraid of the spirits. If she's near, disappear so you don't scare her."

"Very well, sir."

I laughed again.

"We have to get you talking more modern. Try to talk like we do."

"I will. Orion, is it?"

"You can call me Ory," I said.

From that day forward, Cyrus became my shadow—witty, loyal, and ever one clever remark away from landing me in trouble.

My constant companion, Cyrus, stayed by my side as long as I had the amulet. I took him everywhere with me. Amazed by all the modern appliances, vehicles, and television, he wanted everything explained. I could only explain how the cars worked, having maintained them with Walter for several years. Discovering he knew French, we spoke French when he didn't want the other ghosts to understand what we discussed.

His sense of humor was wicked, and he enjoyed getting me in trouble by speaking to me in class and encouraging me to respond. Sometimes I'd end up in a fight with someone who made fun of me for talking when nobody was near. I would be sent to the assistant principal's office for disciplinary action.

We read comic books together, and I had to explain some things to him. He always read over my shoulder, even while doing homework. This helped him learn modern history and improve his English pronunciation. When tasked with writing essays for class, he would assist me in adopting a more mature perspective on describing situations. I consistently received A's. Nanny Helen would be proud of me.

Not long after I began regularly bringing Cyrus's amulet to school, I got my first Finding Job. Jenny Lewis had lost her watch. She cried, surrounded by her friends who were trying to console her.

Cyrus recognized an opportunity.

"Offer to find her watch for her. You can locate it."

I whispered to him, "Yeah, I probably can find it, but they are just going to think I am weird for doing it."

"So what? Tell her you'll find it for her for a quarter."

"Why would I do that?"

"So you can have some money. You never have any cash. Charge for your unique skills."

I stood there watching her cry and the others staring at her.

Approaching her, I offered, "I can find your watch for a quarter."

One of the boys said, "Don't listen to that freak."

I scowled at him and said, "I can find it. I can prove it to you. Follow me."

Jenny said, "If you can find it, I'll give you twenty-five cents."

"Okay."

Having seen her watch on her wrist, I confirmed, "It has a black band, right?"

"Yes."

I closed my eyes and slowly spun in place, waiting for the familiar churn in my stomach. The nausea tugged at me like a string, guiding me down the hall and out of the building. An entourage of six kids followed. Upon reaching the cross hall, I closed my eyes again and moved until the queasiness became more assertive. I headed in that direction down the aisle and out the school side entrance.

I stopped, closed my eyes, and turned until the nausea returned and led me that way. It directed me off the school grounds and down the street. The group continued to follow me.

Stopping at the edge of Madreville Central Park, I closed my eyes and turned around. Nausea led me across the park's lawn and toward a bench. Overcome with nausea, I moved to the seat, extended my hand, and ran it over the wooden bench. Just about to puke, I noticed the watch under the bench, picked it up, and said, "Here it is."

Jenny grabbed it from me, thrilled that I had found it for her. Pulling a quarter from her pocket, she handed it to me.

She said, "Thank you," and returned to the school.

As she walked away, she told her friends, "I sat at the bench to tie my shoe. It must have fallen off then."

A few others stared at me weirdly, unsure what to make of me.

The same guy who called me a freak said, "He probably stole it and hid it there."

They all turned and headed back toward school, some staring back at me.

I told Cyrus, "See, now they think I'm even weirder."

He said, "Now they know you're weird, but in a good way, you can find things. I can tell this is all going to work out."

Shaking my head, I returned to school, was late for class, and received a detention slip, but I had a quarter.

After that, every week or so, someone would approach me and ask me to find something for them and pay me a quarter. The demand for my services was growing, a testament to the increasing significance of my abilities. It was a fascinating journey to observe how my unique talent was becoming increasingly recognized.

As the years went by and I entered junior high school, Cyrus said, "You're older, and all their allowances are higher, so your price for Finding Services has just increased to fifty cents."

By the time I reached high school, my rates had risen to a dollar. My reputation, like my rates, was also on the rise.

A few days after Orion discovered Cyrus, the ghosts held another family meeting regarding his presence and influence on the child. Paul recounted what had happened when he became a ghost and emphasized that the ex-master of the plantation couldn't be trusted. All the ghosts understood how much Orion liked Cyrus and wanted to keep him close at all times. They wished for the child to be happy and to have friends. They feared that taking the amulet away from Orion would upset him. Ultimately, the decision was made to allow Orion to keep the amulet and have Cyrus nearby. This way, they could keep a watchful eye on Cyrus and ensure he wasn't doing anything to harm Orion.

Exhausted and sore from a day of intense searching, I decided to call it an early night. I stumbled into my room, emptied my pockets, took a couple of pain pills, and collapsed into bed.

"I'll keep reading Aunt Gretchen and Aunt Caroline's diaries," Cyrus said softly. "I'll mark the good parts for you."

The anticipation of what we might discover in those pages was almost palpable.

He lit a candle—something about him always clinging to the past—and settled beside my bed. I rolled over, aching and exhausted, and let sleep take me.

# Chapter 26

## Requesting Andrew Butler Sr.'s Journals

When I got up in the morning, I found the diaries stacked neatly, with a few pieces of paper sticking out in various locations.

"You've been busy," I said, eyeing the neat stack of journals, paper markers jutting from their spines.

"I couldn't help myself," Cyrus replied. "Your Aunt Caroline and Aunt Gretchen were extraordinary women for their time. Makes me proud to be part of their legacy—and yours. I flagged anything related to voodoo. There's not much about the Imperatrice, but I found something interesting about Andrew Butler Sr. His surrogate mother was a voodoo priestess called Mama Obeah Oracle."

"Andy Butler told me his father wrote about the Voodoo Imperatrice in his diaries. Maybe we should ask to read those? I'll give him a call later."

The prospect of uncovering more about the mysterious Voodoo Imperatrice kept us on the edge of our seats.

After washing up in the bathroom and applying more antiseptic cream to the cut on my head, I went downstairs for breakfast.

Bertha said, "Good morning, Orion. Here's your breakfast."

It consisted of eggs, bacon, and a stack of corn cakes. After returning to my bedroom, I read the sections of the journals that Cyrus flagged. Aunt Gretchen and Aunt Caroline didn't know much about voodoo or the followers of this ancient practice.

The most significant reference to the Voodoo Imperatrice in Aunt Gretchen's diaries occurred when my grandmother visited the house and Gretchen escorted her around. The other references pertained to the moon ceremony that took place but did not proceed because Marie, my mother, began her monthly cycle, became frightened, and the ceremony was halted. While in the hospital, my mother recounted what happened during the ritual.

*Maybe Andrew Butler's journals can tell me more about my grandmother.*

I decided to go to the garage and inspect the damage from the Jaguar's accident. The moment I stepped into the carriage house, my breath caught. The Jaguar looked worse than I remembered.

"Damn," I muttered. "I didn't think it was this bad."

"Told you," Cyrus said, floating beside me. "You turned that car into modern art. Lucky you were thrown clear."

The front end was crushed inward towards the engine. The driver's side door was missing, and the left fenders were beaten and damaged. The rear trunk area was also impacted. The front right wheel was at an odd angle and may have broken the front axle. Who knows what might be damaged in the engine area? If we can locate the parts, this will cost the trust a lot to repair the vehicle, even if it's just for replacement parts.

Walter approached, holding one of the Jaguar's manual volumes.

"Are you trying to keep me busy for eternity?"

"I'm sorry. I feel bad about this."

"I'm making a list of components we'll have to order. Thank God we have the car's manual; otherwise, identifying all the parts would have been almost impossible."

The relief of having the manual at our disposal gave us hope that we could tackle the repair process effectively.

"Okay, I'll help. I'll start pulling the wrecked components off, and you make the list with part numbers. Make a separate list of items we may be able to repair."

We worked on the Jag for the remainder of the day, with just a brief lunch break. We accomplished a great deal of work, but we still needed to inspect the engine and transmission.

Putting so much stress on my right arm while working on the wrecked Jaguar caused it to throb and ache. Releasing the bent sections, which wrapped around each other at times, caused pain to shoot up my right arm; I was pushing it too far. Returning to the house, covered in dirt, I went upstairs to shower before dinner. As I passed the answering machine in the hall, I noticed the message light flashing on the device. Rewinding the tape, I listened. Andy called, asking how I was doing. I decided to call him after the evening meal.

After cleaning up, I enjoyed a delicious meal, as usual, and phoned Andy at home, knowing his office would be closed now.

"Hello, this is Andrew Butler."

"Hi, Andy. It's Ory."

"How are you doing?

"Okay, but I took it too far today. I went out and inspected the Jaguar. I didn't realize it was so messed up. I removed mangled parts and created a list to be ordered. This will cost the trust a lot. While working on the car, I put too much stress on my broken arm, and it really hurts now when I move it."

"The doctor told you to take it easy."

"Yeah, I know. I went through my aunt's diaries but found little about the Voodoo Imperatrice. You told me your father's journals mentioned her. Would it be possible to read those?"

Andy was silent.

I said, "Are you still there?"

"Yes, I'm here. I'm thinking about it. There are some personal things about my father you don't need to know about in those books."

"You mean because he was gay? Aunt Gretchen hinted at it in her journals. I don't care about that. He was kind to my mother and me—that's what matters."

"Okay, but you can only read the sections about the Voodoo Imperatrice. I'll mark them, and you can come to my office to read them. It'll take me a few days to go through them."

"I won't be able to come for a couple of weeks because I'm not supposed to drive."

"Oh, that's right. I'll bring them over and wait while you read them."

"Great, see you later."

"Sure. Good-bye."

By his tone of voice, I could tell it upset him that someone else knew about his father's personal preferences.

After Andy hung up with Orion, he promptly called Renee Broussard, the Voodoo Imperatrice.

"I just got off the telephone with Orion. He's been reading his Aunt Gretchen's journals. He wants to study my father's journals about you. I told him to give me a few days to review them and mark the parts about you."

She smiled on the other side of the line.

"You bring the diaries here, and I'll make them say what I want. Be here early tomorrow."

"Okay, I'll be there at 7 a.m.," he said and hung up the telephone.

Andy didn't want to make the call—but he had no choice. The last time he refused the Imperatrice, his wife got sick overnight. He still remembered the helplessness and the doctors who couldn't explain it. He stared at the floor, elbows on his knees, hands trembling.

What does she want with Orion now, after all these years?

# Chapter 27

# Encounters with the Voodoo Imperatrice

One month prior to this, the Voodoo Imperatrice entered Andy's office, striding in as if she owned the place. Four towering men followed her—built like pro linebackers, dressed in black, their eyes scanning every corner like business-minded bodyguards.

When they reached the stairs, Doris asked, "Do you have an appointment with Mr. Butler?"

Renee said, "No, darling, but he will see me," and she walked into his inner office.

One of the four bodyguards closed the door and stood in front of it.

Doris exclaimed, "I'm calling the police!" moving her hand toward the phone.

One of the men put his hand on the telephone and said in a strong New Orleans accent, "No, you're not."

She sat back down, feeling worried and wondering what this was about. She rubbed and caressed the crystal on a silver chain around her neck. This always calmed her nerves, and she knew that special forces resided within, helping her when needed.

When Renee Broussard entered Andy's office, he shouted, "Who are you? What do you want?"

He quickly stood from the chair, ready to come around the desk and escort her out of his office.

She smiled and said, "You look just like your daddy. I couldn't do anything to him. Josette put a really good protection spell over him, but I can do something to you and your family if you don't work with me."

A chill ran down Andy's spine. This was her—the Voodoo Imperatrice his father had warned about. He'd dismissed the stories as paranoia. Now, face to face, he wasn't so sure.

He asked, "What do you want?"

He tried to sound in control and unperturbed by her confrontation. Undeterred by his aggressive question, she sat in a chair and looked around the office as if there wasn't a worry in the world.

"I want you to tell me everything Orion is doing."

"What do you mean? I don't know what he's doing."

"You are the closest thing he has to a friend besides the ghosts. He turned twenty-five two weeks ago and is at the peak of his abilities. He is the Spirit Speaker. He can do things he doesn't know yet. He has powerful items he doesn't know he has. I want them. I want his power over spirits."

Andy exclaimed, "I don't know anything about that! He doesn't tell me anything about the ghosts. I think you should leave. I can't tell you what you want and don't want to work with you. My father may have been afraid of you, but I'm not. I don't believe in any of this voodoo bull shit. Leave my office!"

He stood again with his hands on his hips.

"Here's my number. You will call me with information about Orion. You will know when to make the call."

She stood, smiling at him. He got a shiver over his body. She turned and left the office.

Andy watched them drive away from the second-floor window and thought, 'There is no way I'm calling her. I'm glad this despicable woman is gone.'

After the priestess and her bodyguards exited, Doris entered Andy's office and asked, "Who were those people?"

"They were some people my father knew long ago."

He did not want to elaborate on the other information he knew about this woman.

"What did they want?" she pressed, suspicious of his short explanation.

"They wanted me to do something that I refuse to do. Everything is okay. Don't worry about it."

Doris returned to her desk and thought, 'I don't ever remember seeing those types of people come to the office while I worked for Mr. Butler Sr. Something else is going on. I need to keep an eye on this.'

Andy sat behind his desk, hoping these people would never reappear—another shiver coursed through his body.

Two days later, Doris brought a beautiful quartz crystal mounted on a wooden base from home. She walked into Andy's office and placed it on his desk.

Andy looked up from the document he was studying and asked, "What is this?" with a smile.

"I thought your office needed a little something beautiful to spruce it up, and crystals are supposed to give you strength."

"Oh, well, thank you. It is beautiful."

She left his office with a smile. Thanks to the spell she placed on the crystal, she could hear everything in this office whenever she wanted.

Two weeks later, Andy received a call from the Adams family in Masonville, Georgia. They needed Orion to locate jewels hidden in the family mansion by the matriarch forty years ago. The attorney contacted Orion, and he went out on the Finding Job a few days after the call.

While Orion worked in Georgia, Andy's wife, Vivian, inexplicably passed out in the kitchen. An ambulance rushed her to the hospital. The doctors couldn't determine what was wrong with her. Her vital signs repeatedly spiked and dropped for no reason that they could diagnose. If this continued she would not survive.

The worried attorney sat in the ICU waiting room, leaning over with his elbows on his knees and his hands covering his eyes, uncertain what to do and questioning how this event had occurred.

Then he remembered what the Voodoo Imperatrice said, 'You will know when to call me.'

Wiping his face with shaking hands, Andy fled the hospital, the image of Vivian unconscious in the hospital bed etched in his mind. He sped to his office, heart pounding, dread sinking deeper with every mile. In his desk drawer, the number waited. He didn't know why he had kept it—but he had. He phoned Renee Broussard.

Someone answered, "Yes."

"This is Andy Butler. I need to speak with the Voodoo Imperatrice."

"Hold on."

He waited, trembling, sweat running down his back, unsure what to expect.

Renee, a powerful figure in the Voodoo community, came on the line and said, "Yes, Andy. Will you work with me now?"

He exclaimed, his voice trembling and almost shouting, "Okay, I'll tell you what Orion Labauve is doing. Please stop hurting my wife."

"Tell me what he's doing."

"He's in Masonville, Georgia, on a job finding jewelry in a mansion. He'll be back tomorrow. Orion asked me to find his father, but I haven't found anything."

"Thank you, Andy. You tell him that you found his father died of a drug overdose like his mama and I want to meet him."

"Should I tell him you're the Voodoo Imperatrice?"

"No, just tell him I'm a voodoo witch trying to make money from the tourists. You give him my number. Now, go back to the hospital. Your wife will be better."

And she hung up the phone.

Doris lay in bed reading a novel when the crystal around her neck vibrated slightly. She rubbed the crystal with her fingers, closed her eyes, and focused on the crystal in Andrew Butler's office. She overheard Andy's side of the telephone conversation and was shocked to learn that he was talking to the Voodoo Imperatrice, the enigmatic woman who had visited his office a few weeks ago. She was the cause of Vivian's hospitalization and wanted to be informed about everything Orion Labauve was doing. What was going on? The mystery deepened, leaving Doris with a sense of unease and anticipation.

Andy hurried to his car and drove back to Shreveport. He rushed into his wife's room, where she sat up in bed, alert. He was so pleased by this sight that he took her hand and kissed it. She smiled.

The doctor told him, "The strange fluctuations have stopped, but we want to keep her in the ICU for another day to ensure the abnormal symptoms don't return."

Tired, Vivian fell asleep shortly after his arrival. Sitting beside her bed for another hour, he reflected on what had occurred over the last few weeks. What did the Voodoo Imperatrice mean when she came to his office and said, 'He is now twenty-five and at the peak of his power. He is the Spirit Speaker. He can do things he doesn't know yet. He has powerful things he doesn't know he has.'

What have I done? What does she want with Orion? What is she going to do to him?

Andy went home that night and tried to sleep, but he couldn't; the guilt and worry about his wife and Ory piled in on him.

In the morning, Orion called him and asked to be picked up at the Shreveport airport. Andy informed Ory that he couldn't make it because of family issues. Returning to the hospital, he stayed with his spouse all day. The following morning, the doctor released her. He drove her to their house and went into the office, telling Vivian that he had a client to meet that day; Orion would be over later.

When Ory arrived at his office, he appeared happy about the money they would earn from the Finding Job. Andy informed him of what the Voodoo Imperatrice instructed him to say regarding his father, Antoine, and grandmother.

When Orion got into a car accident, he called Renee and informed her of the incident.

He asked, "Did you make this happen?"

She said, "No, this was nothing I did."

He told her which hospital Orion was in. Renee had informants at the medical center to watch him.

The night shift nurse entered Orion's hospital room every hour or so, stood silently for a few minutes, and then left. Cyrus observed this as he waited. He didn't realize it was unusual for the staff to check this frequently unless the patient was in critical condition. Cyrus never mentioned it to Orion. The nurse called to report everything to the Voodoo Imperatrice.

When Orion's brain swelling became severe, the nurse informed Renee. Performing a healing ceremony, the priestess caused the swelling to diminish. She didn't want to lose her grandson until she found the Labauve family signet. The ghost of Rose—a past Voodoo Queen who created the curse against the family who killed her son,

Paul—had informed Renee about the incredible power donated by multiple Spirit Gods held in the signet, and how, if used by a Spirit Speaker during the proper ceremonies, she could control all spirits.

Andy couldn't sleep that night after telling the Voodoo Imperatrice about Orion wanting to read his father's diaries. At 1:30 a.m., he got up, drank a few cups of coffee, gathered his father's journals, placed them in a cardboard box, and set off for New Orleans. Five hours later, he pulled up in front of the Voodoo Imperatrice's small red house.

Andy slid the container off the automobile seat and hesitantly approached the house. He stood with sweat rolling down his forehead and his stomach churning, staring at the most frightening structure he had ever seen.

The small bungalow gave him an ominous, terrifying feeling, making him want to turn and run away. The feathered charms hanging from the porch's rafters swayed back and forth, yet there was no wind. The red building, with one window on either side of the black door in the middle, seemed to stare at him and grow and shrink in his vision as if breathing.

He had to enter this intimidating building to ensure his family's safety. He inhaled deeply and moved forward. The house seemed to swell with his fear and anxiety, intensifying with each step he took along the concrete path. His heart pounded in his ears.

Andy avoided the protective charms hanging from the porch rafters, as his father had informed him in the diaries from when he visited the same house thirty-two years ago. He knocked three times, just as his father had done, and waited. It felt as if insects were crawling up and down his body. A tall, dark woman dressed in white opened the door, and he cautiously stepped inside.

She said, "This way."

He followed the woman toward the back of the house, his knees ready to give way at any second, and she pulled the beaded curtain aside. Andy entered the darkened room. The Voodoo Imperatrice sat at a small table. She gestured for him to sit. He collapsed into the chair, thankful to be seated and not to fall to his knees.

"Give me your father's diaries."

Andy pulled open the box's flaps and placed the journals on the table.

She said, "Wait in the front room. Leave the box."

He placed the box on the chair, went to the small living room, and sat down, trembling and sweating, uncertain of what would happen next.

A massive man carrying a short drum exited a bedroom and entered the divination room. Sitting on the floor in the corner, he beat a rhythm on the instrument. Smoke curled from the brazier as she inhaled deeply, her eyes rolling back. Swaying to the beat of the drum, her voice rose in an eerie chant—half-song, half-prayer.

The journals lay open like offerings. She lifted the effigy, passed it over each page, and whispered in an ancient tongue, bidding the gods to veil her truth. She asked the voodoo gods to ensure that whoever reads these books perceives only good and positive things about her wherever she is mentioned.

Spreading the journals out, she dusted each with a special powder from a bowl on the table. After waving her hands again, she thanked the gods for helping her and blew the powder off the books. Holding the cardboard box, she used one finger to push each journal off the surface into the container. She then went to the corner of the room and washed her hands in a basin full of blessed water.

Renee told the drummer, "Close the box and give it to the white man in the front room. Tell him not to touch the books until after Orion reads them."

He did as instructed.

Andy listened to the instructions, nodded, and took the container. He wondered what she had done to the journals and why he couldn't touch them until after Orion read them, but he knew better than to ask questions because of what his father had written in the diaries. He placed the box containing the transformed diaries on the car's seat and drove away.

During the long five-hour drive back to Madreville, all Andy could think about was what he had done and how this action would affect

Orion. Regret gnawed at his gut with every mile. Twice, he had to pull over and vomit onto the shoulder, the bile thick with fear and guilt. He had betrayed Orion. Worse—he had no idea what came next. At least he had a few days before he promised to take the books to Orion.

# Chapter 28

# Marti's Visit

While anticipating the opportunity to delve into Andrew Butler Sr.'s diaries, I teamed up with Walter to tackle the restoration of the Jaguar over the following days. Together, we meticulously disassembled the vehicle down to its chassis, compiling a comprehensive list of parts that needed to be ordered.

With an extensive list of parts to order, I called Marti Graceland and discussed the project with him. He agreed to contact people he knew in the automobile salvage and restoration business; perhaps they would have access to some of the components needed. Tracking down all the items would require weeks of research. The bills would be issued to the L'Enfant Haven trust and sent to Andrew Butler Jr. for payment.

I asked Marti, "Can you come to the plantation to pick up the parts list?"

He hesitated, reluctant to make the excursion to a haunted house.

I told him, "I still can't drive because of the concussion."

He finally acquiesced.

"Sure, I've never been out there. I'll drop by tomorrow morning," he said.

When it was near the time Marti would arrive, I called a family meeting.

"Okay, guys, my friend Marti Graceland is coming out to pick up the parts list for the Jaguar. I don't want you to appear or move things around while he is here. He is my friend, and I don't want him scared by anything. Is that clear to everyone? Cyrus?"

All the ghosts nodded their heads and agreed.

Cyrus looked shocked that he was being pointed out.

"Why are you pointing to me? I can stay out of the way."

"Because I've seen how happy you can be when you scare people, and I don't want Marti frightened. Is that clear?"

I raised my voice with some conviction and glared at the troublemaker.

Cyrus flinched like he'd been shoved.

"Alright, alright—I get it. No need to push."

"I didn't touch you," I said.

He narrowed his eyes.

"Well… something did."

Cyrus walked away, glancing back over his shoulder at me. The expression on his face suggested that something wasn't right. Why did Cyrus say I pushed him? The others are looking at me strangely as well. Maybe they don't appreciate me telling them what to do.

As Marti's arrival approached, I watched from the living room window. I spotted his car pulling up outside the picket fence. Seeing him evaluate the mansion from a distance, I couldn't help but wonder if he was contemplating whether it was worth venturing inside. I'd seen people do this before, turn around and drive away. He walked up the path and knocked on the door with the lion's head knocker.

I welcomed Marti in with a big smile. I'd never had friends over to the house.

"Come on in," I said. "Glad you made it over. I would have dropped the list by, but the doctor said I can't drive for another week. I still have dizzy spells and headaches from the accident."

Marti said, "That's okay; I've wanted to come out here for a long time, but never made it. The place is beautiful."

He admired the Victorian furniture in the living room.

"How do you keep it so clean?"

"I have people that come in and work on it."

Meaning the ghosts, but I wouldn't say that to Marti.

"Would you like a beer or glass of lemonade? We can go out on the veranda and visit for a while."

"Sure, okay."

I noticed some reluctance in his voice.

With Marti tagging along, I went to the kitchen, pulled two beers out of the fridge, and handed one to him. He was looking around the whole time.

Marti eyed the vintage stove and refrigerator.

"Don't see antiques like these still in use."

"They work fine," I said. "I keep meaning to update them—just never get around to it. I installed a new water heater and clothes washer, though."

I pointed to the cellar door.

We went out the back door, and I sat in one of the wicker chairs while Marti stood and checked out the backyard.

He eyed the cast on my right arm, pointed to it, and asked, "How long do you have to keep that on?"

"For another few weeks."

He nodded.

Seeing the punching bag and weights at the end of the porch, he commented, "I didn't know you worked out."

"Not as much as I should, but I try to keep in shape."

He said, "Nice grounds. Is that a graveyard out there?"

"Yeah, it is the family plot. Many of my relatives are out there."

"You have chickens and is that a vegetable garden? You never told me you garden."

"They keep me supplied with eggs and chicken for meals and fresh vegetables. Those were critical when I was growing up. My mother used most of the monthly allotment on drugs. I might have gone hungry often if it weren't for the chickens and vegetables."

"I never knew it was that bad," he said with a concerned intonation in his voice.

"It was tough at times."

Another sad feeling washed over me, remembering my mother.

Why is everything reminding me of her lately?

To get my mind off her, I said, "Hey, you want to see how far I've come with the Jaguar?"

"Sure."

He followed me out to the carriage house garage.

Marti strolled around, looking at everything Walter and I accomplished.

"You sure have got a lot done. It's pretty amazing how much

you've done alone."

I could tell he wondered how I managed to accomplish so much in such a short time with a broken arm. An unusual look crossed Marti's face. I think he felt someone or something watching him, and he nervously glanced around several times, expecting to see something. I could tell my guest was becoming anxious. I think he sensed Walter, the ghost, remaining quiet and standing in the corner.

Marti said, "Thanks for the beer; I have to get back to the shop."

Marti finished the last of the beverage in the bottle and tossed it into the trash can. We went back to the house, and I handed him the parts list. He examined it and shook his head.

"This is going to take a while. I'll call around and see what I can find."

"Please let me know what you find and can't find. I'll help where I can. Can you keep a log of the time you spend researching the items so Andy can pay you?"

"I will. Thanks. I'll talk to you later."

Marti quickly left.

I stood on the front porch as Marti drove away, wishing he could have stayed longer. It would be nice to have friends over more often.

Walter and I continued working on repairing various components. After a few days, we produced quite a collection of cleaned and rebuilt items. We reassembled several sections of the vehicle but still had to wait for the ordered non-repairable parts.

I went to wash up for lunch and noticed the answering machine light flashing as I walked through the front hall. I rewound the tape. The message was from Andy.

"Hi, Ory. Can I come by this afternoon and drop off my father's journals? Call me and let me know what time is best for you."

I called back and left him a message, "Hi Andy, it's Ory. I got your message. Sure, come by anytime. I'm working in the garage on the Jaguar; just come out if I don't answer the door."

I ate my lunch, returned to the carriage house, and continued to work while waiting for Andy to come out.

# Chapter 29

## Delivering the Journals

Andrew Butler Jr. entered his office after lunch at Martha's Diner down the street and noticed the answering machine light flashing. Doris had gone home for lunch, so the machine recorded the message. He listened to the message. Orion called, saying to come by anytime. Andy sat at his desk, reluctant to take the journals to the estate, but he must. He told the Voodoo Imperatrice that he would do this. He must do what she says, or she would harm his family. He had procrastinated for about a week, telling Orion he had other business to attend to first.

He glanced at the cardboard box in the corner of his office and dreaded what he had to do. He didn't know what the evil enchantress had done to the journals. She told him not to touch them until Orion read them; Andy wondered why she said that. She also said, 'I will make them say what I want.' What did the diaries say now?

This was upsetting his stomach, and he wished he hadn't eaten lunch. Missing meals regularly and not sleeping well at night since his interactions with the voodoo priestess were taking a toll on Andy's health, both physical and mental. He had lost weight and was nervous and anxious all the time.

His wife observed these changes.

"Honey, are you feeling okay? You aren't eating as usual, and I know you're getting up at all hours. Perhaps you should go to the doctor."

He told her, "It's okay, dear. There is just a lot of stuff happening with the business right now. Things will calm down soon."

But he had no idea when things would calm down. He didn't know what the voodoo witch wanted from Orion. How long would this continue?

Andy stood, hesitating, and stared at the box again. The

journals—tainted, unreadable, unpredictable—waited like a loaded weapon. He picked up the box, palms sweating and stomach tightening with dread. The weight of his responsibility was heavy, knowing that if he didn't deliver them, his wife might die. If he did... what would happen to Orion?

He told Doris, who had returned from lunch, "I have to take some books to Orion. I'll be back after a while."

She nodded and watched him descend the stairs, sensing his anxiety.

He placed the container of transformed journals on the front seat of his Chevy and drove to the plantation. Upon arriving at the mansion, Andy's nerves were on edge, heightened by a sense of foreboding as he approached the house. Despite his inner turmoil, he was determined to fulfill his obligation, if only to appease the Voodoo Imperatrice.

When he parked the Chevy in front of the picket fence, a shiver ran over his body as if someone or something was watching him. The atmosphere was thick with unease, causing him to hesitate before leaving the vehicle. All he wanted was to forget about the terrifying events and sleep. Maybe when he woke up, he would discover it was all a dream, but that was just wishful thinking. He hung his head, took a deep breath, and opened the car door.

He looked at the house. It seemed to evaluate him.

Was he worthy of being on this property? Did he deserve to interact with Orion?

He shook his head and pulled the box out of the vehicle. Walking to the front door, the oak trees's shady coolness helped calm him. With the lion head knocker, he knocked on the door and stood waiting, sweat rolling down his back. Was that a flash of a woman's face in the window next to the door? He jerked. No one answered. Orion said he would be in the garage.

He walked around the mansion to the carriage house garage and entered through the side door.

He shouted as he entered, "Orion, are you in here?"

"Over here," Orion called back.

Andy entered and saw automobile parts scattered throughout the place, organized into groups. He found Orion at a workbench on the far side of the garage, hand-sanding some components.

"Hi, Ory. Wow, it looks like you have been busy," he said, admiring all the work Orion had accomplished.

"Yeah, I'm trying to repair and rebuild what items I can of the Jaguar. Marti Graceland came over the other day and is researching parts that must be purchased. You will get some big-ticket bills to the trust for the parts and Marti's time."

"Okay. Thanks for warning me. The trust has plenty to cover it. Here are my father's journals. I'm going to leave them with you. I'm sure you won't say anything to anyone about what you read."

"Of course not. As I said, your father was always good to my mother and me, and that is all that matters. Could you put the box on the counter? I'll start reading them tonight. Would you like to see what I've completed so far?"

"No, I've got to get back. Call me when you're done studying them."

Andy left the garage, hurried to the Chevy, and returned to his office. As he ascended the stairs, exhaustion overcame him.

"Doris, I'm dead tired. I'm going to nap on the couch for a couple of hours."

"Okay. You haven't looked well since those strange people came here a few weeks ago."

She was concerned about what she had learned from eavesdropping on his telephone conversations with the voodoo priestess. He didn't respond. He entered his office, closed the door, removed his jacket, and lay down on the couch. He fell asleep instantly.

The air thickened with smoke. The Imperatrice emerged from the shadows, towering and furious.

"Andy," she hissed, "why didn't you call me?"

He bolted upright with a cry, tumbling to the floor in a cold sweat. Hearing the thud, Doris ran into his office and saw the attorney floundering on the floor. She ran over and helped him up.

"What happened?"

"I rolled off the sofa onto the floor, which scared me."

He did not tell her he had a dream about the Voodoo Imperatrice.

"I'm okay. Thank you."

He stood and walked back to his desk. As he made his way to the desk, Doris sensed that something was wrong, and he wasn't revealing what was happening. She would have to meditate on this tonight.

After his secretary closed the door, Andy called the Voodoo Imperatrice.

Someone answered the phone, "This is Andy Butler. May I speak with the Voodoo Imperatrice?"

"Hold on."

He waited, his hands trembling as he held the phone to his ear.

"Hello, Andy. Why didn't you call me?"

"I didn't know I had to. You said to give Orion the journals and I did."

"You waited a while to get it done."

"I told him it would be a few days before I would take them to him. I didn't want him to think I was too anxious about getting the diaries to him."

"Is he reading them?"

"He was working on repairing the Jaguar. He said he would start reading them tonight."

"Okay. You keep track of what he is doing and let me know."

"I will."

Andy hung up the phone, staggered to the bathroom, and emptied his stomach into the toilet. The bile burned—but not as intensely as the shame.

# Chapter 30

# Reading Spelled Journals

After finishing the day's repairs on the Jaguar, hunger gnawed at me, although the ache in my right arm had lessened compared to previous days. I picked up the box of Andrew Butler Sr.'s journals and took them to my bedroom. After showering, I cleaned up for dinner. Bertha prepared a fantastic meal of étouffée, rice, salad, corn bread, and apple pandowdy for dessert. Back in my room, I read the attorney's diaries.

I settled onto the daybed and cracked open the first journal. To my surprise, Cyrus, finally over his earlier sulk from being called out at the family meeting, resumed his usual reading spot, peering over my shoulder. The cover was dusty and slick, with a strange, oily film that clung to my fingers. The scent was faintly metallic, almost like burnt herbs. As I delved into the entries, I noticed my vision blurring, accompanied by a dizzy sensation. Was it my lingering head injury acting up again? No, this felt different.

The first few entries seemed ordinary enough. Then, a passage caught my eye.

"Oh, here's something about the Voodoo Imperatrice," I murmured. "It says she helped Mr. Butler several times. Seems… likable."

"What are you talking about?" Cyrus asked, frowning. "That's not what it says at all. Josette Montaigne warned him to avoid her. Said she was dangerous."

I blinked. The lines on the page shifted—literally twisting before my eyes. Words melted into new phrases. My stomach flipped.

"No, look here," I insisted, pointing. "She was accommodating—"

"Orion," Cyrus interrupted. "There's a spell on these books. You're not reading what's there. I can see the real text because I'm dead—it doesn't work on me."

I pulled back, my heart racing. My head swam, dizzy as if I had been spinning in circles. I opened another journal—same oily texture, same disorienting vertigo.

"She was generous to Aunt Gretchen," I read aloud, wobbling. "Explained everything about the curse…"

"No," Cyrus snapped. "She misled Gretchen—told her the curse could be broken when it couldn't. Drop the books. Now."

Despite my better judgment, I obeyed, letting the diaries thump to the floor. I stumbled to the bathroom and scrubbed my hands raw. Only when the film was gone did the world stop tilting.

Back in my room, Cyrus knelt over the journals, thumbing through them like a priest deciphering scripture.

"You just rest," he said. "Since you can't touch these, I'll read them and tell you what I find out. You should go to bed and let that stuff leave your system."

"I agree. I still don't feel right."

After taking two pain pills because my arm ached, I stripped and went to bed, where I quickly fell asleep. When I woke the following morning, Cyrus had arranged the books on the floor, open to sections that discussed the voodoo priestess.

I asked, "What have you found?"

"Come and see. Don't touch the diaries. Even though I've wiped them off with a towel, I still don't trust that they are clean." Pointing to a cloth on the floor, he added, "Don't handle that either. I'll have the girls pick it up and wash it."

I moved to the journals, leaned over, and read the exposed pages. I learned how Josette, Andrew Butler's surrogate mother, taught him what to do when around the Voodoo Imperatrice—how to avoid her at all costs.

What happened when Andrew spoke to her about breaking the curse on the L'Enfant Haven plantation? What did her statement ... 'Someone else will come later. We must prepare for his coming.' ... mean? Who was the person they had to prepare for?'

I learned that my mother was the sacrifice to the moon; the loss of her love for Aunt Gretchen and her continuous fear of the ghosts constituted the sacrifice. However, the family attorney never understood why the atonement had to be made.

The revelations echoed the cryptic messages from my mother before her passing, deepening the mystery surrounding my lineage and the Imperatrice's machinations. The enchantress manipulated Gretchen, my mother, and her son Antoine to produce me, but for what purpose?

I asked, "Do you know how the books got a spell placed on them and covered with that dust?"

"The only thing I can think of is your grandmother has something over Andy and somehow got the diaries from him."

"When I first spoke with him about reading the journals, he didn't want me to read them, but when he brought them here, he said to keep them until I was done studying them. What changed? It must be something to do with my grandmother. We'll hold these for a few days before I return them."

I thought about everything and decided I wouldn't learn anything else about my grandmother from the diaries and journals we had read. I had to get closer to the source. I must go to New Orleans and hopefully gather more information about this woman and her plans for me. My mother and father warned me that she wanted me for a purpose, but I still didn't know what that was. I would soon learn what that was.

# Chapter 31

## Ghostly Informants

I took the amulet from the top of the dresser and placed it in my pocket the next morning.

Cyrus asked, "Are we going somewhere?"

"Yes, we're going to New Orleans to do some investigation on my grandmother."

"Wonderful, I'm ready. That woman is a real piece of work."

We hopped into the New Yorker and hit the highway. Five hours and two gas stops later—the New Yorker consumes a lot of gas—we arrived in New Orleans. I pulled into a parking lot and reviewed the New Orleans map stored in the glove compartment. I had never tried this before, but I had thought about it, believed it would work, and decided to go for it.

I unfolded the map across the dashboard and hovered my hand above it, focusing on the Voodoo Imperatrice. A slow churn twisted in my gut—the telltale signal. As my fingers drifted over the inked streets, the nausea sharpened like a punch to the stomach. My skin prickled, and my finger hovered over one street.

"That's it," I whispered. "She's there."

"Are you sure? I've never seen you do this before."

"I'm doing something different, but I'm sure this is right. We'll park a few blocks from away and ask the ghosts in that area about her."

Driving through the unsavory neighborhood, I parked the car, hoping it would still be there when I returned. I wandered along the sidewalks, exploring the streets. Few people were present in the lower-middle-class neighborhood, likely because they were at work or school during that time.

Cyrus slipped into the houses to search for spirits. If any spirits are present, he'd have them speak with me. He vanished as I strolled down the street. A few minutes later, he appeared with the ghost of an old Black man.

Cyrus introduced him, "This is Harry. He's a ghost who lived in this neighborhood all his life."

I continued to walk casually as I spoke to Harry.

I smiled and said, "Nice to meet you, Harry. I need some assistance. Can you help me?"

He nodded.

"Sure, I would like to help you," he said, smiling, happy to have someone to speak with.

"Good. Can you give me information about the Voodoo Imperatrice and her plans? Have you heard anything about her or anyone who may know something?"

Harry got a frightened look and turned to leave.

I said, "Please don't go. I need your help."

He stopped as if he had hit a wall.

He faced me and said, "I can't say anything; if I do, she could hurt my family."

"It's okay, Harry. You can talk to me. Nothing will happen if you assist me."

I smiled, wanting him to feel safe. The spirit relaxed and smiled back.

"Yeah, I guess it is all right to talk to you. I don't know much, but Bernie, the spirit who lives down the street, might know more; his nephew is one of her bodyguards."

"That's great, Harry. Can you ask Bernie to come out and speak to me?"

"Sure, I'll be right back."

I continued to stroll.

A few moments later, Harry and Bernie popped into view.

"Hello, Bernie, nice to meet you. Harry thinks you may be able to help me."

"Harry told me there was something different about you. I didn't believe him, but now I see what he means."

Bernie smiled broadly and looked anxious to help.

"I need to learn about the Voodoo Imperatrice's plans for the L'Enfant Haven plantation. Does your nephew know anything?"

"He doesn't talk much about her, although I did hear him talking to his friend Alan, her bodyguard.

"He said something like, 'She really wants this Orion guy.'"

I didn't flinch when my name was mentioned.

"Is there any way you can get more information about her?"

Bernie appeared reluctant and paused to think for a moment.

"Well, maybe. I can ask Merna, the ghost on the next block; she stays in the house next door to the Imperatrice. She might know more."

"Can you do that for me?"

He looked into my eyes, a big smile appeared, and he said, "I would be happy to."

"I'll be back tomorrow, and if you can find anything, I would really appreciate it, Bernie."

"Happy to help someone like you. I'll do what I can."

He left, and I turned to walk back to the car. Cyrus said nothing during this entire episode.

As we returned to the New Yorker, Cyrus stared at me and said, "Orion, what were you doing to those guys?"

"What do you mean? I was just asking questions."

"Well, yes, but you were doing something else too."

"What on Earth are you talking about?"

"Ory, ever since your birthday, there has been something different about you. When you speak to us ghosts, your voice seems more intense, and I get weird feelings from you. I could sense something from you when you spoke to those guys. I wanted to do whatever you said, and you weren't even speaking to me."

"You're being ridiculous."

I shook my head, wondering what was going through Cyrus's mind. I wasn't doing anything. We were at the car. Thank God it was still parked where I left it. I found a cheap hotel—no sense making the ten-hour round trip.

The next day, we went back to Bernie's street; as I walked up the sidewalk, he appeared with an excited smile.

I said, "Good morning, Bernie. Do you have any information for me?"

He excitedly said, "Oh yes, I have a lot of stuff."

"Great, go ahead."

I was anxious to hear what he had to say.

"The Voodoo Imperatrice has been waiting for the Spirit Speaker to be born. He is now of age, and she is trying to get control of him to use his power. She's obsessed with power. Always looking for ways to get more."

"Who is the Spirit Speaker?"

"Merna had never heard his name; the Voodoo Imperatrice's son, Antoine, somehow helped her."

"How can Antoine have helped the Voodoo Imperatrice? He died of a drug overdose years ago?"

"Oh, no. Antoine Broussard committed suicide last year."

My stomach dropped with this news.

Trying to hold it together and not show how upset I was, I said, "Thank you, Bernie. You have been very helpful. You can go now."

Turning, I headed to the car, feeling confused and upset. So why did Andy lie?

Cyrus said, "But Andy told you that your grandmother said he died of an overdose like your mother."

"I know. That means Andy has been involved with this from the beginning. I can't believe anything he says now, and I have to be careful about what I tell him. He must be telling her everything."

Cyrus agreed, "Yeah, and that one guy said your grandmother has it out for you. Why?"

"I have no idea. But my parents said not to trust what she said and to be careful. Mama said I have the power to fight against her. What power?"

"Well, lately, you seem to have more power over us spirits."

"I still don't understand what you are talking about."

"We all sense it. Ask the others when we get home. Maybe you don't even realize what you are doing."

As we drove home, I reflected on everything that had been shared with me and what had transpired. I still didn't believe what Cyrus said about my power over the ghosts. I resolved to tread cautiously, wary of Andy's potential collaboration and the Imperatrice's manipulations. I returned home with plans to confront both, compelled to unveil the secrets shrouding my past and my grandmother's ominous plans.

When I returned home, the message machine's light flashed. I rewound the tape and listened. It was Andy.

"Hi, Ory. It's Andy. How are you doing with the journals? Give me a call when you can."

A second message was also recorded.

"Ory, It's me again. How are things going? Why didn't you call me back? I hope nothing is wrong."

I turned to Cyrus, "I better phone him back."

I dialed his office number.

"This is Andrew Butler."

"Hi, Andy. It's Ory. Sorry I didn't return your call sooner; I was out at some junk yards looking for parts for the Jag."

"And it took you two days to do that?" he said, sounding a little suspicious.

"Yeah, they were close to New Orleans, so I stayed the night, not wanting to push it because of my concussion."

"Oh, okay. Did you find anything?"

"Nothing I needed."

"Have you finished with my father's journals?"

"I'm about half through them. I'll finish them tonight. So far, my grandmother sounds like a nice lady."

I said this to Andy so he would tell the Voodoo Imperatrice that her spell on the diaries worked.

"I'll bring them over tomorrow."

"Okay, but can you try to come by later in the afternoon? I have clients coming in all day tomorrow."

"Will do. Bye."

I hung up.

Cyrus asked, "Do you think he bought it?"

"I think so. Now the question is, do I confront him about this?"

"I don't think so; if he tells her you know about some of her plans, who knows what she will do."

"I will have to call and confront her eventually, too. I may go back to her neighborhood and ask around some more. Maybe I can find out more information."

As soon as he finished the phone call with Orion, Andy Butler called the Voodoo Imperatrice.

"Hello, this is Andrew Butler. I need to speak with the Voodoo Imperatrice."

"Hold, please."

Andy waited, hating every second of having to do this.

"Hello, Andy. Has Orion read the journals?"

"Yes, he's read half of them. He will finish them today and return them to me tomorrow. From what he said, you are a nice person."

"What else has he been doing?"

"He said he went to New Orleans yesterday to search junk yards for parts for the wrecked Jaguar."

"Oh, he did, did he? Thank you, Andy."

She hung up, suspicious that Orion was in New Orleans yesterday.

She told Jessica, her follower, "Send word around that if anyone finds Orion Labauve in the neighborhood, call immediately and let me know."

Jessica sent two runners to canvas the neighborhood in search of Orion LaBauve. She provided each of them with a photo of Orion, which had been taken while he was unconscious in the hospital. The runners set off and, within two hours, spoke to someone at each house in the area.

# Chapter 32

# Betrayal and Fighting Lessons

When I got up the next day, I was still seething over my lawyer, my supposed friend, who had informed my grandmother about my actions. Why would he do that? Why did she need to know anything about me?

I went out onto the back veranda to drink coffee while contemplating everything, and it made me even more upset. The betrayal stung, especially coming from someone I believed I could trust. I wanted to hit something and glanced over at the punching bag hanging from one of the rafters at the end of the porch. I remembered when Doc Albert hung the first bag in that spot when I was twelve to practice boxing, fighting jabs, and kicks.

⚷ ⚷ ⚷

While in junior high, I frequently found myself in fights. The bullies at school constantly targeted me, hurling insults and taunting me. Although I didn't shy away from a one-on-one confrontation, facing a group of five ready to pounce was a different story.

My ghostly companion, Cyrus, alerted me, "Look out, the Jerk Squad is coming up behind you."

I ducked around the corner of the school, ran to the end of the building, and sought refuge near the trash receptacles. I crouched behind the bins, enduring the unpleasant odors. After sending Cyrus to scout their location, I waited anxiously, knowing I was already late for class.

He returned and said, "They are on the far end of the school grounds."

I sneaked back into the school through the side entrance and was immediately caught by the vice-principal, Mr. Jason. He had been waiting beside the door to catch anyone arriving late.

Grabbing me by the collar with a snide smile, he said, "Ah, I caught you. To my office, young man. You are tardy and getting a detention slip."

He pulled me down the hall toward his office. I looked over my shoulder and watched the Jerk Squad—what Cyrus and I called them—of boys eager for me to enter the door. This was one time I was happy to be caught by the vice-principal. I smiled, realizing they couldn't do anything to me.

Mr. Jason noticed me smiling and smacked me upside the head, saying, "Do you think this is funny?"

The group behind me snickered.

"No, sir."

I kept my head down to look more upset and make him feel like he had accomplished something. He pulled me into his office and looked up the plantation's telephone number, trying to call my mother. Of course, she never answered the phone.

The vice-principal grumbled disappointedly, "Your mother is never home."

"Yeah, she's usually busy," I explained, knowing she was lying on her bed stoned on drugs.

He called Mr. Butler, my secondary adult contact.

"I'm calling you since I can't get hold of his mother. This is to inform you that Mr. Labauve will be staying late for detention because he was late for class again. He will miss the last bus and will require a ride."

Mr. Jason listened to the attorney.

"Okay, I'll tell him."

"Mr. Butler said he can pick you up at 6 p.m. He has clients coming by, so you will have to wait here on the grounds until he comes."

I didn't say anything and just nodded my head. He handed me the detention slip and allowed me to return to class. I walked down the hall to my history class, showed the form to Miss Benson, and sat at my desk, relieved it was over. The rest of the school day was uneventful. I noticed some boys looking at me with disdain, but that was nothing unusual.

After my classes, I went to the designated room for detention. Mr. Jason supervised the troublemakers today, while the teachers took turns handling this unwanted task. I found a spot, plopped down in the seat, and pulled out my homework. After completing all my assignments, I opened the French novel I had with me and began reading. The vice-principal wandered the aisles, peering over everyone's shoulders to ensure they were working on their homework.

He came to me, scowling, and asked, "Why aren't you doing your homework?"

"Because I finished it already."

"What are you reading, some stupid science fiction thing?"

He read the title and opened the book, seeing it was in French.

Not believing I could understand the language, he said, "None of our French classes teach this. Where did you get it?"

"From the library."

"Okay, I want you to read this to the class and translate it for us."

He didn't believe I could do this.

I took the book, and, starting where I left off, read it aloud in French. At the end of each sentence, I translated it into English. I continued this for a few paragraphs until he told me to stop reading. Several other kids in detention had paused their work and turned in their seats to listen.

One said, "Oh, man. It's getting to a good part," wanting me to continue.

I said, "I can keep going if you want me to."

Some of the other detainees chimed in, asking for me to continue.

Mr. Jason agreed, "Okay, keep going. At least you are reading a classic in the actual French."

I was reading *Les Miserables*. I continued to read and translate until the end of detention. I still had an hour to wait before Mr. Butler would come by to pick me up. I went outside and sat on the bus bench, studying the book while I waited.

Cyrus again warned me, "The Jerk Squad is back."

I looked around, and they were coming up fast on both sides. I got up and began running, but they grabbed me. Two held me against the chainlink fence, and the others took turns punching me in the face and stomach. I didn't make a sound the whole time they were pounding on me. This made them angrier, wanting me to start begging and crying. Even though I wanted to cry, I wouldn't give them the satisfaction and gritted my teeth, enduring the pain. It hurt a lot.

The leader emptied my pockets and took my finding money. I had a couple of dollars in quarters. I had been busy earlier in the week.

I managed to loosen their hold on me and swung a fist at the leader; it landed on his right ear. He raised his hand to his ear, yelling in pain. While he was bent over, clutching his ear, I kicked him in the shin and turned to start running, but the rest of the gang knocked me down and kicked me several times. I curled into a ball to protect my sensitive areas from getting hit. Each kick intensified the agony.

Then, an adult voice shouted, "Hey, what's going on here?"

The group scattered. It was Mr. Jason.

He leaned down, pulled me up, and sat me on the bus bench. I was bleeding from my nose and mouth. He took a handkerchief and dabbed the spots, leaving red patches on the white cloth. Now, my eyes welled with tears and began to run down my cheeks. I wiped them off my face with the back of my hand, trying not to appear perturbed by the situation.

He asked, "What was all that about?"

"They don't like me because I'm smarter than them, and they steal my money."

"Is that why you were late to class today? You were avoiding them?"

"Yes."

"Why didn't you tell me?"

Upset, I decided to let it all out.

"Because you don't like me either. And you never listen to me or any of us kids. So, why bother saying something? It won't matter. You won't believe anything I say. And I will probably get another detention slip for this, but I don't care."

The vice-principal sat there, mouth agape. He had never had a student tell him the truth before. At that moment, Mr. Butler drove up and got out of the car. He walked around to the front of the vehicle and saw the blood on my face.

"Oh, my God. What happened?"

The vice-principal explained, "A gang of boys jumped him for his money and beat him up. I know who they were, and disciplinary action will be taken tomorrow. You may want to take him to the doctor to have him checked out."

"Yes, I will."

Mr. Butler helped me up, walked me to the vehicle, and seated me in the front. I winced in pain as I got in. Mr. Jason picked up my books, opened the car's back door, and placed them on the seat.

He leaned in through the open window and said, "Here, take the handkerchief. Your nose is still bleeding. I will take care of those guys tomorrow. And nice work reading *Les Miserables* to the class today."

I nodded my head and didn't say anything.

The attorney drove me to the doctor's office. A nurse was available for emergencies. She examined me and determined I was only bruised in several places.

I asked, "Do I have to go to school tomorrow? Can I stay home?"

She said, "Sure, I'll write a medical leave slip for the school. You will probably be hurting tomorrow anyway."

She gave me the note.

As he drove me home, Mr. Butler said, "I'll call the school in the morning and tell them you will stay home. Take the note to the office when you go in on Monday."

I nodded and sat quietly, feeling depressed about being beaten up. This kind of thing always happened to me for reasons I never understood.

He dropped me off. I retrieved my books from the back seat and entered the house. When I came in, all the ghosts crowded around the front door. I was three hours late getting home, and they were all worried. As I ate dinner, I told them what had happened.

⚷ ⚷ ⚷

After hearing the harrowing story of Orion's mugging by a gang of boys at school, the L'Enfant Haven ghosts held a meeting.

187

Albert said, "We have to do something to help Orion. He has to learn how to defend himself."

Bertha said, "The poor child. Did you see those bruises on him? It made me want to cry. If I could get a hold of those ruffians, none of them would have ears left after I got done wringing them off."

Paul said, "He has always had trouble with others not liking him for some reason. What can we do to help him?"

Albert suggested, "I think this will always happen to him because people don't understand his special abilities. We need to teach him how to defend himself."

Hugo questioned, "But how are we going to do that? None of us know anything about fighting."

Albert answered, "Well, I do. I was the college boxing champion when I was at Harvard."

All the others ooohhhed and ahhhhed.

"Hugo, are there any large bags we can stuff and hang from the porch rafters?"

Milly and Philly piped in, "There are a few old duffle bags in the attic. Would those work?"

Albert said, "Yes, they would," with a big grin.

The ghosts pulled the duffels down from the attic. Albert inspected them and chose one of the appropriate size. It was stuffed with old rags and sawdust that Walter had found in the carriage house. Hugo discovered a long chain in the shed and hung the new punching bag from the veranda rafters.

The ghosts gathered around the new exercise equipment, smiling with joy at their ability to help Orion learn boxing and defend himself. They all cherished the child like a son, always eager to assist in any way they could.

⚷━ ⚷━ ⚷━

When I came down for the morning meal the following day, Doc said, "When you have finished breakfast, come out to the porch. I have something to show you."

I stepped out onto the veranda, where, at the far end, an old stuffed duffle bag hung from one of the rafters by a chain. Doc Albert waved me down.

"I'm going to teach you how to box. You know, I was the college heavyweight boxing champion while in university. You may be unable to avoid all fights, but at least you will know how to protect yourself and get some good hits in."

I smiled, and the coaching began that day. He demonstrated different types of punches, blocks, jabs, the proper stance for optimal balance, and footwork to keep moving, making it harder for an opponent to hit you. I exercised and practiced daily on the duffle bag. Doc held the bag steady so it wouldn't move around much while I punched it, and he coached me for improvement. I grew stronger, and my hits had more power behind them.

I watched the *Green Hornet* on TV when I was younger and wanted to do kicks and jumps like Kato. I tried to replicate them against the duffle. I borrowed a book from the library that explained how to practice martial arts with illustrations. My technique improved, and when fights broke out, I could usually finish them.

The fights in high school were more difficult, but I could still hold my own. While I worked at Marti's, I saved some of the money I made to purchase a more professional punching bag and a weight set to exercise with.

⚷— ⚷— ⚷—

Seeing the black leather punching bag hanging at the end of the porch, I got up and struck the bag with my left arm. It would have been impossible to do that with my injured right arm. I exercised with the weights and the bag regularly, but not as often as I should have. I threw several kicks at the bag and worked up a sweat. I felt better, having released some tension.

While engaging in all these activities, I pondered why Andy would betray me and share information about me with my grandmother. We had always gotten along well. I have known him since I was three, and he was consistently friendly to me throughout my childhood. Though he never did as much for me as his father, Andrew Butler Sr., I always

189

enjoyed his company when he was around. After his father died when I was thirteen, he continued right where his father had left off.

I reflected on the last few times we spoke face to face. I sensed something was wrong when I visited his office, and he informed me about my father having passed from an overdose. I now realize this was a lie. That must be why I felt something was off that day. He must have been collaborating with my grandmother at that time. How far back does this go?

I admit I was short with him when I said, 'No, you don't understand. But, maybe one day, I'll tell you everything.'

Why haven't I told him or his father everything I know about the ghosts in the house? I guess I always thought they would think I was crazy and wouldn't understand. People are always terrified of spirits. I don't know why; I never have been. Compared to everyone else, I'm weird, and people sense it, always giving me suspicious stares. When I was a child, they wanted to beat me up. People never want to be friendly; even Marti is a little standoffish with me. I would love to have friends. The specters are my only friends.

After contemplating all of this and feeling quite down, I decided to return to my grandmother's neighborhood and conduct further investigation to discover what this mad woman was planning.

I took a shower to wash the exercise sweat off, dressed in clean clothes, and said to Cyrus, "We're out of here."

"Where are we going?"

"Back to the Voodoo Imperatrice's area to research more."

"Okay," he smiled, glad to leave the house.

As I walked out the door, I picked up the box of Andrew Butler Sr.'s journals and placed them in the car.

Cyrus asked, "Why are you bringing those?"

"I'll drop them off at Andy's office on the way."

We took off in the New Yorker. I drove to Andy's office and took the tainted journal box upstairs.

Doris said, "Did Mr. Butler know you were coming?"

"No, he thought I was coming by later this afternoon, but I have other things to do, so I decided to drop this box off now."

"He is with clients right now."

"That's okay. I'm just dropping this off."

She moved to open the box, and I informed her, "I wouldn't do that if I were you."

"Why not?"

She always opened Mr. Butler's mail; why couldn't she open this box?

"Andy might not want you reading or touching them."

She sat back down, looking disappointed, "Okay. Should he call you when he's done?"

"No, I'll be gone for a while."

"Where are you going?"

"To some junk yards to look for parts for the Jaguar."

"All right, have a fun time."

I left and headed for New Orleans.

As Orion left, Doris passed the crystal around her neck over the box and concentrated. She felt an unusual vibration from the box. Whatever was in the container had some sort of spell on it, but it wasn't for Mr. Butler; it had been for Orion.

Was this what Mr. Butler took to New Orleans and the Voodoo Imperatrice? What was the spell's connection to Orion?

192

# Chapter 33

# The Woman From My Dreams

Andy opened the door for his client.

"I'll get on that as soon as possible."

They shook hands and the man disappeared down the stairs.

Doris said, "Orion Labauve dropped this off for you while you were with Mr. Osborn," pointing to the cardboard box on her desk.

He snatched the box with a sudden urgency.

"Did he say anything when he dropped this off?" he asked Doris.

"Not much. Just told me not to open it. Said he was heading to some junk yards looking for Jaguar parts."

"Damn it. I told him to come by later."

Taking the container, he returned to his office and closed the door. As he shut the door, Doris's crystal necklace began to pulse. She touched it, closed her eyes, and concentrated.

Andy immediately called the Voodoo Imperatrice.

"This is Andrew Butler. I need to speak with the Voodoo Imperatrice."

A pause.

"Hold, please."

He waited, his hand trembling on the receiver.

Then her voice: smooth, cold.

"Andy. What do you have?"

"Orion is heading for New Orleans. He said he is going to junk yards again."

"Thank you, Andy."

She hung up the phone.

He collapsed into his chair, wringing his hands. Dread curled in his stomach. Moments later, he lurched toward the bathroom and vomited into the toilet. He hoped this would pass. He still had another appointment with a different client coming soon.

After leaving Andy's office, I drove straight to New Orleans—to the neighborhood where my grandmother, the Voodoo Imperatrice, lived. I figured I would speak with the spirits on the backside of my grandmother's street. I pulled up near the area and parked the New Yorker in a small shopping center parking lot, hoping it would still be there when I returned.

Cyrus wandered in and out of houses as I strolled down the cracked sidewalks. None of the ghosts we encountered knew anything about what the Voodoo Imperatrice planned. As I walked down the sidewalk, a few faces peeked through curtained windows, their wary eyes tracking my movements. Not thinking much of it, I continued to the car. Unfortunately, our trip yielded no new information and wasted my time.

Cyrus remained vigilant for anyone suspicious approaching me to soothe my paranoia.

He said, "A huge guy is coming up the side road toward you on the right."

I nodded, not wanting the stranger to observe me talking to someone who wasn't visible.

I approached the vehicle, and Cyrus said, "There are three more behind the car."

I quickened my pace, palming the car keys and Cyrus's amulet from my pocket. I unlocked the New Yorker as quickly as possible and hopped in, locking the doors from the inside. I pretended to drop the keys and slid the charm under the seat.

"Stay with the car," I whispered. "If they take me to her, I don't want her sensing you. Aunt Gretchen's journals say she can detect spirits. I don't want her to see you if they take me to her. There's no telling what she could do to you."

Cyrus protested, "No, don't do that. I want to go with you."

I inserted the key into the ignition, and WHAM! The window shattered into glittering shards. One of the goons had swung a baseball bat and smashed the driver's side window. Two of them seized me and pulled me through the broken glass. I fought back, landing a few awkward left-handed punches and a kick—but with a fractured arm and these guys built like linemen, I barely made them grunt. My struggles were futile.

One said, "The Imperatrice wants to see you. Come along nice and quiet."

Through the broken window, one unlocked the door, got into the car, and unlocked all the other doors. They threw me into the back seat and sat on either side of me. The other two climbed into the front seats. The driver brushed the glass shards off the driver's seat, started the New Yorker, and drove the few blocks to my grandmother's house. The gorillas dragged me out of the car.

The house was just as Andrew Butler Sr. had described—small and red, with crimson and black bone-and-feather charms swaying from the porch rafters. The place exuded an oppressive energy that prickled my skin, awakening old nightmares of the woman who haunted my childhood dreams. My stomach dropped. I struggled to escape, but these ex-football defensive backs weren't allowing me to.

Her bodyguards dragged me into the house, through the tiny living room, a curtain of beads, and into a dark room lit only by candles. A smoky haze and the pungent odor of unidentifiable herbs permeated the room. They pushed me onto a hard wooden chair beside a table and stood on either side.

She emerged from the shadows with a broad, unsettling smile, leaned in close, and kissed both of my cheeks, saying in the sweetest voice with a slight lisp, "It is so good to meet you finally, Orion."

My grandmother was the woman with unsettling facial deformities from my dreams when I was little. She wore a multi-colored scarf around her head and multiple necklaces that jingled as she moved. The bridge of her nose displayed a large knot, and two front teeth were missing. Additionally, her left eyelid drooped, making her eye appear half-closed all the time. As a child, I woke from dreams of her screaming, drenched in sweat. That fear surged back now, vivid and raw. I recoiled in surprise, not expecting this; the fear resurfaced from my terrifying childhood dreams.

I must have had a weird expression because she asked, "Did they hurt you? I told them not to hurt you."

Not sure how to react, I replied, "They were pretty rough."

She reprimanded them and to the guards said, "I told you not to injure him."

They all bowed their heads and said, "Sorry, Imperatrice."

They looked at me and said, "Sorry."

Despite my confusion, I played along, acknowledging their apology and nodding.

"Thirsty?" she asked, then turned to a goon. "Bring us both a Pepsi."

He returned moments later, popping the caps with a church key and handing one to me. I held it, still shocked by what I had just discovered.

"I have wanted to meet you for so long. I knew my son had a child, but your mother took you away, and I could never find you. But look, you found me."

She took a drink from the bottle.

"Well, kind of. It seems like you found me," I said.

I took a swallow of the Pepsi. It tasted great because my throat was parched. I didn't trust her but figured the freshly opened bottle should be safe.

"What happened to my father?" I asked.

She echoed Andy's lie with perfect ease.

"He died of an overdose of drugs. He had been addicted to drugs for years. I tried to help him, but he would never listen to me. It broke my heart when he passed on. You look a lot like him."

I knew this story was a lie.

"Where is he buried?" I asked and took another drink of the Pepsi.

"In the Holt Cemetery."

She freely offered the information.

"Why did you want to meet me so badly? My mother wasn't hiding. You could have found us anytime."

A strange dizziness crept in. I took another sip before the realization hit.

"You are my grandson; why wouldn't I want to meet you? You

have grown into such a fine-looking man. Your father was very nice-looking as well. Did you ever get to meet him?"

What was she saying? I couldn't make it out.

I said, "What?" and something in my mind realized she had drugged me. I glanced down at the Pepsi, and the bottle appeared distorted and out of shape. I dropped it, and the strangely bent glass container fell to the floor slowly.

I wasn't sure if I thought it or said it aloud: "I have to get out of here."

I stood, stumbled—then the floor rushed up to meet me.

My grandmother leaned over me, her face going in and out of focus, and said, "Ah... now it's working," she whispered, her face flickering in and out of view. "He lasted much longer than most."

I blacked out.

# Chapter 34

# Captured and Waiting

Cyrus stood frozen on the porch, blocked by an invisible wall. He pressed against it, desperate to follow Orion inside, but it held firm. Through the window, he saw the guards dragging his friend through a curtain of beads—and then, nothing.

Worried, he waited, hoping Orion would return. Suddenly, a cold force yanked at his arm, trying to pull him away from the house. Snarling, Cyrus twisted free and shoved it off.

Then, movement. Orion reappeared behind the beads—slumped between two towering men, unconscious. A sharp-featured woman followed them like a shadow.

"ORION!" Cyrus screamed, beating on the glass.

The window trembled under his fists.

Far off, the wind echoed, carrying his cry: "Orriionn!"

Inside, the Voodoo Imperatrice paused as she passed through the dining room. The glass rattled. A voice called her grandson's name, faint and distant. She smiled. Her wards were working. Whatever spirit attempted to reach Orion would never breach her walls.

Outside, Cyrus seethed. He couldn't protect his friend. His eyes darted to the porch charms—bone-and-feather talismans dangling from the rafters. Rage flared within him. He ripped them down one by one, shredding them with ghostly hands. Each one wailed with a tiny scream as it was destroyed.

Again, the force tugged at him—trying to drag him from the porch. He braced himself, summoning every ounce of strength to remain. When he stopped tearing the charms, the attack ceased.

He stood there, silent and watchful. He had waited over a hundred years in that attic at L'Enfant Haven. But this was different. This time, someone he cared about was in real danger.

They dragged Orion's unconscious body into the bedroom and tied his wrists and ankles to the bed with a rough rope that irritated his skin when he moved. Once they tied Orion to the bed, the Voodoo Imperatrice waved them off.

"You may leave."

They left, and she closed the door. She circled the bed, studying her son's child with distant affection, thinking, 'He looks so much like his father, only lighter-skinned with soft curls from his mother.'

She sat on the edge of the bed and ran her fingers through his silky black curls. She noticed the dark, scabbed line on his forehead from the car accident.

Even though he didn't know she was there, "I'm sorry, Orion," she whispered. "But I need this power. I did terrible things to your father, too, but it had to be done. I took it too far with him, and he slit his wrists while highly dosed on drugs, so I couldn't tell what he was doing. He released himself from the pain I caused him. I will try not to do the same thing to you. You seem much stronger than your father; I'm sure you will make it through, and I'm sure you will want to help me once you hear why I need it."

Orion stirred and whispered, "Mama?"

"No, baby," she said softly. "I'm not your mama."

The priestess rose and quietly exited the room.

She approached one of the bodyguards and instructed him, "Wait in the bedroom with him and tell me when he wakes up."

"Yes, ma'am."

He entered the room and sat on the chair, staring at Orion.

The Voodoo Imperatrice, Renee, entered the divination room, sat at the small table, and stared at the sputtering candle. She attempted to center herself in the flickering candlelight, but meeting her grandson—and sensing his immense Spirit Speaker gift—had rattled her faith in her plans. He was so much stronger than she had anticipated. Would she be able to control him?

# Chapter 35

# Vengeance Required

The reason Renee needed Orion's power never left her thoughts. Her past haunted her—the screams, the blood, the betrayal. Her mother's murder and the horrors inflicted on her Aunt Bernadette demanded vengeance.

Webster Turner, the man who raped her and killed her mother, had already paid. Renee had cursed him with slow, excruciating cancer. Even in death, she bound his spirit in place, refusing him passage to the other side. His ghost still lingered in agony. But that was only the beginning.

After her mother's death, Renee was taken in by her mother's sister, Bernadette Benson, and Bernadette's husband, Jeremiah. Bernadette helped her niece survive the devastation—her mother's death, the trauma of the rape, the unplanned pregnancy, and later, the birth of her son, Antoine. She sat with Renee through endless nightmares, held her when she screamed, and offered comfort when the darkness overwhelmed her.

Bernadette, who could never have children of her own, poured her love into Renee and Antoine. She encouraged Renee's pursuit of voodoo, a calling that ran deep in the Broussard family. In every generation, at least one Broussard had served as a priest or priestess. Bernadette drove Renee to her private lessons, and with each visit, Renee's abilities deepened. She could feel her power growing.

After Antoine's birth, Bernadette joyfully cared for the baby while Renée attended school and studied the craft. Even as an infant, Renée sensed that her son possessed something rare—an aura of unique spiritual potential.

But not everyone welcomed their presence. Jeremiah resented the added burden. With another mouth to feed and growing tension, arguments between him and Bernadette became frequent. In addition to working as a janitor, Jeremiah also delivered drugs for Earnest Charbonnet's cartel. He wasn't discreet. He wanted out, but with Renee and the baby in the house, he felt trapped.

Their problems escalated when a rival gang, the Blays, moved to seize Charbonnet's territory. They tracked Jeremiah during his rounds and eventually captured him outside the house. Bernadette witnessed it from the living room window and frantically called Charbonnet. He refused to help. Desperate, she went directly to the Blay gang's headquarters to plead for her husband's release.

Joseph Blay offered a deal: reveal the location of Charbonnet's stash and he'd let Jeremiah go. Bernadette understood the risk—if Charbonnet found out, she was as good as dead. Yet, she accepted the deal, hoping the Blays would eliminate the cartel. Jeremiah was released.

Soon after, Blay's men dumped Jeremiah's battered body on the Bensons's porch. Renee and Bernadette dragged him to bed, horrified by his injuries. With no money for a doctor, they did what they could. Renee promised to beg her voodoo mentor for a healing spell.

The Blay gang launched a raid that night, but they had grossly underestimated the defenses. Charbonnet's men were ready; someone had warned them. Many died in the crossfire, but Charbonnet kept his territory.

A few days later, while Renee was away, Charbonnet's enforcers came. Armed and brutal, they burst into the house. Jeremiah, weak in bed, heard the noise and sat up. A gunman entered the room.

"No, don't! I didn't say nothin'!" Jeremiah cried.

The bullets hit him in rapid succession. Blood soaked the sheets. In the living room, Bernadette screamed and ran toward the sound. One man grabbed her. Another slammed her to the floor. As she kicked and cried, they ripped her shorts off. The men took turns raping her, laughing as she begged for them to stop.

When they finished, she lay sobbing on the floor, her eyes wide with disbelief. The baby's cries echoed from the other room. One man peeked into the nursery, then returned.

"Just a baby," he said.

They didn't kill Antoine. Charbonnet had a rule: no children. His men followed it.

Bernadette whispered thanks to God.

Then the leader raised his gun. Pressed the barrel to her forehead. Pulled the trigger. Blood and brain matter sprayed across the wall. She collapsed in a growing pool of red.

The men left, slamming the door behind them.

When Bernadette didn't arrive to pick her up, Renee asked a fellow student for a ride home. The moment they turned onto her street, dread seized her. Everything looked normal—but she knew something was wrong. As she approached the porch, the world shifted. Her vision swam with red. Antoine's wails pierced the silence.

When she opened the front door, the horror met her like a blow.

Bernadette's lifeless body sprawled on the floor. Her eyes stared glassy and vacant. A dark hole marred her forehead. Blood covered the floor and splattered the wall behind her. Renee turned—Jeremiah lay in the bedroom, riddled with bullets.

She collapsed to her knees, screaming.

"NO. NOT AGAIN!"

Grief transformed into fury. Rage surged through her veins like fire. She vowed to the Lwa Spirits that she would avenge them.

Antoine's cries pulled her back. She scooped him up, rushed next door, and banged on the neighbor's door.

"Please open up! It's me, Renee! Please—let me in!"

No one came. No one wanted trouble. Eventually, a neighbor named Robert cracked open the door and let her inside.

Gunshots had echoed through the street—but no one called the police. Renee did.

Once again, she endured questioning. This time, she didn't know what had happened—only the aftermath. When the truth surfaced, her rage turned cold and calculating.

She cursed the Blay gang first. It was easy. One by one, each member was captured, imprisoned, and tormented through supernatural means.

Charbonnet was more formidable. A devout voodoo follower, he paid powerful practitioners to safeguard his operation. Worse yet—he had a Spirit Speaker in his employ, someone who could command ghosts. That made him untouchable.

Renee had mastered nearly every branch of voodoo—but not the Spirit Realm. She could sense ghosts but could not speak with or control them. For that, she needed a Spirit Speaker of her own.

She had waited, planned, and studied for decades. Nothing would stop her—not time, not blood, not even family. With the Labauve signet's power and her grandson Orion's abilities, she would finally obtain what she needed.

She would destroy Charbonnet's empire. And this time, no one would be spared.

# Chapter 36

# Meeting the Duke

While I was unconscious—drugged by the poison the Voodoo Imperatrice had laced into that bottle of Pepsi—Mama came to me. Whether it was a dream or a vision, I couldn't say. But she was there, clear as day, as if she had never left. She brushed back my curls with the same tenderness I remembered from childhood, her fingers warm, familiar, trembling slightly with urgency.

"Be brave, baby. Be strong. What she's about to put you through—" Mama's voice cracked, "—you can survive it. She doesn't know the full extent of your gifts, the ones the Duke gave you. You're twenty-five now. Everything he gave you is yours. Learn how to use it."

She paused.

"I have to go."

"No—don't go yet, Mama. Please. Tell me more."

"He'll tell you what you need to know," she said softly. "Just know—I'm proud of you."

And then she was gone.

I woke up with a horrendous headache, and flashes of pain shot through my right arm from struggling with the bodyguards. One of the goons sat across the room. He got up and left the room, returning with a glass of dark liquid.

He said, "You woke up too soon. We aren't ready for you yet. You must have a strong system to fight this stuff off so fast."

"Ready for what?" I sluggishly asked.

He grabbed my lower jaw and pulled my mouth open. I tried to move my head, but this guy's vise-like grip held it in place. I thought my jaw would break. He poured the mixture into my mouth, and I attempted to spit it out, but I couldn't because he forced my mouth closed. The liquid spilled out and down the sides of my face and I choked.

He waited a few seconds.

"It will be easier if you swallow it and get it over with. I can do this all day."

He poured more in and closed my mouth. I swallowed. It tasted like Pepsi. He released my jaw and left the room. By the time he returned, the substance was making me dizzy again.

I asked, "Why is she doing this to me?"

"You never ask the Voodoo Imperatrice why she does anything."

Everything went black again.

As Cyrus waited on the porch, many people dressed in white came to the house. The door opened instantly for them. He tried to follow some people in, but the invisible barrier blocked the ghost's entrance.

The spirit became enraged, picked up the charm pieces he had destroyed earlier, and threw them at the followers as they approached the house. The people yelled and screamed as the protective bits of bone and wood struck them when they ran toward the house. Having never experienced such frightening occurrences, they were apprehensive about what to expect from the evening's ritual.

Men took Orion out of the bedroom and into the kitchen while Cyrus peered through the window, worried about his friend. Orion was in terrible shape, half walking and half being dragged through the house. His head lolled, and his eyes fluttered at the top of his head.

The ghost screamed Orion's name and beat on the glass. The apparition tried to enter the backyard but couldn't get through or over the fence. The thrum of the drums and the voices singing and yelling came over the barrier. At one point, a familiar laugh from long ago echoed out of the backyard. But no, it couldn't be him. Orion wasn't dead; he would know if she had killed him. He sat on the porch stairs and waited with his chin in his hands.

When I woke up, two creeps made me drink some other vile-smelling concoction in a wooden bowl. One held my mouth open, and the other poured the stuff in. When it went in, they closed my mouth, "Swallow, or else we'll do it again."

I swallowed.

They released me and I lay on the bed while they whispered near the door. I began to feel strange. I wasn't passing out this time, but things looked distorted. There were auras of multiple colors of light around the thugs. The walls seemed to breathe. I lay there blinking. An ugly man approached and stared into my eyes.

He said, "He's ready."

All the guys had somehow turned ugly. Their faces twisted—grotesque and wrong, like masks half-melted in fire.

They untied the ropes from my wrists and ankles. I tried to roll off the bed to make a run for it, but my legs wouldn't cooperate and I fell to the floor. It was a long way down before I hit with my knees. The two guys grabbed me and half-dragged me through the kitchen and out the back door. We moved in bursts of speed and slow motion. I struggled to keep up with my surroundings.

I could hear my name echoing from far away.

Was that Cyrus' voice?

We emerged into the backyard, where a circle of people dressed in white, each surrounded by colored lights, stood around a huge iron pot in the center, filled with fire. Forced to my knees, two unsightly goons held my arms out to each side. I struggled to pull my arms away, but there was no way I was going anywhere in my current state. Drummers crouched in the shadows, their hands a blur over taut leather as they pounded out a rhythm that made the earth itself seem to pulse.

I looked around, and everyone was drinking from wooden bowls and swaying back and forth to the rhythm of the drumbeats. The bowl came to me, and I turned my head, unwilling to have more of the foul-tasting liquid. Once again, the ugly guys pried my mouth open, poured the liquid in, and held it closed. I swallowed. Things got even stranger.

The Voodoo Imperatrice shook strange dolls before me and spoke in an unfamiliar language. The dolls transformed into miniature people with hair sticking out in all directions, wriggling in her hands.

I said, "Let them go. Can't you see they want to be released?"

My grandmother laughed.

Something struck my head; my neck bent back, and the stars above in the clear sky swirled in figure-eight patterns. A snake writhed inside me, trying to grasp onto anything to remain.

I closed my eyes, yelled, "No! No!" and pushed it out.

A tall, thin Black man in a dark tuxedo with tails and a top hat, his face painted white like a skeleton's, stood beside the giant brazier and grinned with a toothy smile.

He said, "There you go, boy. Push it out."

I thought, 'Who the hell is this?' which was amazing since I was having trouble thinking coherently.

He stared straight at me and said, "I'm Duke Shamedi, your spirit protector and God father, so to speak."

I thought, 'Some protector you are.'

He laughed uproariously and it echoed around the circle of dancers, causing their hair and clothing to move as if stirred by a strong wind. I guess he read my thoughts. I could tell the Voodoo Imperatrice felt the unusual wind and heard the laughter. She turned and glared at me with a scowl as if it were my fault. I was the only person who could see this Duke.

'Was this the Duke my mother mentioned?'

Voodoo Imperatrice motioned to someone and they forced another bowl of the putrid mixture down my throat. I coughed and gagged and vomited most of it onto the ground. They poured a second bowl down my throat and I swallowed it. I had no idea how long I knelt there. Time ceased to mean anything; I hit a new level or state of otherworldliness.

Staring at a row of ants moving across the patio flagstone, I could read their thoughts. Could ants think? Their tiny voices whispered in unison: 'Follow. Don't stop. Never break the line,' I thought, 'What if they moved in a circle? With those thoughts, they would never stop.' A group of ants broke the line and marched in a circle. I wondered how long this would last.

The thing attempted to enter me again, hitting me with such force that my entire body jerked and I almost pulled away from the gorillas holding my arms. I pushed and pushed to expel the entity. Was it more vigorous this time or was I weaker? I don't know.

The Duke laughed again, saying, "You're doing good, boy. I knew there was a reason I chose you."

My body twitched and I had no control over my actions. The dancing and singing, if you want to call it that, became faster, reaching a fever pitch, or was that my hallucinations going wild? Another bowl of the foul stuff appeared, and I drank it. Loaded on the unsavory solution, I didn't know where or who I was anymore. The Duke laughed like a crazy person, or was that me laughing? The thing entered me again; this time, it wriggled straight past me and went somewhere else. I blacked out.

⚷ ⚷ ⚷

The Voodoo Imperatrice approached Orion's hanging head. Suddenly, his head shot up, and he gazed into her eyes.

Her grandson's mouth said—but it wasn't Orion, "I'm in" in a different female-sounding voice.

The priestess jumped and laughed with joy, while all the followers leaped with happiness.

⚷ ⚷ ⚷

I semi-awoke while all this madness unfolded, but all I saw was the Duke getting closer and closer. With his hand out in front, he touched my head, and I gasped and shivered from the deathly cold chill that ran through my body. Icicles stabbed into my head. His face loomed closer and closer until I entered the dark abyss of his eyes, and everything went black.

209

210

# Chapter 37

# Taken Home

At the Voodoo Imperatrice's nod, the bodyguards released Orion's arms. He collapsed to the floor like a puppet with cut strings, his limbs twitching in erratic spasms. His eyes fluttered wildly, and low, guttural moans slipped from his throat. She studied her grandson thoughtfully.

'That took longer than I expected. Rose struggled to gain control—he's stronger than I gave him credit for. I gave him more of the Spirit Opening Mixture than anyone before. I hope it doesn't damage him too much... I still need him.'

She told her henchmen, "Take him and his car back to the plantation and drop him off at the front door. Don't go in. The spirits may not like what we have done to him."

The lead bodyguard, Alan Christian, pointed to two other guards and commanded, "Take him to his car and drive him to his house. James and I will follow."

The largest guy grabbed Orion's twitching body and roughly hoisted him over his shoulder in a fireman's carry. All the guards exited the red house through the front door. They unceremoniously dumped him into the back seat of his Chrysler New Yorker. His limbs jerked as though invisible needles stabbed into his nerves—tiny, relentless shocks rippling across his skin. Two men took the front seats and drove off.

The driver glanced at the gas gauge and complained, "We've got to stop for gas before leaving. These old cars suck gas like crazy. I hope I have enough money to pay for this trip."

His traveling companion said, "I have some cash. I can loan you for a fill-up."

They stopped at the first gas station they encountered.

During the drive, the men spoke only a few times. The man in the passenger seat glanced back at Orion, who was twitching, and said, "Man, I have never seen anyone take so much of the Spirit Opening Mixture before. He looks fucked up. I wonder if he will come out of it?"

The driver said, "Who knows? It is not for us to question her methods."

The other thug nodded.

After a couple of hours, the guy in the passenger seat, sniffing the air, said, "What is that smell? Did he ..."

He glanced back at Orion and exclaimed, "Damn," the man said, wrinkling his nose. "He pissed himself."

From the back seat, a faint voice slurred, "Mama's gonna be mad at me...."

The driver asked, "What did he say?"

The other guy said, "Mama's going to be mad at me...."

The two men glanced at each other and burst out laughing.

"You're right—she probably is."

He chuckled again as he rolled down the window to let the odor of urine escape.

The men remained silent for the rest of the trip with the only sounds in the vehicle coming from the moans of Orion in the back. They stopped once for gas and when they arrived at the plantation, the gauge was on the empty line.

The two ruffians pulled Orion from the back of the New Yorker, one under each arm, and carried him with his feet dragging along the path to the front door. They seated him on the porch and leaned his back against the door. The black Ford that followed them drove up.

One of the other guards in the front said, "Look at that."

They both turned, shocked and terrified at what they observed.

The front door creaked open—by itself. No one stood there. Orion's limp body slumped sideways, twitching faintly. Then, unseen hands gripped his arms and dragged him across the threshold. The door closed behind him with a soft click. No one was there.

The two guys who drove Orion to the house quickly jumped into the back of the Ford, slammed the doors, and shouted, "Get the fuck out of here!"

Alan Christian sat in the driver's seat. His eyes widened, and his mouth hung open at what he had just witnessed. He skidded the car around and slammed the gas pedal. Dirt and dust flew up behind the vehicle as it raced down the plantation's private drive.

I could feel someone throwing me into the back of a car. I was in and out of consciousness, experiencing the weirdest dreams I've ever had while small electric shocks coursed through my body. Many of the images terrified me. Someone held my hand, and I squeezed it tightly, not wanting to let go for fear of floating away and not coming back.

During one of my semiconscious moments, I pissed my pants and thought, "Mama's going to be mad at me." People were laughing at me about it and I wanted to find somewhere to hide. I continued having strange dreams, with the Duke laughing, people in white jumping and dancing, and drums that kept pounding in my head.

I woke up for a short while and called for Cyrus, but instead, Andy showed up. Then, I seemed to float up the stairs to my room and bed.

Was this all a dream?

214

# Chapter 38

# A Ghostly Phone Call

Cyrus sprang to his feet the moment the red house door creaked open. Four guards stepped out, the largest of whom had Orion slung over his shoulder like a sack of flour. The young man's body hung limp, twitching involuntarily, with moans leaking from his throat.

"You heathens!" Cyrus bellowed, his voice thick with fury.

His ghostly form trembled.

"What have you done to him?"

In his rage, his speech slipped back into the formal cadence of the nineteenth century. Two of the guards glanced around uneasily, as if they had heard something behind them, but the large one tossed Orion into the back seat of his Chrysler New Yorker without a word.

Cyrus leapt in and crouched low beside his friend, taking Orion's hand.

"Orion, it's Cyrus. I'm here with you. I won't leave you."

He squeezed tight.

Orion stirred faintly, his eyes fluttering, his breath ragged. But he squeezed back.

"That's it," Cyrus whispered, gripping tighter. "I've got you."

When Orion urinated in the seat and the thugs complained, Cyrus snarled, "You aren't worthy to smell his piss!"

The car rattled along the rural road. During the long, tense ride, Cyrus never let go of Orion's hand.

Cyrus followed the goons carrying Orion to the house. He squatted next to Orion and held his hand. Milly peeked through the window beside the door and he motioned for her to open it. She opened it slowly, causing Orion's body to slide down until his head landed on the floor in the vestibule. All the other ghosts crowded around, staring at Orion and they spoke all at once.

"Oh God, what happened to him?" Milly gasped.

"Lordy, lordy!" Bertha cried. "Why's he shaking like that?"

"Look at his wrists," Hugo said grimly. "He was bound."

"If I had a body," Paul muttered, "I'd knock their teeth out."

"Silence!" Cyrus shouted. "Get him inside. I'll explain."

Doc and Hugo seized Orion's arms and pulled him deeper into the house while Milly shut the door. Doc came back with his stethoscope and examined for signs of life.

"Pulse is weak but steady. I think he's been drugged."

"That makes sense," Cyrus said. "They gave him something. He was twitching the whole time."

"You weren't with him?" Doc asked.

"No. A spell blocked me. I couldn't follow into the Imperatrice's house."

Doc frowned.

"We need to know what was in him."

"Some kind of Spirit Opening Mixture," Cyrus said. "One of the thugs said no one had ever taken as much as Orion did. He wasn't sure if he'd come out of it."

"Sounds like a hallucinogen," Doc muttered. "No way to tell how long it'll last or how deep it's gone. This could damage his brain."

Orion groaned.

"Wait!" Bertha said. "I think he's waking."

His eyes rolled beneath fluttering lids.

"Cyrus? Where are you?"

"I'm here," Cyrus whispered, face close to his friend's.

But Orion stared through him.

"He's not seeing me," Cyrus said, turning to the others.

"Drugs," Doc replied. "Same thing happened with his mother when she was sedated. She couldn't see us either."

"How long will this last?" someone asked.

"I don't know," Doc said.

Cyrus stood.

"We need someone alive to reach him. I'll try Andy."

"But Orion said not to trust him," Walter reminded.

"He's all we've got."

Cyrus zipped to the phone, flipped open the book, and dialed.

"Andrew Butler speaking."

Cyrus yelled, "Andy, Orion needs your help! Come to the plantation."

"Who is this? Talk to me. If you aren't going to speak, I'm hanging up," and he hung up the telephone.

Cyrus slammed the receiver down and dialed again, screaming three words with everything he had: "ORION! HELP! PLANTATION!"

On the other end, Andy froze. Something—just barely—echoed through the receiver.

"Orion... help... plantation?"

"I'm coming!" Andy shouted.

Andy hung up the telephone. He grabbed his coat and ran out of the office.

Doris stopped him and asked, "What's going on?"

"I think Orion needs my help. I've got to go to the plantation."

"I'm coming, too."

She picked up the crystal from her desk and placed it in her voluminous purse.

"What can you do?"

"I have skills. Let's go."

"Okay," he said, not wanting to waste time arguing.

They both quickly descended the stairs and hopped into Andy's Chevy. He drove down Main Street too quickly, but luckily, the sheriff wasn't around.

At the plantation, Andy pulled in behind the New Yorker. They ran to the already open front door. Lying on the floor, Orion twitched and moaned. Andy knelt beside him and touched the young man's sweaty face, covered in three days of dark stubble.

Orion opened his eyes, shaking.

"Andy, is that you?"

"Yes, Orion. I'm here."

Orion whispered, "Why did you tell her what I was doing? You asshole."

"I'm sorry. If I didn't, she would hurt my family. She almost killed Vivian."

All the ghosts standing around and Doris heard this revelation.

"Why didn't you tell me what was happening?" Doris asked. "I could have helped."

"How could you have helped? It would have put you in danger, too."

"I told you I have skills."

Doris knelt beside Orion, pulled a large quartz crystal from her purse, and set it gently on the floor. Then, she drew a smaller one from beneath her blouse—this one dangling from a silver chain—and closed her eyes. Humming softly, she rubbed the pendant between her fingers. Light pulsed from both crystals—first faintly, then intensifying. Around them, the air shimmered. One by one, the ghosts took shape—translucent outlines glowing with faint silvery-blue auras. Concern etched into their ethereal faces.

"There you all are," Doris whispered. "So worried for Orion. Good."

Andy stumbled back, stunned.

"My God," he breathed. "My father was right.... There really are ghosts in this house."

# Chapter 39

# Recovering From the Ceremony

Andy snapped into action and said, "Okay, we have to do something about Orion. Let's get him upstairs to his room."

He leaned down and sat Orion up. From behind, Andy wrapped his arms around the front of the young man's chest and locked his hands together. He lifted with his legs and raised Orion's torso off the floor.

He complained, "He is a lot heavier than he looks. If you ghosts can help, please do."

Orion's legs bent at the knees and lifted off the floor. Andy moved to the stairs and ascended them backward. Some other ghosts must have lifted Orion at the hips because he felt a little lighter.

He reached the top of the steps and asked, "Which way?"

Doris could still see Cyrus's reflection on the main floor, pointing to Andy's right.

Doris said, "To your right."

He moved in that direction and the door opened by itself. A gush of cool air washed over him.

He said, "Oh, God, does that feel good."

They placed Orion on the bed, where he lay twitching and moaning. Andy leaned over and panted, realizing that he was not in as good shape as he thought.

Andy flinched as unseen hands began to undress Orion. The shirt peeled away, followed by his shoes and jeans—each movement precise and eerily gentle. They removed his underwear, which reeked of urine and appeared damp. Orion lay naked and continued to twitch and moan.

Doris walked in, smiled, and commented, "He reminds me of Ronni. He was beautiful, too."

She placed her massive bag on the floor and rummaged through it.

She pulled out two crystal necklaces. She gave one to Andy and put the other around Orion's neck. The crystal around Orion's neck began to glow.

Doris said, "He has power. I've never seen the crystals glow that brightly immediately upon attachment."

Andy held his necklace.

"What's this for?"

"It has a protection spell on it. Please put it on; it'll help protect you from the voodoo witch. It may not protect you from everything she can do, but it'll probably diminish whatever she's trying to do."

He put it around his neck.

"It feels warm."

"See, it's already doing something."

A sheet from the notepad on the night stand floated over to Andy. He read it out loud.

"It says he needs to drink lots of water and tea to flush the hallucinogens out of his system. Doc."

Andy asked, "Are you a doctor?"

"Yes," appeared at the bottom.

An invisible hand wrote another statement on the sheet.

"Can one of you search for the amulet? It's probably in the New Yorker. Then Cyrus can come up here."

Doris volunteered, "I'll go do that."

She left, going down the stairs, out the front door and to the New Yorker. She remembered that her father owned this automobile model. She rummaged through the front seat floor and under the seats, carefully pushing aside the broken glass bits, and touched something. She pulled it out, and the beautiful fleur-de-lys with the jewel in the middle flashed as the light from the porch hit it.

To herself, she said, "This must be it."

She returned to the house and proceeded up the stairs.

"I found it."

When Doris entered the house with the amulet, Cyrus popped straight to Orion's bedside.

He took Orion's right hand and said to his best and only friend, "I'm here, Orion. If you don't recover from this, I swear to God I will haunt that voodoo bitch for the rest of her life and after.”

Doc stared at Cyrus after hearing this statement and thought, 'I have never heard him so upset.'

As Doris entered Orion's bedroom, Andy lifted Orion's head and assisted him in drinking some warm tea.

As the night passed, Andy and Doris took turns helping Orion drink water and warm tea. The ghosts fashioned towels into diapers and quickly changed them after he urinated. The urine-soaked towels would float away, and a new, clean, dry towel would replace them.

Orion continued to toss, turn, jerk, and moan throughout the night. Sometimes, he cried out. He calmed down in the early morning hours. The tossing and turning stopped, and only an occasional twitch and moan occurred. Andy fell asleep in a chair he moved close to the bed from the hearthside, while Doris lay on a bed in one of the spare bedrooms. Earlier in the evening, Andy called his wife to inform her that Orion was sick and that he would spend the night helping him.

⚷⚷⚷

I woke up and was disoriented for the first few moments. My eyes focused on Andy, who was asleep in a chair with his arms crossed over his chest.

Why is he here? Is he going to tell my grandmother how fucked up I am?

My head pounded, and my mouth was so dry it felt like I could spit sand.

I called his name, but it came out as a whisper, “Andy, Andy.”

He didn't wake.

I tried again, “Andy.”

An invisible hand shook his shoulder back and forth, and he awoke.

“What? What?” and he rubbed the sleep from his eyes.

I repeated his name, “Andy.”

He jumped and moved to the bed, “Orion, you're awake, at last.”

“Not quite. I still feel weird and super tired, and I have a horrendous headache. Can I get some water?”

“Sure. Can you see any of the ghosts?”

221

I looked around, and none of the ghosts were visible, yet someone was squeezing my hand.

"No, I can't see them, but someone squeezes my hand."

Andy said, "I think that's Cyrus."

I squeezed back. Two phantom hands wrapped around my right hand and—was that a kiss?

"Okay, Cyrus. Let's not go overboard."

Andy said, "From what Doc wrote to me, Cyrus told them that your grandmother drugged you and performed some voodoo ceremony on you in her backyard. There was a spell on the house, and he couldn't enter to get in the backyard."

"Yeah, that sounds right. I can only remember bits and pieces. Why are you here? To keep tabs on me for my grandmother?"

"You don't remember what I told you yesterday? She threatened my family if I didn't tell her everything you were doing. Cyrus called me because you couldn't see any of them. They needed a live person to talk to you."

"Oh, yeah, now I kind of remember calling you an asshole."

I felt the warmth of the crystal necklace around my neck, rubbed my fingers over the gem, feeling a tingle from it, and asked, "Where did this come from?"

Andy explained, "Doris gave each of us one."

He pulled his crystal out from under his shirt.

"She said they have protection spells on them."

"Okay, I think I need some protection right now."

Two pain pills and a glass of water floated over. I knew they were from Doc.

"Thanks, Doc."

I took the pills and drank the water. I closed my eyes and fell asleep quickly.

I woke up standing in the middle of the bedroom.

How did I get here?

All the dresser's drawers were scattered on the floor. Clothing was strewn everywhere. The items atop the dresser had been swept onto the floor.

What's going on? How did I end up here?

I suddenly felt dizzy and sick. I bent over and vomited. The dizziness intensified, and I blacked out. When I opened my eyes, the ghosts were crowded around me, helping me to bed. Confused and not understanding what was happening, I slipped on some water on the floor and began to shake.

"Where did that water come from?"

Doc said, "It looks like you lost control when you fainted—but don't worry, it's just your body processing the last of the drugs."

"Oh, God. What is going on? How did all my stuff get pulled out and thrown everywhere?"

Doc replied, "We thought you did it."

"I was asleep, and when I woke up, I was standing in the middle of the room, sick and dizzy, and everything was thrown everywhere."

Doc said, "You lay down. Bertha is making you some chicken soup. You haven't eaten anything for days. Your blood sugar level must be at rock bottom. That is probably why you're dizzy."

I lay on the bed with my arm over my eyes; I think I fell asleep for a bit.

Bertha called my name.

"Orion, child, sit up and have some soup. You need to eat something."

I looked up at her and smiled, "Okay. You're right. I should eat."

I sat up, and she placed the tray with a large bowl of soup on my lap. It smelled wonderful. With the first spoonful, I thought it was one of the best things I had ever eaten. I slurped the soup down as quickly as I could.

Bertha warned, "Child, don't eat it so fast, or else you will make yourself sick, and it will come back up."

"You're right."

I slowed and savored each mouthful.

After I finished, she took the tray away, and I lay in bed for a while. My mind raced from question to question.

What's happening to me? Why is she doing this? How do I fight back?

# Chapter 40

# What Did That Bitch Do To Me?

I needed to calm down. A hot shower might help—God knew it had been nearly a week. I shuffled to the bathroom, turned on the water, and waited for it to warm as it traveled from the basement to the second floor.

In the mirror, my reflection stared back: sunken eyes, days of stubble haunted me. I tried to load a fresh razor blade, but my hands were shaking too badly. I gave up.

Stepping into the shower, I raised my casted arm out of the spray and let the warm water cascade over me. With my eyes closed and head bowed, I tried to breathe through the mounting panic.

Then I opened my eyes and I wasn't in the shower anymore.

I was in my bedroom, staring out the window, watching Paul mow the lawn.

It had happened again.

My heart thundered in my chest. Fear engulfed me. I felt nauseous and dizzy. My vision blurred. I lost consciousness.

When I awoke, the ghosts crowded around, helping me up. Shaking with tears streaming down my cheeks and not understanding what was going on, the ghosts walked me back to bed. Wet footprints and water spatters were evident on the floor, demonstrating my trajectory from the shower into the bedroom without drying.

I lay on the bed, shaking in shock.

"I was in the shower, and the next thing I knew, I was back in here watching Paul mow the lawn through the window. What's happening?"

I grabbed for the crystal that should have been around my neck.

"Where's the crystal that Doris gave me? It is supposed to protect me from spells."

Cyrus said, "The girls found it on the floor in the corner, with the chain broken. It looks like you tore it off and threw it over there."

I shook my head, not understanding what was happening to me. I stayed in bed and fell asleep. When I woke up the next day, I felt as though I had gotten some natural sleep. Cyrus sat on the daybed, reading one of my French novels.

He asked, "How are you feeling today?"

"I feel better and I'm hungry."

"Nothing happened last night. I stayed here all night. You slept like a baby. I'll go down and get you some breakfast. Don't move; I'll bring it right up."

I lay with my eyes closed.

And I heard, "ORION, what are you doing?"

My eyes jerked open, and I found myself in my mother's bedroom, lifting the bed and tipping it over. I turned around to see all the dresser drawers scattered across the room. My stomach lurched as fear flooded back, my head spun, and I trembled all over, confused. Cyrus stood in the doorway, holding the food tray and staring at me. Then I passed out and fell to the floor.

I was alone in my bedroom when I woke up in bed. I got up and went to the door, turning the handle. The door wouldn't open. I twisted the knob back and forth, but it didn't turn.

'The old lock must have jammed.'

I pounded on the wood panels and shouted, "Hey, you guys find the key—the lock is jammed! I can't get out."

No one came to the door.

I yelled louder, "Cyrus, Doc, unlock the door!"

Cyrus came to the other side.

"We aren't letting you out. Every time you are out, you destroy something."

"What are you talking about? I didn't do anything."

"What about the dressers and clothes that were thrown everywhere? Last night, you woke up and trashed your old bedroom."

"That was Mother's room, and it wasn't me. It is something else."

"That was yesterday. After you passed out, we put you back to bed, and later that night, you got up and trashed your old room and passed out again,"

I stood with my mouth open in shock, unable to recall any of this. I turned and leaned my back against the door, trembling and terrified. I slid to the floor and drew my knees up.

I cried with my forehead on my knees.

"I'm sorry. I don't understand what's happening. What did that bitch do to me? I don't remember any of it."

As I sat afraid of what I might do next, I thought, 'At least I can't hurt any ghosts, but I'm destroying the house for some reason. Why would my grandmother want this done? What is she trying to accomplish? She tortured her son to the point where he committed suicide. Is she trying to do the same thing to me?'

After a while, I picked up a T-shirt from the floor and blew my nose. Naked and cold all this time, I dressed in jeans and a T-shirt I found near the dresser. I returned to bed, lay down, and fell asleep again.

When I woke, I found myself lying on the floor in the center of the room. Frantic, I looked around. Oh no. It happened again. The room was utterly trashed; everything was overturned. Dressers, tables, chairs, and mattresses were flung across the room from where they normally would be. Two fist-sized holes in the wall next to the door were visible. Everywhere, tossed clothing lay on the floor, much of it ripped and torn.

Only the armoire stood upright, like a silent witness. I crawled to it, shaking as I remembered the times I'd hidden in places like this as a child—during the worst of it, when Mom was high and men I didn't know pounded on the walls.

I opened the doors. The clothes had all been thrown out. There was room.

I climbed inside, pulled the doors shut, and curled up in the dark. I hugged my knees, my face buried, sobbing quietly. I wasn't afraid of some monster anymore—I was the monster. And I didn't trust what I might do next.

The door lock jiggled, and a soft knock came on the bedroom door.

A voice said, "Orion, are you okay?"

It was Andy. He must have been reading a note because I heard paper rustling.

"We'll be downstairs in the dining room if you need anything. Cyrus."

Andy poked his head in, and his eyes widened in surprise upon seeing the devastation in the room. He inched his way inside, not seeing Orion anywhere.

The odor of vomit and urine permeated the room, and small puddles of unidentifiable liquids were visible on the floor. He searched the room for Orion and noticed the armoire door cracked open. A scratching sound came from inside the cabinet. He opened it an inch and saw Orion crouched inside. Having wet his pants while hiding, the odor caused Andy to scrunch his brow in disgust as he opened the cabinet door wider.

"Orion, how are you doing, buddy?"

Andy's face tightened. Orion looked wrecked. His hair hung in damp clumps, matted to his scalp. His week-old, scraggly beard had pieces of vomit stuck in it. His filthy, stained T-shirt was smeared with vomit down the front.

Andy stood and stared down at me. I turned my face away, trembling, not wanting him to see me this way, a disgusting thing that had caused all this devastation.

I sniffled, "I don't know what's happening to me. The ghosts tell me I'm destroying everything, but I don't remember it."

I hit the back wall of the armoire with my fist and shouted, "What the fuck did that bitch do to me?"

"Why don't you come out, lay on the mattress, and tell me what you remember?"

Andy took my arm and gently helped me out of my hiding place. I stepped out, shaking, and he led me to the mattress on the floor.

Why was it there?

I shuffled toward it. Then everything went black.

Andy guided Orion to the mattress. His friend closed his eyes and lowered his head.

Andy asked, "Orion, Ory, are you okay?"

The crystal Doris gave him vibrated. He looked down at the spot on his shirt where the charm hung for a split second, and a fist flew at his face.

# Chapter 41

# Release

Orion's eyes snapped open—and his fist shot upward. The uppercut landed squarely under Andy's chin, dropping the attorney with a single, sickening thud. Orion's possessed body grabbed Andy's limp shoulders and silently laid him down on the mattress, careful not to alert the ghosts with any loud noises.

Rose—the vengeful ghost of the voodoo priestess—had taken control of Orion's body. Frustrated by her failure to locate the signet, she rampaged through the house, leaving destruction in her wake. She waited for the next opportunity to escape the locked room.

She looked up and approached the unlocked door. She cracked it open and surveyed the area for the ghosts. Cyrus mentioned they would be in the dining room. Barefoot, she descended the steps like a shadow. She thought, 'I've got to find the signet to release Paul from this curse. It has to be somewhere in this house, or the ghosts wouldn't still be here. The Voodoo Imperatrice said she would ensure my son was released once she had the seal in her possession. The Spirit Speaker is so strong; I should have been able to take control for much longer periods.'

As she reached the bottom of the stairs, she paused to listen for the ghosts. They were conversing in the dining room.

Cyrus said, "I wonder how Andy is doing up there?"

Doc commented, "It was good he stopped by to check on Orion. Maybe Ory will pay attention to him since he is alive."

"The poor boy has been through so much. I don't know how much more he can take," Bertha remarked, concerned for Orion's well being.

Cyrus continued, "Maybe I should go and see how things are going."

"I'll go with you," Paul offered.

Doc replied, "Give Andy a few more minutes."

Rose recognized her son's voice and thought, 'I'm going to get you out of here, Paul. I promise.'

As the ghosts continued speaking, Rose retreated into the library. She inspected the room and thought, 'There is so much to go through here.' She decided to begin with the desk.

Pulling open the drawers, she rummaged through each, searching for the seal she hadn't seen for over 170 years. She still remembered its appearance: a one-inch silver filigree hemisphere with a silver handle and blue-carved Labauve crest meant to be pressed into hot wax to seal letters and official documents. She had stolen it after they hanged her son and created the most intense, powerful charm she could, imploring all the Voodoo Gods to add to the power of the gris-gris. Several responded in some way, but many did not. She didn't know why some gods added power and some didn't. The Lwa had their reasons.

The search of the desk yielded nothing. Glancing at the books, she thought, 'It's small enough; maybe it could be hidden behind a book.'

Rose approached the bookcase, taking books out and tossing them onto the floor.

Bertha went into the kitchen to start a pot of coffee for Andy, recalling that he preferred coffee when he and Doris were here a few days ago. Thumps came from the library. Looking through the kitchen doorway across the hall and into the library, she saw Orion pulling books off the shelves and tossing them onto the floor.

She hurried back through the swinging door into the dining room and whispered, "Orion's in the library, throwing books around."

Doc asked, "Where's Andy?"

Bertha said, "I don't know. He's not in the library."

Doc said, "Milly, Philly, go upstairs and find Andy. The rest of you, let's go in and stop Orion."

Cyrus ran into the library. He approached Orion from behind, grabbed his arm, and pulled him around. He could tell that he wasn't making eye contact with Orion. Orion pushed him away and continued pulling out books and throwing them down.

Milly and Philly quickly went upstairs and entered Orion's room.

Andy was sitting up on the mattress, rubbing his chin, where the pain was more intense from Orion's punch.

8—x 8—x 8—x

Andy rubbed his chin where Orion had struck him. Something on each arm helped lift him off the mattress and guided him out of the bedroom, down the stairs, and into the library.

Andy listened to Orion speak in a different, almost feminine voice.

"Cyrus Labauve, I cursed you once. I'll curse you again."

He pointed his finger at something.

He waited a moment, and the voice emanating from the young man's mouth said, "Yes, it is me. I have to find the Labauve signet. Don't stop me."

Orion's body convulsed. His head snapped back, mouth gaping, eyes rolling to the ceiling. A low, guttural cry escaped his throat—then turned into a scream. Orion's body jerked violently multiple times. He fell to the floor and thrashed about, beating the hardwood with his fists and heels. He screamed, and his back arched at an incredible angle. He held that position for a few seconds before collapsing back down. His friend opened his eyes, rolled to the side, projectile vomited across the room, and fell onto his back, unconscious.

Andy covered his mouth as he watched the frightening actions Orion performed, not understanding what was happening to the young man.

8—x 8—x 8—x

Cyrus pulled Orion from the bookshelves and shouted, "Why are you doing this? Stop!"

Rose in Orion's body yelled, "Cyrus Labauve, I cursed you once, and I'll curse you again."

In shock, recognizing the voice, Cyrus said, "Rose? You are the one possessing Orion?"

"Yes, Cyrus. I have to find the Labauve seal. You can't stop me," she yelled and turned, continuing to pull books off the shelves.

Cyrus shouted, "No, you don't!"

He leapt straight for Orion's chest and vanished into the man's body.

The two spirits struggled inside Orion, but Cyrus couldn't force Rose to release her hold on his friend. Cyrus lifted his head from Orion's chest and yelled at the other ghosts, "I need some help here! We have to pull her out of Orion."

The other ghosts exchanged glances before jumping into Orion's body one by one. With each ghost that entered, Orion's body jerked violently. All the ghosts tugged at Rose, pulling her out of Orion's body, until they finally leaped out, dragging Rose along, kicking and screaming.

I came to on the library floor. My body thrashed uncontrollably—something inside me howled and clawed, trying to stay. Screams rang in my ears, but they weren't mine. Not entirely. I thought my head would explode from the shouting and screaming inside. Other things jumped around in my body. I battered, beat, and kicked the floor with my fists and feet. Something was being ripped from me, but it didn't want to leave. My insides were being shredded in my chest, and I screamed.

Then it stopped, I gasped for air, and I fell back. My stomach flip-flopped. I turned and vomited. Lying on the floor, panting, my head spinning, I blacked out.

# Chapter 42

# The Duke Comes Forward

When I opened my eyes, the world was blurred. My mouth felt dry, my throat parched, and a foul, metallic taste coated my tongue.

"Water, please," I rasped, the words barely more than a whisper.

I blinked several times until my vision cleared. Tears ran down my cheeks—not from pain, but from relief. It was over. The possession had ended. I could feel the absence—like a weight had been lifted from my soul. The menacing presence that had haunted me was gone.

Around me stood my ghost family—the spirits who had cared for me throughout my strange life. Their faces were etched with concern and quiet vigilance after the harrowing ordeal.

Cyrus stepped forward, holding a glass of water. He gently cradled my head and brought the rim to my lips. I drank greedily; the water tasted like heaven.

"What happened?" I asked.

My voice was hoarse. My last memory was blacking out in my bedroom.

Beaming, Cyrus replied, "We got Rose out of you! We all jumped in together and pulled her out."

"You jumped in? What? Into me? How? Rose? Rose, who?"

I was confused, not understanding what he was telling me.

The others nudged a woman forward. An unfamiliar Black woman, wrapped in a dark scarf and a simple black dress, stepped hesitantly toward me. Paul hovered protectively at her side, one arm around her.

"Who are you?" I asked.

She gave a regretful smile.

"I'm Rose. Paul's mother. I was the one who possessed you."

My body tensed.

"Why? Why would you do that?" I asked, bewildered and not

comprehending the purpose.

Her voice trembled.

"The Voodoo Imperatrice promised me—if I found the Labauve signet and gave it to her, she'd send Paul to the other side in peace. I didn't mean to hurt you. I possessed you during the ceremony at her place. I remembered what the seal looked like—I had to find it."

A sudden chill swept over me. I shuddered, then gasped as a powerful cold entered my body. My vision dimmed. In the next instant, I found myself in a dark, wind-swept place, frost biting into my bones. Somewhere in that endless cold, I caught a glimpse of the Duke's smile—just for a moment—before his voice echoed around me.

Andy and the ghosts watched helplessly as Orion convulsed. His eyes rolled back. When they returned, they were no longer blue—but a glowing, inhuman gold. He spoke in a guttural, ancient language that only the voodoo priestess recognized.

Her eyes widened.

"He's speaking the tongue of the Spirit Gods... the Lwa."

She listened carefully, then gasped.

"It's the Duke. Duke Shamedi."

The golden-eyed Orion turned to her and grasped her arm. In a deep, bone-chilling voice, he spoke English.

"Rose, you hurt my boy. I chose him because he's special. He has work to do for me. You must stay and help him. When the curse is broken, I will take Paul to the other side. Renee will never help you. But I will. Serve the boy. Teach him. You'll go when he goes. And when he recovers from what you've done, I'll return and show him how to use everything I gave him."

With her eyes wide in amazement that the Spirit God would possess a non-practitioner, she answered.

"Yes, Duke. I understand."

Andy could only stare, dumbfounded. He didn't see Rose or grasp the full meaning of what he was hearing—but the weight of it chilled him.

He thought, 'Poor Ory, so many odd, horrible things have happened to him over the last two weeks.'

Then the Duke turned Orion's head and fixed Andy with a stare. The golden eyes pierced through him like a branding iron of ice.

"Son of Andrew Butler... Josette Montaigne loved your father like her own. Her offerings to me were pure and of the highest quality. Because of her devotion, I extend the protection spell she cast on your father to you and your family. In return, you must help my boy."

Shocked that this entity knew him and his father, Andy could only nod, feeling overwhelmed.

"I will."

"Good. I must go now."

Orion convulsed once more. His eyes rolled back, and when they returned, they were light blue again. He collapsed onto the sofa, shivering and gasping for breath.

⚷— ⚷— ⚷—

Back in my body, I whispered, "Was that... was that the Duke? It was so cold. I was in a dark place. Wind... always blowing."

Rose nodded solemnly.

"Yes. That was him."

She turned.

"Walter, bring that blanket."

Walter appeared and placed a heavy quilt over me. Rose draped it around my trembling shoulders.

I closed my eyes.

"When is all this shit going to stop?"

I rubbed my palms over my face, trying to scrape away the lingering cold and grit that had blown onto them. When the Lwa Spirit God took me over, a gust brought grit against my face. I wrapped my arms around my body and squatted against the freezing wind, but it didn't help. The cold seeped right into my bones. I thought I would turn into a popsicle. Even back in the real world, the cold clung to my bones.

"God, I'm so tired I could sleep for a year."

237

Doc stepped forward.

"Hugo, Paul, girls—go fix Orion's room. Bertha, make Orion some chamomile tea."

The ghosts vanished to carry out their tasks.

Andy knelt beside me, placing a comforting hand on my shoulder.

"Looks like we both have protection from the Voodoo Imperatrice now."

I nodded, too weary to speak.

"I'll come back in a few days," he said softly. "We'll talk then. We've got a lot to sort out."

Again, I nodded.

Andy rose and walked to the door. It opened by itself—something that would have terrified him a few days ago. Now, it barely raised an eyebrow.

He paused and turned to the space behind him.

"Good night," he said. "Take care of Orion. I know you will—like you always have."

Then he left.

Driving his tan Chevy through the quiet streets, Andy reflected on everything that had happened—Rose, the Duke, the possession. Even the bruise on his chin didn't seem important now. Despite all of this, things finally seemed to be turning in the right direction.

When he got home, he felt more exhausted than he could remember ever being. He dragged his aching body across the carpet and into the bedroom. Knowing that he and his family now had the same protective spell his father had he could rest without worrying for the first time in weeks. He didn't feel the need to double-check the locks or sleep with the lights on. He undressed, climbed into bed, and curled up beside his wife. Sleep claimed him immediately and held him deep into the following morning.

When he finally stirred, Vivian smiled at him.

"I didn't want to wake you. You were really out."

"I know," he said, stretching. "And I feel good." He reached for her. "Come here."

As she approached the edge of the bed, he grabbed her arm and pulled her down on top of him. He wrapped his arms around her and kissed his wife deeply and passionately—something they hadn't done for quite a while.

She grinned.

"So... you're definitely feeling better."

They kissed again, and this time, neither of them let go. They continued to kiss and make love.

240

# Chapter 43

## Spirit Speaker Revelation

Doc helped me upstairs. As we ascended, I recalled the wreckage of my room—the stink, the mess, the broken furniture. I hesitated.

"Do I have to return there?" I asked.

Albert gave a reassuring smile.

"It's okay. The girls cleaned it."

The transformation shocked me. Everything was back in place. The furniture had been reset, the sheets replaced, and the air no longer reeked of rage and possession. A couple of the dresser drawers hung at odd angles, but the room was livable again. I released my breath with a long sigh, grateful that I didn't have to endure the previous disastrous state of my room.

Doc guided me to the bed, where I sat, still a little chilled and shaken. I noticed the holes in the wall by the door. My knuckles were bruised, the skin scraped raw. I'd done that—or at least, my body had.

Hugo caught my glance.

"I'll fix those tomorrow," he said, nodding toward the damage.

I nodded back, grateful. I shouldn't blame myself for this; it wasn't me who caused all the devastation. Rose performed all the carnage. Yet, for some reason, I felt a part of me was responsible for these actions. Rage welled up from the dark recesses of my soul, and she was able to channel and release it. If it did come from deep inside me, I never wanted that to happen again. I'd have to ask her about this when I felt better.

The girls returned with a basin of warm water and a washcloth. They gently cleaned me, wiping away the sweat, vomit, and everything else. As they worked, I felt layers of filth—physical and emotional— being peeled away. When they were done, Bertha handed me a mug of chamomile tea. It soothed my irritated throat and warmed my stomach.

I was barely able to keep my eyes open.

Doc gave me two pain pills. I slid under the covers and sank into a dreamless sleep—the first genuine rest I'd had in weeks.

I woke up late the next afternoon. Disoriented, I lifted my right arm and accidentally bumped my head with the cast.

"Doc," I groaned. "Can this thing come off?"

Albert appeared moments later with a pair of pruning shears. He carefully cut the cast and peeled it away. At last, fresh air touched my arm. My skin looked pale and shriveled.

He rubbed my arm to encourage circulation and told me, "You'll need to build strength back slowly."

I nodded. When I stood, Cyrus came in and helped me to the bathroom. I urinated into the toilet and frowned while doing it, thinking, 'This is the first time I used the bathroom to do this in at least a week.' How revolting my life had been for the last couple of weeks, and I wanted to wash away all the foulness from my body.

I told Cyrus, "I'm going to shower and shave."

Cyrus raised an eyebrow.

"You think so?"

He pointed to my trembling hands.

"I'll get the girls."

I stood holding onto the edge of the sink and looked at myself in the mirror. I had dark circles around my eyes. My hair was greasy and desperately needed washing. My beard stubble had a white spot on my right cheek. I don't think I had that there before the craziness started with the Voodoo Imperatrice. Was that a white curl hanging above my right eye? That definitely wasn't there before these hideous events. And the scar, angry and red, across my forehead.

The girls entered quietly.

"You know what to do," Cyrus told them with a wink, then vanished.

Milly ran the water. I sat, waiting. Philly laid out soap, shampoo, a razor.

"This is weird," I said.

Philly smiled.

"We used to give you baths, remember?"

"Yeah. With toy boats."

Milly grinned.

"No boats this time."

The water warmed; I stepped into the tub and leaned against the wall, letting it run over my body. I closed my eyes and submerged my head to wet my hair, luxuriating in the warmth, while one of the girls shampooed and scrubbed my mane and scalp.

Milly said, "Back under."

I rinsed the shampoo out of my hair. I put my hands against the wall next to the shower head and let the water run over my back as the girls rubbed soap all over, their hands massaging all parts of my body. These sensations seemed to bring some life and energy back to it. Then a soapy hand wrapped around my cock and began moving up and down.

I jumped, "What are you doing?"

Philly said, "Making you happy. We know how to do this. We did this for your great-great-grandfather, Gregor Labauve. He placed us in a house where we were taught the things that men enjoy. You know this. We taught you what to do with girls when you were sixteen."

"I understand what happened to you then and what you taught me, but you don't have to do it now. I don't expect anything like this."

"We know, but we want to do it for you. Let us make you happy. It is no different than doing it to yourself while in the shower."

I blushed. Sometimes, I forget that the ghosts know everything I do while I'm in the house. She rubbed my shaft with an expert hand. Then Milly ran a finger around my anus and inserted two fingers. Startled by this action, I exclaimed, "What the fuck?"

"I'm doing something else that you'll enjoy. Many men like to be stimulated this way."

Her fingers glided along my prostate gland—remembering this from the medical training Albert gave me—and it gave me a shiver. I let them continue these sensual and well-practiced actions to fruition. I stood there panting in ecstasy afterward.

My knees were giving out, and I said, "I need to sit down."

The girls lifted me out of the tub, and I sat on the toilet seat.

"Thank you. But you don't ever have to do that again. Cyrus put you two up to this. Didn't he?"

Milly said, "It is okay, Mr. Orion. We enjoyed making you happy and would love to do it again whenever you want."

I considered this tempting offer but didn't want to exploit the girls. I remembered what I had witnessed when I touched them on their death anniversary many years ago. When they were alive, they never had a say in the matter, and my ancestor forced them to do as he wished, or else they would be back living on the streets. I suppose what he offered was better than living on the street, but I didn't want to continue where Gregor had left off.

They dried me with a soft towel, then shaved me, removing the beard that reminded me of days I wanted to forget. When I looked in the mirror again, I saw a man still recovering—but returning.

Back in bed, Bertha came in with a tray of food.

She placed it on the table next to the daybed and said, "Doc told me to make you nothing greasy and only a very light breakfast, even though it is dinner time. So, I made you scrambled eggs, toast with no butter, and chamomile tea."

I sat down to eat and said, "This is just like being in the hospital."

I put some eggs on a wedge of toast and took a bite. It tasted fantastic. I hadn't eaten anything for quite a while.

"This is so much better than the hospital's version. How do you do it?"

She smiled.

I filled my mouth, realizing how famished I was, but I remembered what she said about eating too fast a few days ago—or was that last week? My sense of time was still whacked out—so I slowed my eating. I managed to get through about half the food on the plate and felt stuffed. I sat back on the daybed, holding a warm cup of tea.

I said, "That's all I can do. I'm stuffed."

I sipped the soothing liquid and emptied the mug. Still holding the cup, I closed my eyes and drifted off to sleep once more.

A light blanket covered me when I woke, and the mug sat on the table. Cyrus stood over me, wearing a concerned expression.

"How're you doing?"

"Better."

I got up, and, taking careful steps, headed to the bathroom to relieve myself.

When I came out my friend asked, "Do you want to come downstairs and relax? Bertha has some chicken soup for you when you want it."

"I'm still full of the eggs and toast, but maybe some tea would be good. That seems to calm everything down."

My knees felt unstable and weak, so I leaned on Cyrus as we descended the stairs. We entered the living room and I sat on the sofa. He turned on the television and Milly brought me a mug of tea. I accepted the cup and smiled at her. She curtsied and stepped back.

Then he asked, too casually, "So… did they make you happy?"

I said sharply, "Yes, you know they did, but don't ever ask them to do that again."

"Okay, okay! You're doing it again. The pushing thing."

"Oh, I'm sorry. From what the Duke said, I guess I do have special powers he gave me. I had no idea. But why did it start now and not earlier?"

Having heard the question, Rose approached and said, "Because you turned twenty-five. Most Spirit-Speaking abilities aren't complete until the person reaches twenty-five. That is why your grandmother wants you and the Labauve signet. She knows you are the Spirit Speaker, and the signet holds all the power the Gods put into it.

"What do you mean, I'm the Spirit Speaker? Some ghosts I talked to said something about that, but none knew what it was."

She explained, "A Spirit Speaker is someone with the ability to see, hear, and speak to spirits and be possessed by them."

Listening to this, Cyrus said, "Orion can do all that and more since he turned twenty-five."

I said, "The Duke said he would teach me how to use all my powers when I am recovered. How is he going to do that?"

Rose answered, "I don't know."

"When I feel better, I want to hear your story. You have to tell me how you returned from the other side and why you decided to work for the Voodoo Imperatrice.

"I'll tell you everything."

I nodded.

"Later. For now, I need sleep."

The next morning, I woke up at a normal hour and felt stronger. I brushed my teeth, shaved, and descended the stairs slowly.

In the kitchen, a simple breakfast waited. I ate it all.

I lifted a small weight outside on the veranda to rebuild my arm. Rose approached and sat in the chair next to me while I carried out this exercise.

She said, "I'm sorry for everything I put you through with the possession. Paul told me you have always treated him well and appreciated his work on the property."

"I have always liked Paul. He played with me in the yard when I was little and he taught me about gardening."

"I always worried about him being left here. He got caught in the curse I placed on the plantation. I didn't realize he was still here."

"So, you were the one who created the curse on L'Enfant Haven?"

"Yes. I can tell you everything now if you want."

"Tell me your story," I said. "But let me try something first."

I touched her arm. She closed her eyes and her life unfolded in my mind like a storm of memory and pain.

# Chapter 44

# From Slave to Priestess

Born a slave on a plantation in Haiti, Rose worked in the fields. The plantation's voodoo priestess noticed that the girl possessed exceptional sensibilities. The child always sensed when the overseer or the master approached the road or the slave quarters before anyone else and would alert everyone to appear more diligent with their tasks.

The voodoo priestess took Rose under her wing, teaching her the voodoo religion and its practices. The child showed a natural talent for creating powerful gris-gris charms. Rose assumed the role of priestess when the old woman passed away.

When the master died, his wife, hailing from a high-class European family, decided to sell the plantation, all the slaves, and the property before returning to Europe. Rose and twenty others were sold to the Labauves' Oak Manor plantation in Louisiana, a French territory.

The journey across the Gulf of Mexico was horrific. A sudden tropical storm battered the ship for days, leaving many in the hold violently ill. Rose tried to calm the seas through prayer, but without the proper materials for the ceremony, the storm raged on.

The storm finally subsided and they landed in the New Orleans harbor. The overseer and master of Oak Manor arrived with a large covered wagon to transport the acquisitions back to the estate.

Martin Mason, the overseer, was an unattractive man. His face had suffered severe burns at some point in his life, and a large, distorted scar covered the left side. His greasy brown hair, with streaks of gray, revealed his age in his late forties.

He yelled at the slaves, "Get into the wagon and be quick about it!"

As they climbed in, he approached the three women from behind and grabbed each of their backsides, pushing them into the conveyance.

He appeared to be helping them but was actually evaluating them for other duties he would enjoy having them perform.

The master, Ambrose Labauve, approached on his black horse, leaned down, and asked the overseer, "How are the goods?"

Mason said, "The bucks look strong enough, and the femmes are fine."

He moved his eyebrows up and down with a smile.

Ambrose smiled.

"It looks like the new agent, Mr. Jonas, made excellent purchases. We can keep him in mind for future deals."

The overseer jumped into the back of the wagon, placed manacles on the slaves's ankles, ran chains through the rings, and attached the chains to the wagon floor with padlocks. He hopped down, climbed into the driver's seat, shook the reins, and clicked his tongue to the horses. The buckboard moved away from the harbor, heading north. It took them two days to reach Oak Manor plantation.

The Labauve family arrived to see the new acquisitions when the wagon rolled up to the carriage house. Ambrose jumped down from his horse, and his ten-year-old son, Cyrus, ran up to his father and hugged him.

Ambrose said, "Come, boy, inspect the new bucks and femmes. Let me know where you would place them to work on the plantation."

As the slaves hopped off the carriage, the boy scrutinized every aspect. He grabbed the men's arms and legs, running his hands up and down their muscular limbs. The women he turned around with a cursory glance, showing less interest in them.

After his inspection, he stood before his father with his hands on his hips and an air of mastery, reporting, "The men are all strong bucks and should be put to work in the fields. The youngest woman is pleasing to look at and should be placed among the house staff. The other women can be placed wherever needed."

Ambrose stood and considered his son's recommendations.

He turned to Mason and said, "You heard the boy. Do as he says."

"Yes, sir."

He gathered the new slaves, told them, "Follow me," and guided them to the slaves' quarters for assignments to their sleeping pallets.

Ambrose smiled at his son and thought, "He will run the plantation well when I'm gone," unaware that this was only a few years away.

Rose became a housemaid and the cook's assistant at the manor house. Oak Manor did not have a voodoo priestess, so she became the slaves' s priestess. Ambrose and Mr. Mason took advantage of her just a few days after her arrival, when the master's wife, Miss Victoria, left for a week to visit her sister at another estate.

Rose had learned from her mentor about the special herbs used to brew a mixture that could prevent pregnancy. She took this regularly and dispensed it to other slave women who did not want children from the White masters.

Rose and Caesar, the head houseman, were attracted to one another and engaged in regular intimate relationships. She allowed herself to become pregnant from these encounters. She named her son Paul, but Miss Victoria referred to him as Jupiter. The plantation mistress insisted on naming all the slave children.

Paul grew strong and tall, and by the age of ten, he became a valet to the young master, Cyrus, who took a liking to him. Paul accompanied Cyrus on trips as his personal servant.

Cyrus took control of the plantation at the age of sixteen when his father died of a heart attack. The young master was wild and frequently sought his pleasures with both slave men and women, although he preferred the males. Martin Mason observed this preference but never commented on it. He enjoyed the spectacle of two men together and realized he would be fired if he said anything about it.

At eighteen, under pressure from his mother, Cyrus married Miss Judith Beauregard from a nearby estate. They had two children, Cyrus Jr. and Anna.

Cyrus's younger brother, Joseph, married young at sixteen, and the couple had seven children. Their oldest boy was headstrong and spoiled, always wanting everything his way. He suffered a terrible fall down the stairs and died. Did he fall, or was he pushed? No one knew for sure.

Cyrus accused Jupiter of pushing him. Rose was sure that Paul did not push the boy and suspected the master of doing it. The men quickly apprehended Jupiter, dragged him to the front yard, and hanged him from the oak tree.

Rose screamed as they took Paul; she had to be held back. She struggled to be released and protect her son. The slave housemen held her back, knowing that if they didn't, she would also be killed. After her son died and they released his body from the tree, she ran and fell on top of his limp form, crying in agonizing sobs and swearing vengeance on the house of Labauve.

They buried Paul in the slaves' graveyard. The voodoo priestess vowed to make the Labauve family pay, particularly Cyrus Labauve. She firmly suspected he had lied about Paul pushing the child down the stairs. Over the next few weeks, she gathered everything needed for a ceremony to create the most potent gris-gris she had ever produced.

She called all her followers to meet in the forest at midnight for the ceremony. On the day of the ritual, she stole the Labauve signet from Master Cyrus's desk while cleaning the room.

During the voodoo ceremony, Rose summoned all the Voodoo Spirit Lwa Gods to contribute their powers to the charm. Several did. The Spirit Lwa Gods possessed Rose, allowing her to transfer their contributed power to the signet; then the Lwa would leave her, and the next would enter. This occurred five times, but no more contributed. When the ceremony finished, everyone returned to the plantation.

Possession by the Lwa exhausted the priestess. She overslept and was late in performing her daily duties. While cleaning Master Cyrus's office in the library, she planned to return the cursed seal to the desk. As she opened the drawer where it was usually kept, Cyrus entered and caught her replacing the signet, mistakenly thinking he had found her taking it. He silently approached from behind and grabbed her hand.

"What do you think you are doing?"

Rose answered, "Putting it back in its proper place, sir. It was on top of the desk."

As she said this, Mr. Mason, the overseer, entered the office.

Cyrus pulled the jeweled signet from her hand and the overseer seized her shoulders.

Mason said, "We can see where Jupiter got his attitude. He pushes children, and his mother steals from the master. I'll take her out and shoot her in front of all the slaves as an example."

He turned to go, dragging her with him.

"No, don't do that. Sell her. Just get her off the property. Don't say why we are selling her; say she wasn't good at her job."

In shock, Mason stared at Cyrus.

"Why would you do that?"

"Don't argue with me. Just go and do it, or else I'll get rid of you, too."

"Yes, sir."

He left with a confused look, pushing Rose in front.

Transported to the nearest slave market and sold at a low price to a tobacco farmer, she remained on this farm for the rest of her life, becoming the voodoo priestess for all the local slaves until her death.

After a few years, through slave gossip, she learned that Cyrus Labauve had died while intoxicated, falling down the stairs and landing in the same spot as the child who had passed away years before.

She smiled when she learned this, knowing that his spirit would be trapped there for eternity unless he could save a child or someone broke the curse. This would never happen.

⚿⚿⚿

Orion pulled his hand away from Rose's arm and sat back, tears streaming down his cheeks. He wiped them away and turned to Rose, who was sitting in the chair next to him.

She said, "Thank you for understanding and crying for me."

Orion said, "I always cry when I experience a ghost's life. There's always so much tragedy involved, which is why you are a ghost. I wasn't shown anything about you working with the Voodoo Imperatrice."

"That must be because that happened after I was dead, and you are only seeing what occurred while I was alive."

"What happened? How did you get pulled back to the side of the living and start working with my grandmother?"

Rose continued her story.

252

# Chapter 45

# A Call From the Voodoo Imperatrice

Rose should have been happy, but her son Paul was not there to greet her. Unjustly killed, his ghost lingered at the plantation, trapped by the curse placed on the estate.

She begged the Lwa Gods, "Please send me back so I can help my son."

The Lwa said, "The only way that can happen is for someone living to call you with the proper ritual."

The call came from Renee Broussard, the Voodoo Imperatrice for the entity that initially placed the curse on the L'Enfant Haven plantation. Rose stepped forward, recognizing that this was what she had been waiting for to free her son Paul.

The voodoo priestess and Rose discussed the actions needed for Renee to harness the power of the gris-gris. A Spirit Speaker, also a Labauve heir, would be necessary to connect all spirits to the talisman. A special ceremony involving multiple sacrifices over three days must be conducted to create the links to the power residing in the signet. A Spirit Speaker heir to the Labauve estate needs to be established.

The Voodoo Imperatrice devised a plan for her child, who possesses the ability to see ghosts, to produce offspring with a Labauve woman who can also perceive apparitions. This would enable the child to become a Spirit Speaker.

Renee contemplated this plan for months to find the ideal Labauve woman. Marie Labauve would become the mother of the Spirit Speaker.

When Andrew Butler requested an exorcism of the ghosts from the L'Enfant Haven plantation, both priestesses recognized this as an opportunity to implement their agenda. The Moon ceremony triggered the girl's menstrual cycle and ignited her ability to sense apparitions earlier than expected. Antoine accompanied his mother to the mansion to ensure that he would meet the girl and that they would bond.

After the birth of the Spirit Speaker, the next step was to ensure that the child would live at the plantation and engage with the spirits trapped there. Because each ghost felt guilt about the death of a child, they were compelled to protect Orion upon his arrival. Gretchen Labauve would need to die for Marie to inherit the property.

Using her unique abilities, the Voodoo Imperatrice psychically implanted the idea in Gretchen's mind to sell most of the property and create a mechanism to ensure that only a Labauve heir could ever reside at the manor. Gretchen Labauve and Andrew Butler Sr. established the L'Enfant Haven Trust with stringent stipulations.

After the trust was established, the matriarch had to die. Renee Broussard placed a curse on Gretchen Labauve to contract cancer. When she died two years later, Marie Labauve inherited the right to live on the plantation. They had to wait until the Spirit Speaker came of age and acquired his full abilities at twenty-five. Only then could they move forward.

The gris-gris signet with spirit power had to be found. It needed to be at the plantation because the ghosts were still present. The house retained its opulent appearance because one of the Spirit Lwa had placed the power to slow time on the property, ensuring that the house would not deteriorate as long as a Labauve heir resided there. Thus, the house provided a place for the ghosts to remain almost for eternity until someone broke the curse.

I listened as Rose continued to explain, "When they captured you, they gave you the Soul Opening Mixture to make you more receptive to a complete possession by a ghost. It took far more of the mixture than anticipated to allow my occupation. I finally got in and found that the only thing I could hold on to was your repressed anger that you buried deep in your subconscious."

My eyes widened upon hearing this.

"So, when you came out, you also pulled my anger and rage with you, and things were destroyed because of it."

Shaking my head and looking at the floor, I continued, "When I saw the devastation, I knew it came from me. All those years of neglect from my mother and people shunning me because they could always sense there was something different about me produced a lot of anger. I always tried to hold it in and rarely allowed it to surface.

"It's all because of my grandmother manipulating my entire family, both alive and dead. She forced my father to leave my mother, leaving her alone, and when Aunt Gretchen died, she had to return to the plantation to claim the monthly allotment and ensure a roof over my head. At my conception, the Duke granted me extra Spirit Speaker abilities, which helped me survive."

Tears welled in my eyes and streamed down my cheeks. The spirits of my mother and father tried to warn me, but I didn't understand. Now I do. It makes sense now, but how will I stop the Voodoo Imperatrice?

"What you have told me about the gris-gris power over the house also explains why the house looked run down when my mother and I first came here. The house hadn't had an heir for over six months, and the power maintaining the structure was dissipating. That also explains why the ghosts move more slowly when I'm gone for a few days."

Rose nodded her head.

256

# Chapter 46

# Searching For The Signet

Rose left me sitting on the back porch, staring at the family graveyard, my mind reeling from everything she had just revealed. The Voodoo Imperatrice wanted the Labauve signet—but where was it? It had to be in the house. We had to find it.

Bertha approached and said, "Lunch is ready."

"I'm not hungry."

I sat with my head in my hand, processing the information I had just received.

"Orion, child, you must eat to regain strength. Come and eat now."

"You're right. Okay."

I got up and followed her into the kitchen. The light lunch included chicken soup, soda crackers, and sliced apples. As I took a bite, I realized I was hungry and the food tasted delicious.

Afterward I drifted into the living room and sat at the piano. Playing calmed my nerves and quieted the chaos in my head. As my fingers moved across the keys, Andy walked in. He no longer flinched at the spirits in the room; instead, he smiled, listening.

I stopped playing and turned toward him.

Sitting on the sofa, Andy said, "Don't stop playing; you play beautifully. I want to listen."

Smiling, I resumed playing Schumann's *Arabesque*. My right arm ached from disuse, but I made it through.

When I finished, Andy asked, "Who taught you to play so well?"

"Nanny Helen. She started teaching me at three when Mother and I moved in."

"I don't think I've met her."

"That is because she's gone to the other side. When I was eleven, she saved my life when the creep George hit me and I almost went over the railing from the second floor. Because she prevented a child from dying, the curse was broken for her, and she was able to go to the other side. I was upset when she left. She was like a second mother to me."

"I remember my father telling me about some guy named George hitting you and your mother for money and stealing her car."

I nodded.

"After Nanny saved me, she was so angry that she appeared to him; all the ghosts appeared to him. It scared him so badly that he ran right through the picket fence out front."

Andy gestured to my hair.

"Where'd the white curl come from?"

"Possession trauma, I think. I've also got a white patch in my beard now."

He gave a half-laugh.

"Fits. Still... what your grandmother might do is terrifying."

"Rose showed me her life and explained how she came here from the other side and some of my grandmother's plans."

I outlined the information Rose had told me to Andy.

Andy sat there in shock at how this despicable woman's mind worked.

"What are we going to do?"

"We must find the signet before she can get her hands on it."

"What then?"

"We have to keep it away from her or destroy it. But if we destroy it, then my whole family will be gone. They'll all go to the other side. It may sound selfish, but I don't want to lose them. They are the only thing I have."

Andy leaned forward.

"I think your grandmother is counting on you feeling this way. If you find the seal, her only card to play is to convince you how alone you will be when they are all gone. She will attempt to manipulate you into working with her to keep your ghost family intact."

"You're right. I know. I don't know if I can do it."

"If you can't, I'll destroy the signet for you."

Andy wore an intense expression, having regained his

self-confidence and strength of character knowing that Josette's spell protected him and his family.

"That's wonderful that you would volunteer to take care of it, but I think I have to do it because I'm the Spirit Speaker."

"How do you know this?"

"I don't know. I just do. I understand things now that I never did before. I guess it must be an ability the Duke gave to me."

"Well, we need to find the seal. Can you call everyone together to set up search teams and locations?"

"Sure, okay."

I closed my eyes, concentrated, and said, "Everyone, family meeting now."

The ghosts entered the living room one at a time. I glanced around and confirmed that they were all present. Paul stood beside his mother.

I said, "Okay, we have to find the Labauve signet. It must be somewhere in the house because you are all still here. We can't allow the Voodoo Imperatrice to get her hands on it. If she does, she will use the power it holds along with my abilities to control any spirits she wants to. This cannot happen. Rose, please describe the seal for everyone."

Rose described the signet, and all the ghosts nodded their heads except for Cyrus, who remembered its appearance, having owned it.

I continued, "We need to check every square inch of this place. Andy is going to assign search teams and locations. Listen to him."

All the spirits agreed.

I told Andy, "They are ready to start searching."

The counselor pulled a notepad from his briefcase and created a chart with the ghost names listed in a column on the left and the room names along the top. He assigned two ghosts per room and held up the chart. The apparitions crowded around, studied the lists, and set off for their designated locations.

I told him, "Okay, they are off searching."

Andy asked, "Can you use your Finding abilities to locate the seal?"

"I don't think so because it is too close to my family, but I'll try again."

I closed my eyes and concentrated on the signet. I turned around in a circle, and no stomach distress manifested.

"Nope, nothing."

The counselor nodded, understanding.

Andy and I waited in the living room for the spirits to finish their search. When someone knocked on the door, I went to open it.

As Doris rushed in, she was already mid-sentence, saying one statement after another and not allowing me to respond.

"I'm so glad you look better than the last time I was here. Where did that white curl come from? It looks good on you. I have to show you and Andy something."

Surprised to see his secretary here, Andy asked, "Why are you here?"

"I need to show you this."

She pulled a massive nine-inch clear crystal from a bag over her shoulder, unwrapped the towel around it, and set it on the end table next to the sofa. She then removed five other smaller crystals, each a different color and shape.

As she arranged the crystals, I asked my attorney, "What is she doing?"

He explained, "Doris is a Crystal Witch. They channel energies between realms. She can use the energy frequencies that crystals focus from the ether and the various Spirit Realms. I never knew this about her. I don't think my father knew it either. She explained it to me after you came back from being drugged by your grandmother."

Surprised by this revelation, we both watched as she carefully arranged the crystals at precise angles. She took the hexagonal gem from around her neck, rubbed it with her thumbs, hummed, and concentrated. The charm in her hand began to glow, and white light shot out and struck the clear crystal in the center of the configuration. From there, the illumination emitted from other facets of the quartz and flashed onto the surrounding five crystals. These crystals then emitted light connecting to the next gem. The most significant facet of the quartz crystal pulsated, and an image appeared projected above the crystalline cluster.

Andy and I stared in amazement.

I said, "That's incredible."

Doris shushed me and said, "Listen."

My grandmother's image appeared. She paced back and forth in a room, wringing her hands. Her expression conveyed her concern.

She shouted, "Jennifer, has Rose called yet?"

Jennifer stuck her head through the doorway, appearing unnerved. "No, Imperatrice."

"Why hasn't she called? What is going on out there? She had better call soon, or I must go out there myself and take over."

The projection faded. The light pulsated three times and went out.

I asked, "Were we actually seeing and hearing my grandmother?"

Looking concerned, Doris said, "Yes. She has been doing this for the last forty-five minutes. We have to keep her from coming out here."

262

# Chapter 47

## Possessed Again

I yelled, "Rose, come here immediately!"

She popped into view and wobbled, seeming to lose her balance.

She said, "Oh my God, you are strong. You pulled me here before I could respond to your call."

I said urgently, "Rose, Doris just showed us that the Voodoo Imperatrice is about to come out here if we don't stop her somehow. Do you have any idea what we can do?"

The priestess replied, "I was supposed to call her and keep her informed, but I never had a chance because I could never stay out for more than fifteen or twenty minutes before either your family found me or you came back out."

"Can you tell her exactly that? You have been stopped but are still searching and will call her as soon as you find the signet."

"Yes, I can do that, but I'll have to do it while inside you or I won't be able to speak over the phone. She will recognize my voice through you. I'll have to go back inside you."

"You mean you will have to possess me again?"

I didn't like the sound of that.

"No, I can just enter you, but you have to allow it and allow me to use your voice to speak. Afterward, I can leave—the same as when the ghosts went inside you and pulled me out."

"Well, that hurt a lot; I thought my insides were being torn out."

I grimaced, remembering the excruciating pain I experienced.

"That's because I was trying to hold on. I won't do that this time."

"Okay, if we must. What do I have to do?"

"Just relax and let me enter and take over."

I nodded. Andy and Doris looked confused, having only heard half the conversation.

Andy asked, "What is going on?"

"Rose will enter me again and call the Voodoo Imperatrice and tell her everything is all right, and she is still searching."

"Oh, is that all," Andy said sarcastically.

I turned to the priestess and said, "Okay, go ahead."

I closed my eyes and relaxed. I jumped when she entered and opened my eyes, still able to see through them. She was inside me, but it wasn't like before. She was at the surface, not deep inside. She walked me over to the telephone and dialed the Voodoo Imperatrice's phone number. Someone answered the phone.

Rose said, using my voice, "Hello, this is Rose. I need to speak with the Voodoo Imperatrice."

My voice sounded more feminine.

"Hold, please."

We waited. Andy and Doris stood behind me. As I held the receiver, I saw the other ghosts begin to appear, eager to ask questions. I raised my hand and halted them. They immediately ceased coming toward me.

My grandmother said over the phone, "Hello, Rose. It is about time you called. Have you found the signet?"

Rose answered, "No, I haven't. The Spirit Speaker is so strong that I can only be out for short periods and the other ghosts keep stopping me. They even locked Orion in his bedroom for a couple of days. I've convinced them that we're better, and they let us out, but I have to be careful, or they will lock us back up. It will take much longer than I thought to find the seal. I've got to go before they catch me on the phone. I'll call when I can."

And she hung up.

She stepped out of me with a pull as she exited. The other ghosts approached with curious expressions.

Rose said, "See, that wasn't too bad, was it?"

I said, "No, I can handle that. Do you think she bought it?"

"I don't know. Let's hope so."

I turned to Doris.

"Can you hook that crystal system back up so we can observe what my grandmother is doing?"

She said, "I'll try, but she may figure out we are watching her."

Doris returned to the crystals on the table, closed her eyes, and concentrated. This time, the light and images emerged more slowly.

My grandmother spoke with one of her followers.

"Rose seems to be having a hard time keeping control of the possession. The Spirit Speaker is too strong for her. I'll give her a few more days, and if nothing happens, then I'll have to go out there and take control."

The Voodoo Imperatrice turned around with a scowl and said, "Who is that?"

Doris broke the link by blocking the light from her crystal with her hand.

"She sensed us. I had to break the link, or else she may have been able to trace us."

I said, "At least we have a few more days to find the seal. I'm sorry I stopped you guys, but I didn't want you distracting Rose while she was making the call. Did anyone find anything?"

They all shook their heads.

Doc asked, "So, you can now allow a possession? And how did you stop us like that?"

"It wasn't a possession. She was just under the surface so that she could speak through me. I don't know exactly how I stopped you; I just knew I could."

I sat on the couch and closed my eyes.

Cyrus asked, "Do you feel okay?"

I said, "All of that made me tired again."

Albert said, "You are still recovering from all the stress that your body has suffered. It would be best if you went back to bed and slept. We can continue to search for the signet."

Not hearing what the Doc said, Andy said, "You should go back to bed and rest."

"That is what the Doc said."

I stood and headed up the stairs.

Andy and Doris left, saying, "Good night."

As he walked out the door, the counselor said, "I'll be back tomorrow."

I returned to my room, undressed, climbed into bed, and fell asleep, but that didn't last long.

# Chapter 48

# The Spirit Realm

I awoke to the Duke's voice, commanding me, "Boy, come with me. I need to show you things."

I found myself back in the dark, chilling place with the wind howling around me. Naked and shivering, I hugged myself tightly while the Duke, unaffected by the cold, stood nearby, his tuxedo jacket undisturbed by the wind.

I asked, "Why is it so cold here?"

"Because this is the cold in between the grave and the other side."

"What is all the sand blowing around? It hurts my eyes."

"You've heard of the sands of time; that is what you feel."

"I don't think I can last long here."

It was difficult getting the words out with my teeth chattering.

"I know; follow me to the Spirit Realm."

As he led me toward a distant light, the Duke moved quickly, taking elongated strides that contrasted with my feeble attempts to keep pace. I jogged to keep up with him. The illuminated orifice grew to ten feet wide. The Lwa Spirit God stepped through. I stopped, looking at the multi-colored undulating orifice, unsure where the Duke had led me. Warmth emanated from the light, and I moved through, needing to escape the grave's cold.

The cold instantly disappeared. I glanced down at myself and found that I was now dressed in a magnificent purple tuxedo jacket with tails adorned with a few lines of shifting symbols and pants but no shirt, hat, or shoes. I also had an erection, making the pants tight across my groin.

The Duke, now towering over me at eight feet tall, smiled with his broad, toothy grin and said, "Welcome to my home, boy."

The Duke's tuxedo displayed strange symbols written in an

unknown language, darker than the coat fabric. The symbols adorned the coat—on the arms, the lapels, and the tails—all in constant motion.

I looked around. A bright, ethereal light illuminated everything. No sun was evident; only a continuous golden glow remained. The landscape consisted of lush, vibrant gardens of plants, none of which looked familiar, but all were incredibly beautiful, and the air's aromas were the most fragrant I had ever smelled. On top of a hill stood the most perfectly formed tree you've ever seen, adorned with flowers and fruit of various kinds hanging from its branches. A silver stream meandered at the base of the hill, following its curve and disappearing behind it.

Orbs of various colors, sizes, and textures floated everywhere. One approached me. Its image continuously shifted, reminding me of a face that could never entirely focus. Was that a giggle it made?

Duke said to the orb, "Leave the boy alone for now. He has a lot to learn first."

The orb zipped off into the distance.

I asked, "What was that? What are all the orbs floating around here?"

"They are the minor Lwa spirits. You'll learn more about them later. First, we must get you fed and refreshed so you can stay here for a while."

I didn't understand what he was talking about, so I followed him. We walked toward the hill with the perfect tree. My bare feet moved through the one-foot-tall, multi-colored grass, and silk ran over my feet and toes. My steps didn't crush the grasses; they sprang back up after I passed by.

He stopped in front of the stream and said, "Drink."

I asked, "What is it? It doesn't look like water."

The silver creek shimmered like water covered in an oil slick, undulating in a rainbow of colors across the surface.

Duke said, "It is the Nectar of the Gods. It will refresh your body completely. Drink."

I knelt and dipped my hands into the beautiful liquid. The fluid in my palms didn't run through my fingers as water would have; instead, it remained a pool. The colors swirled in patterns, as if still part of the stream below, being moved by an unknown force.

I inhaled the delectable aroma of the nectar, and a slight tingle flushed through my body. Staring at the liquid, the urge to imbibe was overpowering, and I slurped it down my throat. I drank another handful; it was the most exhilarating thing I had ever drunk. I went for a third handful, but the Duke stopped me.

"Don't take too much, or you won't be able to leave this realm."

I stood, and a buzzing sensation coursed through me from head to toe, energizing me so much that I felt I could run a marathon effortlessly. I looked up at the Duke with a broad smile.

He said, "Feels good. Doesn't it?"

I enthusiastically nodded my head.

"Let's continue."

Three rocks jutted above the stream surface. He stepped onto the stones with his long legs and easily crossed to the other side. I had to jump to reach each rock to get across.

We ascended the hill and arrived at the base of the tree. The massive trunk was as large as one of those giant sequoias in California, but it wasn't a pine. It resembled a deciduous tree, but the branches stretched at least one hundred yards from the trunk, three times its height. The iridescent leaves swayed without any wind. I touched a leaf, and silk flowed across my fingers; I could feel life pulsing through it.

Both flowers and fruit hung on the tree simultaneously. The flowers and fruits were of various types, displaying different colors, shapes, and sizes. It was the most beautiful sight I had ever witnessed. The aromas wafting from the tree consisted of every fruit I had ever known, along with many unfamiliar scents, so delectable that my mouth began to salivate.

As I admired the tree, several Lwa orbs flitted among the branches, and fruits vanished upon contact. Other entities moved within the tree's branches. Like twinkling lights, tiny orbs zipped around, accompanied by creatures six inches high with gossamer wings and glowing, almost human-like bodies that flew between the branches.

I asked, "What are those tiny lights and the creatures with wings?"

"Those are pixies and the lower fairies from over there."

He pointed to the right to a green glow on the horizon.

While studying the green shimmer, he whispered, "I wonder where she is right now?"

I asked, "Who is?"

He came out of his reverie, attempting to deflect my attention.

He said, "Over there is the Angel Realm."

He pointed to the side of the tree opposite from where we stood. I peered around the trunk, and a golden glow shone on the horizon in the distance.

When he said Angel Realm, it shocked me.

"Do ... do you mean heaven?"

As if discussing angels was of minor importance and a common everyday thing, he said, "No, no; it's where they hang out until Bondee, or Yahweh as they call him/her, orders them to do something."

Pointing to other locations on the horizon, he said, "Over there is Asgard, and over there the Gens congregate. Many realms are here."

"Can I go to these other realms?"

"Not until you are invited by one of the higher orders that live in those realms."

I returned to staring in awe at the tree with my mouth hanging open. Laughing, the Duke pulled a fruit off the tree and stuck it in my mouth. The second the unusual-looking item touched my tongue, I tasted the most delicious thing I had ever had, even better than the nectar I had just drunk. I bit down and chewed the flesh of the fruit with my eyes closed in ecstasy and swallowed. My body flushed, and my erection throbbed, wanting to escape the pants. Close to having an orgasm, I opened my jaw to take a second bite, but the Duke pulled the bitten fruit away from me and gobbled it down in two bites.

He said, "One bite is all you can have."

I asked, "What is this tree?"

"It is the Tree of Life. All life stems from this tree."

I knew my body had changed from eating the small piece of spirit fruit. I glanced at my chest, and my form, which had been thin and weak from the possession, was now in the best shape it had ever been, showcasing muscle definition and considerable enhancement. I ran my hand over my chest; the muscles were real, not an illusion. My perpetual aches and pains since the possession had dissipated.

Duke said, "Follow me."

I could now keep pace with the God as we moved down the hill and across the stream toward an area that existed in perpetual twilight, illuminated by a glowing bonfire.

As we approached, I noticed many unusual spirit entities sitting around—some engaged in conversation while others lounged casually on comfortable-looking couches and pillows. Each entity was of a different type: some appeared mostly human, like the Duke; some were part human and part animal, while others were just odd.

Duke said, "These are the Lwa Spirit Gods."

Several turned and scrutinized me in minute detail. They scanned me inside and out. Their scans crawled over my body like snakes and insects scurrying everywhere. I inhaled, shivering. Some didn't seem interested and paid no mind to me.

Duke Shamedi yelled, "Enough!" and the scans stopped.

I exhaled, almost collapsing.

He continued, "This is my boy. None of you can touch him. He works for me."

One of the gods, who appeared partially human with a human head and hands, but the rest of him animal-like—an animal I couldn't identify—said, "Are you sure about this? Giving a sacrosanct anointment to a human hasn't happened for over two thousand years, and you know what resulted from that."

The Duke said, "Legba, that was a different time and circumstances. We were following what the Bondee instructed us to do then. This boy works only for me. Too many human souls are not passing over; many things in the world hold them there. Someone must be of the living world to find these lost souls and correct the reasons they haven't passed on. Orion is the beginning of a lineage of Lwa Spirit Speakers."

Legba said, "But you already tried this once."

The Duke said, "I made a mistake and have learned from it."

Another God with a dog-like head said, "Okay, but I think this will lead to other problems. Uncertain images are forming in the distance."

"I will deal with them when the time comes."

Duke turned to me, saying, "Boy, come, stand next to me and look into the sacred flames."

I did as he said, not understanding most of what was discussed between the Gods. I peered into the flames. It was not an ordinary fire, with white, red, orange, and yellow colors in the conflagration, but rather many different colors floating and swirling together, and no heat emanated from them. Images appeared and focused on the flames.

The Duke said, "Here is how you were conceived."

I said, "I don't want to see this," not wanting to observe my mother having sex with my father.

The image appeared, and I was in the room as it happened.

My mother and father shared a joint on an old, dirty couch in a dilapidated room. They kissed, and it was evident that they had incredible passion for each other. I could feel the love between them. My father took my mother's hand and led her to the bedroom. They continued to kiss and fondle one another. They removed their clothes.

My father peered into my mother's eyes and passionately said, "I love you. I've never loved anyone as much as you."

Tears ran from my mother's eyes, and she said, "I love you too. I have never had anyone say this to me, and I have never felt this way about anyone before."

They kissed intensely and hugged, never wanting to let go.

My father said, "I need to wash up first."

He went into the bathroom and washed himself. While in the bathroom, the Duke possessed his body. My father shook and his eyes fluttered at the top of his head. When my father exited the bathroom, the Spirit God was in control. He proceeded to make love to my mother, giving her an incredible orgasm. The Duke allowed my father to experience the lovemaking, not realizing that the Duke was in control.

Duke Shamedi said, "That was when you were conceived. I sensed that your mother was at her most fertile point and it had to happen then. Antoine conceived your body, but I conceived your Lwa Spirit Speaker abilities. As I told you at the ceremony your grandmother put you through, I am your *God* Father."

I turned away from him, thinking about what I had been shown. My emotions were on the edge, ready to burst out. Could this be the fruit and liquid I ate and drank? Usually, I could keep my feelings in check, but something was happening, and my anger erupted like lava, forcing its way to the surface. Driven by resentment toward my tumultuous past, I lashed out at the Duke.

I faced him and scornfully said, "So, you are the reason for all the weird things I can do, why I never can make friends, because people always sense there is something different about me. My grandmother put my mother through hell, and she turned to drugs to escape it, and because of that, she was never around for me. Now I find out that it is you who put me the rest of the way through hell, not allowing any other living person to want to be near me. I would be alone if it weren't for my ghost family."

My anger and rage surged to the surface in futile fury. I picked up a log from a pile beside the fire, swung it around, and struck him with it. The log shattered against his arm, yet he stood unfazed and calmly stared down at me. I swung a fist at his stomach, and it felt like hitting a brick wall. The bones in my hand broke, and I screamed in pain. My hand healed in seconds.

I dropped to my knees, beat the ground, and yelled, "God damn you!"

I bent my head to the ground and screamed, angry that I could do nothing to him or about the situation. After a few minutes, I calmed down, leered up at him, and said, "I hate you," with intensity.

He said, "That's been said before. Are you done with your childish temper tantrum?"

"I guess so," I said, still feeling angry at him for my fucked-up life.

One of the Gods said, "My, he has a temper, doesn't he? It's a good thing he was on this side when it happened. He would have destroyed many things on the living side."

The Duke said, "Come boy, I must teach you how to use your powers properly. We don't have much time left."

As we progressed, I followed him to an outcrop of boulders, wishing I could shoot laser beams of hatred at his back from my eyes. He pointed to the ground and I sat.

He said, "I know you have figured out how to use some of the abilities I gave you, but you need to learn the rest and how to control them better. Since we don't have much time left, I'm going to do this the 'quick and dirty' way, as you humans say."

He scooted around to face me. We sat cross-legged and looked at each other. He placed his hands on either side of my head and gazed into my eyes. Cold icicles pierced the inside of my brain, and I shuddered as I inhaled. Images flashed in my mind at incredible speed. He released my head, and I thought it would freeze solid from the intense cold that burned and swirled. I raised my hands to my head and screamed. Everything went black.

The Lwa God the Duke called Legba recognized the scream and said, "I guess he anointed him the quick way."

The Duke picked up my limp body and flung me over his shoulder. Somehow I knew this was happening without being conscious.

He headed for the human world portal and said, "You're right, boy. Your life has been hard and will continue to be difficult, but I will make it up to you. You won't be alone forever."

He stepped through the portal and transported my soul back to my body.

# Chapter 49

# Returning From the Spirit Realm

It was late morning, and Orion hadn't gotten out of bed yet. Doc Albert decided to wake him. He entered the bedroom and could tell that something was off.

The young man lay on his left side, his eyes open and staring. Albert shook him but received no response. He moved the young man onto his back and he continued to stare at the ceiling.

Doc called his name, "Orion, Orion! Wake up!"

No response.

Albert called Rose, hoping she would understand what was happening to him.

"Rose, please come to Orion's room. There is something wrong."

She materialized in the room, looked at Orion, and said, "The Duke must have his soul. He's in a trance."

She pushed the sheet aside and recognized his erection.

"He has a continuous erection, one of the signs in men."

Doc asked, "What can we do?"

"Nothing until he returns. He may be in pain and will want to have sex. His erection won't stop until that is completed."

"We can have the girls take care of that for him."

Cyrus stepped in and overheard the conversation about Orion.

"He may not be happy about that. He was pretty upset when I asked the girls to do that for him the other day."

Rose said, "I don't think he will complain too much when he returns. The urge will be intense. I've seen possessed men return ready to rape the first woman they can get their hands on."

The day passed as the young man lay in a trance-like state. His soul was ensnared in the Spirit Realm. Concerned for his well-being, the ghosts anxiously awaited his return.

Rose said, "I have never seen a soul possession trance last this long. I hope he is okay."

In the early morning, Orion's soul reunited with his body, with flashes of light transforming it into a vessel of strength and power. Despite the pain he felt, he was reborn and ready to embrace his destiny as a Lwa Spirit Speaker.

I awoke in agony, screaming, my head pounding. The ghosts crowded around the bed.

I moaned, "Oh, my head."

Doc gave me two pain pills and a glass of water. I swallowed them and gulped down the water. I lay with my eyes closed and rubbed my erection.

"God, I want to fuck something."

Rose glanced at the Doc with a 'I told you,' so look.

Doc pointed to the girls and the others all left the room.

Milly raised her skirt and crawled onto the bed. I opened my eyes and knew what she was going to do. I urgently wanted it—no, I needed it. I rose to my knees, grabbed her by the waist, pushed her down on her hands and knees, and forcefully inserted myself. I pumped hard, wanting it so badly. I yelled out and shuddered; the sensation was incredible.

Milly asked, "Should we continue?"

I vigorously nodded my head, ready for more. I pulled Milly around and pushed her onto the bed on her back. I mounted her fast and hard. Her head was banging on the headboard. It was a good thing she was dead or I might have severely injured her. I moaned and cried out loudly; the sensations were incredibly intense. I was in such a state of arousal that everything seemed more extreme.

Still erect, my penis was ready to continue. I rolled over onto my back, breathing hard, and the girls traded places. Philly began performing oral sex—God, that girl could suck. I grabbed Philly's head and pushed her further down onto my cock. It took longer this time to climax, but I was still ready for more afterward. Philly continued with the blow, and it felt amazing.

After I came the fourth time, my dick went limp. I knew it could be restimulated, but four orgasms were more than enough, and I had calmed down. The immediate and aggressive need for these actions had been quenched.

I told the girls, "Thank you again for doing that for me," embarrassed by what had just happened.

Both maids said in unison, "Any time, Mr. Orion," giggling.

They left the bed, and the other ghosts returned to my bedroom.

Doc asked, "How do you feel?"

"Better now, but super tired."

Rose asked, "Did the Duke take you and teach you how to use your powers?"

"Yes, kind of. It wasn't so much taught, but more like he injected the knowledge. It was a painful process. But what I saw in the Spirit Realm was spectacular. I'll tell you all about it later. I can barely keep my eyes open."

I scooted under the sheets and fell asleep.

# Chapter 50

# New Abilities

While I slept, my mother visited me in a dream. She ran her fingers through my hair and gently touched my head.

Seeing the white curl, she whispered, "I'm so sorry you went through all that trauma with the possession. But you got through it—just as I knew you would. I'm proud of you, baby. There's still more to learn about your father. Find his grave. You'll get the answers you need to fight the Voodoo Imperatrice." She stopped stroking my hair and said, "Goodbye, baby."

I reached for her, crying, "Mama, don't go. Please stay."

"I can't, baby, but I'll see you later," she said before fading away.

Upon waking, I was surprisingly rejuvenated despite the emotional weight of my dream visitation from my mother. My body felt renewed and my strength was amplified. I hopped out of bed and headed for the bathroom. I showered, shaved, and brushed my teeth. A glance in the mirror revealed the absence of the scar from the car accident—a testament to the transformative power of the spirit fruit.

As I descended to the kitchen, I found that Bertha had prepared a hearty breakfast, which was a comforting gesture that eased the ache of my mother's departure.

I said, "I'm so glad you made me a full breakfast. I'm starving."

Bertha said, "Rose told me you would be hungry when you woke, so I made a full meal."

I asked for coffee, and she prepared a pot.

While it percolated, I stepped onto the back porch and began my workout. I effortlessly lifted the heaviest weights I owned. My punches into the bag were sharper and more powerful than ever. Each hit released tension, anger, and especially the resentment I still felt toward the Duke.

My energy level was sky-high, and I worked up a sweat. When Bertha arrived with the coffee, I calmed down and sat in the wicker chair.

The ghosts gathered around, eager to hear what had happened to me. I told them everything, struggling to describe the magnificence of the Spirit Realm. They all listened in awe. Rose was the only one who seemed concerned.

As the ghosts listened to my experiences in the Spirit Realm, I wondered where the Lwa were that should be associated with each ghost's curse. I had learned that every curse and spell has at least one Lwa associated with it, and complex curses or spells may have a small regiment of Lwa with various powers and abilities. The Spirit Gods can assign them to these duties, or the Lwa can choose to accept tasks requested by a human.

Where is the Lwa for the curse on the L'Enfant Haven plantation?

I noticed a concerned expression on Rose. I asked, "Rose, what's wrong?"

"It's what the Gods said. The comment about the anointed one two thousand years ago, and doing as instructed by Bondee. I think they were referring to Jesus."

"Oh, come on. That can't be right."

"Maybe so."

I didn't believe this and asked her a question.

"Rose, from what I saw in the sacred fire, my father loved my mother and never wanted to leave her. My grandmother forced him to leave. Do you know anything about this?"

She said, "I wasn't with the Voodoo Imperatrice when she visited her son. I don't know what she did to him. I do remember that she was angry when she found out he had committed suicide. She had some plan for him to meet you."

"Do you know where he's buried?"

"Yes, she had him buried in the Holt Cemetery under the name Antoine Turner, his father's last name."

"I need to go to his grave. Mother visited me in a dream last night and told me I must find my father's grave, where I would find information to help me fight my grandmother."

"Are you sure you should go back to New Orleans? Your grandmother still wants to get her hands on you."

"With what I understand now, I think I can take care of myself. I have to go to my father's grave and find the information my mother told me to find."

I went to the garage. Walter had moved the New Yorker to the carriage house after the goons left it out front. He had a piece of plastic tarp duct-taped over the broken window, and all the fractured glass shards were removed from the inside. I hopped into the driver's seat and turned the key, but the engine wouldn't start.

Walter said, "It's out of gas, and I don't have any more here."

"Damn!"

I went into the house and called Andy.

"Hi, Andy. Would you be willing to come by with a can of gas for the New Yorker and a couple of hundred dollars in cash?"

"What do you need that for? And how are you doing?"

He sounded concerned.

"I'm doing great since I returned from the Spirit Realm, but I must go to my father's grave. Something is there I need to see."

"What are you talking about? The Spirit Realm? What do you mean you have to go to your father's grave?"

"Andy, just get over here with the gas and the money, and I'll explain everything."

Half an hour later, Andy and Doris walked in the door.

Andy said, "I left the gas can on the porch. I didn't want to bring it in and smell the place up."

I said, "That's okay; I'll have Walter take it to the garage."

I looked to the side and mentally told Walter, 'The gas is in the can on the porch.'

"Okay, he's taking care of it," I said.

My attorney asked, "So, you can talk to them now without having to be near?"

"Yes, and many other things. Come here. I want to give you a gift."

Andy walked over with a curious expression.

I told him, "Close your eyes."

He followed the instructions and I took his hands in mine. I lowered my head, closed my eyes, and focused on opening Andy's Spirit Sight, whispering the incantation. I released his hands and hovered my palms over his eyes and ears for a few seconds.

"Okay, now open your eyes and look around."

He glanced around and his jaw dropped. He could now see, hear, and feel all the ghosts in the house.

I said, "This is my family. Please introduce yourselves to Andy while I open Doris's Spirit Sight."

Each ghost approached Andy, shook his hand, and told him their name. He was all smiles, happy to meet them after fifty years of hearing about them.

I repeated the ritual on Doris and she was thrilled to meet all the ghosts.

Andy asked, "Will I be able to see all ghosts everywhere I go?"

"No, I only opened your and Doris's Spirit Sight for the ghosts directly associated with me."

"Okay, that's good. I don't think I want to see ghosts everywhere."

I smiled at this statement, half wishing it was the same for me.

Doris told Rose, "I would like to sit down with you one day to discuss the differences between the voodoo and Crystal Witch practices."

Rose smiled and said, "I would enjoy a conversation on that subject."

I stared at the Lwa next to Andy's shoulder, and the attorney noticed me looking at him.

"Why are you staring at me like that?"

"I'm not staring at you, but at your Lwa."

"My what?"

I explained, "Each spell has a Lwa or power spirit from the Spirit Realm that controls the spell. The blue Lwa at your shoulder controls the protection spell you have."

I extended my hand and performed the finger movements to summon it. It floated over and landed on my palm. My fingertips tingled from the energy it radiated.

I commanded it, "You had better protect my friend well, or else there will be hell to pay. You tell the others who are protecting his family the same thing."

In a respectful tone that only I could discern, it said, 'Yes, Small Duke.' I laughed at being called 'Small Duke' and released it. It returned to Andy's shoulder.

Andy looked puzzled.

"What were you laughing at? And how can you speak to these things?"

"It called me 'Small Duke.' I must find my human father's grave; important information on how to fight the Voodoo Imperatrice is there. The ghosts can tell you what happened to me while I was in the Spirit Realm with the Duke and other Gods. I explained it all to them."

"Human father? Do you have a non-human father as well?"

"Yes, I do. They'll explain it. I've got to go."

As I left out the front door, Andy said, "Why am I not surprised?"

# Chapter 51

# Visiting My Father's Grave

The New Yorker idled at the front gate, warmed up and ready. I jumped in, turned it around, and floored the gas pedal, heading straight for Marti's to fill the tank.

Once full, an urgent, restless energy urged me to reach my father's grave—fast. But speeding meant risking being stopped. I summoned a few Lwa and instructed them to distract any police officers along the way.

In unison, they replied, 'As you command, Small Duke,' and vanished.

Without worrying about getting stopped for speeding, I barreled down the highway at 95 mph. The Lwa would create distractions for the police, such as knocking over a thermos of coffee or a can of soda, causing the officer to drop their keys, pencils, or notepads—just small, ordinary things. I would be long gone when they came up from retrieving the dropped item or cleaning up the mess.

I still had to stop for gas twice on the way. While waiting for the tank to fill at the last gas station, I pulled the New Orleans map from the glove compartment and ran my hand over it, concentrating on Holt Cemetery. I located it and determined the fastest route to get there.

A closed sign was on the gate when I pulled up to the cemetery. I exited the New Yorker, walked to the gate, and rang the bell hanging from a post. I waited and rang it again. A grizzled old man with mostly gray hair and several missing teeth meandered to the entrance.

"It's closed. Can't you read, boy?" he said in a strong Southern drawl.

"I know what the sign says, but I've got to get in."

"What for?"

"Personal business. I need to visit my father's grave."

"Come back tomorrow."

I took my wallet from my back pocket and pulled out three twenty-dollar bills. I passed them through the gate's poles and said, "Can't you help a fella out and let me see my father's grave?"

The old man grabbed the bills and unlocked the gate. I hurried through.

I said, "Thank you."

"You had better not be vandalizing any graves or I'll call the cops. I'll be in the guard shack when you want to leave," he said warningly, pointing to an old wooden structure at the end of a path.

I nodded and said, "Thanks."

Not knowing where Antoine's resting place was, I put out my Finding Senses for Antoine Turner and hoped they would work now that I had my full power.

Yep, they worked. My stomach became queasy.

I moved down the concrete walkway. Mausoleums and large marble gravestones with ornate carvings lined both sides, positioned closely together. The nausea subsided, indicating I was no longer heading in the right direction. I turned in a circle, the nausea returned, and I continued down another walkway.

A few ghosts wandered among the graves, always stopping and staring at me as I passed, sensing that I was different and possessed spirit power.

I made two additional course corrections, and the stomach ache intensified. I walked along a flagstone path to a remote corner of the cemetery, and the nausea increased. I found the stone with Antoine Turner engraved on it. I touched it, and the nausea disappeared.

I stared at the stone but couldn't identify anything unusual, only his name and dates. A spirit was nearby; I could sense him.

I said, "Show yourself."

The ghost stood behind my father's gravestone. I didn't recognize him.

I asked, "Who are you?"

"I'm Webster Turner."

"Oh, you are the ghost that always followed my father. You are his father."

I hesitated momentarily, realizing ....

"And my grandfather."

"Yes, Orion. I am."

"How do you know who I am?"

"Your father watched you for years, so I was always present."

"What do you mean my father watched me?"

"Sit down and I'll tell you everything that happened to your father."

I sat on the stone bench beside the path to listen to my grandfather.

Seated on a weathered bench, I listened intently as my grandfather recounted the untold truths of my father's past, unraveling the tangled threads of my lineage. With each revelation, I felt propelled forward by an unyielding determination to unearth the secrets buried in the shadows of the past.

Webster didn't even know he had a son until the day he died—ravaged by cancer, writhing in pain for months. But instead of stepping toward the tunnel of light, something yanked him away—across town to a small, crumbling house in a working-class neighborhood.

Webster watched the boy sleeping in bed; he could only stand by and observe him. Antoine woke up, and the ghost terrified the boy. He became frightened and called out for someone named Josephine. A woman rushed into the room and wrapped her arm around the boy's shoulder.

"Antoine, what is wrong?"

"That white man—he's just staring at me! Who is he?"

Josephine scanned the room but saw nothing.

She said, "It is okay. I will tell your mother."

Antoine pulled the blanket over his head and shivered, fearful of emerging.

Renee Broussard entered the bedroom and immediately noticed Webster.

She said, "Ah, so you have died, Webster Turner. I have cursed you never to be able to have peace and go to the other side. You killed my mother Angelique and raped me, producing Antoine."

She indicated the shivering figure beneath the blankets.

"You are cursed to watch what you produced from your actions forever and never have peace."

The ghost attempted to communicate with her, but she couldn't hear him. The voodoo priestess approached the bed and removed the blankets from over her son.

She sat on the edge of the bed, put her arm around Antoine's shoulder, and said, "This is your father; he will follow you and be next to you for the rest of your life. This is his curse, never to have peace. He can do nothing. Do not be afraid of him; ignore him."

"But Renee, I don't want a white man watching me all the time. Make him go away, please."

"I cannot do that. You will get used to it as time goes by. Now, go to sleep."

She left the room and turned off the light. The boy cowered under the covers throughout the night.

Denied peace and tethered to his son, Webster grappled with the anguish of terrifying Antoine, maintaining a cautious distance to alleviate the boy's fears. Bound by the curse, Webster was never more than fifteen feet away—no matter how much he wished to grant his son peace.

Webster's presence upset and distracted the boy so much that he couldn't concentrate, causing his school grades to plummet. He continuously peered over his shoulder. The other kids at school called him "Fraidy Cat," believing he was always afraid of someone coming up behind him, which was true—he was always scared the ghost would be close to him.

He begged his mother, "Please make the white man go away. I don't like him always there."

She shouted at him, "I told you he must stay there as punishment! Stop bothering me about this."

He continued to beg her, "Please, Renee. Please make him go away."

She wouldn't allow him to call her mother, or mommy or mama, anything that reminded her that he was her son and how he had been conceived.

"I told you to stop bothering me. Now, you will be punished along with him."

She seized his arm, thrust him into a closet, and secured the door lock.

Antoine screamed and beat on the door. Even though he couldn't see the ghost in the dark, he knew it was very close, which terrified him even more.

"Let me out! Let me out! I won't ask again to make him go away."

This went on for an hour, and finally he quieted and cowered in the corner with his knees pulled up to his chest and his arms wrapped around them.

He cried, thinking, 'I hate her. I hate her so much.' He glanced at the opposite corner where the ghost stood and thought, 'And I hate you too.'

After a few hours, Renee told Josephine to let him out of the closet. She unlocked the door, and the boy jumped up and ran across the room with a terrified expression. Josephine went to the boy and hugged him. He cried into her dress. That night the Voodoo Imperatrice's follower took him to her home and he stayed there until he was sixteen and ran away.

Whenever Renee needed him to spy on a spirit, she summoned him without warning—her pawn, her instrument. At thirteen, she called for him to come to her home. Marcella drove over, picked him up, and took him to the house.

During the drive, he asked Marcella, "What does she need me for? To see another ghost?"

"No, I don't think so. I'm not sure why she wants you."

After they arrived, he was instructed to remain in the bedroom until the White man departed. He stood in the room and listened to the conversation between Renee and Marcella.

Renee asked, "What time did you tell him to be here?"

"8 a.m."

"This is Josette's adopted son? She produced powerful protective spells. I could never break her spells, and I'm sure—What's his name?"

"Andrew Butler."

"I'm sure Andrew will have one on him."

"Yes, he does."

"I wanted you here because you were close friends with Josette and him. He will feel more comfortable with you here."

Marcella nodded her head.

The white man came but wasn't there for long. When he left, Antoine exited the bedroom and asked his mother.

"Why did you want me here when that man came for a reading?"

"He will take us someplace important. You will meet a person who will be special to you."

A few days later, Marcella and his mother drove to Josephine's house. Marcella approached the house and knocked on the door. Josephine answered.

Marcella said, "The Voodoo Imperatrice wants to speak with her son."

"Okay, I'll get him."

Antoine walked out to the vehicle and the Voodoo Imperatrice lowered the car's window.

"I need you to come with us. Get in the car."

He knew he shouldn't ask, but he did anyway, "Why do I have to come?"

"You don't need to ask questions. Just get in."

She spoke with a furrowed brow, angry that he dared to ask her a direct question. The scowl on her face and the drooping stare of her left eye scared him, prompting him to open the door and climb into the back seat. Marcella drove the Ford and sped off toward the L'Enfant Haven plantation. The ghost sat in the back seat next to his son. Antoine scooted as far away from the spirit as possible, pressing his body against the opposite door.

From the passenger seat, the Voodoo Imperatrice turned to look at her son, who stared out the window. She glanced at the ghost with a scornful smile. She didn't turn to view them for the entire five-hour trip to the plantation in the middle of nowhere.

Antoine and the ghost followed his mother into the mansion. When the beautiful blonde girl, Marie Labauve, came down the stairs, she resembled an angel. He joyfully followed her out to the yard. They conversed while in the yard and back in the house. He appreciated her company.

Two weeks later, they returned to the plantation with the entire ceremonial entourage and performed a moon ritual. Marie descended the stairs again while the teen waited outside in the hall, eager to observe the ceremony.

He told her, "You shouldn't do that."

But she insisted and paid the price. She screamed upon seeing the blood on her pajama bottoms.

At sixteen, Antoine ran away from Josephine's and lived in a drug flophouse. He discovered that he didn't see ghosts while using drugs, and after that, he tried to be high most of the time. Despite the drugs, the ghost of his father was always near Antoine.

One day, Marie Labauve walked into the flophouse where he lived. They were instantly attracted to each other and fell in love. Webster was present when the Duke possessed Antoine and made love to Marie. Something remarkable happened then, but he wasn't sure what it was. The girl became pregnant, and both Antoine and Marie reduced their drug use.

One day, a blue Ford pulled up beside Antoine as he walked to his new job, and a big guy yelled, "Get in the car! The Voodoo Imperatrice wants to see you."

"I can't; I have to go to work," he said and kept walking.

The guy got out of the vehicle and grabbed him. Antoine struggled, but the goon was too strong, throwing him into the back seat. The car screeched down the street as they drove to his mother's house.

They forced him into the house and to the back divining room, pushing him onto a hard wooden chair and holding him in place. The two men restraining him pressed down on his shoulders.

His mother sat in a chair at the other side of the table and leaned toward him.

She said, "Marie is pregnant with your son. The child will be exceptional."

Shocked that his mother was aware of Marie's pregnancy, he struggled to leave, but the enormous henchmen prevented him from doing so.

She continued, "You have to leave her and never return. I have somewhere else you can go."

"No, I don't want to leave her. I want to stay with her always."

Defiance glared in his eyes.

"If you don't leave her, I will make her life hell. You know I can do it. Don't return to Marie. She and your child will be cared for, but you can't be with them."

"But why must I leave her?" he shouted.

He asked a question. You don't ask the Voodoo Imperatrice a question. One of the big guys punched Antoine in the face, knocking him out of the chair. They picked him up and placed him back in the chair. Blood dripped down his chin from the cut lip.

He yelled, "You can beat me all you want, but don't hurt Marie or my baby!"

"I promise I won't, as long as you leave her now and never come back."

He nodded, looking down at the floor, again having no choice in his life.

They took him away and dropped him off at a flophouse in New Orleans with cash in his pocket. In an attempt to avoid thinking about the woman he loved and the child, he used drugs for weeks. Webster feared that Antoine might kill himself.

While at the drug dealer's, Antoine learned that Marie was inquiring about him. He instructed the dealer to never disclose his address and that he would pay him extra for this service. The dealer agreed.

Antoine's mother sent him cash each month, and he paid people to keep him informed about what Marie, and, after several months, his son were doing. Then word reached him that Marie and the boy had moved back to the plantation in Madreville. The aunt she hated had died, and she had inherited the estate. He remembered Renee's words, 'They would be provided for.'

He wanted to keep tabs on them, but he had no contacts in that area. He moved to Madreville and worked at Jordan's Grocery store, stocking shelves and making deliveries. He delivered groceries to the plantation once a week and hid behind the trees across the driveway when the yard ghost wasn't looking, hoping to catch a glimpse of Marie and the boy. He never saw Marie, but a few times the door opened and he saw Orion standing nearby as the ghosts took the groceries in.

The first time he viewed his son with his mop of black curls, he cried. The boy was excited that the food had been delivered and looked for the small bag of candy that was always left in the box for him. It was evident that the boy could see and speak with ghosts. Orion had more extraordinary abilities than either he or Marie. That must be why the Voodoo Imperatrice was interested in him.

Antoine, now named Anthony Turner, worked at the store until Orion turned six and began school. He got a job as a day janitor at the school, which allowed him to keep an eye on Orion during school days. All the kids sensed that his son was unusual; he did not want to play or associate with them. They would call him names, and he often got into fights. However, he was proud that the boy did well in his classes and received good grades. He would check through the files after everyone left and read how exceptional his son was in his classes.

At eleven, Orion gained a ghost friend to accompany him to school. They would talk, leading him into even more trouble. A group of toughs had it out for Orion and always chased him.

One day while mopping the hall floor, Orion came running down the corridor at full speed and passed him in a flash. Antoine could hear the rapid footfalls of the gang approaching quickly behind him. As they neared the corner, he kicked the bucket of water on the floor ahead of them. They all slipped and fell, sliding across the surface and crashing into the wall at the end of the hallway. The boys yelled at him and he apologized. Antoine smiled as they got up to chase after Orion, knowing he'd helped his son escape the gang.

Antoine continued working as a janitor at the school while Orion secured a job as a mechanic. He secretly watched his son every day as he walked home from work and learned about Marie overdosing and dying one day while talking with Marti Graceland. That night, he cried all evening in his rented room for the only woman he had ever loved.

Webster was always around over the years, and Antoine learned to ignore him. However, he would occasionally speak to him in his room during the evenings.

Then his mother's goons showed up and again forced him into a car, driving him to the Minute Motel near his mother's house. Forced into one of the rooms, he found her sitting at the table when he entered.

His mother asked, "How are you, Antoine?"

He defiantly said, "You know exactly how I am."

"You're right. I do. How is your boy? I know you watch him all the time."

"He is good, perfect."

"Yes, I know. I want you to meet your son and tell him who you are and how you have been watching him all these years, afraid to say anything to him."

"Why would I do that?"

One of the thugs scowled at him, prepared to punch him, but the Imperatrice raised her hand.

"He has something I want; I need you to find it. By becoming friends with him, you will have access to the plantation and can search for the Labauve signet."

"It must be something you want. You care nothing about how Orion or I feel."

"You are wrong. I do care about Orion."

"I don't believe that. If I do this, what is in it for me?"

"You will be able to meet your son up front and never have to work again."

"Let me think about it. Can I tell you tomorrow?"

"Okay. I'll be back tomorrow." She scowled at her guards and said, "Let's go."

Antoine understood that his mother desperately wanted the Labauve signet; otherwise, she would never allow him to meet his son. She also seemed interested in Orion, probably because he could see and speak to ghosts. He didn't think she would harm him, as she wanted him intact to use his abilities somehow. There was a connection between Orion and this seal. If he could keep her from getting her hands on it, it would buy his son some time before she got her clutches on him. Only one option remained available.

Antoine called the drug dealer he worked with in New Orleans and ordered a pizza with very specific toppings, which served as a code for a drug delivery hidden in the pizza box. His mother's guards would be watching out front but might not notice anything unusual about a pizza delivery.

The box came and he paid with the cash in his pocket. He had just cashed his paycheck before the goons picked him up. He opened the box. They were in a baggy under the cheese layer. The twenty pills delivered were enough that he wouldn't sense pain when he made the cuts.

After filling the bathtub with warm water, he took the pocketknife from his pants pocket and set it on the tub's edge. With a glass of water, he swallowed all the capsules, tasting the bitterness of drug residue on the outside of the encasements. He stepped into the tub and immersed himself in the warm water.

As he lay waiting for the drug to take effect, he thought about his son and all the times he had watched his beautiful boy. He loved his son, even though he had never interacted with him. He often daydreamed about playing with his young son, never having had the chance to experience this joy.

The pills were taking effect, and a light-headedness, a distant feeling of the world, came over him.

He picked up the knife and said, "I do this for you, Orion, to save you from her, at least for a while."

And he made a deep slice across his left wrist almost to the bone and felt no pain. He took the knife with the hand with the severed wrist and attempted to make a slice to his right wrist, but the severed tendons prevented him from holding the blade properly. He could only make shallow surface cuts on his right wrist. Unable to make deeper cuts, he dropped the knife into the water. The blood ran out of his left arm, turning the water red. The warm water allowed the wound to continue to bleed with no clotting.

Antoine smiled as he lay in the tub, awaiting the end—a final act of sacrifice to shield his son from Renee's clutches. He closed his eyes, and the tunnel of light appeared; Marie's golden hair glowed in the light. She held her arms out and beckoned him to the other side. At last, he found peace and escape from his mother.

Webster stayed with his son's body and watched as Antoine moved down the tunnel. He tried to follow his son, but something held him back. The next morning, the Voodoo Imperatrice arrived and discovered her son's body in the bathtub. Furious, she threw items around the room. Webster stood and smiled. She noticed his snide look and became even angrier. She left with the guards.

# Chapter 52

## Betrayal

As I listened to the tragic account of my father's life, a profound sense of loss washed over me. I finally understood the depth of his sacrifice and the love he had silently given me all those years.

I remembered Anthony, the janitor at school, a quiet Black man with a beard. He had always been around Madreville for as long as I could remember. Now, realizing that he was my father and had committed suicide to protect me from my grandmother, I sat on the bench with tears running down my cheeks. It began to sprinkle rain while I sat crying for a father I had never met, and now I understood why my mother loved him.

All these years, I resented my father for leaving my mother. When she told me she found out he left her because of my grandmother, I didn't feel quite as bad toward him for never being around for me. But now, knowing the whole story, I feel guilty and selfish for never considering what he must have been going through. This information cemented my resolve to confront my grandmother and put an end to her incessant manipulations.

I sniffled and said, "I guess this was the information my mother wanted me to find out. But how can this help me fight the Voodoo Imperatrice?"

I sat thinking about all of this and asked, "Why did the Voodoo Imperatrice hate you so much and curse you?

Webster stared at the ground and explained, "I was a greedy, selfish man. All I cared about was money. I got involved with voodoo, thinking it would help close a major deal. When it failed, I lost millions. I was furious and drank too much. I went to Angelique's house and kicked in the door, demanding that she fix everything. She said she couldn't do it, so I started beating her. I went off the deep end and kept beating her. Her daughter, Renee, tried to stop me. This enraged me, and I beat and raped her. I left, and the next day I expected the police to show up and arrest me for assault and rape, but they never appeared. I read in the newspaper about Angelique dying and again expected the police to walk in and arrest me for murder, but nothing happened.

"After several years, I contracted cancer. I know now that it was Renee who cursed me with that, and then, after I died and found that I couldn't go to the other side, I understood that this was also a curse and the consequences of my stupid actions. I wish I could go back and change everything."

I said, "Well, that explains why my grandmother hated Antoine and me, her grandson. We remind her of all the horrible things you did to her and her mother."

"You're right. I'm the cause of it all."

We both sat on the stone bench, staring at the ground, leaning forward with our elbows on our knees, and wringing our hands. Like teardrops falling from the sky, the rain fell on our heads—or at least my head—as we sat contemplating our traumatic lives.

Webster asked, "Did you ever find the Labauve signet she wants?"

"No, we never have. We have searched every square inch of the mansion."

"I used to collect family seals. It was a hobby of mine. Of course, it was a selfish hobby; some of these signets had expensive jewels and were worth a lot. Many families would remove the jewels and place them in other jewelry: necklaces, pendants, etc."

"Amulets?" I asked, wide-eyed, the jewel with a carved symbol on Cyrus' amulet flashing in my mind.

"Yeah, sure. Amulets."

"Oh my God," I whispered. "I know where the seal is."

My pulse surged. I leapt to my feet and ran for the cemetery gate, with Webster close behind.

"What are you doing?" I asked.

"I was cursed to stay with Antoine, but he is gone. You are part of Antoine, so now I must stay with you."

"Okay, let's go."

I rushed to the caretaker's shack and pounded on the door. The old man gradually opened it, rubbing the sleep from his eyes.

"What the fuck? Oh, it's you."

"Yeah, I'm ready to leave. Please unlock the gate."

The caretaker shuffled to the entrance and unlocked it. I dashed out and jumped into the New Yorker. I performed the hand and arm movements and called the Lwa again, instructing them to distract the police as I drove by, just as before. Webster stared at me in amazement, not understanding what I was doing. We sped off with tires screeching, returning to the plantation. It rained the entire way home.

A man parked across the street, watching the New Yorker pull up and park in front of the Holt Cemetery entrance while a young man with black, curly hair entered the graveyard. The Voodoo Imperatrice would want to know this. The man assigned as a lookout drove to the nearest pay phone and called her about Orion's appearance.

When she hung up, she realized something was amiss. If Rose still possessed Orion, why would they come here? If Rose no longer had Orion, what could have happened to her? How could she have been exorcised? She had to go to the plantation to find out for herself.

As I sped down the highway, the sprinkling that had begun while I was in the cemetery transformed into a fierce, steady downpour. I had to reduce my speed from 95 mph to 65 mph on the way from the graveyard, and even that felt like tempting fate, given the intensity of the rain.

Webster asked, "Aren't you afraid of getting pulled over by the police?"

"No, I sent the Lwa out ahead to distract the cops as I pass."

"The what?" he asked, not understanding what I was referring to.

"Lwa are power spirits from the Spirit Realm. They are the entities that perform curses and jinxes and also protect people when ordered by the Spirit Gods."

"Are you a Spirit God?"

"No, I am a Spirit Speaker—to be exact, a Lwa Spirit Speaker, because Duke Shamedi, a Lwa Spirit God, is my *God* Father. He possessed my human father when my mother was impregnated, and I was conceived with Lwa Spirit Speaker abilities. These only came to full power on my twenty-fifth birthday in March. I didn't understand what that meant until a few days ago when the Duke took my soul to the Spirit Realm and showed me everything."

"So, does that mean you're like a demi-god?"

"I don't think so, although the Lwa call me 'Small Duke.' I'm upset right now. I can't believe that Cyrus would keep this information about the signet from all of us."

"Who's Cyrus, and what information did he keep?"

"Cyrus is one of the ghosts that live at the plantation. The amulet he's attached to has the sapphire, which I now think is from the original Labauve signet. That has to be why the curse is still active and all the apparitions are still at the house. He knew this all the time and never told me. Why? Why?"

My voice got shrill and loud.

"Why would he do this? He knows the Voodoo Imperatrice wants it and what she can do with it. He knows we have to keep it from her. I will probably have to destroy it. God damn him!"

I pounded my palm on the steering wheel several times as I yelled. It finally stopped raining and I stomped on the accelerator.

Webster didn't ask any more questions for the rest of the trip. He recognized how upset I was.

The revelations of the past few weeks churned in my mind, leaving me to question the very foundation of my closest relationship. Cyrus, my supposed best friend, had kept the most critical secret from me and everyone, shattering my trust in him.

The New Yorker fishtailed on the rain-slicked road, tires spitting gravel as I raced up the drive toward the plantation. I wasn't thinking—I was just feeling. Anger. Betrayal. Urgency. Panic surged as I approached the mansion too quickly; I stomped on the brake, closing my eyes and holding my breath, realizing I might have waited too long to stop. The brakes could not slow the heavy automobile quickly enough, and it careened through the plantation's front picket fence, smashing it to the ground, pickets snapping and breaking, crushing beneath the vehicle's tires.

I opened my eyes and inhaled, relief washing over me that I had missed the massive oak tree's trunk by inches.

I threw open the car door and ran to the plantation house; with trembling hands, I fumbled for the door key in my pocket. My mind was consumed with apprehension and thoughts of losing everyone I cared for, and I was unsure how to stop it.

Bursting into the vestibule, I urgently yelled, "CYRUS!" willing him to appear.

The ghost materialized, and I shouted, "Where is it?"

I was angry with him about what I had discovered at my father's grave.

"Where is what?" he replied, displaying his irritation at being forced to appear.

"You know what I'm talking about."

I was tired of Cyrus's constant deflection.

He feigned ignorance, a façade I refused to entertain.

"It's in the bedroom where you left it this morning. Orion, why is that so important?"

Ignoring his question, I sprinted up the stairs two at a time to my room and desperately searched every surface until I spied the precious item and seized it. My hands trembled as I stared at it, having difficulty believing it had been in plain sight all along. This curious object possessed the power my grandmother craved and obsessed over for years. She would do anything to possess it, even putting both living and deceased family members through hell.

Cyrus followed me upstairs and stood in the doorway with a worried look.

"Orion, what is going on? Why do you need that old thing?"

Cyrus was trying to make me believe that it was of no importance.

"You know exactly why I need this. You've been lying to me and all of us about it."

Holding the amulet in front of his face, he looked surprised I had discovered the secret. My grandmother had devised several plans to find the seal, even capturing me and having a spirit possess my body to search for the item, nearly driving me insane. It had been in the amulet all this time and no one recognized it except Cyrus. I couldn't discover it with my Finding abilities because it was too closely associated with my family and me.

Cyrus turned, saying, "I don't have to listen to these accusations," and disappeared.

With my left arm and hand outstretched, I yelled, "Come back here!"

He reappeared with a terrified expression. I clenched my hand into a fist and pulled his spectral form toward me; his feet didn't touch the floor. When he came closer, I seized his arm and threw him into the chair beside the fireplace.

Upon hearing the yelling and commotion, the other ghosts appeared and observed the heated conversation. Webster was also present, and a few spirits glared at him with furrowed brows, unsure of who he was or where he had come from.

"Cyrus, why didn't you tell us that the sapphire in the amulet was from the Labauve signet?"

Cyrus couldn't leave because I was forcing him to stay. His look was pathetic—a child caught stealing from the cookie jar. He leaned over, wringing his hands, and stared at the floor.

I yelled, "Cyrus, tell us why you lied!" mentally pushing him harder.

He sat up and was flung back into the chair. The windows in the bedroom rattled from my display of anger. The other ghosts all stumbled back, moved by my rage. A few Lwa hovering in the corner zipped out to escape any escalation of my agitation.

He yelled, "Because if I told you...You'd destroy it. And that would mean losing you."

His voice cracked.

"I don't want to leave. I love you, Orion. I've loved you for longer than I can say."

Spectral tears ran down his cheeks.

I stood over Cyrus, confused, taken off guard, not anticipating this type of answer.

Bewildered as to why he would say something like this, I asked, "What do you mean?"

"In this day and age, people would call me gay. I have always been a sodomite, gay or homosexual, whatever you want to call it. Paul knows —he was my regular lover when we were both alive."

Paul jumped in and exclaimed, "Yeah, I remember. And I hated it."

Paul's voice was venomous.

"You think that was love? You forced yourself on me. Then, when you pushed your nephew down the stairs and accused me of doing it, that was your way of getting rid of me and the evidence I had over you."

My knees buckled, and I sank into the chair across from him. My thoughts raced—part fury, part heartbreak.

"You'd better tell us everything. No more lies."

Cyrus closed his eyes and nodded his head.

304

# Chapter 53

## She's On Her Way

Trouble stirred at L'Enfant Haven—Renee could feel it in her bones. The watcher she'd stationed near her son's grave had finally reported back: a tall young man with a mop of curly black hair had bribed his way into Holt Cemetery, spent an hour inside, then raced away in an old New Yorker.

It had to be Orion.

She clenched her fists.

Had he found the signet? Had he exorcised Rose? There were too many possibilities—and she couldn't afford any of them to be true.

She snatched her phone and called her head bodyguard.

"Alan, bring the car. Now. We're going to the plantation."

He hesitated and stammered, not wanting to return to the haunted estate after what he had seen when they dropped off her drugged grandson.

"I... I can't today," he stammered. "I have to take my mother to the doctor."

Liar.

"Get your ass over here," she snapped. "Or something will happen to your family."

A beat of silence, then: "Yes, Voodoo Imperatrice."

Renee yanked a heavy canvas bag from the closet. One by one, she packed it with spelled items—clay balls smeared with blood runes, feather-wrapped bones, and pouches that writhed faintly with trapped energy.

She walked out to the front porch. She stepped off the edge, got on her hands and knees, and reached under the porch floor until she touched the container. She retrieved the black-latched box that housed the protective gris-gris and her Lwa. With a whispered chant, she nestled it deep inside the bag. She was ready.

During the long drive north, she thought about why she needed to enlist the Spirit Speaker's help to gain control over all spirits. This was the final piece in her ultimate plan to control all aspects of the voodoo practice—control of ghosts and spirits. When she had mastery over all elements of the voodoo practice, she would be able to successfully fight against the Charbonnet cartel's army of voodoo priests and priestesses.

The pressure in Doris's head and chest bloomed like the storm outside—a warning. Something was coming. She decided to check up on what the Voodoo Imperatrice was doing. The Crystal Witch arranged her quartz crystals in the familiar observation pattern, the air tingling with static. Holding the gem pendant at her throat, she hummed and focused, attuning it to her frequency. A soft blue glow pulsed from the gem, then shot toward the table's centerpiece: a nine-inch quartz crystal. An image shimmered into view—Renee, the Voodoo Imperatrice, scowling in the passenger seat of a rain-slick car.

The voodoo priestess agitatedly snapped, "Can't you go faster?".

"Not unless you want to skid into a ditch," the driver muttered.

"How much longer till we get to the plantation?"

"An hour and a half. If it stops raining, maybe an hour."

She stared out the window, angry that it was taking so long.

Doris covered the pendant, cutting off the feed. Her brow furrowed.

Why is she coming to the plantation now? Something must have happened…something tied to Orion.

She called Andy's home phone number. It rang several times before someone picked it up.

Andy answered groggily, "Hello."

"Andy, it's Doris. The Voodoo Imperatrice is coming—she's on her way to the plantation."

A pause. Shuffling.

"What? Now?"

"Yes. Something's happened. We need to help Orion."

"Right. Okay. I'll pick you up in a few. Call him now."

He hung up the phone, ran to his bedroom, and hurriedly dressed.

Vivian, his wife, asked, "Who was that on the phone?"

"It was Doris; she needs my help. Her car is stalled out on the highway."

He felt terrible about lying to his wife, but he had to. He didn't want her worrying and knowing about all the unusual things that had been happening for the last several weeks.

"I hope she is okay. Be careful."

"I will."

He kissed her forehead and ran out the door.

The secretary called Orion's number and listened as the telephone rang several times before he answered.

※ ※ ※

Cyrus was about to start telling his story when the phone rang downstairs.

"Shit! I've got to get an extension up here. Hold on, I'll be back. You aren't off the hook yet," I said, pointing a finger at Cyrus.

He stared up at me, looking so distraught that I almost wanted to let him go. But I had to understand why he had lied and kept such important secrets all these years. He nodded, staring down at the floor, not wanting to see my disappointment in him, knowing he must spill everything he had been holding back all this time.

I ran down the stairs and answered the phone. It was Doris.

"Orion, I just checked up on the Voodoo Imperatrice through the crystals, and she's on her way to the plantation. She'll be there in about an hour."

"Oh, great! She must have figured out I know where the signet is."

"You found it?"

"Not exactly. Some information I got at my father's grave helped me realize that the sapphire in Cyrus's amulet is what is left of the seal. I've had it all this time. I'm talking to Cyrus about this right now."

"Andy and I are on our way. What are you going to do when your grandmother gets there?"

"I don't know, but I think I can slow her down to give me more time to figure things out. I'll talk to you in a few. I've got to go."

I hung up the phone.

⚷— ⚷— ⚷—

All the ghosts except Cyrus, who was still forced to remain in the chair, came out onto the second-floor landing and listened to the conversation with Doris.

Albert looked over at Webster and asked, "Who are you? Where did you come from?

"I'm Webster Turner, Orion's grandfather through his father. We met at the cemetery."

Albert nodded, understanding that it was appropriate for Webster to be here, and continued to watch Orion below.

⚷— ⚷— ⚷—

I had to slow the Voodoo Imperatrice down so I could listen to Cyrus's story and figure out what to do. I quickly called a few Lwa from the Spirit Realm with the appropriate hand and arm gestures. Magic filled the area, a glowing portal appeared, the Lwa popped through and floated in front of me, vibrating with excitement.

"Find the car my grandmother is in and stop or slow the vehicle down in any way you can—flat tires, overheated engine, out of gas, blocked road. Those sorts of things."

They simultaneously said, 'As you command, Small Duke,' and zipped through the front door with flashes as they passed through the physical material.

I went back upstairs and sat in the chair across from Cyrus. He looked like he was about to melt into the chair, not wanting to be seen.

I said, "Okay, get started. We don't have much time."

# Chapter 54

## Cyrus's Shove

Cyrus Labauve had always been drawn to the young male slaves working shirtless in the cotton fields. Their rippling muscles, the sheen of sweat across their backs—it stirred something in him he didn't fully understand at first. At thirteen, hidden behind a tree on the edge of the fields, he watched and fantasized, overwhelmed by urges he didn't yet have words for.

At fourteen, he watched his father and Mr. Mason, the overseer, in the barn, demonstrating their power over the slaves and having their physical way with them. These acts both horrified and excited him in equal measure. Seeing the tight muscles and smelling the sweat rolling down the slave's back was too intoxicating.

From the hayloft above, Cyrus watched, his breath quick and shallow, his body reacting in ways he couldn't control. They brought over another slave for Mr. Mason. While watching Mr. Mason with the male slave, he came again, and he realized he enjoyed the sexual acts with men more than women. He wanted to do the same thing with a man. He would have to figure out how to do this. He couldn't let his father or Mr. Mason know this.

Over time, rumors spread among the enslaved men. The young master was not to be trusted. He pursued the men more than the women, and though they could never outright refuse him, they learned to avoid being alone with him whenever possible.

After his father died when he was sixteen and he became the master of the plantation, he no longer had to sneak around and did what he wanted when his mother, brother, or sisters weren't close by.

He liked the slave Jupiter (Paul), the son of the housemaid, Rose. He took the boy as a personal valet on top of his daily chores as a yards man. Cyrus taught him how to perform sexually, praised him when he pleased, and told him he was special. Paul played the part, smiled when expected, and obeyed every command, because refusal meant punishment.

By fifteen, Cyrus decided Paul was ready for more. That night, Paul did not cry or scream. He did what he had been taught—accept everything. When Cyrus reversed their roles, asking Paul to penetrate him, Paul agreed. It was the only time he felt any power in their twisted relationship.

But Paul wanted out. Desperately.

But the slaves were not the only sexual encounters that Cyrus had. Cyrus's secrets extended beyond the slaves. He carried on a clandestine affair with his brother-in-law, Bernard Beauregard. They met under aliases—Jonathan Barbier and Adonis Glenford—exchanging erotic letters and meeting secretly in Shreveport.

Cyrus hoarded the letters, reading them aloud in his room, whispering Bernard's name while pleasuring himself. He burned the letters after each reading, but Paul listened to his master read these letters several times and knew about the secret love affair between the two men. He also knew that Cyrus Labauve and his family's reputation would be ruined if others found out.

One day, the Labauve family went for a country ride on a rare day when the weather was pleasant, not too hot and muggy. Cyrus declined the outing, pleading excessive work. As soon as the family left the plantation, Paul entered the master's bedroom, having been told to come up after they departed. Cyrus was reading a love letter from Bernard. Paul heard the entire letter.

Cyrus threw the letter into the fireplace, turned, and left the room, saying, "I'll be right back."

He left and went downstairs for a new bottle of wine from the locked cabinet in his office. Paul saw his opportunity; the letter had just started to burn on the edges. He quickly grabbed it by the opposite side, removed it from the fire, and stomped on the burning end. He picked it up, staring at the letter, thinking, 'This is my way out,' and put it in his pocket.

Cyrus reentered the bedroom and saw Paul place the letter in his pocket. He came up behind Paul and grabbed his hand, still holding the letter half in his pocket. The two men struggled.

Paul wrenched free, the singed letter clutched tight in his fist.

"I know what's in this," he said, his voice trembling but defiant, "about you and Mr. Beauregard in Shreveport and the letters. If anyone else saw this, your name would be mud in every corner of this parish."

Cyrus's face darkened.

"What do you think you're going to do with it?"

"Nothing. If you leave me alone—no more valet, no more touching me, having me do things I hate. I just want to work the yard, not be your secret."

Cyrus took a step closer, his voice suddenly soft.

"I thought you liked what we did together. You always sounded enthusiastic. Paul… I always cared about you. I never called you Jupiter. I honored the name your mother gave you."

"You honored no one," Paul spat. "I smiled because I had to. You would've had me beaten if I didn't."

The moment cracked. Cyrus lunged. They struggled. The letter slipped from Paul's hand and fluttered toward the open doorway.

Richard Labauve, Cyrus's nephew, came up the stairs as the shouting started in his uncle's bedroom. He snuck over and stood beside the entry, listening to the confrontation. He was shocked by what was revealed.

He didn't like his uncle. His father's brother always yelled at him and accused him of doing things he didn't do. Then the letter that the slave Jupiter said had all the evidence slid next to the door jamb. He picked up the fallen letter and read just enough to realize its scandalous contents.

Cyrus saw his nephew reading the letter and shouted at him, "Richard, stay right there!"

Holding the letter, Richard said, "I'm going to tell Papa."

Cyrus shouted at the boy, "No, you're not! Don't move."

He grabbed the child by the arm. Richard struggled and managed to pull his arm away. He ran for the stairs with Cyrus right behind him. His uncle grabbed for the boy again and caught hold of his shirt. He never liked his nephew, a spoiled child who was always doing things he shouldn't and denying them.

He pulled the letter out of the child's hand, and with a smirk, he pushed the child. Richard teetered at the top step. Cyrus's shove—with more instinct than intent—sent the boy over the edge.

Richard's body crashed down the staircase. His head struck the fourth step with a sickening crack. Silence followed, then a slow, spreading pool of red.

Paul ran to Cyrus and said, "What did you do?"

He stood in shock with the crumpled letter in his hand.

"I didn't mean to do it. It was an accident."

At that moment, the front door opened, and the entire family, having returned from the morning outing, entered and saw Richard lying on the bottom steps, his eyes open and a pool of blood oozing from the boy's head and dripping off the step to the one below. Several of the women screamed.

Joseph, Richard's father and Cyrus's brother, ran to the boy and picked up the child's limp, dead body, pulling him to his chest with tears welling in his eyes.

He looked up at Cyrus and Jupiter on the second-floor landing and shouted, "What happened?"

Cyrus quickly stuffed the incriminating letter into his pocket, pointed to Paul, and said, "He pushed Richard down the stairs. I came out of the bedroom and saw it."

All the men in the group ran to the second floor toward Jupiter. He turned to run, but there was nowhere to go. They grabbed him and pulled him out front.

The house slaves, hearing the commotion, rushed from the back porch, where they had been enjoying some relaxation while the family was away. Rose viewed the child crumpled on the stairs and heard Cyrus accuse her son of pushing the boy. Paul would never do such a thing; Cyrus was lying.

The men dragged Paul downstairs and out to the front yard. One of the young boys ran to Mr. Mason's office in his small cottage and told him what had happened. Mason grabbed the hanging rope with the tied noose and ran around the mansion to the front yard. He threw the rope over one of the oak tree's branches, and the men holding Jupiter placed the noose around his neck. Pulling on the rope, the men held the slave off the ground while he struggled to be released, but the noose did its job too well and cut off the air passage.

Rose shrieked, fighting against the arms holding her back as the noose tightened around her son's neck.

"No! Not my baby—please, not my baby!"

But the men held firm. Paul's legs kicked once, twice. Then stopped.

The house slaves held Rose back, knowing that if they didn't, she would also be killed.

Through all of this, Cyrus never came down. He watched through the second-floor window as they hanged Paul. He really did care about the boy, but he couldn't let him stay with the knowledge the slave had about... his preferences. He threw the letter into the fire and waited for it to turn to ash. After the letter had burned, he hurried downstairs. Two house slaves were cleaning the blood from the steps. The boy's body had been placed on the back porch.

Cyrus went outside and hugged his brother and sister-in-law. The family believed his upset expression to be only for his nephew. As the days went by, the entire family was distraught over the loss. Cyrus began to drink all the time. The guilt of pushing the boy and being the actual cause of the death of his nephew ripped and lashed at his conscience.

A few weeks later, Cyrus caught Rose stealing the Labauve signet from the desk drawer. She denied this accusation. Mason was ready to kill her, but Cyrus stopped him. He couldn't bear the thought of having Paul's mother killed after what he had done to her son.

He told Mason, "Get her off the plantation, sell her immediately."

The overseer asked, "Why would you do that?"

"You don't need to know. Do as I say, or I'll get rid of you, too."

Confused, he said, "Yes, sir."

Rose was sold within a few days.

A few months later, Cyrus took the Labauve signet and had the sapphire turned into an amulet he always wore, thinking the new adornment would make him feel better, but it didn't.

He continued to drink wine and brandy every day. Drunk most of the time, he staggered around the house and yelled at everyone, whether slave or family member. The plantation management suffered. His brother Joseph took over most of the plantation business activities, with Cyrus always accusing him of doing it all wrong.

After two years, the hell Cyrus put the family through ended. Heavily intoxicated, he came out of his bedroom, yelling for the slaves to bring him more brandy. He stumbled and fell down the stairs, with his head crashing onto the same step edge as Richard's. He died shortly afterward, again with a pool of blood dripping off the edge onto the step below.

He found himself standing over his own broken body. Blood on the steps. Family crowding. His mother and wife sobbed, but his brother whispered to himself, "At least we don't have to listen to him anymore."

Paul's ghost appeared across from him, arms folded.

"Welcome to hell."

Cyrus turned to flee, but couldn't. His feet locked, bound by something unseen. The amulet. He would learn later that he could never stray more than fifty feet from it. Not in life. Not in death.

The amulet and his other belongings were packed into a massive chest and stored in the attic. Cyrus's ghost couldn't go beyond fifty feet of the amulet, so he never left the loft. He didn't know why he couldn't move beyond that point.

He didn't know about the curse until years later when some of the servants coming up the attic stairs talked about it. Two maids had died because of botched abortions, and their ghosts started appearing. He stayed in the loft for 156 years, scaring people who came near his chest of belongings to amuse himself.

One day, a boy came up the attic stairs. Somehow, he knew the boy's name, Orion. The boy was special. He wasn't afraid of ghosts and spoke to him. The child took the amulet and Cyrus could now leave the attic and see the world with the boy.

⚷—⚷—⚷—

"I loved being with you," Cyrus confessed to Orion. "When you're near, I don't have to relive the horror of my life. The other ghosts— well, they only suffer on the anniversary of their deaths. But I suffer every day except when I'm with you. Maybe it's because you're the Spirit Speaker. I don't know. But as you grew into a beautiful man, I realized... I loved you.

"Then this whole situation with your grandmother, the curse, and the signet came to light. Yes, the sapphire is the only thing left of the seal; you must destroy it to break the curse. I saw what happened with Helen Jones and how she went to the other side when she broke the curse by saving your life. We would all go to the other side if you destroyed the sapphire and stopped the curse. I don't want to go. I want to stay with you forever."

Rose's voice rang out.

"You relive it daily because you are the cause of the curse, Cyrus. Orion shields you from it—because he is the Spirit Speaker. But your time is coming. And you must choose what kind of spirit you'll become when that curse breaks."

316

# Chapter 55

# Confrontation Preparations

After Cyrus's story ended, silence stretched in the room like a held breath.

I turned to him, my voice low but shaking with fury.

"How incredibly selfish of you. You'd sacrifice the peace of every other ghost—risk what my grandmother might do with that sapphire—just so you could stay with me?"

Cyrus flinched.

"I—"

"No. I can't believe I ever called you my best friend. I don't even want to look at you."

Without another word, Cyrus stood and walked away, head bowed. The ghosts parted solemnly as he passed, their expressions filled with judgment and sorrow. He climbed the stairs to the attic and disappeared.

Andy and Doris had entered during the story and now sat silently on the edge of the bed, absorbing the weight of what had just been revealed.

Doris stepped forward, "The sapphire was where the curse resided. You said that there are Lwa spirits that control curses. I think the Lwa controlling this curse live inside the sapphire, probably many of them. That type of gem can hold an incredible amount of energy."

"That would explain why I don't see any Lwa near the ghosts. They're trapped. All of them."

Doris nodded.

Andy looked at me.

"What happens when your grandmother arrives?"

I exhaled.

"I'm not sure. I'll call several Lwa to safeguard the house and everyone inside. I'll have to wait and see what she will do."

I descended the stairs. The others followed. I stood in the parlor, centered myself, then began the summoning. My arms traced sacred shapes through the air—ancient gestures taught to me by the Duke.

A shimmer opened in front of me. One by one, the Lwa slipped through—a cascade of vibrant beings, pulsing with color and sound. They flickered like will-o'-the-wisps, hovering, waiting. The Lwa floated, vibrated, and pulsed in multiple hues before me, waiting to be told what to do.

Neither Andy, Doris, nor any of the ghosts could see the creatures.

I told the Lwa, "My grandmother, the Voodoo Imperatrice, is coming here."

When the Lwa heard her name, some pulsated to a much smaller size and flew toward the back of the room.

I asked, "What is wrong? Are you afraid of her?"

A collective voice came into my mind: 'Yes, Small Duke, several of the Gods have given her much power. We may not be able to stop her.'

I said, "I understand this, but we all must do our best to keep her from using the power from the amulet to control spirits everywhere."

'Yes, Small Duke.'

"That's good. Then it would be best to learn to work together as a team. I will help where possible, and the ghosts will assist."

'Yes, Small Duke.'

The Lwa all clustered into an amorphous mass and seemed to be discussing strategies.

One of the larger golden Lwa floated over, 'We have a plan.'

"That is good. Are you the leader?"

'Yes.'

"What is your name?"

It communicated in a way that transcended human understanding, speaking in the divine language that echoed in my mind.

I said, "I'm going to call you Bob."

'Yes, Small Duke.'

Andy and Doris approached me.

The counselor asked, "While doing those arm and hand movements, your eyes changed color to a golden color, the same as when they changed while the Duke possessed you."

"Are they still that color?"

"No, they changed back to blue when you stopped talking to whatever you were talking to. Are those spirit things going to help?"

"Yes, Bob said they have a plan."

"One is named Bob?" Andy asked, not believing a spirit entity could have such a name.

"That's what I'm calling him. I can't pronounce his name."

"What do you want us to do?"

"Stay out of the way. If she unleashes spells, she could kill you. I might be able to block some with what the Duke gave me, but she's been gifted by other Spirit Gods. I don't know if I can stop everything."

Doris scoffed lightly.

"She's not killing us. I brought protection."

She ran to Andy's car and pulled a cardboard box from the back seat. She carried the box into the house and began pulling out crystals of various sizes, colors, and types.

She said, "I will place a protective barrier around the house." She looked up and continued, "Everyone, I need your help."

The ghosts crowded around.

She handed each a few crystals and said, "Place a crystal at the house's foundation every twenty feet. Surround the house."

The apparitions swept outside and got to work. Moments later, they returned, confirming the task was done.

Doris placed the largest quartz crystal on the front porch. She rubbed the gem that hung from her neck, closed her eyes, concentrated, and hummed a series of tones. Her crystal glowed brightly, and a beam of light shot out toward the quartz; from there, rays of illumination extended from the large quartz crystal to the smaller crystals surrounding the house, creating a continuous shaft of light linking all the crystals. When the final link was established, the Crystal Witch changed the tones of her hum, and a wall of soft, semi-transparent light of various colors rose into the air, encompassing the house, curving over the roof, and meeting in the center, thus creating a protective bubble around the mansion.

She stopped humming, turned, and said, "There, that should stop her from getting inside."

Amazed, I asked, "What did you do?"

"I have set a power shield around the house. It won't be easy to pass through. She may be able to break it, but it will take some work."

She smiled, proud of herself for creating the largest crystal shield she had ever manifested.

Outside, the Lwa organized themselves into concentric circles, each ring spinning in a different direction. Their bodies hummed with power, forming a living barricade.

I smiled, thinking, 'That looks wonderful.'

In my mind, Bob said, 'Thank you, Small Duke.'

Andy again asked, "Is there anything I can do?"

He could not contribute anything to the defensive preparations but wanted desperately to be involved.

"Just keep out of the way. I don't want you or Doris harmed if the Imperatrice starts throwing spells around. I may be able to block some of them with the power the Duke gave me, but from what the Lwa said, she has an exceptional amount of power given to her by some of the other Spirit Gods. I don't know if I'll be able to deflect everything. I don't understand how the other Gods' powers work. I only know what the Duke gave me, and he didn't give me everything he has control of."

The ghosts gathered around and asked what they should do.

I said, "If she gets past all the barriers, my only option is to break the sapphire. That's what she is after."

Rose said, "And she wants you and your powers, so she probably won't kill you, but she might do some serious damage and put you out for a while."

I said, "The only thing you guys can do is try to slow her down somehow if she breaks through."

Everyone nodded, but their uncertainty was palpable. They were unsure of what they could do in the face of such a powerful threat.

Andy, filled with determination, declared, "I have to help somehow. If they come into the house, I will find something to use as a weapon."

He went to the front closet under the stairs and rummaged around for anything to use as a weapon. All he found was an old croquet set. He pulled it from the closet and set it next to the stairs.

He said, "If the Voodoo Imperatrice enters the mansion with her bodyguards, I should be able to get some good hits in with the mallets. I can also throw the balls at anyone who comes in. I was an excellent baseball pitcher in high school and college, and I taught my sons how to throw a ball for accuracy and power. I should be able to do some damage with these hard wooden balls."

I said, "Okay, that sounds good."

We left the front door open for easy sighting of the Voodoo Imperatrice. I stood by the door, and the Lwa I had sent to slow my grandmother's car down came rushing in, circling my head, frantically saying, 'She's coming.'

"Thank you. Now go and join the others out front."

They flew out and found positions in the moving circles.

Walter stood by the road. Headlights appeared at the far end of the driveway.

He burst into the house, his voice filled with urgency, "She's coming! A car is approaching."

The impending danger was intense.

A hush fell over the house as the energy shifted. Everyone—living and dead—braced for the Voodoo Imperatrice's arrival.

# Chapter 56

# Spirit Orbs, Spells, Crystals
# & Croquet Balls

A Ford Fairlane pulled up beside the splintered picket fence. The Voodoo Imperatrice stepped out, slinging a heavy canvas bag over her shoulder. Her eyes narrowed as she spotted the New Yorker crashed in the yard, and a smile tugged at her lips. Orion had been rattled.

She scanned the property, and with her psychic sight saw the shimmering crystal light dome cloaking the house.

'So, he has help. Must be that presence I've sensed watching now and then,' she thought. 'But I brought things to handle this.'

She stomped across the shattered gate with a sneering smile and advanced boldly toward the house.

⚷— ⚷— ⚷—

Standing in the open doorway, I watched her bold, determined approach to the house.

I shouted at her, "That's far enough!"

She stopped, smiled, and replied, "Orion, can't a grandmother come to visit her grandchild?"

"One who drugs her grandchild, tortures him, and has him possessed doesn't deserve a visit. Turn around and leave."

"You aren't possessed any longer. How did that happen, and where is Rose?"

"Rose was removed with help from some friends."

Rose stepped out from behind me.

"I'm here."

"Rose, why didn't you return to me?"

Rose answered, "Because I'm now working with Orion. He will

323

assure that Paul goes to the other side in peace."

"Oh, now you can send Spirits to the other side, can you?"

"Something like that."

I didn't want to give her too much information.

She took a few more steps forward, and I said, "I wouldn't get any closer if I were you."

She definitely continued. A few Lwa moved toward her and pushed her back. She stumbled backward with a surprised look.

"Ah, so you have acquired some Lwa to help you. I didn't know you could perform ceremonies to conjure that kind of help."

"I don't need to perform ceremonies; they work for me."

She pulled a small purple bag from the large tote and opened the drawstrings. She poured powder into her hand and blew the dust before her. My Lwa troops floating in the air became semi-transparent and visible.

She said, "Oh, my, you have a small army of little helpers, don't you? That must have been what caused the car to have problems."

She revealed a black container, held it before her, and said, "I've got my own army."

She opened the box and screamed in the God language, "Destroy Orion's Lwa!"

Her box burst open, releasing dozens of monstrous Lwa into the yard—larger, shrieking beasts of light and color. The air split with flashes and sounds as my Lwa clashed with hers in a chaotic aerial melee. It resembled fireworks and lightning colliding mid-air.

Behind me, Andy and Doris gasped as explosions crackled and screams pierced the boundary between worlds.

While the Lwa battled, the priestess withdrew clay spell balls. One struck the crystal barrier—BOOM!—sending a ripple through the light wall. Another—CRACK!—punched a hole. A third created a jagged tear.

She laughed and said, "Your protection spell isn't going to last long. Give me the signet, come with me, and I'll leave your ghost family and friends unharmed."

I bellowed at her, "There's no way I'm coming with you, you fucking bitch!"

Doris attempted to step onto the front porch, but I stopped her.

She shouted, "I may be able to close some of the holes in the shield."

"It's too dangerous. Get back inside."

She reluctantly backed off.

My Lwa were losing ground; their smaller bodies were no match. Some fell onto the lawn, leaving scorched patches of grass. The shield continued to tear.

Smoke and sulfur choked the air. The high-pitched screams rattled my brain—inaudible to others but deafening to me. This battlefield existed in a reality that only she and I fully perceived. A tense standoff ensued, and despite our efforts, she began to breach the defenses.

The others only saw what appeared to be miniature fireworks in the space above the yard, alongside the small explosions that occurred when the spell balls and pouches struck the light shield. This was enough to frighten both the living and the dead.

A two-foot-diameter hole was rent open in the shield wall after one of her power bags ate at it. I closed my eyes and focused. Spirit energy surged through me. A lavender orb formed in my palms, humming, six inches wide. My hands trembled.

I'm sure my eyes must have turned golden while doing this. My sight became more pronounced, and I could see energy waves flying through the air from the battle outside. The energy I held wanted to escape my hold. I threw it through the barrier hole at the Voodoo Imperatrice. It blazed through the hole with a tail of colored particles behind it, like a comet, but was blocked by one of her Lwa and exploded mid-air.

I created another spirit energy orb, drawing even more energy from the other side. This orb was larger and a deeper purple. I threw it through the hole, but again, it was stopped by a large, orange Lwa. The explosion knocked her Lwa warrior out of the air and onto the ground, burning the grass. This blast caused my grandmother to stumble back a few steps.

One of my grandmother's spell balls came through the wall hole as I formed an energy orb. With the orb still in my hands, I extended my arms, and the ball struck the orb, knocking me back and causing me to land on my ass.

Andy stepped forward, and with a pitcher's movements, he threw a yellow croquet ball through the shield hole toward my grandmother. The ball quickly flew through the air but was stopped by one of her Lwa. It was deflected toward the oak tree, struck the tree trunk and ricocheted off toward the house, where it hit the light shield. The ball exploded into flames and fell to the ground.

I quickly got up and continued creating energy orbs while Andy occasionally threw a croquet ball. We kept lobbing energy orbs, croquet balls, spell balls, and pouches at each other. We seemed to be about even in our abilities.

Doris had been watching the battle through the living room window and suddenly ran toward the back porch.

"Where are you going?" I shouted.

"Something's not right!" she called back.

I didn't have time to pay attention and went back to making spirit energy balls.

Later she told me what she saw: a feathered talisman floating toward the rear, eating through the light wall. She pulled out her personal crystal, hummed, and cast golden light across it. The charm fizzled and died. More came, but she neutralized each with skill and resolve. When the attack ceased, she returned to the front.

Meanwhile, I was failing. My Lwa were dwindling. The barrier was disintegrating. Sweat streamed down my face. Forming the spirit orbs took a lot of my physical energy. I was breathing hard as if I had been jogging for several miles; my heart was racing, and I was frantic, unsure of what else to do to stop her.

My only option was to destroy what remained of the signet. I had to do it or she would break through and take it. The gem's destruction meant I would lose my ghost family, but at least they would find peace on the other side. I would have to learn how to live without them.

I turned and ran to the kitchen.

When my grandmother saw me leave, she laughed and yelled, "Oh, look, the boy runs away."

She threw two small pouches, and they burst into a cloud of golden sparkles, creating tiny holes in the crystal light barrier.

I opened the kitchen junk drawer and grabbed the old ball-peen hammer.

Running back to the open front door, I knelt and leaned down, pulling the amulet from my jeans pocket. Holding it by the ribbon with the sapphire exposed, I placed it on the flagstone porch and smashed the gem hard with the hammer.

CRACK—first blow. The earth trembled.

I glanced up at the Voodoo Imperatrice; she felt it too, as demonstrated by her surprised look. She knew what I was doing and threw several more spelled pouches. The crystal wall was coming down fast.

CRACK—second strike. A flash. The porch shook.

One final blast from her hit the quartz crystal, and the shield collapsed. The light links disconnected with a final flash and the entire barrier went down. She pulled her arm back to throw another spell ball at me, and the next thing I knew, Cyrus jumped in front of me to deflect the projectile. I pushed him aside with the amulet ribbon still in my hand. The spell ball continued flying toward me; all I could do was raise my arms in front of my face.

When the spell ball exploded, the sapphire in the amulet hanging from the ribbon cracked open, and a wave of power tore through the air. Windows rattled—a scream—inhuman, endless—burst from the gem. Light exploded in every direction. The ground heaved. Ghosts and people alike were thrown backward.

The extreme force pushed me off my feet and back through the air into the house. Something entered me midair—warm, electric, divine. I was so dazed and shocked that I couldn't tell what it was.

I crashed onto the stairs. My right arm smashed into the balustrade of the staircase, breaking it severely again, bones pushing through muscle and skin, gleaming white and red. The back of my head bashed onto the fourth step edge—the same one that both Cyrus's and his nephew's heads had hit—cracking my skull. Blood immediately started flowing from my head onto the step and dripping onto the ones below. Two ribs in my back hit the stairs and were also broken.

When I landed on the stairs, everything went black. I opened my eyes and moved toward the beautiful tunnel of light, with peace and love emanating from it. My mother, father, and Nanny were there, ready to take me to the other side. I was happy and wanted to go, but a firm hand touched my shoulder and stopped me. I glared over and up, not wanting to be stopped. It was Duke Shamedi.

He said, "Boy, it's not your time yet. I have work for you to do."

I pleaded, "But I want to go."

"I'm sorry, but you have to finish your work first."

"Fuck you!" I yelled at him, not wanting to return to a life that would be hell.

Then I gasped for breath, wracked with agonizing pain, as he forced me to drink from a small vial. I choked down the liquid. It was Nectar of the Gods from the stream in the Spirit Realm. A shiver ran through my body, and everything went black again.

# Chapter 57

# Confrontation Aftermath

The explosion from the shattered sapphire sent the Voodoo Imperatrice tumbling across the lawn. She groaned, pushing herself up slowly, pain radiating from her bruised knee where the blast had struck hardest.

"Where the hell is Alan?" she muttered.

Looking over her shoulder, she spotted him crouched low in the front seat of the Ford Fairlane. Coward.

'He's done. I need someone braver,' she thought bitterly.

Limping toward the mansion, she found the front door unguarded and stepped inside. Her eyes landed on Orion's crumpled form at the bottom of the stairs. Blood pooled beneath his head. His right arm was twisted and shattered, white bone gleaming through torn flesh. Andy Butler knelt beside him, fingers pressed to Orion's neck.

"I can't find a pulse," Andy said, pale. "I think he's gone."

Doris stood nearby, trembling.

"Oh no. Orion is dead."

Tears welled in her eyes.

Ghosts surrounded them, silent and stunned.

The signet was gone. Its power spent. And her grandson—her key to everything—was dead. Renee Broussard's grand designs to harness the Spirit Speaker and dominate the spirit world lay in ruin.

Anger boiling in her chest, she turned and limped back to the car, each step sending fresh jolts of pain up her leg.

She yanked open the car door and snapped, "Get up, you pathetic coward! Drive me home!"

Alan straightened, eyes wide.

"Yes, Voodoo Imperatrice."

He started the car and quickly drove back to New Orleans, unsure of what had happened. He heard the yelling between the Voodoo Imperatrice and the Spirit Speaker, but all the high-pitched screams and explosions drowned everything else out. He held his head down and shook, terrified, not understanding that an actual battle had occurred. He felt the earthquake, the car shaking, and then silence. Despite her yelling at him when she told him to take her home, he was relieved it was over.

⚷— ⚷— ⚷—

The blast wave from the destroyed gem on the amulet lifted Andy so forcefully that he flew ten feet, hit the floor, and slid to the back door, where he banged his head. Feeling dizzy, he shuffled toward the entrance and saw his friend's battered body on the stairs with blood dripping off the edge. His right arm was also bleeding, with bones exposed. Andy couldn't tell if Orion was breathing or not.

Doris was pushed into the living room and luckily fell onto the couch, making her landing the softest of everyone in the house. The ghosts were all knocked to the ground. Doris got up off the couch and shook her head. The power blast knocked her hard, and she felt dizzy. She slowly left the living room, saw Orion's body on the stairs, and gasped.

The attorney said, "I can't find a pulse. I think he is gone."

Doris cried, "Oh no, Orion is dead," and started to cry. "Albert, is he dead?"

Doc Albert leaned down, checked for a pulse, listened for a heartbeat, inspected the pupils in his eyes, and sadly said, "Yes, he's gone."

No one noticed the Voodoo Imperatrice standing in the doorway and listening to these statements. She turned and left.

Through all this, Cyrus stood off by himself in shock when Doc Albert said Orion was dead. He couldn't take it. It was all his fault. If he hadn't jumped in front of Orion, thinking he was protecting him from being hit by one of those spell balls, Orion would have had time to hit the gem a third time and destroy it. Instead, Orion pushed him away to save his sorry ass, and a spell ball hit the man he loved, blowing him onto the stairs and killing him.

Cyrus popped into the attic, sat on his old storage chest, rocking back and forth, and sobbed. He was sure he would be going to hell for everything he had done in his life and after and would never see Orion again.

Duke Shamedi popped into existence and pushed Albert out of the way. His sudden appearance shocked Andy, and he fell backward onto his butt away from Orion's body. The Duke put his hand on Orion's chest, and the young man's clothes changed from jeans, a T-shirt, and tennis shoes to a purple tuxedo with tails and no shirt or shoes.

The Lwa's Spirit God closed his eyes and said, "Boy, it's not your time yet. I have work for you to do." He paused and continued, "I'm sorry, but you have to finish your work first."

With his free hand, he removed a small vial from the inside pocket of his coat.

Orion's eyes opened and he gasped for breath. The Duke put the vial in his mouth and forced him to drink the shimmering fluid. Orion drank and choked some down. He shivered and fell unconscious. He was breathing again.

Andy stood and questioned the Duke, "What did you do?"

"I resurrected him and gave him the Nectar of the Gods to assure that he would recover. I have work for him to do. I can't have him lollygagging around and dying on me right now. When he wakes, tell the boy I said he did good."

He smiled and disappeared with a pop and a flash. Several remaining Lwa followed him to the Spirit Realm, but the humans and ghosts never perceived this. After the Duke left, Orion's clothing changed back to jeans, a blood-stained T-shirt, and the tennis shoes he had previously worn.

Andy shouted, "Doris, call the ambulance! We have to get him to a hospital."

As Cyrus sat in the attic, he felt that something was happening. He manifested back downstairs and heard Andy telling Doris to call the ambulance. Orion was alive. How did that happen?

He asked Rose, "What happened? I thought Orion was dead."

Rose answered, "The Duke came and resurrected him."

Cyrus moved back to a corner and silently cried, thanking the Duke for returning Orion. He stayed silent and out of the way, knowing the other ghosts hated him for what he had done in the past and what he almost did.

Doris ran to the phone, called the ambulance, and gave them the address.

She returned and said, "It will be at least forty-five minutes before the ambulance arrives. Should we phone Dr. Wilson in town?"

"Yes, call him."

The secretary hurried back to the telephone and called the doctor. She gave him all the information and told him that Orion had fallen down the stairs.

The doctor said, "Okay, I'll be out there in about fifteen minutes."

"Dr. Wilson is on his way. Everyone, stay out of the way. Wait a minute. Why are you all still here?"

Albert offered, "When Helen Jones saved Orion at eleven years old, it was a little while before she left. Maybe we have to wait. It'll happen soon."

Dr. Wilson arrived and checked over the young man.

He asked, "What happened to him?"

"He fell down the stairs."

"With this much trauma… he's lucky to be alive."

The doctor wrapped Orion's head and arm, stabilizing him. When the EMTs arrived, they transferred Orion onto a stretcher and rushed him to the hospital.

Andy said, "Thanks, doctor, send your bill to my office."

The doctor nodded.

"Let me know what the hospital finds."

The attorney said, "I will."

The doctor left.

"I have to call Vivian and tell her something. She must be worried sick right now."

Doris said, "Tell her when you pickd me up that I needed to deliver some special family items to Orion. I had been returning from New Orleans when the car conked out. We went to Orion's to make the delivery and helped him at the house. Tell her he was moving some furniture around. Then he fell down the stairs, and we called the doctor and ambulance, and we are going to the hospital now."

"Wow, you are really good at this type of thing."

She shrugged.

"When you're a witch and get involved with weird things, you learn to think on your feet."

"You've been involved with other weird things?"

"I'll tell you sometime when we have more time. Now call your wife."

"Yeah, right."

Andy called his wife, relaying the story that Doris concocted.

Vivian was very sympathetic as usual and told him to call and let her know how Orion was doing.

As Andy and Doris were leaving the house and heading to the hospital, Andy said, "You'll probably all be gone by the time we get back. It's been nice meeting all of you. Good-bye."

Andy and his secretary drove to Shreveport and the hospital. It started to rain again.

The battle was over. But the war wasn't finished yet.

334

# Chapter 58

# Pain Levels

I woke in excruciating pain. My right arm was throbbing worse than the first time I broke it in the Jaguar crash. My head pounded and it was hard to breathe without spasms shooting across my back.

Andy leaned over the edge of the bed and said, "Finally, you're awake."

Gasping through the agony, I managed, "How long have I been out?"

"Five days. The doctors are amazed you're alive. I guess it was the Nectar of the Gods the Duke gave you."

"Is that what he forced me to drink?"

"He wants you to know that, in his words, 'You did good, boy.'"

"Hmm. I guess that's the closest thing to a compliment I'll get from him."

I groaned and scrunched my eyes closed as flashes of pain shot through my right arm.

Andy said, "I'm going to tell the nurses you are awake and in pain."

He returned to the room a little later, with the nurse following him with a syringe in her hand.

She asked, "How would you rate your pain level from one to ten?"

"Eleven," I groaned.

She smiled and proceeded to inject the medication into the IV drip connected to my left forearm and exited the room.

The counselor said, "Orion, you died for about two minutes, then the Duke showed up, resurrected you, and made you drink the nectar."

"Yeah, I know. I was in the tunnel of light. Mama, my father, and Nanny were there to take me to the other side. I wanted to go with them so badly. I was ready to go."

My eyes welled with tears, which began streaming down my face.

"Then the fucking Duke came up and said, 'Boy, you can't go now. I got work for you.' What an asshole!  And now I'm back—in this mess—hurting like hell."

I wiped the tears from my face with my left hand.

Andy was saying something else, but I couldn't make it out. Thank God the pain reliever was kicking in. I closed my eyes. When I opened my eyes, the brightness made it almost impossible to keep them open.

I said, "Can someone shut off the light? It's hurting my eyes."

Doris said, "Sure, I'll close the curtains. That should help."

Thinking I had only just closed my eyes, I asked, "What happened to Andy?"

"He went to work—two days ago. You've been drifting in and out from the meds. How do you feel now?"

"Still hurts like hell but it's better than before."

"I'll tell the nurse you are awake and still in pain."

She exited the room.

Someone was holding my left hand.

I asked, "Webster, is that you?"

My hand shook up and down. I nodded. I couldn't see him because I still had too many drugs in my system.

I said, "When I'm healed, we'll see about breaking that curse my grandmother placed on you."

My hand moved up and down again. I smiled.

Doris and the nurse returned, carrying a glass of water and a paper cup with two pills.

She said, "We want to get you off the other pain medication, so we're changing to this."

She set the two containers on the rolling tray and pressed the bed controls until it was up to a half-sitting position. Handing me the paper cup, I popped the capsules in my mouth and took the glass of water, sucking it through the straw, swallowing the medication.

She said, "These might make you a little sleepy."

As she left, a doctor came in. He smiled broadly and said, "We get to meet you, Mr. Labauve. I'm Dr. Marsters; I operated on your arm."

"Operated? Why, I thought it was just broken?"

"Because you had recently had the same arm fractured, it hadn't fully healed and was still weak. When you fell down the stairs, as I understand it, you shattered the bones and forced them through your skin, tearing the muscles in the process. I had to place small metal plates on your radius and ulna to hold them together. We reattached what we could of the muscles, but they may never be as strong as before. It will take several months for the bone to regenerate. I'm sorry, but your right forearm may never be the same."

"Wonderful, now I'll have a gimpy arm. At least I'm left-handed."

"We'll have to wait and see how it goes. I've signed you up for physical therapy. After you leave, you'll have to come in once a week for that, and there will be exercises you will have to do each day at home."

"Okay, doctor, just another thing I must learn to live with."

"Just another thing?" the doctor questioned.

"A lot of shit has happened in my life these last few weeks."

The doctor peered at Doris, and she nodded, confirming what I had said.

He patted me on the shoulder and said, "At least you're still alive. We were amazed that you made it through with the cracked skull. That seems to be healing nicely, though."

"Thanks, doctor."

Dr. Marsters left.

I told Doris, "This will cost a mint. It's going to take me years to pay this off."

"Maybe not."

"What do you mean?"

"Andy and I have been talking with Webster. He has a sizeable sum of money and stock certificates in a private, high-security bank vault. He wants it all to go to you."

"How can it go to me if he didn't have me in his will?"

"Apparently, this is a special type of bank. You only need the passcodes to enter the vault and safety deposit box. He'll give you the codes."

"How much is it all worth?"

"He's guessing around ten million, depending on how well the stocks are doing."

I shouted, "Ten million dollars?"

The shouting made my head start to pound.

I scrunched my brow and continued, "Why wasn't this included in his will?"

"From what he told Andy and me, he was paranoid and never trusted anyone. He had a standard will that included his business partners, leaving them his part of the business they had all invested in. He figured he would leave the cash and stocks in the safety deposit box until he found someone he trusted to pass on the codes. Now he wants to give it all to you."

I still couldn't see my grandfather because of the pain medication, but I could feel him holding my left hand. I looked over in that direction and smiled at him.

"Thank you."

He squeezed my hand.

Doris continued, "Andy and Webster have been discussing how to transfer the funds without having to claim it all on taxes. Webster has some contacts who would be willing to create a second will with your mother or her heir as the beneficiary for the right price. This should keep the IRS off your back."

"So... I wake up after a week, and I'm a millionaire living alone in a haunted mansion."

I gazed at my right hand, envisioning the vacant rooms. The silence. The ghosts who had been like family.

I closed my eyes, heart aching, and fell asleep.

⚷— ⚷— ⚷—

The next day, Doris returned to the estate to retrieve her crystals. The front yard had changed. The New Yorker was gone. The picket fence, once shattered, now stood whole and freshly painted. Burn marks scarred the lawn, but grass had begun to regrow.

'Who cleaned all this up?' she wondered.

She parked on the grass and walked to the door. The large quartz crystal was missing from the porch.

The door opened. Rose smiled, welcoming her inside.

338

She asked the priestess, "Who moved the New Yorker and fixed the fence?"

"Walter moved the car to the carriage house, and Hugo fixed the fence."

"I thought they would be gone?"

"Come in. We'll explain."

The crystal witch entered the living room and all the ghosts appeared.

Cyrus anxiously asked, "How is Orion?"

She answered, "He's doing okay. He was in a coma for five days; then, when he woke, he was in so much pain that the doctors kept him on strong pain meds, and he was out most of the time. Yesterday, he woke up feeling better. They had to operate on his arm. The doctor said it will probably never be the same. It will still be a while before he comes home."

Cyrus said, "At least he's still alive."

"But why are all of you still here? I thought you would have passed to the other side."

Albert came forward and explained, "After you guys left, the tunnel of light appeared with the Duke standing beside it. We all thought he was there to escort us to the other side. He told us that because the curse was broken and we had all helped Orion all these years, he was giving us a choice: to stay with Orion until he passed or to pass on now. We all decided to remain with Orion, except for Bertha."

Doris saw Bertha standing beside the fireplace.

"But Bertha, you're still here."

The cook said, "Yes, I wanted to wait until Orion came home and tell him myself that I needed to go be with my children. He has been like a son to me all these years, and I need to say goodbye in person. The Duke agreed to this."

"I'm sure Orion will understand and appreciate that. I stopped by to pick up the crystals. Did you guys retrieve them?"

Hugo said, "Yes, here they are."

He held out a wooden crate containing the crystals wrapped in newspaper to prevent them from rattling around.

"Thank you so much for packing those for me. Orion will be so excited when I tell him that you are still here."

Rose said, "Please don't tell him. We want it to be a surprise."

"Oh, okay. I can tell he's been depressed, thinking you're all gone. It will definitely be a pleasant surprise when he walks in and you are all still here."

She left with a smile.

# Chapter 59

## There Till The End

I stayed in the hospital for two more weeks before the doctors cleared me to leave. Their biggest concern was my fractured skull. Aside from a lingering headache, it didn't bother me much. What troubled me most was my right arm. It ached constantly, making it hard to sleep.

Andy drove Webster and me home. This time, he brought clean clothes from the plantation—a blessing, since the hospital had to cut off my blood-soaked T-shirt.

The day was gray and rainy, echoing my mood. I stared out the window, dreading the return to an empty house. No Paul waiting in the yard. No Milly or Philly ready to carry my bag. No scent of home-cooked food wafting from the kitchen. No Albert smiling from the library. Nothing would be the same.

I rubbed my aching arm, still in a sling. A tear slipped down my cheek. I quickly wiped it away.

As we pulled up, I noticed that the New Yorker was no longer in the yard and that the fence had been repaired.

"Did you move the car and fix the fence?" I asked.

"No," Andy replied. "I had someone do it."

'Guess I'll be taking care of things on my own now,' I thought. 'Well, I'm a millionaire, I could hire someone. But no, I'll do it myself.'

Andy came over to assist me out of the car. My balance was still wobbly. The doctor had advised against driving for a while, especially since my right arm was still nearly useless.

We walked slowly to the front door, which opened before we reached it. Rose stood there, smiling. I rubbed the lion-head knocker as I passed, smiling back. Andy guided me to the couch.

"Would you like something to drink?" Rose asked.

"Coffee, please."

As she walked to the kitchen, I rested my chin on my left hand, deep in thought. Andy sat at the other end of the couch, smiling gently. A moment later, Doris entered through the front door.

"I'm so glad you're home," she said. "How are you feeling?"

"Okay, I guess. Small headache. My arm still aches."

She nodded, then looked behind me.

"Here comes your drink."

I turned, expecting Rose—but it was Bertha.

She smiled that warm, familiar smile—the same one I fell in love with at three years old.

I stammered, "Wh... what are you doing here?"

Then all the others appeared, materializing around me. My jaw dropped.

Doc Albert stepped forward.

"After you left for the hospital, the Tunnel of Light appeared. The Duke told us that, because the curse was broken and we'd helped you all these years, we had a choice—to go on or stay with you until your time came. We all chose to stay. Except Bertha."

Tears filled my eyes.

Bertha stepped close.

"I need to go be with my children. But I had to say goodbye in person. I hope you're not upset."

I set the mug down and hugged her with my left arm.

"Of course, you have to go and be with your children. I understand completely, and I'm happy for you."

I kissed her on the cheek and the Tunnel of Light appeared behind the group of ghosts. They all moved aside so that Bertha could leave. The silhouettes of her children, with their hands out, could be seen in the tunnel. She took two steps toward it, then turned back.

"I love you like a son, Orion Labauve. I'll be waiting when it's your time."

"I love you, too, Bertha."

Tears streamed down my face. She stepped into the tunnel and embraced her children as they vanished together into the light. The tunnel then closed.

I stood there, head bowed, still crying.

Raising my head, I said, "And all of you... I love you, too. I can't believe you stayed."

I held my left arm wide, motioning for them to come in.

The ghosts rushed in. We all embraced.

Cyrus stood off to the side, unsure whether he was welcome after everything that had happened. He gave me a pathetic puppy-dog look, and I motioned with my head for him to join. He smiled and grabbed the edge of the pile, joining the family hug. I openly sobbed with joy that my family was still here with me.

Looking at Andy and Doris, who were standing to the side and smiling, I said, "Come on, you two. You're part of the family now, too."

They both joined the family hug. We all embraced for a minute before I pulled away and asked, "What's for dinner? An excellent meal is always waiting when I get home."

I wiped the tears off my face.

Rose said, "I'll be cooking now that Bertha is gone. I might not be as good as her, but I'm not bad. She told me your favorite meals, and gave me the recipes, so I'll make fried chicken for you."

I smiled and said, "It sounds wonderful. I can't wait."

I turned to Andy and Doris and said, "You two are staying for dinner. I've never had dinner guests before."

They both smiled and said, "Sure."

Andy said, "I'll call Vivian and let her know I'm remaining here longer to help you with things."

I sank onto the couch, knees shaky, sipping the now-warm coffee with a smile.

Albert said, "Another thing the Duke said is that he is reinstating the Lwa to slow time on the house as long as a Labauve heir lives here. This will keep the house from deteriorating."

"Gee, I guess he can be a decent guy if he wants to be, but we shouldn't let that out and ruin his reputation."

Everyone laughed.

Webster came up behind me, patted me on the shoulder, and said, "Are you happy now, son?"

"Yes, I am," I said, nodding.

"I worried about you at the hospital. You looked so depressed."

"I was. But now that I know my family is here until the end, everything is wonderful. Too bad my mother and father couldn't be here. But they deserve the peace of the other side after all the hell my grandmother put them through."

Andy returned from calling Vivian and heard my comment.

He said, "So, do you think that is the last we will see of the Voodoo Imperatrice?"

"No. From everything I have found out about her, she doesn't give up. Once she finds out I'm alive and out of the hospital, she'll probably start devising new plans. We'll have to keep an eye out for her."

We chatted until dinner. Milly announced it was ready. The table had three place settings—for the living. I sat at the head, while Andy and Doris flanked me.

Before we began, Doris said, "I think we should give thanks."

We clasped hands.

"We thank all Gods and Goddesses who helped us through these past trials," she said. "We're grateful to be together and for this meal."

Andy and I echoed, "Thank you."

Then we ate—hot mashed potatoes, golden fried chicken, buttery biscuits.

I hadn't felt this happy in weeks, perhaps months. I hoped it would last. However, I knew the Duke wasn't finished with me yet. He said there was work to do. I believed him. But I found peace here—in my haunted home, surrounded by the dead who raised me and the living who joined me.

What do you do when you're raised by the dead? You learn to live with it. You love them. You protect them. And that's what I've always done.

⚷ ⚷ ⚷

A few Lwa Spirit Gods stood before the sacred bonfire, watching Orion Labauve return home. When the Small Duke said, "Gee, I guess he can be a decent guy if he wants to be, but we shouldn't let that out and ruin his reputation," the Spirit Gods all laughed.

Legba said, "Yeah, you don't want that stellar reputation of yours ruined."

Duke Shamedi laughed uproariously.

With his arms crossed and a big smile, he said, "I chose well this time."

The End

# Acknowledgments

I would like to thank my friends and family for the support and encouragement they gave me on this project.

I would like to thank my Beta Readers (Jim W., Mark B., Mary G., and Nancy J.) for reading my first novel and giving me valuable feedback.

I want to express my heartfelt thanks to Rose B. for the initial edit of this novel and for making me rethink certain aspects of it, which resulted in a better story.

And thanks to Laura G. for the wonderful cover design. Somehow, she caught my protagonist's image perfectly. My mind is still blown by this.

# About the Author

L.L. Blacke is an author specializing in science fiction, paranormal fiction, and horror literature. From an early age, she has been an avid fan and voracious reader of these genres, which have inspired her imaginative and captivating storytelling.

With over thirty years of experience in the science fiction and fantasy community, L.L. Blacke has not only attended numerous conventions but has also played a significant role in organizing them. Her deep involvement in these events has enriched her understanding of the genres and provided her with a wealth of inspiration and connections within the literary world.

Now, in her retirement years, L.L. Blacke has embraced her passion for writing, finding it to be one of the most fulfilling and enjoyable pursuits of her life. Her works reflect her lifelong love for the fantastical and the eerie, drawing readers into richly woven narratives that challenge the boundaries of reality.

When she is not writing, L.L. Blacke enjoys exploring new books, participating in literary discussions, and sharing her experiences and insights with aspiring writers and dedicated fans of speculative fiction.

# A
# Preview
of
# Spectral Promises

**Orion Labauve Novel 2**

I jolted awake, tears scorching down my face. The nightmare hit me again, an unending loop of a frightened child trapped in a shadowy house, desperately waiting for his mother's return. In that intensely vivid dream, it felt like I was the boy, helpless and forsaken.

Wiping my eyes with my left hand, I sat up, my right arm cradled in its cast, a constant reminder of the battle scars from the psychic conflict two months ago with my grandmother, the Voodoo Imperatrice.

My arm was still in a brace from being shattered during the destruction of the Labauve signet sapphire. This dynamic artifact was part of my family's twisted legacy. The magical conflict with my grandmother nearly cost me my life, and my right limb would be in a cast for months. Even after surgery and weeks of physical therapy, the constant pain remained a cruel companion. I could barely move my fingers and most nights sleep was hard to come by.

Webster Turner, the ghost of my paternal grandfather, sat vigilantly in a chair beside my bed. His spectral image was that of a frail, balding 70ish old man with a hunched back. He may have been good-looking in his youth, but now his face and body were gaunt, just as they appeared at the time of his death from cancer.

Bound to me by a curse—punishment for killing my great-grandmother, another capable voodoo priestess—he could never stray more than fifteen feet away, which forced him to follow me everywhere, just like he did with my father for thirty-five years. When I visited my father's grave, Webster had to stay close, since I am part of my father. The curse, a legacy of my family's tangled and violent history with voodoo, kept us linked until I could break it. Once my right arm healed enough to perform the necessary magical movements,

I would set him free.

Webster's spectral presence flickered as I wiped away the tears.

"Orion, did you have it again?" he asked gravely.

"Yeah," I muttered. "It has to mean something. Why else would I keep dreaming about this kid? The Duke said I had work to do, so this has to be part of it. I need to figure out where the boy is. I'm sure he's dead and a ghost."

My determination to unravel this mystery remained unwavering despite the challenges. Duke Shamedi, the voodoo Lwa Spirit God, and my *God* father, never makes things easy, as shown by the cryptic dreams that provide no clues about where the spirit child is or who he is.

"Can't you use your Finding ability to track him down?" Webster asked.

I possess a unique talent, a gift from the spirit God, to locate people and objects, which has been my profession for the past seven years. This ability allows me to find even the most difficult targets. It's a form of supernatural tracking. However, it doesn't work on ghosts, which has been a source of agitation in my current situation.

Frustration simmering, I shook my head.

"You think I haven't tried? It doesn't work on spirits. It's useless in this case."

The dream started haunting me three weeks after I returned from the hospital. They weren't a nightly occurrence, but each time they came, they left a deeper scar. I still couldn't grasp how Duke Shamedi believed I could achieve anything with an almost useless arm.

The aching in my arm flared. I hunched over, grimacing, cradling it close, wishing it would cease.

Webster leaned forward, his ghostly brow furrowed.

"Why don't you take those pain pills the doctors gave you?"

Bitterness spilled out before I could block it.

I snapped, "You know why! I'm not ending up like my mother, hooked on pills and worse."

My deceased mother died of a drug overdose. Pain meds were her drug of choice for several years, and later, after developing a

tolerance for them, she switched to heroin. This addiction proved
to be too much for her heart and she passed on five years ago. After
seeing what these drugs did to her, I refuse to use them unless
necessary.

I took deep breaths to calm myself and stop yelling. He was only
concerned about me.